Tough Cookie

Diane Mott Davidson

Tough Cookie

WHEELER
PUBLISHING, INC.
ROCKLAND, MA

★ AN AMERICAN COMPANY ★

Published in Large Print by arrangement with Bantam Books, a division of
Random House, Inc. in the United States and Canada.

Wheeler Large Print Book Series.

Set in 16 pt Plantin.

Library of Congress Cataloging-in-Publication Data

Davidson, Diane Mott.
    Tough cookie / Diane Mott Davidson.
        p. (large print) cm.(Wheeler large print book series)
    ISBN 1-56895-892-7 (hardcover)
    1. Large type books.
I. Title. II. Series

[PS3554.A925 T68   2000]
813'.54—dc21

To Triena Harper
Chief Deputy Coroner,
Jefferson County, Colorado,
who serves the citizens
of our state with dedication,
hard work, and
compassion.
Thank you.

ACKNOWLEDGMENTS

The author wishes to acknowledge the assistance of the following people: Jim, J.Z., Joe Davidson; Jeff and Rosa Davidson; Kate Miciak, a brilliant editor; Sandra Dijkstra, the most energetic agent in the business; Susan Corcoran, a phenomenal publicist, and Jessica Bellucci, also fabulous in that department; Lee Karr and the group that assembles at her home; my sister Lucy Mott Faison, for testing and retesting the recipes at low altitude; John William Schenk, JKS, and Karen Johnson, Ravens Catering, for their unceasing willingness to answer questions; Monica Koziol, the Front Range Chef, for her help, guidance, and support in teaching the author how a personal chef operates; the extraordinarily knowledgeable and helpful Wayne Belding and Jeff Mathews of the Boulder Wine Merchant, for sharing their expertise; Katherine Goodwin Saideman, for her close readings of the manuscript; Emyl Jenkins; Commander Debra Grainger, Arvada Police Department; Richard Staller, D.O.; Triena Harper, chief deputy coroner, and Jon Cline, coroner's investigator, Jefferson County; John Lauck, Criminal Investigator, District Attorney's Office, First Judicial District of Colorado; Linda Gustafson, Vail; Greg Morrison, Chief of Police, Vail; Allan Stanley, member, Colorado State Parole Board; Carol Devine Rusley; Julie Wallin Kaewert; Kevin Devine, Lake Tahoe Ski Patrol Avalanche Control; Nicole Mains, personal trainer, Boulder Country Club; Jim Gray and Shirley Carnahan, Boulder Renaissance Consort; Elaine Mongeau, King Soopers Pharmacy, Evergreen; Janine Jones, Chris Wyant, and Mark Kimball, The Alpenglow Stube, Keystone Resort; Nate Klatt and Tiffany Tyson, public relations, and Sally Reed, floor director, KRMA-TV, Denver; Jim Buchanan; Keith Abbott; Bob Egizi, security manager, Vail Associates; Suzanne Jarvis, Village Security, Beaver Creek Resort; Tim Batdorff, Toscanini, Beaver Creek; Alan Henceroth, mountain manager, and Jim Gentling, Arapahoe Basin Ski Area; Meg Kendal, Denver-Evergreen Ob-Gyn; Russell Wiltse, Department of Film Studies, University of Colorado, Boulder; and as always, for his knowledge, patience, and suggestions, Sergeant Richard Millsapps of the Jefferson County Sheriff's Department, Golden, Colorado.

Greedily she ingorg'd without restraint,
And knew not eating Death.

JOHN MILTON, *PARADISE LOST*,
BOOK IX, 791-792

Nate Bullock Memorial Fund-Raiser
Front Range Public Broadcasting System

"Cooking at the Top!"
FILMING FROM
THE SUMMIT BISTRO

Killdeer Ski Resort, Killdeer, Colorado
December the Seventeenth

Mexican Egg Rolls with
Spicy Guacamole Dipping Sauce/
1996 Cline Ancient Vine Zinfandel

♦

Chèvre, Teardrop Tomatoes, and Poached
Asparagus on a bed of Frisée;
Shallot Vinaigrette Sancerre

♦

Chesapeake Crab Cakes with Sauce Gribiche/
1997 Les Monts Damnés Sancerre
Sauvignon Blanc—Chavignol

♦

Crisp Italian Breadsticks

♦

Ice-Capped Gingersnaps/
1983 Château Suduiraut Sauternes

CHAPTER 1

Show business and death don't mix. Unfortunately, I discovered this while hosting a TV cooking show.

Up to then, I'd enjoyed being a TV chef. The job didn't pay well, but this was PBS. Arthur Wakefield, the floor director, had crisply informed me that most chefs made nothing for guest visits, much less five thousand clams for six shows. He could have added: *And what's more, those chefs' kitchens haven't been closed by the county health inspector!* But Arthur said nothing along those lines. Like most folks, he was unaware that my in-home commercial catering kitchen had been red-tagged, that is, *closed until further notice.*

So: Bad pay notwithstanding, I was lucky to have the TV job. Actually, I was lucky to have any food work at all. And I certainly didn't want more than our family and a few friends to know why.

I could not tell my upscale clients—those who'd made *Goldilocks' Catering, Where Everything Is Just Right!* the premier food-service busi-

1

ness of Aspen Meadow, Colorado—that our plumbing wasn't up to code. And of course, I could *never* let it be known that my dear husband Tom was ransacking the house for valuables to sell off, so we could buy fancy drains and thereby get my business *reopened*. No plumbing? No drains? It sounded nasty. Sordid, even.

In September, things had gone badly. The county health inspector, giggling from the shock engendered by his surprise visit, closed me down. The bustle in our kitchen immediately subsided. Calls for catering gigs stopped. Suppliers sent letters asking if I wanted to keep my accounts current. *Yes, yes,* I always replied cheerfully, *I'm looking forward to reopening soon!* Soon. Ha!

Without my business, an enterprise I'd lovingly built up for almost a decade, I entered a spiritual fog as thick as the gray autumnal mist snaking between the Colorado mountains. I gave up yoga. Drank herb tea while reading back issues of *Gourmet.* Spent days gazing out the new windows in our beautifully-remodeled-but-noncompliant kitchen. And repeatedly told Tom how gorgeous the kitchen looked, even if I couldn't work in it....

Truly, the place *did* look great. So *what* if it didn't meet new county regulations mandating that every commercial kitchen sink have backflow protection? Months earlier, Tom had rescued the remodeling job after a dishonest contractor had made our lives hell. During time away from his work as a Homicide Investigator for the Furman County Sheriff's Department, he'd put in marble counters, cherry cabinets, expensive windows, a solid oak floor. And the wrong drains.

To fix the problem, Tom was now tearing out the guts of three new sinks and prying up the floor beneath. He insisted we should heal our temporary cash-flow problem by selling a pair of historic skis he'd bought years before in an odd lot of military memorabilia. In October, I'd started calling antiques dealers while wondering how, during a prolonged closure, I could keep my hand in the food business.

There'd been no takers for the skis. How else to get money? I'd wracked my brain for other ways to work as a cook: Volunteer at a school cafeteria? Roll a burrito stand up and down Aspen Meadow's Main Street?

Eventually, it had been my old friend Eileen Druckman who'd come through with a job. Loaded with money and divorced less than two years, Eileen had just bought the Summit Bistro at Colorado's posh Killdeer Ski Resort. Eileen—fortyish, pretty, and blond, with cornflower blue eyes and a full, trembling mouth that had just begun to smile again—had hired a good-looking young chef named Jack Gilkey, whose food was legend in Killdeer. To Eileen's delight, she and Jack had quickly become an item personally as well as professionally. When I told Eileen my business woes, she and Jack had kindly offered me the position of co-chef at the bistro. But I couldn't work restaurant hours—seven in the morning to midnight—fifty miles from home. Restaurant workers, I'd noticed, had a high mortality rate, no home life, or both.

Eileen, ever generous, had promptly pitched a cooking-show idea to the Front Range Public Broadcasting System. They'd said yes. I'd demurred. Eileen argued that my cooking on TV, at her bistro, would boost her business plus give her a huge tax write-off. Meanwhile, I could use my television exposure to publicize the new culinary venture I'd finally hit upon: becoming a personal chef. That particular avenue of food work requires no *commercial* kitchen; it only requires a wealthy *client's* kitchen. Just the ticket.

So I'd said yes to show business. The Killdeer Corporation had offered free season ski-lift passes to me as well as to my fourteen-year-old son, Arch. Shot through with new enthusiasm and hope, I couldn't wait to cook and ski. I gave up herb tea for shots of espresso laced with whipping cream. In November, I plunged eagerly back into work.

Every Friday morning, I would appear at Killdeer's Summit Bistro to do my bit before the camera. At first I was nervous. And we did have a few mishaps. Thankfully, *Cooking at the Top!* was taped. Viewers never saw me slash my hand—actually, sever a minor artery—while boning a turkey during the first episode. The spray of blood onto the prep counter had been distinctly unappetizing. The following week, I produced a meringue so sweaty it needed antiperspirant. I also dropped two roasts—one of them stuffed—and splattered myself with a pitcher of Béarnaise. But with glitches edited out, even I had to admit the Saturday morning broadcasts looked pretty good.

On the upside, I told jokes on-screen and mixed cream into smashed garlicky potatoes. I chatted about the rejuvenating properties of toasted, crunchy almonds while folding melted butter into almond cake batter. I gushed about the trials and joys of learning to ski as I chopped mountains of Godiva Bittersweet Chocolate. I swore to my viewers that my recipe made the darkest, most sinfully fudgy cookies on the slopes. I even assiduously followed Arthur's tasting instructions: *Take a bite. Moan. Move your hips and roll your eyes. Say M-m-mm, aaah, oooh! Yes! Yes!* Watching the footage, Tom had quipped that the program should be called *The Food-Sex Show.*

All in all, the first four weeks of taping went well. By Week Four, though, my personal-chef business still had not taken off. I only had one upcoming job. Arthur Wakefield himself had offered me a gig the following week: preparing food for a holiday in-home wine-tasting. Arthur supplemented his floor director income by working as a wine importer. He needed to showcase some new wines—and serve a gourmet meal—to high-end customers and retailers. So, even in the personal-chef department, things were looking up.

Unfortunately, in Week Five, *Cooking at*

the Top! hit a snag, one occasioned by a predictable Colorado crisis: blizzard.

"Don't get hysterical on me, Goldy!" Arthur wailed into the telephone December the sixteenth, the night before we were due to tape the fifth episode. I held the receiver away from my ear and pictured him: Short, slender, with a handsome face and a head covered with wiry black hair, Arthur was single and, with the income from two jobs, well-off. Unfortunately, no matter whether he was fretting about the show or his precious wines, he wore an air of gloom. Sporting a band-collared black shirt, black pants, and brown rubber-soled shoes, he strode everywhere hunched forward with apprehension. *That guy is stuck in a Doppler shift,* my son—currently studying ninth-grade physics—had commented. As Arthur quacked into the receiver that night, I imagined him tipping forward precipitously, straining to peer glumly out his condo window, anxiously assessing the thickening wash of snow.

Without taking time to say hello, he'd launched into his late-night communication with a grim update on the severe winter storm bearing down on us. The weather service was predicting four feet of white stuff. Nevertheless—Arthur tensely informed me—despite problems with transportation and prepping, Front Range PBS *had* to shoot the show the next morning. I told him that it would take me an hour just to ready the ingredients on the menu. Arthur didn't want to hear it.

"Then leave an hour early so you can deal with the *roads!*" he snarled. So much for sympathy.

I gripped the phone and glanced out the bay window Tom had installed during our remodeling. An old-fashioned street lamp illuminated fast-falling flakes swirling from a black sky. In the living room, wind whistled ominously down our fireplace flue. I sighed.

"Sorry I snapped," Arthur moaned. "I've got a blizzard and a crew in revolt. Plus, my boss says our show has to raise money. The annual fund-raiser got canceled, so we're up." He moaned again, pitifully. I registered the clink of a bottle tapping glass. "One of our PBS people was killed a while back. This fund-raiser is a memorial for him. We *have* to do it."

I sighed and murmured a few consoling words. I didn't ask why it would be a good idea for us to risk *our* lives remembering someone who was *already* dead.

"Killdeer's been dumped big time," Arthur reported dourly. "We've already got thirty-five inches of new snow. I couldn't open my door this morning." He stopped to drink something. "Are you getting any?"

In Colorado, this meant snow, not sex. "About a foot today," I replied. Our mountain town lay forty-five miles east of the Continental Divide and forty miles west of Denver. Five to six feet of snow over the course of a six-month winter was normal. This was much less than the snowfall registered in Vail, Keystone, Breckenridge, and Killdeer—all ski resorts west of the Divide.

7

Arthur groaned. "The snowboarders and skiers? They're ecstatic! They've got an eighty-inch base in December! How'm I supposed to get our van up a road covered with seven feet of white stuff? My crew's having a late-night drinking party, like a farewell before our broadcast." I heard him take another slug of what I assumed was wine. "Know what that crew's thinking, Goldy? I'll tell you. They're thinking *Donner Pass.*"

Tucking the receiver under my ear, I started heating some milk: It was definitely a night for hot chocolate. "Arthur," I answered calmly, "why does the show have to be *live*? Why don't you just postpone the taping?" I adjusted the flame under the milk. "Better yet, why not tell me exactly what's going on?"

"Look." I heard another gulp. "High winds closed the bistro early tonight. Whenever gusts reach forty miles per hour, Killdeer Corp closes the gondola, so tonight's telethon was canceled. That's why the kitchen crew couldn't do your prep."

I tapped the gleaming new Carrara marble counter and glanced at my watch: half past ten. "So we have to *raise money* during our show?"

He cleared his throat. "The show was an annual telethon. It brings in about ten thousand bucks each year, and the station uses the money to buy equipment. So tonight, when the telethon got canceled, my boss announced to viewers that instead of seeing *our* show *Saturday* morning, viewers could tune in *tomorrow morning* for a live version of *Cooking at the Top!*" He took a gulp. "We *have* to do it tomorrow, Goldy. The professional fund-raiser folks say that if you put people off for long, they'll stow their checkbooks. Don't worry, I've got phone-bank volunteers."

"You said it was a memorial," I reminded him.

"Haven't you ever watched it?"

"Never. I can't take telethons. Too much tension."

"It's in memory of Nate Bullock. *High Country Hallmarks*, you must have watched *that*." Arthur took another desperate swig. *Nate Bullock*, I thought. A pang of regret wormed through my chest. Yes, I had watched *High Country Hallmarks*. And I'd known Nate. His wife, Rorry, had once been my friend.

"Wait a minute," said Arthur. "My other line's ringing. Probably a supplier telling me he slipped into a ditch with a truckload of champagne. Can you hold?"

I said yes. I gripped the phone cord, glanced out at the snow, and thought back. Eleven years ago, Nate and Rorry Bullock had been our neighbors in Aspen Meadow. *Rorry*. She and I had had good times teaching Sunday school at St. Luke's Episcopal Church. But our work and our relationship had ended when the Bullocks moved to Killdeer. *High Country Hallmarks*, Nate's hugely popular, locally produced PBS show, had covered exciting aspects of Colorado life, from tracking cougars to evacuating in advance of flash floods. Safe at home, snuggled inside cocoons of comforters and sipping cocoa, Arch and I had watched it together often when he was little.

Tragically, Nate had been killed in an avalanche three years ago—tracking lynx for one of his own shows, reports said, although the television station denied knowledge of such a dangerous project. The papers had reported that the cause for the avalanche, and the reason for Nate's being in its path, were a mystery. Investigations had led nowhere, and his death remained shrouded in unanswered questions and pain. Poor Rorry. The thought of my widowed friend brought sadness. Although I'd written to her after Nate's death, I'd received no response.

Arthur returned to the line and announced he'd just calmed one of his cameramen. He tried unsuccessfully to conceal a burp and went on: "All right. At six, two cameramen, a handful of volunteers, and I will drive up our equipment van on the—*plowed,* they promised me—back road. Is your van four-wheel drive?"

"No. And my tires are marginal." Another side-effect of my cash-flow problem.

"Then take the gondola up the mountain. Since the bistro staff couldn't do any of the prep, the owner and her head chef,"—here he sighed—"will be helping you. Now listen, *going live* is just a bit different. People expect mistakes. Don't worry, it's part of the fun."

"Oh, gee, Arthur. It doesn't sound like fun." Overseeing a close friend who knew nothing about food prep and her chef-cum-boyfriend chopping mountains of scallions in time for a live broadcast? *Fun?* A wave of queasiness assaulted me.

"Just be there by seven, Goldy," Arthur said, ignoring my protests. "Don't come early. I have too much to do and you'll be underfoot. When you get there, you can tell Eileen and Jack what you need and I'll run you through the telethon scenario. We'll start filming at eight. *Ciao!*"

He hung up. The wind wailed around the house. I whisked cream and sugar into a heap of dry Dutch-style cocoa, beat in the steaming milk, and liberally doused the cocoa with whipped cream. Worries about the next morning crowded in as I set two fragrant, filbert-studded fudge cookies on a china plate. I took a bite of cookie and nearly swooned over the combination of life-restoring dark chocolate and crunchy toasted nuts. *Forget the show! Consume chocolate! Oh, and get some sleep,* I ordered myself. *Otherwise, people will call in to complain that the chef looks half dead.*

The phone rang again.

"Hey, Goldy, honey, how you doing?" Doug Portman's obnoxious greeting sent ice down my spine. "Coming up to Killdeer tomorrow?"

"Yes, Doug." What strange bedfellows failed remodeling makes, I thought as I sipped the cocoa. Doug Portman and I had history. We'd dated unhappily after I'd rid myself of The Jerk, my abusive ex-husband. But pretentious, penny-pinching Doug was a well-known collector of military memorabilia, and our drains-crisis had brought him back in our orbit.

11

"Still want to sell those World War Two skis?" Doug asked imperiously, his voice as gruff as ever. "The ones Ike signed?"

"If the price is right." Tom's historic skis had belonged to a veteran, a member of the 10th Mountain Division. On the skis, the soldier had carved the names of each of the Alpine towns where he'd fought. More importantly, the trooper had somehow convinced Eisenhower himself to carve *Ike* onto the left ski. An antiques dealer had told Tom the skis could sell for as much as ten thousand dollars, of which we, unfortunately, would get only *half*. Remembering Doug and his insatiable passion for military memorabilia, plus the fortune we'd need to replace the drains, I'd called him two weeks ago and offered him the skis for nine thousand. He'd turned me down.

"I've changed my mind. Eight thousand. Cash." Doug said triumphantly. "Take it or leave it."

"Great," I said, surprised and pleased.

"Meet you at your cooking show, then." Doug lived in Killdeer. "And hey. If I'm going to buy your skis, I want some of those goodies you're making." He paused. "I heard they charge nine bucks for spectators. Suppose you could leave me a free ticket at the restaurant desk? We'll ski down together afterward. It'll be fun."

Everybody promised fun. I sighed and told him no problem. A free ticket? Eight thousand dollars to spend, and Doug couldn't spring *nine* bucks for public television? But this was typical. Doug never paid for what he could scav-

12

enge for free. I told him I'd see him the next morning and signed off.

With my hopefully soporific hot drink in one hand and the second oversized chocolate cookie in the other, I strolled to the kitchen's back wall. Gusts of wind plastered icy flakes against our new windows. I put down the cocoa and placed my palm on the cold glass. The snow relentlessly batted against the pane, *tat-tat-tat-tat*. A whirling curtain of snow streamed past our deck light. The deck itself boasted at least eighteen inches of new powder. I prayed for Tom to be safe. He was down in Denver, working a fraud case. His Chrysler's snow tires were in pretty good shape. Piloting my own rear-wheel-drive van to Killdeer the next morning would be another story.

I wanted to do the show. I pulled my hand away from the window and sipped my creamy drink. With my catering business shut down, the program's wide audience still showcased the personal-chef venture, for which I refused to give up hope. Now, with Doug's offer, I finally had a deal for the skis. Plus, knowing the show was dedicated to remembering dear Rorry Bullock's husband, I *had* to get to Killdeer in the morning.

I bit into the cookie and watched the snow. Christmas was only nine days away, but the Yuletide spirit eluded me. I'd bought a snowboard for Arch—his heart's desire—and a new revolver for Tom. I was no gun-lover—far from it—but I'd learned a great deal about firearms from Tom. The dangers and risks of his work had convinced me he needed another weapon, even if all he used it for was practice. So: We had some gifts. Our tree sparkled in the living room. We had plans to bake Christmas cookies together, as a family. But without a job after the New Year, I felt a lack of purpose, and Christmas was just one more landmark on a calendar I didn't want to face.

Things could be worse, I consoled myself as I drank more cocoa. I could be out in this weather. I could be facing the holidays without a husband, like Rorry Bullock. My heart ached for her.

Handsome and effervescent, Nate Bullock had always been one to court—and then miraculously escape from—the perils of mountain life. *Had* he secretly been tracking Canadian lynx, reintroduced to the Front Range after the native lynx habitat had been destroyed by development? Who knew? One fact everyone agreed on was that Nate Bullock had strayed—or hiked intentionally—into Killdeer Valley, an area that was off-limits for all humans, not just skiers, because of the possibility of avalanches. The avalanche, that killer tide of snow that sweeps the unsuspecting to their death, was much to be feared in the Colorado mountain winter.

That's why the Valley is out-of-bounds, Killdeer officials had solemnly intoned, ever wary of their liability insurance. *Avalanches in the high country happen without warning.* Of course, this had not prevented Killdeer Corporation from recently deciding to expand the resort

14

onto the slope *adjacent* to the Valley. Next season, a new lift would take skiers and snowboarders right over the area where Nate had died. Poor Rorry, I thought again, with guilt. Would she be at the fund-raiser? Would she want to talk to me, when all I'd done was write her a sympathy note? Why hadn't I been more persistent in checking up on her after Nate's death?

I finished the cookie and downed the cocoa. Late at night, problems loom large. I had to crawl to bed and get some beauty sleep. Or, as I checked my pudgy, curly-blond-haired reflection in the frosted window, just some sleep, period.

Early the next morning, in an impenetrable, windy, predawn darkness, I loaded the historic skis into my van. It was still snowing hard. A torrent of flakes iced my face as I stamped inside. I left a note for Tom, whose large, warm body had finally snuggled in next to mine around two A.M. I packed up my boots and skis, traipsed out to check the tread on my radial tires—barely adequate—and set out for Killdeer.

As my van negotiated the snow-crusted expanse of Main Street, the wind lashed fresh snow across my windshield. When I pulled over to scrape it off, I was hit in the face with a swag of holiday evergreen and a strand of white lights. Convulsing in the wind, the decorations had torn loose from a storefront. I climbed back

15

into the van, shivered, and started the slow trek to the highway.

Once the van was headed west on Interstate 70, I cranked the wipers as high as they would go to sweep off the relentlessly falling snow. Traffic was light. Beside the road, a herd of bighorn sheep clustered below a neon sign warning of icy roads on both sides of the Eisenhower Tunnel. When I passed Idaho Springs, a radio announcement brayed the news that an avalanche had come down late the previous afternoon at the Loveland Ski Area. Cars slowing down to watch the cleanup were clogging the road, the announcer solemnly declared.

"Perfect," I muttered.

Twenty minutes later, I braked behind a long line of cars. Through the snowfall, I could just make out dump trucks laboring in the Loveland parking lot as they scooped away a three-story-high heap of snow, rocks, and broken trees. Under the pile was a maintenance building. The radio announcer passionately recited a rumor of a scofflaw skier who'd ducked a boundary rope and precipitated the slide. The avalanche had raced down the hillside, snapped a stand of pines like matchsticks, and buried the vacant building. Passengers riding up the high-speed quad lift had seen the skier schuss to safety—and away from being caught.

Concentrate on your driving, I warned myself, as I entered the neon-lit purgatory of the tunnel, that deep, dark passageway bored

16

beneath the Continental Divide. After a few minutes, the snowpacked descent from the tunnel loomed ahead in the early morning grayness. When I emerged, a sudden wind whipped the van, rocking it violently. Another thick shower of snow blanketed my windshield.

I thought: *What would it be like to die in an avalanche?*

CHAPTER 2

At six-twenty, my van crunched into the snowpacked parking lot of the Killdeer resort. To the east, the sky was edged with pewter. My fingers ached from gripping the steering wheel. When I turned off the engine, flakes instantly obscured the windshield. I hopped out onto the snowpack. A frigid breeze bit through my ski jacket and I stumbled to get my footing. Righting myself, I tugged up my hood, cinched it tight, and donned padded mittens.

I struggled to get my bearings. Through the swirling drapery of flakes, the parking lot's digital display flashed the happy announcement that the temperature stood at 19°. Windchill −16°. *Welcome to ski country!*

Lights from the ski area cast a pall across the imposing face of Killdeer Mountain. Columns of snow spiraled around the lampposts. A lead-colored cloud shrouded the runs. The digital sign went on to proclaim that the mountain now boasted an *Eighty-five-inch base* topped with *Thirty-three inches of new!!!*—ski-talk for *how much snow we've got.*

I pulled out my Rossignols, bought on sale long ago. I'd need them to follow Doug down from the bistro at the end of the show. The other skis, the valuable pair, I would be selling to him in less than three hours. I tossed down my poles and put on my boots. Another blustery breeze stung my eyes. The sign joyously screamed: *More SNOW on the way!* followed by a smiley face and the words *Ski with CAUTION!*

In the back of the van, I pulled out three blankets to hide the precious skis. The carved names glowed briefly: *Abetone, Della Vedetta, Corona.* They were a glorious find, and I would have loved for Tom to keep them. Arch, who was obsessed with learning about the Second World War, was extremely unhappy with us for thinking of selling them.

I was supposed to pick up Arch after the show. With his teachers out for a faculty conference yesterday and today, he had stayed overnight with his best friend, Todd Druckman, Eileen's son, in her gorgeous Killdeer condo. The boys loved to snowboard together. I was dreading one of his adolescent bad moods when he heard these skis were actually sold.

It was not something I wanted to think about. I spread out the blankets, threw a tarpaulin over the whole pile, and locked the van.

I could just hear the muffled jangle and clank of the gondola, half a mile away. Apparently, this morning's winds had not been strong enough to delay the six o'clock start-up, when the ski patrol ascended the mountain. Resignedly, I shouldered my skis, poles, and backpack, and crunched across the mammoth lot. *Buck up!* I ordered myself. *Doing the show and selling the skis will get you closer to reopening.* I breathed in tangy wood smoke and blinked away stinging snowflakes. An arctic breeze whipsawed my scarf, and my boots cracked and slid on the hard-pack. I trudged along in the semidarkness, determined to get out of the cold wind that had whipped to a fury in the lot's open space. Despite my resolution to be cheerful, I wondered why people thought hell *wasn't* frozen over.

Panting, my thighs and toes numb, I finally arrived at the artfully carved wooden sign welcoming me to Killdeer. I leaned my skis and poles against the signpost. Under my bundled clothing, my body felt slick with sweat. Ahead, snow tumbled steadily around gold-glowing street lamps lining the walkway to the gondola. Extracting a tissue from my pocket, I wiped my eyes and blinked at Killdeer's just-like-Dickens row of brightly-lit Victorian- and Bavarian-style shops. The street lamps, I'd learned, stayed on until the sun was completely up. In my month doing the cooking show, the days had become shorter; the pale, cold sun had risen later and later. I'd teased Arthur that by the close of the year we'd be

19

doing the show in the dark. Arthur had sighed glumly and then suggested we could do a champagne breakfast show, bubbly supplied—like all the other vintages we featured—by Wakefield Wines. Now, thinking of my frozen fingertips, I wondered if Arthur had schnapps up at the bistro. If so, did I dare drink some before "going live"?

Actually, I didn't want champagne or schnapps. I wanted *coffee.* I cared not a whit about the admonition that caffeine constricts skiers' cells and lowers their body temperature. If I wanted to be awake to cook at the top and raise money as well, I desperately needed several shots of the good stuff.

Luckily, I knew there would be one place open at this hour. My spirits rose as I schlepped my load down the short, charming avenue. Storefronts twinkling with thousands of holiday lights made Aspen Meadow's Main Street, fifty miles away, look as stark as a Shaker living room. In several hours, these brightly festooned boutiques would become a hive of commercial activity. *I* wouldn't be trucking in high-priced commerce, but never mind.

I sniffed the scent of the dark, fragrant brew even as I rejoiced at the Open sign dangling from the door of Cinda's Cinnamon Stop. I dropped my equipment near the covered decking that ran by the shops and clopped up the wooden steps.

"Hey, Goldy!" bellowed Cinda Caldwell from her steamy walk-up window. Cinda's hair, dyed in a range of pink hues from cotton-candy to scarlet, was luminous behind the swirl of fat white flakes. "Come in, come in, I need to talk to you about something!"

I'd come to know Cinda—tall, athletic, endlessly enthusiastic and energetic—during my stint with the program. "You look worse than usual!" she cried cheerfully. "You're still doing your show?"

"Yes, but I need *your* coffee to transform me into a chipper TV personality. Make that a *warm*, chipper TV personality."

She guffawed. "Want three or four shots? Need a pastry with your espresso? On the house! C'mon!" she hollered impatiently. "There's something I really need to tell you!"

"Okay, okay, triple shot, thanks," I called back dutifully. "And I'd love a cinnamon roll." I congratulated myself on being *too early* to appear at the bistro. What else could I do while I waited for Arthur's crew to finish setting up, but indulge in free treats at Cinda's?

I stuck my head into the warmth of her shop. The Cinnamon Stop boasted a short counter and eight round wooden tables plastered with snowboard stickers. A higgledy-piggledy assortment of plastic and wooden chairs bunched around and between the tables. The huge screen that showed snowboarding videos during working hours was dark. Cinda, who had gained unexpected renown as one of the first female snowboarders in the state, whisked back and forth in her minuscule working space. She wore a bright yellow turtleneck and purple ski pants. A fluorescent purple-and-

21

yellow headband held her tangle of pink hair in place. On the wall behind her, a poster of a snowboarder catching air vied with old-fashioned Christmas bulb lights strung around a fluorescent Burton snowboard. The board hung at an angle beside a row of Cinda's freestyle trophies. "Almost there!" she promised me. She was so upbeat, you'd never know she'd blown out her knees several years ago on the Killdeer half-pipe—that long, snow-covered half-cylinder favored by boarders—and hadn't touched a board since.

"Drink." Cinda thrust a paper cup of steaming dark liquid at me, then a paper plate topped with a twirled roll glazed with cinnamon sugar. "Listen, before I get into the serious stuff, I have to ask you something." Her brown eyes, set in an elfin, freckled face, sparkled. "Do I hafta use Grand Marnier in your chocolate truffles? I've got some bargain brandy left over and was hoping I could substitute." She gave me an open-mouthed smile.

I took a healthful swig of caffeine and wondered if you could chug an espresso, slam down a roll, lie politely, and still get the heartwarming effects of caffeine and sugar. Probably not. "The truffles will turn out better if you use high-quality liqueur. Cognac yes, brandy no."

She surprised me by leaning in close. She smelled like vanilla. "How about this question, then. Didn't I read in the paper that you're married to a cop? He works for the Furman County Sheriff's Department?"

"Yes. He does." *Crime alert.* Regardless of what the thermometer said, my mind was not so frozen that it didn't recognize the coffee, the roll, and the truffle question as an introduction to something else altogether. I gave her an innocent look. "You need help?"

She fiddled with the psychedelic headband. "It's probably nothing. But a guy came into the shop a few nights ago, plastered, wanting coffee. My waiter, Davey, gave him some Kona. I used to know the drunk guy. Name's Barton Reed. He was a snowboarder until he got into some kind of trouble and had to go away for a while. He's a big-bruiser type with about twenty earrings in each ear, all little crosses and saints' medals. Not that he's religious—I heard he gave up *that* a long time ago. Anyway, Barton boasted that he'd gotten hold of a poison that could kill you if you just *touched* it."

I pondered the espresso in my cup before answering: "Did he say he was going to use it?"

"He said he'd put patches of the poison in a *letter,* if you can believe that. You open the letter, you're dead."

"Did he show the letter to Davey?"

She paused and looked cautiously around the empty shop. "No. Here's the bad part, Goldy. Barton said he was going to deliver this poison-in-a-letter soon. To a cop."

My skin prickled. I heard my tone sharpen as questions tumbled out. "Do you know where this Barton guy lives? Did you report what he said?" She shook her head. "How about the cop? Did you get *his* name?"

Cinda picked up a rag and wiped the counter beside my half-full coffee cup. "Nah, I figured it was a hoax. So did Davey. Plus, who'm I going to report it to? Ski patrol? Forest Service? I couldn't imagine the sheriff's department traveling way over here, to the edge of the county, to hear about some drunk who claims he's going to send a poisoned Christmas card to a cop." She shrugged. "So I figured if you came by for coffee today, I'd tell *you* about it. See what you thought."

It was getting on to seven o'clock. Still, this was very worrisome and I *had* to call Tom. Unfortunately, I'd left my cell phone in the van. I asked Cinda for her phone; she hoisted one to the counter. Quickly, I pressed the button for a Denver line and dialed first our home number, then our business line. Tom must have left early: Both calls netted answering machines. I pressed buttons for his sheriff's department line and left a voice-mail asking Tom to call Cinda Caldwell about a threat to a policeman. Hanging up, I rummaged through my backpack full of culinary tools, pulled out my dog-eared wallet, and extracted one of Tom's cards. "Call this number in thirty minutes, Cinda. Tell Tom everything you told me. Thirty minutes. Promise?"

She looked at me uncertainly. She took the card and fingered it cautiously, and I could imagine her telling Tom, *Goldy told me to call*

24

you, it's probably nothing, but she figured it might be kinda important—

I put my mittens back on. "Need to hop. They're doing our show *live* today. It's a fund-raiser dedicated to Nate Bullock, remember him?"

Still staring at the card, she nodded her rainbow-pink head. "Sure. The TV tracker dude."

"I'm doing Mexican egg rolls. Crab cakes. Gingersnaps."

Now she looked at me, perplexed. "I'll try to catch it. But you know my customers would rather see an extreme ski video than a cooking show." She shrugged.

I finished the roll—flaky, buttery, and spicy-sweet—polished off the coffee in two greedy swallows, and thanked her again.

When I ducked out of the warm shop, another fiercely cold wind struck me broadside. I struggled past the brilliantly lit facade of the Killdeer Art Gallery. In the Christmas-plaid-draped front window, black-and-white photos of backlit snowboarders making daring leaps off cliffs vied with garish, romantic oils of Native Americans beside tipis. A third of the window was devoted to watercolors of mountain villas. Just visible behind these were collages made up of images of ski equipment. When Coloradans enthused over Western Art, they weren't talking about Michelangelo.

The last shop on the row was *Furs for the Famous*. Ah, fame. Fame was much desired by the *hoi polloi,* much despised by celebrities, much avoided by the infamous. As I clomped back down the steps toward the gondola, fueled by Cinda's rich coffee, I reflected that I had no use for fame. Doing a gourmet cooking show had spawned neither gourmet cooks nor ardent fans. But *complainers*—who wrote and called and stopped me in the grocery store to ask if they could substitute margarine for butter, powdery dried muck for fresh imported Parmesan, and blocks of generic *je-ne-sais-quoi* for expensive dark chocolate—these I had in abundance. Tom had given me an early Christmas present: a T-shirt silkscreened with: *DON'T ASK. DON'T SUBSTITUTE.*

And speaking of Tom, being married to a police investigator had also brought me recognition, as Cinda's question demonstrated. Sometimes I felt like the pastor's wife who is told of incest in a church family. Nobody wants to bother the pastor with it, right? Somebody's sending a poisoned letter to a cop? *Don't bother the cop! Let Goldy handle it.*

I walked down the snowpacked path and tramped across an arched footbridge. Four feet below, Killdeer Creek gurgled beneath its mantle of ice. Christmas and the promise of more snow would soon bring an onslaught of skiers. I trudged onward resolutely, not wanting to think about the holiday, and all the parties I would miss catering.

Sell the old skis. Get the new drains, I told myself. *Develop the personal chef sideline, then reopen your business. And quit worrying!*

I clambered up the ice-packed pathway to the clanking gondola. The car manager, his hair swathed in an orange jester cap, his face spiderwebbed from a decade of sun, stopped a car for me. I heaved my backpack and poles into the six-seater while the car manager whistled an off-tune Christmas carol and clanked my skis into the car's outside rack. The car whisked away.

Up, up, up I zoomed toward the bistro. Even though snow continued to fall, the sky had brightened to the color of polished aluminum. The muffled grinding of the cable was the only sound as the car rolled past snow-frosted treetops and empty, pristinely white runs. This early, an hour and a half before the runs officially opened, I was alone on the lift. Our small studio audience usually rode up at quarter to eight. Early-bird skiers who couldn't brave the cold would still be guzzling cocoa at Cinda's or the Karaoke Café. Or they could be poring over maps of Killdeer's back bowls, those steep, ungroomed deep-snow areas braved by only the hardiest of skiers. Or maybe they would be having their bindings checked at the repair shop, or just staring out at the snow-covered mountains. In other words, *they* could be anticipating *real* fun.

I shifted on the cold vinyl seat and peered downward. Below the new blanket of flakes, groomed, nubbled snow had frozen into ridged rows. The grooming was left to the snow-cats, those tractor tanks that churned and smoothed the white stuff after-hours. By the time I skied down at nine, I knew, the new powder would be lumped into symmetrical rows of moguls: hard, tentlike humps of snow arrayed across the hill like an obstacle course. As much as I loved skiing, and I did, this might or might *not* be fun.

Halfway to the top, the car stopped. This happened occasionally, when children failed to make the hop onto the seats and their parents went nova. But it shouldn't be happening now. I glanced back at the base; the gondola station was out of sight. A sudden wind made the cable car swing. I shivered and looked down at the runs. How far down were they, anyway?

Think about something else, Goldy. What you're doing later. Selling Tom's skis. I tightened my grip on the cold bars and took my mind off the distance to the ground.

Tom's skis, I reminded myself. Yes. The buyer was Doug Portman. Not exactly a happy thing to think about, but never mind.

Doug Portman was a social-climbing accountant who had somehow become a rather large cog in our state political machine. Dressed in dapper seersucker or corduroy, he was always a hobnobbing presence at law enforcement picnics and other events. I didn't know what he did to earn his living now, and didn't want to know. The only thing I knew was that he had married for money and could now indulge in his collecting hobby. Still, I felt guilty about selling him Tom's skis, since I had not told Tom to *whom* I was selling them. You didn't exactly say, *Uh, honey? I'm selling one of your most prized possessions to a guy I used to date...oh yes, I still have his number....*

Outside, the snowflakes whirled and thickened. My face was numb with cold. I briefly released my death-grip on the metal bars to tighten my hood. The time before Christmas should be full of laughter, parties, shopping, decorating, baking, family gatherings. So why was I dealing with the loss of my beloved business, a live television fund-raiser for a kind, outdoorsy fellow who'd died in an avalanche, and—as of twenty minutes ago—a crazy earring-studded guy sending poisoned love notes to a cop? Not to mention the sale of a valuable collectible item, more or less under the table, to a man I'd vowed never to see again?

But I was seeing him again. So much for *never*.

CHAPTER 3

The gondola inexplicably started again and I sighed with relief. At the top, I popped through the doors, shouldered my skis and pack, and headed onto the mountain's flat peak. A bitter wind blew me into the snow before I could don my skis. I gasped as my body hit the hard-pack and pain exploded up my knees. *Poor Cinda,* I thought as a red-clad ski patrol member gently helped me up.

When she wrecked her knees, had it hurt as much as this?

"You all right?" the tanned patrolwoman asked, her voice tight with concern. "Need help getting to the show?"

"No, thanks. I'm fine." I struggled to my feet, slung on the backpack, then conscientiously slotted my boots into my skis. *Eventually, today's show will be over,* I consoled myself as I reached for my poles.

I skied cautiously to the racks by the Summit Bistro. The restaurant occupied the eastern third of an enormous blond-log edifice known as the Chapparal Lodge. Snuggled within a stand of pine trees, surrounded by a wide apron of log decking, the lodge housed the bistro, the kitchen, a cafeteria, and mountaintop ski patrol headquarters. The lower level contained a storage area, rest rooms, and pay phones. I racked my skis and reflected that until a few moments ago, I'd had no dealings with the patrol, who were summoned if you had a crisis on the slopes. Patrol members, expert skiers who wore red uniforms emblazoned with white crosses, brought injured skiers down on sleds, closed dangerous runs, and yanked lift tickets from reckless skiers and snowboarders. Apparently, they also felt they should pluck a mid-thirtyish woman to her feet when she did a face-plant in the snow.

I sighed and surveyed the sprawling lodge, where I now prayed *someone* had thought to start a coffeemaker.

The bistro's heavy wooden door was locked.

Banging on it hurt my frozen knuckles and produced no response. Blackout curtains covered
the windows. The crew's bustle inside must
have muffled my knocking. Then again, maybe
they hadn't made it up the back road. This was
not something I wanted to contemplate.

How was I supposed to get in? Eileen had
told me that the rear part of the lodge's basement contained the mammoth trash- and
food-storage areas, plus railroad tracks leading
to the gondola. The gondola's cars were
removed at night, so that a second crew could
run canisters of trash down the mountain,
and unpack the food supplies that ran back up.
I moved along the decking and peered down:
the TV van, complete with chained tires and
a hood of snow, was parked by the rear entry.
So the crew *was* here. This was good.

Melting snowflakes trickled down my cheeks
and lips. It would take another ten minutes to
struggle downhill to the lower entrance. I
retraced my steps past the bistro door to the
cafeteria entrance, yanked on all six doors, and
finally found one open. *Eureka.*

The darkened cafeteria was empty. But at
least I was inside the building. There were two
ways of looking at Killdeer security, I thought
as I readjusted my backpack and made my way
to the kitchen entry. With all the locked
doors, computerized scanning of lift tickets,
and red flags screaming *Danger! Run Closed!*,
you'd think Killdeer was an outpost of the Pen-
tagon. On the other hand, in the last five
weeks I had repeatedly seen boundary ropes

down, run signs askew, office doors unlocked, and scofflaws ducking lift ticket scanners. Add to this: untended kitchens left open.

I pushed through the doors and looked around hopefully.

"Hello?" I called into the gloom. No answer. No Eileen Druckman and Jack Gilkey chopping egg roll ingredients. A single fluorescent bulb cast a pall over the cavernous space. Rows of steel counters lined with cutlery, pans, and bowls, alternated with shelves burgeoning with foodstuffs. My footsteps echoed and re-echoed on the metal floor.

Through the kitchen's swinging doors, noisy hustling and shouting was suddenly audible. I stripped off my snow-coated jacket and boots, opened my backpack, and slipped into the sneakers I wore for the show. Then I whipped past the walk-in refrigerators and deep sinks and pushed through more swinging doors to the restaurant.

The glare of TV lights blinded me. Mysteriously, the lights did not diminish the intimate feel of the dining room. Chandeliers elaborately twined with fake deer antlers, stucco walls stenciled with painted ivy, plush forest-green carpeting, a moss-rock fireplace with a glowing hearth—all these gave the bistro the air of a ritzy hideaway. Silk roses and unlit candles topped pristine white damask tablecloths. Along one wall, a blond woman was hanging an arrangement of artworks. *Elegant Gourmet Restaurant at Eleven Thousand Feet Above Sea Level? No problem!*

About five and a half feet in height, wearing his usual black shirt and ski pants, Arthur Wakefield tucked his clipboard and ever-present bottle of Pepto-Bismol under his arm and barreled in my direction, leaning forward at an acute angle. His taut, no-nonsense air made him look older than the twenty-nine I knew him to be. The director, Lina, a paraplegic woman who rarely left the production van, I had only met once. She gave her cues to the two cameramen and to Arthur via headsets. I had a full plate dealing with Arthur himself: He worried and complained enough for three people.

Clean-shaven down to the cleft in his dimpled chin, Arthur wore his ultracurly black hair combed forward, Roman-emperor-style. Dark circles under his eyes made me wonder about the hangover quotient. I braced to hear the latest crises.

"Here you are, then. Four minutes late." He *tsk*ed, then added, "Rorry Bullock was supposed to be here at seven. Nobody's seen her. Eileen Druckman should have arrived with her chef. So we're in a bit of a pickle. A gherkin, maybe."

"Just tell me what I need to know so I can get ready." I hesitated. "No Rorry?" Again, I felt guilt. I should have called her, maybe offered her a ride...

"Do you know her?"

"She and Nate used to live near us. Rorry and I taught church school together." Glancing around at the chaos in the dining room, I had a sudden memory of the fun Rorry and I had had with our fourth-grade class, as we acted out the story of the Valley of Dry Bones. All of us had leaped wildly around the narthex floor once the boy playing Ezekiel prophesied....

Arthur asked, "Did you know she was pregnant when the avalanche happened? They'd been trying for ages. Right after Nate died, she lost the baby." He sighed, and I wondered if the miscarriage, with all its attendant physical and emotional pain, was the reason Rorry had not responded to my letter. Why hadn't I followed up? "Everybody at the station loved Nate. And his shows were popular with the granola set." Arthur searched his pockets fruitlessly for an antacid. "So every year we do a memorial fund-raiser for him. The Federal Communications Commission only lets us raise money on air for *ourselves*. Sad, because Rorry needs money." He raised a black eyebrow at me. "I was hoping you, Goldy, could introduce Rorry. I wanted her to say a few words at the beginning of the show. She said no to me."

"I haven't seen her in a long time—"

He smoothed the top of his curly hair. "Just ask her yourself, will you? Do you have your script?" I nodded; he glumly assessed the top page of his clipboard. "Live fund-raising is not that different from taping. Just crack a joke if something goes wrong. Most important: If the phones stop ringing? We've got *zip*. If that happens, the camera will focus on the silent telephone bank. I'll cue you. Watch your screen. Be out here and ready to go at quarter to eight. Got it?"

I nodded compliantly. Arthur again consulted his clipboard. I gazed at the far wall in search of dark-haired, slender Rorry Bullock. What would I say to her? Why hadn't I known about the baby?

Arthur waved at the row of grills and stovetops along the back wall of the restaurant. Called the *hot line,* this was where I did my work before the camera. Then he pointed to a row of empty chairs against the far wall of the bistro. "That's where the phone bank will be. We'll get you wired when you come out."

I nervously made for the hot line. Five weeks earlier, Arthur had impatiently explained that broadcasting from Killdeer presented too many technical problems to go live for all six weeks. But we *were* doing it today. Although the term for my persona on camera was "the talent," this talent was definitely afraid of committing more bloopers. I suspected I was the cause for Arthur changing from Rolaids to an extra-large bottle of Pepto-Bismol. Did that affect his taste buds, I wondered?

When I finished arranging plates on the hot line's tile bar, I whisked back to the kitchen. Thank heavens: Eileen and Jack had finally arrived.

"Goldy!" Eileen Druckman called and rushed to hug me. "You made it." She had newly short, newly blonder hair and was wearing a clingy royal blue turtleneck and black ski pants. She looked terrific. "Think the boys will be able to snowboard in this mess?"

"When did snow ever stop two fourteen-year-olds?"

In the background, Jack Gilkey smiled bashfully as he looked up from chopping scallions. Jack was pale and thin, and possessed craggy good looks, sort of *French Cro-Magnon man*. His dark eyes were earnest, and his long, mahogany brown hair was woven into hundreds of thin braids pulled into a ponytail.

"Thanks for helping, Jack," I said sincerely. He nodded, and I wondered again why Arthur had been adamant that I should do the show alone, without help from the bistro's excellent chef. Jack had fixed a stupendous dinner for Eileen, Arch, and me at Eileen's condo, so I knew he was a great cook. Plus he was *much* cuter than I was.

Ah, well, who was I to decipher the mysteries of PBS? The three of us set to work filling glass bowls with black beans, shredded cooked chicken breast, grated cheddar cheese, and egg roll wrappers. I fished out my script, peered into the dark interior of the larger of two walk-in refrigerators, and retrieved a bag of delicate frisée greens and a head of crisp radicchio. Because I prepared only two longer or three shorter recipes per show, I wouldn't actually be tossing the salad today, although I would talk about it. Arthur had told me to instruct folks to use the meal's *wine,* rather than lemon juice or vinegar, as the acidic ingredient in the dressing. Easy enough, as were the crab cakes, which I had urged Arthur to include. They were made from pasteurized crab, and sent my clients to heaven. Make that my *former* clients.

"Any progress on getting your business reopened?" Eileen asked, once we'd set up the ingredients so they didn't obscure the large portable screen where I watched the camera's movements. The babble of voices from the telephone bank almost drowned her out.

I mumbled, "Not yet," and scanned the row of chairs set up behind the two cameras. I was startled to see the face and shoulders of Rorry Bullock emerge from just behind the screen. *Now that I saw her, what should I say?* I didn't know.

I sighed and turned my attention back to my work. Fifteen minutes to showtime. I still needed to be wired. A bubble of panic rose in my throat. Arthur nodded to me, then in Rorry's direction. While Jack and Eileen leafed through the script to make sure I had every single ingredient, I hurried over to the screen.

"Rorry?" I asked nervously. "Remember me? Goldy? Fellow church school teacher? Supervisor of kids carving clay tablets of the Ten Commandments?" One of our more memorable projects, the tablet-making had been surpassed only by the blowing of horns to bring down the Sunday school walls, à la Jericho.

Rorry turned and faced me. She was wearing a sagging gray sweatshirt, and looked uneasy and out of place. She was dunking a tea bag into hot water. Her look was unexpectedly defiant.

"I'm sorry," I stumbled on, wishing I hadn't tried to be funny. "This day must remind you of Nate—"

"Long time no see, Goldy." Rorry's face was unreadable, her tone bitter. She slurped some tea. "Don't feel sorry for me."

"I'm so sorry," I repeated, in spite of what she'd said. "Didn't mean to upset you—"

"I'm not upset," she interrupted. "Just puzzled."

"About what?" My question sounded stupid, even to me. I shakily wired the microphone Arthur handed me through my double-breasted chef's jacket.

"Two minutes," he warned. "Mrs. Bullock, I don't suppose we could convince you to say a few words for PBS—"

"No!" Rorry's reply was nearly a shout. The hand holding the plastic cup trembled; pale green tea slopped out. Arthur rushed away.

"Rorry," I murmured. "I just heard about the, your, other loss. I didn't know about the baby, and I know you loved Nate—"

"Nate is the only man I've *ever* loved," she cut in fiercely.

Why the rudeness? I didn't get it. My cheeks reddened. Why did I always make things worse when I was nervous? "I *know* you did—"

Rorry lifted her chin. "You don't know a *thing*, Goldy."

She walked away from the screen, toward the spectators' seats. Slowly, she seated herself. I gaped, stunned. During my years of marriage to my first husband, Doctor John Richard Korman, a.k.a. The Jerk, I'd seen plenty of his ob-gyn patients. I could read them pretty well. Why had no one told me about Rorry?

Three years after the death of the only man she swore she'd ever loved, Rorry Bullock was nine months pregnant.

I didn't have time to reflect on Rorry and her condition, though. Arthur raced back and sternly ordered me to test my mike. I nodded, swallowed, and rasped, *one, two, six.* My tongue was dry. When Arthur moved away, I poured myself a glass of water from the hot line sink. Had Rorry remarried? Did she have a lover? What was going on?

Don't be preoccupied while you're on TV; everyone will be able to tell something's wrong, Arthur had warned when we'd first begun shooting. After the turkey-boning and sauce-spilling incidents, I'd concentrated harder. Now Arthur—clutching Pepto and clipboard—murmured into his headset about the sequence of shots. He rechecked the audio for the six-person phone bank. Then he trotted over and delivered a last set of directorial laws: "Never admit you've made a mistake. We'll break at the halfway point to show a clip from one of Nate's old shows. Watch the screen, watch your time, but don't be obvious. I'll signal you."

Finally he backed away. I blinked into the bright lights, forced myself to clear my mind, and shuffled through my notes. *Do the egg rolls first.* On the counter, the delicate wrappers lay next to the glimmering bowls of stuffing. *Quickly, the crab cakes. Talk about how satisfying a hot, succulent shellfish dish is after skiing.*

On the hot line's closest stovetop, a finished set of crab cakes was waiting for the final shot of the entrée. *Last, do the dessert.* I would have preferred a chocolate treat, but Arthur said chocolate was too tricky with dessert wine. So I was making gingersnaps. The wine Arthur had paired with them cost seventy-five dollars a pop.

Arthur morosely called for silence, then counted down loudly from five to one. The red light on top of Camera One blinked on. I took a shaky breath.

"Greetings from Killdeer!" I began, and hoped I was the only one who could hear the wobble in my voice. "A very special show today commemorates the loss of a dear friend of the Front Range Public Broadcasting System...." And I talked on about how we remembered Nate, how special his show had been to those of us who'd been regular viewers. Then I gave the phone number where folks could call in, and segued into a cheerful review of the show's menu.

My screen showed the visual for the egg rolls. When the camera returned to me, I mixed the cheeses with the other south-of-the-border ingredients and swiftly rolled them into the wrappers. I slid the egg rolls into a deep-fat fryer that Chef Jack, hovering on the sidelines, had set to the proper temperature, and we were on our way. If I could only ignore the two cameras intimately focused on me, I thought, I'd be fine. I'm never happier than when I'm cooking.

I launched into my patter about buying crab and mixing it with easy-to-find ingredients. I smiled at the camera, mixed the ingredients for the sauce, and patted rich cracker crumbs on both sides of the soft, luscious cakes. Then I dropped them into the hot sauté pan with a tantalizing *splat.* The phones rang; I gabbled on about food and love going together.

Standing beside Jack Gilkey, Eileen grinned crazily when I commented that the Summit Bistro was a cozy, romantic spot to enjoy lunch during a day of skiing. Arthur shot Jack a dark look and swigged Pepto-Bismol. I rolled on.

You could offer a rare, old-vine zinfandel with the appetizers, and a sauvignon blanc with your main course, I sang out gaily. At this, Arthur, bless his heart, finally cracked a smile. Then he guzzled more Pepto. The camera panned to the phones, where three of the volunteers were chatting with donors. Off-camera for a moment, I scanned the crowd and bit back my second gasp of the morning.

Doug Portman, buyer of Tom's historic skis, had arrived. Looking older, pudgier, and balder than the last time I'd seen him, he waggled his fingers at me, despite the fact that I'd forgotten his free-food ticket. Just then all the phones rang. I made Rorry Bullock's face out in the crowd. Her eyes were slits, her face tormented. Why? The fund-raiser was going well. Why was she so upset? Arthur wrote on his clipboard: *10 seconds to* BREAK! I quickly moved the crab-cake pan to the sink and introduced a clip from one of Nate's programs.

Once the five-minute spot was underway, I sat, drank more water, and reviewed my script. *A live show.* While the audience shifted in their seats, my palms sweat and my heart jogged in my chest. Still, I was beginning to think I might survive this ordeal. I had just finished readying the dessert ingredients when Arthur waved his clipboard. *30* SECONDS!

I could hear the crack in my voice when I announced, "The aphrodisiacal qualities of ginger, cinnamon, and nutmeg in these gingersnaps will spice up your love life, no question about it! Especially if you pair them with a luxurious dessert wine." I raised my eyebrows naughtily at the camera and started up my hand-held mixer. Plasterlike blocks of butter stalled the mixer's motor. *Hnnh, hnnh,* the engine growled. I pressed the button again, again, and yet again. The beaters refused to move. I glanced up: The live-show disaster I'd feared had struck. The cluster of folks closest to me—Eileen and Jack, the two cameramen, and Arthur Wakefield—were gaping at me. I felt like the pilot of the *Hindenburg*.

My ears buzzed and I heard Rorry say, *You don't know a thing, Goldy.* The seconds ticked off; the camera eyes glared. I pressed the mixer button hard. *Hnnh! Hnnh!* The bank of phones fell silent.

I grinned at the red light on top of Camera One, quickly unplugged and replugged the mixer, then pressed the Restart button. The beaters strained and moaned, as if they were blending cement. Hadn't Jack or Eileen softened the butter? Did "room temperature" at eleven thousand feet mean *forty degrees*? The butter was hard as a brick.

Arthur's gloomy visage loomed behind the camera. He looked as if his best friend had just gone *down* in the *Hindenburg*. The mixer ground gears, stuttered, and made a small sound along the lines of *kerpow!* before spewing a cloud of dark smoke in my face. I coughed and choked. What had Arthur said to do? *Tell a joke.* Somewhere in my brain, I had surely stored half a dozen funny stories of culinary mishaps. Unfortunately, I couldn't think of one.

Fanning away the smoke, I blinked at the bank of lights. Arthur furiously scribbled a command, then, scowling, held up his clipboard: COOK!!!

I locked the bowl into the behemoth backup mixer. Bigger, more powerful beaters roared into clumps of butter and dark brown sugar. Encouraged, I tentatively cracked an eggshell

Mexican Egg Rolls
with Spicy Guacamole
Dipping Sauce

2 tablespoons vegetable oil, plus
   additional oil for deep-fat frying
1½ pounds chicken breast, trimmed
   of fat and finely chopped (½-inch
   square pieces)
2½ cups chopped onions
1 to 2 tablespoons prepared dry chile
   mix, to taste
1 cup canned black beans, well drained
4 ounces (1 small can) chopped
   green chiles
1 cup grated Cheddar cheese
1 cup grated Monterey Jack cheese
½ cup finely chopped cilantro
½ jalapeño chile, seeded and finely
   chopped
3 tablespoons of picante sauce
1 teaspoon salt
1 pound egg-roll wrappers (16 in a
   package)

In a frying pan, heat the 2 tablespoons
oil over medium-high heat until hot
but not smoking. Add the chicken and

onions, stir well, then add the chile powder and stir again. Stir for several minutes, until the onions turn translucent and the chicken is just cooked. Remove the pan from the heat, and add the beans, chiles, cheeses, cilantro, jalapeño, picante sauce, and salt, and set aside. On a very lightly floured surface, place 1 egg-roll wrapper at a time and, following the directions on the wrapper package, roll ¼ cup of the filling into each egg roll. Complete the 16.

In a wide frying pan, pour vegetable oil to a depth of ½ inch. Heat to 370°F, then place no more than three egg rolls at a time into the oil and fry for 3 minutes per side, or until golden brown. Drain on paper towels. Serve with sauce.

Makes 16 egg rolls

Guacamole Dipping Sauce:

1 avocado, peeled, seeded, and
   chopped
juice of 1 lime
1 cup fat-free or regular sour cream

½ cup medium-hot picante sauce
⅓ cup finely chopped cilantro
1 tablespoon grated onion
½ very finely chopped jalapeño chile, whirled in a small blender or food processor

Either mash all ingredients together until well combined, or whirl in a food processor until smooth. Chill and serve with egg rolls.

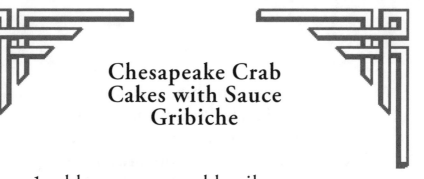

Chesapeake Crab Cakes with Sauce Gribiche

1 tablespoon vegetable oil
½ cup finely chopped celery
½ cup finely chopped onion
2 cloves garlic, crushed
⅔ cup lowfat mayonnaise
¾ teaspoon dry mustard
½ teaspoon paprika
1 teaspoon salt
⅛ to ¼ teaspoon cayenne pepper, to taste
1 pound crabmeat (can use refriger-
    ated pasteurized crab)
1⅓ cups club cracker crumbs,
    divided in half
2 additional tablespoons vegetable
    oil, divided in half, plus extra to
    oil baking pan

In a frying pan, heat 1 tablespoon oil over medium heat, add the celery and onion, lower heat, and add garlic. Sauté over medium-low heat, stirring frequently, for 3 to 5 minutes, or until translucent but not brown. Remove from the heat and set aside.

In a large bowl, combine mayonnaise with spices. Add crab, ⅔ cup cracker crumbs, celery, onion, and garlic. Stir until well combined. Using a ½-cup measure, scoop out crab mixture and form into 6 cakes about 4 or 5 inches in diameter.

Spread the last ⅔ cup cracker crumbs on a plate. Dredge the cakes in the crumbs.

Preheat oven to 300°F. Lightly oil a 9x13-inch baking pan.

In a wide frying pan, heat 1 tablespoon vegetable oil over medium heat until it shimmers. Place 3 crab cakes into the pan and cook approximately 4 minutes per side, until golden brown. Place the cooked crab cakes into the baking pan and put them in the oven while you cook the rest of the crab cakes. Add the second tablespoon of oil to the hot frying pan and cook the last 3 crab cakes approximately 4 minutes per side, until golden brown. Place in the baking pan in the heated oven while preparing the sauce.

Makes 6 crab cakes

Sauce Gribiche:

1½ teaspoons finely chopped shallots
2 gherkins, minced
1½ teaspoons capers, drained
1 tablespoon finely chopped parsley
1½ teaspoons minced fresh tarragon
1 teaspoon fresh lemon juice
½ teaspoon Worcestershire sauce
¼ teaspoon dry mustard
½ teaspoon salt
¼ teaspoon sugar
freshly ground black pepper, to taste
1 cup lowfat mayonnaise
1 large egg, hard-boiled and finely
  chopped

In a small electric mincer or well-cleaned coffee grinder, combine shallots, gherkins, capers, parsley, and tarragon. Pulse for about 5 seconds, or until thoroughly combined and well minced. Set aside. Stir together lemon juice, Worcestershire sauce, dry mustard, salt, sugar, and black pepper. Stir into mayonnaise along with egg and minced shallot mixture. Serve with crab cakes.

Ice-Capped Gingersnaps

½ pound (2 sticks) unsalted butter,
   softened
1½ cups dark brown sugar
2 eggs
½ cup dark molasses
2 teaspoons apple cider vinegar
4 cups all-purpose flour
4 teaspoons ground ginger
1 teaspoon ground cinnamon
¼ teaspoon freshly grated nutmeg
¼ teaspoon ground cloves
¼ teaspoon ground allspice
½ teaspoon baking soda
1 teaspoon baking powder
½ teaspoon salt
Frosting (recipe follows)

Preheat oven to 350°F. Butter two
cookie sheets.

Beat butter until creamy. Add brown
sugar and eggs and beat until well combined, then add molasses and vinegar
and beat thoroughly. Sift together all
the dry ingredients and add gradually

to butter mixture. Using a 1½-tablespoon scoop, space cookies out 2 inches apart on sheets. Bake 10 to 12 minutes, until cookies have puffed and flattened and appear slightly dry. Allow to cool on sheet 1 minute, then transfer to racks and allow to cool completely.

Frosting:

1½ cups confectioners' sugar
2 tablespoons whipping cream
2 tablespoons milk
¼ teaspoon vanilla extract

In a shallow bowl, mix all ingredients well with a whisk. Holding the cooled cookies upside down by the edges, dip the tops into the icing. Allow to cool, icing side up, on racks until the icing hardens. Store between layers of wax paper in an airtight container.

Makes 5 dozen cookies

on the bowl's rim. Although I expected the egg to rupture, the first yolk and white plopped politely into the swirling mixture.

"As easy as cookies are to prepare," I announced nonchalantly to the crimson camera light, "some skiers would prefer to spend their day on the slopes. So they'll turn dessert preparation over to their personal chef!" I added with a two-hundred-watt smile. I was prevented from further self-advertisement by Arthur, who was waving his clipboard at me. *Faster!!!* it screamed.

The second egg was uncooperative. When I cracked the shell, the egg exploded. Arthur went to overhead cam in time to shoot errant eggshell daggers floating briefly on the batter before being gulped into the creamy vortex. I could imagine perplexed viewers calling in to ask: *Does the recipe call for eggshells? How long has this woman been in the food business?*

Cursing silently, I stirred molasses into the batter and slapped in a tumblerful of vinegar. I brandished a flat grater and insisted that grating whole nutmeg was essential. While demonstrating, I unfortunately grated three of my right knuckles, and blood spurted onto the nutmeg flecks. Without bothering to sift or whisk the flour and spices together, I dumped the whole mess into the molasses mixture and clicked the mixer over to "stir." The mixer moaned and sent up a windspout of spicy flour. I groped for a towel to wipe the powdery mess off my face. My microphone squealed.

I wondered if Arthur had opened the bottle of dessert wine, and if he'd let me chug it after the show.

Muttering, I scooped the fragrant dough into Ping-Pong-ball-size spheres. The phone volunteers raised eyebrows at each other: *Some caterer!* I slapped the uncooked cookies into what Arch called the "pretend" oven and struggled to compose a last enthusiastic pitch about new equipment for PBS.

Two lights above the phone bank flashed as the ringing halfheartedly resumed. I rinsed my hands and wiped them on the towel. Volunteers murmured to the donors. *How much longer?* My watch was obscured by ginger-snap batter. I plunged back into my monologue, urging viewers to tuck crab-cake sandwiches into their packs before a full day of skiing.

Camera One swept a wide-angle panorama of the hot line burgeoning with the completed, cooked dishes. Then the cameraman focused on the volunteers manning the phones, which had once again, drat them, gone dead. Arthur, pale with panic, shifted to a visual with the phone number viewers could call. He then ran a prepared tape of avalanche-avoidance safety tips. *Shun steep, leeward slopes. Listen for broadcast warnings of avalanche danger. If you're caught in unstable snow, grab a tree and hold on. And never, ever ski out of bounds.*

Too bad Arthur hadn't run safety tips for cooking live. I felt acutely, painfully embarrassed. *You don't know a thing, Goldy.* No kidding.

I looked for Rorry Bullock.

She was gone.

CHAPTER 4

As the credits rolled, I scanned the interior of the bistro. Arthur was talking urgently into his headset. Jack was handing Eileen a champagne glass filled with orange juice. Or perhaps it was part orange juice, part champagne. Eileen cupped the glass in her hands and beamed Jack a grateful smile. No one was hustling up to offer congratulations or tell me how much money we'd made. True, the show had been flawed by the cookie fiasco, and had lacked the public support of the pregnant widow. But there should have been *some* good news. Wasn't that what public broadcasting was all about?

Unfortunately, the only news coming my way was in the shape of pudgy, self-aggrandizing Doug Portman. His pate shone in the bright lights as he waved and shouldered toward the set through the dispersing crowd of spectators. I swallowed. How did you greet someone you'd had three dates with, eight years before?

"Hey, Goldy?" Doug bellowed. "You forgot my ticket!"

"Sorry, I—"

"Ready to rock?" he hollered. "It's really coming down out there!" People stared at him.

"Yeah, okay, I'm coming." I yanked off my microphone and surveyed the mess on the hot line counter. Fortunately, the bistro staff cleaned up after each show.

"Arch and Todd decided to take a group snowboarding lesson," said Eileen, suddenly at my shoulder. "Want a mimosa before you take off? Jack made them."

"No, thanks, I've got some business to conduct. Need to be sober. Are you skiing down?" Eileen replied that she was staying to talk to the PBS people.

The kitchen was jammed with folks, so I couldn't change there. I nabbed my clothes and Eileen and I walked together down the hallway to the bistro's ladies' room. While I was taking off my chef duds and slipping back into my ski clothes, Eileen sighed. "Sorry about the butter," she said ruefully. "It was almost frozen in the walk-in. Our microwave isn't working, and I was afraid to smash it to soften it, 'cuz that would have looked bad."

"Not to worry. Is Jack skiing down now? He was awfully nice, and I wanted him to know how much I appreciated his help."

"He has to do lunch prep, sorry." She looked at me solicitously. "Goldy, are you sure you're okay?"

"Yes, and thanks." We left the ladies', then paused outside the Lost and Found and glanced outside. The sky had turned a bright nickel. Swirling snow powdered Widowmaker Run. With a pang, I thought of poor Rorry.

"You can always stay with us, if the weather gets really bad," Eileen told me cheerfully. "We've invited Arch for another night."

"Thanks. But I promised Tom I'd be back this afternoon. I can pick Arch up tomorrow when I do my contract with Arthur, my one and only personal chef client."

"Friend, if you make a round trip to Aspen Meadow in this weather, you'll be one tired caterer."

"I'll be okay." Impulsively, I hugged her. Eileen was always a thoughtful friend, the best kind there is. "Thanks again."

Outside, I could just make out Doug Portman's glimmery black metallic ski suit and leather cowboy hat. He was stamping over to the snow-covered ski rack. Before pulling down his skis, he scanned the exterior of the lodge. Seeking me, no doubt. He doffed the snow-gorged cowboy hat and whacked it against his thigh. *Ride those skis, pod'ner!* Would Doug's hat make it to the bottom of the mountain, or would it join the fifty other cowboy hats I'd just glimpsed in the Lost and Found?

"Gotta split," I told Eileen. I zipped up my sensible down jacket and knotted the string on my waterproof hood. Eileen finished off her drink and handed me my scarf. I glanced at her empty champagne glass and hoped *she* wasn't skiing down anytime soon.

In the bistro dining room, the arriving

restaurant staff was clearing away the last vestiges of the show. The phone volunteers were wolfing down the food, without benefit of forks and spoons, no less. Hey! Fund-raising is an appetite-building business. One of the phone-answerers, a wife of a member of the Killdeer Hunt Club—they shot elk and deer, not foxes—stuffed a Mexican egg roll into her mouth and called out that we'd raised six thousand dollars in half an hour. She added, "That's pretty good." I didn't know if she meant the egg roll or the money. Scooping up two more egg rolls, she yelled to me, "And that was in spite of everything!"

Doug Portman had returned to the bistro and was looking around impatiently. I felt annoyed to be hurried. But I slipped my hands into my new padded mittens—a gift from Tom—donned my ski boots, and walked as gracefully as possible to the front door. Of course, walking gracefully in ski boots is like waltzing on cannonballs.

"It's snowing harder," Doug informed me, ever the weather reporter. "We'll take Widowmaker to Doe's Valley to Hot-Rodder to the base. I'll meet you at Big Map."

"Big Map," a familiar landmark at the base of Killdeer Mountain, was a large, plastic-covered map of the entire ski area's terrain. I could find the map without a problem, but when I mentally reviewed the runs Doug was talking about—a mogul-laced "black" run—i.e., a steep ski trail covered with big bumps, designated for expert skiers—followed by a "blue"—intermediate, that would no doubt be treacherously icy under the new snow, followed by another precipitous black slope— I thought: No dice.

"You go ahead," I told Doug politely. "I'll take an easier route, probably be a few minutes after you."

He scowled and shifted in his ski boots. "I don't have time for you to come *after* me. I want you to come *with* me," he insisted, still macho to the core. "I'm running late already." He hesitated. "Does Tom know we're meeting today?"

"Er, sure," I lied.

"Great. I've got something for him in my car. Don't let me forget to give it to you." He squeezed my elbow meaningfully. "It's great to see you again, Goldy, after all this time."

I pulled my arm away and wordlessly clopped to the door. If it hadn't meant so much to Tom that he sell the skis to make up for the expense of the new drains, I'd probably be skipping this whole encounter. *Great to see me again,* sure. I'd go down the runs Doug wanted me to, but *very* slowly. If he didn't like that, tough tacks.

Outside the entrance to the lodge, giant icicles hung from the roof, their thick bases as solid as tree trunks. The snow was now falling in thick pale sheets. Doug pulled his skis from the rack, snapped them on, and shoved off without so much as a backward glance. Once he whizzed away, the heavy snow instantly enveloped him.

With more caution, I started down the smooth side of Widowmaker. *Weight on the downhill ski, press through the arch of your foot,* my first ski instructor had taught me. I'd do my best.

The new powder on the slope, the falling snow, the lack of sunshine, my gray-tinted goggles—all these made seeing difficult. As skiers whizzed past, I concentrated dutifully on the slope five feet in front of my skis. Usually, I found skiing an invigorating escape. This was not true, however, when the slope you were on was too challenging. The curtain of snow enclosed me tightly. I could hear my labored breathing and feel every creak of my bones.

Most runs are set up like slant-sided wedding cakes. Long sloped sections alternate with narrow flat areas. On the flat sections, you can meet up with friends, figure out where you are, or just plain rest. At the first opportunity, I pulled over to a flat area by a sign marking the beginning of two more blue runs. One was Doe's Valley, where Doug had said he was going. It led to black runs. Right next to it, and feeding into the bottom of Doe's Valley, was the easier-sounding Teddy Bear Run. I decided to take it. I could catch up to Doug on Hot-Rodder.

Teddy Bear Run was smooth and dreamy, yet still steep enough to present a challenge. Feeling less apprehensive, I let loose with some speed. After the pressure of the show, the release was exhilarating. I surged down the slope, and felt as if I was flying.

I hockey-stopped dramatically, flushed with the thrill of my run, on the last flat area.

At the top of Hot-Rodder, neon yellow ropes stretched on bamboo poles across the entry to that particular slope. One of the ski patrol's *Closed! Hazardous Conditions!* signs swung from the middle of the ropes. Which way would Doug have gone? Beyond Hot-Rodder lay a double-black diamond run—the most challenging and dangerous—with the happy name of Coffin-Builder. Few skiers were bold enough to vault down *that* turnoff. The ones who did were lean and fast; they hung briefly in the air and then plummeted from view. *That* was probably where Doug had gone. It was where I would *not* go.

To my left, a blue run named Jitterbug beckoned. Before deciding which way to go, I waited for a noisy class of snowboarders on its way down Teddy Bear. Their instructor, clad in a bright blue ski school uniform, led the group as it artfully carved the snow. The kids balanced on their boards, adjusted to nuances in the terrain, extended their arms, and leaned into the hill—all as graceful and quick as surfers. I thought I spotted Arch in his new burgundy jacket, but when I called his name into the blowing snow, there was no response. Without a glance in my direction, the young snowboarders slid swiftly past.

I was cold. Icy pinpricks of snow fell on my cheeks and lips. I shivered inside my jacket and headed toward Jitterbug, which I knew to be a curvy blue run without too many surprises. At the base, Doug would be ticked off with me.

But there was no way I was skiing down Coffin-Builder.

The few straight stretches of Jitterbug were bordered by trees on the left and a yellow cord to the right. After a few moments, I stopped on the right side of the slope to rest. Snow obscured the far mountains, but the vista downward was breathtaking. The yellow cord marked a no-man's-land of rocks and pines that led down to two steep mogul fields, Hot-Rodder closest to me, Coffin-Builder beyond. On Coffin-Builder, a handful of expert skiers zigged and zagged through the bumps. I certainly hoped that it *was* Arch I'd seen at the top of Jitterbug. If I thought he was boarding down a black run, I'd probably have a heart attack.

I skied fast down the next section of Jitterbug. When I careened around a bend, I spied a crowd of people clustered ahead of me. Digging in my skis, I sent up a cloud of snow as I came to an abrupt halt.

Why was everybody stopped?

Something scraped my cheek and I pulled back. It was a large shred of ash. Or a torn chunk of map. Without thinking, I tried to catch it. It was indeed a wadded piece of paper. That's when I realized that, along with the snow, this large confetti was coming down everywhere. It was as if someone had torn up a newspaper and carelessly dumped the crumpled bits of litter from the lift.

Litter?

"Mom, hey, Mom!" Arch's voice sailed past me. "Over here!"

61

I turned, but did not see my son. All around, gaggles of skiers had halted and were scooping up the tumbling papers. I did not see any snowboarders. "Arch!" I cried into the mêlée. "Where are you?"

"Here, Mom!" Suddenly my son scraped his snowboard next to my skis. Swathed in his dark red outfit and a stay-warm ski mask that made him look like an escapee from a horror movie, Arch clutched a handful of the paper. His prescription goggles had been pulled up at an angle on the top of his head, and I could just make out his merry brown eyes above the mouth mask. "Money!" he announced. "Hundred-dollar bills! It's falling with the snow! Here," he squawked as he thrust a fistful of bills at me. "Put these in your pocket, would ya?" Before I could protest, he scooted off on the board to retrieve more of the falling cash.

There was squawking and yelling among the skiers now, as a sudden updraft swirled the precious bills heavenward, where they mixed with a new tornado of flakes. A member of the ski patrol showed up and started hollering ineffectually for order.

Still uncomprehending, I stood grasping the wad of bills Arch had handed me, then stuffed them into my pocket. I dug in my poles and scooted to the slope's right side. An abrupt shift in the wind spun up a fresh storm of bills. The money smacked my goggles and I was momentarily blinded. I wiped the bills away and strained to see their source. They seemed to be blowing up from somewhere below where I stood.

To my right, the yellow boundary cord had torn loose from its moorings. The cord lay in a loop, then disappeared under the snow. Past the boundary pole, a row of boulders obscured the drop to the lower slope. I hesitated, then cautiously skied to the torn yellow rope. With great care, I glided down to the edge of the rocks that stood between Jitterbug and the steep drop-off to Hot-Rodder.

The view of the lower run was obscured by more boulders and a cluster of pines. Several sets of tracks led through the trees, while more circled the rocks. Money continued to fall. *Damn.* I had a very sinking feeling, despite the gleeful cries from the skiers downslope. Using the perpendicular-to-the-mountain two-step taught to all beginning skiers when they need to get uphill, I maneuvered up and around the rock pile.

On the far side of a boulder below me, a cowboy hat lay at the base of a small, barren aspen tree. A chill ran through me. Squatting cautiously on my skis, I slid carefully to the edge of the drop-off.

Sprawled next to a mogul, Doug Portman lay motionless in the crisp white snow. His legs seemed to be tangled with one of his skis. Beside the sharp half of a broken pole, his left arm was impossibly contorted. A splotch of blood was spreading on the snow.

"Ski patrol," I whispered, as I turned and

worked my way back up to Jitterbug run. "I—we—need help."

The crowd of skiers on Jitterbug were still grabbing at the whirling shreds of paper tumbling down with the snowflakes. "Help!" I called. No one paid attention. The bills swirled and landed on the slope, on moguls, on boulders, on branches of pine trees. Greedy hands reached impatiently for them.

I unsnapped my bindings, hefted up my skis, and crammed them into the snow in the X-position, the emergency signal for ski patrol to stop and give assistance. Then I lunged back through the snow to the edge of the run, below the coiled yellow rope and the row of boulders. Surely Doug would be all right... They would send in a chopper and take him to safety....

"Mom!" I recognized Arch's ski mask bobbing toward me. He was scooting himself forward, one foot on the snowboard. "Mom, what's wrong? Where are your skis? Mom?"

I put both hands straight out in front of me, warning my son to stop. Then, praying even as a stone formed in my chest, I glanced over the cliff. From this vantage point, I could see Doug Portman. He hadn't moved.

I didn't want Arch to see him. I knew Doug Portman was dead.

CHAPTER 5

"Mom!" Arch's voice had grown desperate. "Why are your skis crossed? Mom? Are you hurt?"

I shook my head. Unnerved by my silence and outstretched hands, Arch finally skidded his snowboard to a stop.

Around us, the snow fell. Where was the patrol? Another torrent of bills swirled up from the lower run. More jubilant skiers joined those already on the plateau. They stretched, bent, fell, and rolled out of their skis as they merrily dived for cash.

"Agh!" A woman's shriek cut through the din. I could not make out who had screamed. "That's disgusting!" shouted a tallish woman as she flung bills onto the snow. "That's *blood*! There's *blood* on it!" Her eyes searched the slope above. She saw me, my crossed skis, and my son, motionless on his snowboard. She took off down the hill.

The skiers hoarding the bills slowed their grasping movements. Heads bent to inspect the money. Suddenly, mittened hands were throwing down fistfuls of cash. More blood-stained bills blew upward, swirled with the snow, then resettled on the slope. In places, the money left erratic pink trails. Skiers pushed off queasily, suddenly eager to be away.

"Mom! What is *wrong*?"

"What's going on?" barked a man who'd skied

up to Arch. Tall and lean, he wore stylish wrap sunglasses and a uniform. Ski patrol, I thought, in numb relief. A thick red headband held back his gray hair. "Are you all right?" he asked my son. "Whose skis are these?"

Arch gestured and I waved my hands over my head. Another skier hockey-stopped six inches behind me, churning a wave of snow into my face. He too demanded to know what was happening. The ski patrolman shunted away this intruder by assuring him he had the situation completely under control. The skier took off and the patrolman addressed me. "Can you talk? Where are you hurt?" The patrolman's light blue eyes, gray eyebrows, and well-tanned, deeply wrinkled skin conveyed a seriousness I felt I could trust.

"Send my son away," I said tersely, as if *I* knew exactly what the situation was, which I didn't. "Please. I need to show you something. My son mustn't see it."

There was a fractional hesitation in the patrolman's shrewd eyes. Then he pivoted to Arch. "Young man, could you please proceed to the ski patrol office at the base?" he called. "Wait there. I'll bring your mother down."

Arch cast a worried glance in my direction. I nodded to him that it was all right. Only then, with a last concerned look, did he reluctantly move away.

"Are you injured? Can you tell me who you are?" demanded the ski patrolman.

I told him my name, what I'd seen on the

lower run, then motioned to my former perch. As I traipsed up clumsily in my ski boots, the patrolman, a deft skier, quickly two-stepped to the spot. He peered over the edge of the precipice, whistled softly in surprise, then pulled out his walkie-talkie and spoke rapidly.

A moment later, he snapped his radio shut. "Mrs. Schulz, Goldy Schulz," he said when I arrived at his side. My feet were so cold I couldn't feel them. The patrolman touched my shoulder. "Did you see this man fall?" I shook my head. "Did you see someone hit him?" Again I indicated a negative. "There's no one else on that run down there, Hot-Rodder."

I swallowed. "It's closed."

"Have you talked to any other patrol members? When was the run closed?"

"I haven't seen or talked to anybody." My voice seemed to belong to someone else. "I have no idea when the run was closed."

"How long have you been here?"

"About fifteen minutes. Listen, I'm freezing. I need to be with my son. And—" I hesitated, then added, "I should tell you, I... I know that guy down there. We...started off skiing together at the top, and I was supposed to meet him at the base, but he was skiing faster—"

"We're getting help for him. What's his name?" I told him, and the patrolman nodded grimly. "Mrs. Schulz. I need you to look over the side again, please. I need you to tell me if this is *exactly* the way the man appeared when you first saw him." Snowmobiles were roaring up the lower part of Hot-Rodder. "Please, look one time. Try to remember *exactly* what you saw. It's important."

His voice faded away as I leaned over the edge of the run. I could not imagine what kind of terrible spill Doug Portman had taken. His large body was sprawled crazily, like a bulky scarecrow blown off its support. He lay half on his back, half on his side. Snowflakes had not yet completely covered his face, but heavy clumps of ice and snow virtually obscured his shiny black jacket and pants. Below him on the slope, his skis lay twenty feet apart. One of his poles had landed clear across the run. What looked like his goggles stuck crazily from the top of a mogul. Odd. Two things had indeed changed since I'd first seen him. More money littered the slope. And by Doug's left shoulder, the ugly blotch of blood had widened. I pointed out these details to the patrolman.

One of the patrolman's questions buzzed in my brain: *When was the run closed?* I stared down at the lower slope of Hot-Rodder, its moguls lined up in icy rows. Had Doug Portman ducked the rope that closed the run? How fast had he been going? What kind of maneuver had he been trying to make?

Three snowmobiles arrived at Doug Portman's body. Shouted orders carried up through the snowfall. *Get out the... Move the... Easy....* With great ease and speed, the rescue team hustled around in the snow and prepared the sled. *But,* my mind supplied, *there's so much blood...money everywhere....*

Who closed the run? When?

Had anyone known Doug was carrying so much cash?

I stared down mutely at the patrol members moving a floppy, unconscious Doug onto the sled. Maybe my experience living with a homicide investigator made me too paranoid. Still, I wondered, what if Doug had been hit? If he *had* been hit, intentionally or no, all the patrol's traipsing around on the mountainside would make it impossible to tell exactly what had happened.

"Can you ski to the bottom, Mrs. Schulz?" The patrolman eyed me skeptically. "Do you need me to go with you?"

"Wait a sec. Doug Portman, the man in the snow. Why are they transporting him down the hill? I mean, without waiting for...medics or for...law enforcement?"

"They're following procedure." His calm blue eyes studied me. "Don't worry about Mr. Portman, we've got the situation under control. Let's go now, all right?" I nodded. He murmured into his walkie-talkie, moved with enviable agility back to the right side of Jitterbug, and waited patiently while I stomped over to my skis and painstakingly snapped them back on. Ten minutes later, chilled but in one piece, we arrived at the ski patrol office at the base, a small log building with green trim located next to the rental shop. Arch, watching out the large window, instantly opened the door.

"Mom." His voice was hoarse with anxiety. "Are you okay?"

"Call Tom," I told him. "Please, hon, ask Tom to come to Killdeer. Can you manage that? Tell him we're okay but that it's an emergency."

Arch nodded and made for the bank of phones on the countertop of the bustling office. A wall of detailed maps, complete with colored pins, gave the place the appearance of a battle-control center. A group of patrol members standing in one corner eyed me before going back to their conversation.

"Into the far room, Mrs. Schulz," said my escort.

I followed my silver-haired companion through the crowded room. He opened a door and I walked into a small office. The patrolman told me to take a seat; he'd be back in a minute.

I had just struggled out of my ski gear when Arch poked his head into the room. His hair had become matted on one side, wildly skewed on the other. His cheeks were bright red.

"I got Tom. I told him you were all right but you'd been in a ski accident. He wanted to know what happened, and I said maybe you could come talk." He grimaced. "Those patrol guys by the phone said you couldn't come out yet. Tom said, 'Why not?' I said I didn't know, and Tom said he was leaving right away to come get you. He'll be here in about an hour and a half." My son pushed his glasses up his nose. He looked me over curiously. "*Are* you hurt?"

"No, hon. Thanks."

"So what happened? Somebody with a bunch of money had an accident?"

"I think so." I frowned. A needle of anxiety poked my chest...poor Arch. "Somebody was skiing and had a bad fall."

He glanced at the front office, then turned back to whisper, "They're really arguing about something out there. Gotta go."

A moment later my silver-haired companion returned. He was accompanied by a taller, massively built, grim-faced fellow who was carrying a covered paper cup. The big guy—fortyish, thinning dark hair, lumpy face—wore a belted maroon ski suit with the Killdeer logo across the chest. He introduced himself as Joe Magill, from Killdeer Security, before placing the cup on the desk in front of me.

"Your son said you liked coffee, so we brought you some."

"Thanks." I looked at the drink but did not touch it.

Magill, who had an oddly diffident air about him, announced that he was in charge. He gestured at the silver-haired man, said I already knew Patrolman Ted Hoskins, and that he and Ted had a few questions, if I didn't mind. I said nothing as the two men sat down. But I knew protocol: If there was any kind of investigation, the Furman County Sheriff's Department was in charge. Their efforts would be aided by the Forest Service, which leased land to the ski resorts, and by the ski patrol, a group of trained volunteers. In terms of *who was in charge,* Killdeer Security was fourth down the list.

"Now, Mrs. Schulz," Joe Magill began smoothly, "what we'd like you to do is talk to us about your day, beginning with when you got up this morning—"

"Excuse me," I interrupted. I took a shaky breath. "Mr. Magill? You're from Security?"

"Yes, Mrs. Schulz. Anytime there's an accident on the slopes, we're responsible for investigating. Did you witness the accident?"

"Could you please tell me where Doug Portman is now?"

Magill inhaled impatiently. When he leaned back in his chair, his ski suit made a silky, scratching sound. His opaque eyes widened. "Portman died in the ambulance, I'm sorry to say."

"I see...."

"Your son told us your husband is a police officer." Magill again.

"Yes, that's correct. He's on his way."

"This is not an official questioning, Mrs. Schulz. But we need your help. The sheriff's department and ski patrol will conduct an official interrogation as soon as a deputy arrives. The ski resort just needs to know if you witnessed the accident."

"Why does the ski resort need to know that?"

Magill cleared his throat. "In a case like this, with a prominent Killdeer citizen killed, we're probably going to be facing litigation of some kind. We need to know precisely what happened."

"Mmm." I probably should have drunk some coffee, but I held back. Accepting a drink from Magill felt as if I were conceding points to a man I did not know well enough to trust. Plus, I'd been at enough crime scenes to know that we should *wait* before I started answering questions. Not that this was a *crime* scene, but...Tom, I felt confidently, would want me to wait for a sheriff's deputy to arrive.

"Mr. Magill," I said finally, "have you contacted Mrs. Portman?" I stared at the paper-covered bulletin board and tried to conjure up a mental picture of Doug's wife. I'd met Elva Portman at a crowded law enforcement cookout several years ago, and had had a chance to talk to her for a few moments at a gallery opening I'd catered in Killdeer. She was sophisticated and wealthy, with glossy dark hair and porcelain skin, a young Rose Kennedy. Loved paintings with bold brushstrokes. Couldn't eat bell peppers.

Again I got Magill's flat eyes, the uncomfortable shift of the squeaky suit in the chair. "Elva and Doug Portman have been divorced for a couple of years. Elva lives in Italy now. So, you knew Portman, but haven't been in touch with him for a while? Patrolman Hoskins said you were skiing together?"

I looked up at the water-stained ceiling. *This guy does not need to know my story.* I hadn't even told *Tom* I was selling his skis to Portman. I was suddenly conscious of how badly Portman's death might play out in the media. *Prominent citizen dies on way to rendezvous with cop's wife.* I wished desperately I'd never contacted him about the damn skis.

Magill inhaled noisily through his teeth, a gesture of impatience. "Patrolman Hoskins told me that you claimed to be *acquainted* with Portman. But your son said he *didn't* know him—"

"My son? My *son*?" I snapped to attention, enraged. "You should know you can't question a minor without a parent present!"

Magill's suit squeaked as he leaned forward. "I'm not here to hurt you, Mrs. Schulz. I know you're a caterer, I know you do the TV cooking show." He gnawed the inside of his cheek, then asked in a perplexed tone, "Does your reluctance to talk to us mean you're here in some official capacity for your husband?"

"In some official capacity for my *husband*?" I echoed, bewildered. I remembered Doug Portman's words: *I've got something for Tom in my car.* I'd thought it was a book about the 10th Mountain Division, or a magazine on military memorabilia. But what would make Magill think I was here in an *official* capacity? He knew I did the show. I wish Magill also realized that I'd endured a snowstorm, a TV show that had to rank high in the annals of disastrous live performances, and a lethal accident. That was *enough* for one morning, thanks. This security guy's unofficial and inept interrogation had not impressed me favorably. Where were the police?

At that moment, as if in answer to a prayer, a short, dark, mustachioed man in a green sheriff's department uniform walked into the cramped office.

"Mrs. Schulz, forgive me for taking so long," said the deputy, whose name tag announced he was Sergeant Bancock. "I happened to be near the Eisenhower Tunnel when the call came, so I got here as fast as I could." He nodded to Magill and then dismissed him with an impassive, "I'll call you. Hoskins, you stay."

Magill, angry to be banished, banged the door shut with a little more energy than required. Pulling out a notebook, Sergeant Bancock sat down and began to ask me a routine set of questions: my name and address, what I was doing at Killdeer, and so on. Like Magill, he asked me to describe my day. This time, I did. I had just come to the part where I looked over the slope at the run below, when my husband strode in. *Thank God.*

Tom, a handsome, bearlike man with gentle green eyes and thick, sandy-brown hair, didn't need to announce that he was in charge. He just *was.* I felt thankful for it, and for him.

Bancock stood and shook Tom's hand. "Schulz. We're just getting going here."

"This is Ski Patrolman Hoskins," I said, getting to my feet. Tom nodded at Hoskins, hugged me, then searched my face.

"You all right, Miss G.? Want to go outside for a bit?"

"Thanks," I whispered. "I just want to get this over with. Is—"

"Arch has gone back to the Druckmans' condo," Tom reassured me, anticipating my question. "He's spending another night. I'll take you home, if you want. We can leave the van here."

I had to bite my lip not to exclaim: "Oh, yes, take me home, please!" Instead, I told him I was fine. Tom smiled tenderly at me, tilted his head at Ski Patrolman Hoskins, and sat down beside me. Sergeant Bancock smoothed out a fresh page in his notebook.

"Not much longer, Mrs. Schulz," he said. "Of course, the coroner may have more questions for you later. You want to talk more to Killdeer Security, that's up to you." Bancock reviewed his notes. "You told Patrolman Hoskins that you were meeting Douglas Portman later this morning. Is that correct?"

I gave Tom an apologetic look. If he saw I was sorry—deeply sorry—that I hadn't told him who the buyer of his skis was, maybe he'd forgive me.

But Tom did not look angry. Instead, he looked dumbfounded. "Meeting Doug Portman? You were selling *Portman* my skis?"

"I knew Doug collected stuff, and—"

"How did you know Portman?" Bancock interrupted sharply, with a warning look at Tom.

"Sergeant Bancock, Tom and I have been married not quite two years. Before that, I was a single mother. Every now and then I would go out. On a date. I spent a couple of evenings with Doug Portman, enough to know he collected military memorabilia. And I knew he'd become involved in politics. Something in law enforcement, right? I saw him every now

76

and then at the picnics." I paused. Bancock, Hoskins, and Tom all waited, too. "When I went out with Portman, he was a forensic accountant. I'd hired him regarding divorce proceedings from my first husband. I hadn't really talked to him for years," I went on. "I knew he'd married, now apparently divorced. When Tom said he wanted to sell some World War Two skis, I called Doug. We agreed to meet this morning after I did my cooking show."

Bancock made another notation in his notebook, then leaned forward, his expression impenetrable. "And did you?"

"Yes. He came to the bistro, where I was doing the show. Afterward, it was snowing hard. We agreed to ski down and meet at Big Map." I faltered. "That's how I knew what he was wearing...the black suit and cowboy hat. That's how I recognized him on the slope, when he'd...fallen."

Bancock stopped scribbling. "Did you see him drink any alcoholic beverages?"

"No," I replied without hesitation. "Nor did I see him eat anything."

"Did he complain of headache, nausea, chest pain, anything like that?"

"Nope."

Hoskins interjected, "But...did he seem drunk?" When I shook my head, he continued: "Did he seem tired?" No. "Have you skied with him before?"

"Never."

Bancock was writing again. "Had he skied any runs prior to coming to the bistro?"

I thought back to the morning. Had Doug been pink-faced, sweaty, breathing hard? Had he seemed tired? "Don't think so. Why?"

"Was Hot-Rodder one of the runs you were supposed to go down together?"

"Yes. But it was closed."

"It *was* closed," Bancock repeated crisply. "Bamboo poles with ropes and red flags were pulled across the top. But we can't find anyone on the ski patrol who shut the run."

Patrolman Hoskins glanced at Bancock; Bancock nodded at Hoskins to go ahead. "How about his equipment?" Hoskins asked me. "Did you see anything wrong with his skis or boots? Maybe his poles or bindings? Did he complain of anything not working, being loose?"

When I shook my head again, Bancock took up the questioning. "All right. Now, please describe once again everything that happened once you left the bistro. We need to know every detail you can remember."

This I did, including seeing Doug disappear into the snowfall, my own slower skiing as I followed, getting caught up with the crowd trying to catch money. Suddenly remembering the wad in my pocket, I pulled out the bloody bills and placed them in a paper bag offered by Hoskins. Then I recounted how I'd looked for the source of the cash and seen Doug on the run below.... Total time elapsed from the bistro to the death scene: about twenty-five minutes, I concluded.

"Please describe the exact appearance of the

victim," Bancock said, in a chillingly matter-of-fact tone.

This I did: ski suit, hat, skis off and broken, one pole down the slope. Doug, covered with snow, sprawled motionless, looking as if he'd taken a spectacular fall and landed like a grotesque rag doll. The blood. I shuddered.

"And what did you think when you first saw him, Mrs. Schulz?"

"That he'd hit his head."

"The money," said Bancock thoughtfully, tapping his notebook. "Did you request he pay you in cash, instead of by check?"

"He said he was paying cash, and I didn't ask why. Eight thousand dollars." I thought again of the blizzard of falling currency on the mountainside, and swallowed.

Tom rolled his eyes and Bancock snorted.

The latter went on, "Did anyone else but you know he had the money for the skis on him?"

"I don't have a clue." How much of that scattered eight thousand would the authorities ever recover? I shot another apologetic look at Tom. My husband's face was blank. I said, "What's going on here?" An awful suspicion dawned on me. I turned to Tom. "Did *you* know Doug Portman in some official capacity? What did he do exactly?"

Tom exhaled before replying. "He was in corrections. And yes, I knew him in an official capacity." He checked Hoskins' face, which revealed nothing, then Bancock's. The sergeant nodded.

"Doug Portman was the chairman of the state

parole board," Tom told me. "You didn't know?"

"No." Why would I? Belatedly, I remembered Cinda Caldwell, and her customer who'd mouthed threats about poisoning a cop. Did a parole board chief qualify as a cop? "Wait, there's something else—" I told them of this morning's interchange with Cinda. "Tom, didn't you get the message I left?" He shook his head and said he hadn't yet retrieved his messages. Bancock wrote down the name of Cinda's café. He asked Patrolman Hoskins if he had any further questions; Hoskins replied in the negative. The young deputy reviewed his notes, then asked for our phone numbers. While Tom recited them, I walked to the outer office to check on the snow. It was still coming down hard.

Does your husband know I'm meeting you?

I've got something for Tom in my car....

Doggone. I dashed back to the office. "Sergeant Bancock. There *is* something else I forgot to tell you. This morning, just before we left the bistro? Doug told me he had something for Tom."

Bancock gave me a curious look, then transferred the curiosity to Tom. "Had something for your husband?" he asked me. "What?"

"I have no idea. He mentioned it was in his car."

"Know what kind of vehicle he was driving?" Bancock asked.

I did not. Hoskins and Bancock went out to phone Portman's office, in search of a description. Tom asked, "Have you received any mail from the Department of Corrections lately?"

"No. Why?"

"The DOC sends out notices to a convict's victims and relatives of victims, before the convict comes up for parole. The board holds a hearing before parole is granted, so the victims can give their opinion on the guy getting out. Or not getting out." He shook his head. "If the DOC sent you a notice about John Richard, it might mean trouble for you. You see that, don't you?"

"Why? What trouble? What does this have to do with The Jerk? Look, Tom, all I did was go *out* with Doug Portman, eight years ago. Today I was just going to sell him some skis. Which one of those is a crime? What could that have to do with my ex-husband?"

Tom gnawed the inside of his cheek. "John Richard has been in the Furman County Jail for how long, four months?"

Blood rose to my cheeks. *No. Not parole for The Jerk. Not yet. Please.* I counted back. In September, John Richard had finally been convicted of assault—not of me, but of another woman. With the state penitentiary operating at double capacity, he was currently serving his two-year sentence in the Furman County Jail. "Almost four months." I searched Tom's face. "That's *got* to be too early for parole."

"Sorry, Miss G. I haven't memorized all the statutes."

81

"He couldn't be. Anyway, Tom, no matter what's going on with John Richard, Doug Portman *died while skiing*. This can't have anything to do with John Richard. End of story."

But I knew all too well that wasn't quite the end of the story. Why would Doug insist on buying Tom's skis with cash instead of a check? Wasn't that foolhardy? And speaking of foolhardy, if the run was closed, why was Doug Portman on it? People who died skiing usually suffered heart attacks. Or they collided with an obstacle and died of internal injuries. If Doug suffered an *internal* injury, there was an awful lot of his blood on the slope.

I knew, too, that a suspicious death raises questions first about the person who discovers the body. Say a woman finds the body of a parole board member. Say she has an abusive ex-husband, now in jail. The ex-husband is no threat, *until he comes up for parole.* If he's granted parole, what happens if the formerly abused wife takes exception to the decision of the parole board?

My body felt numb. This time, however, it wasn't from the cold.

CHAPTER 6

Hoskins and Bancock reappeared to say they had a description of Portman's BMW and were going to search for it. When the door closed behind them, Tom scraped a chair over, clasped my elbow, and spoke in a gentle voice.

"Look. I shouldn't have said anything."

"They were *your* skis. I *should* have told you—"

"Goldy, please. There's a lot going on here that's out of whack."

"No kidding." I finally took a sip of my coffee. It was cold.

"For one thing," Tom went on calmly, "why would Portman give you something for me?"

"I don't know. Maybe it's an article discussing the rising values of collectible skis. Wouldn't he have called the sheriff's department directly if he'd had something to give you from work?"

He waved a hand. "We'll know pretty soon. If this is work-related, if it has to do with a case, you shouldn't be acting as courier."

"What could he have had for you, relating to one of your cases, that couldn't wait until Monday morning?"

Tom raised his eyebrows. "Portman was kind of an eager beaver, very self-impressed. Of course, maybe on your *dates*, he didn't give that impression—" He chuckled.

"That's not funny," I said as he smiled.

"If some guy *I* put behind bars and *he* let loose out on parole has become a troublemaker, then we have problems." Tom moved his hand up to my shoulder. "I know you don't want it, but it might be a good idea for somebody to be with you."

"I don't need pampering, Tom. I'm fine."

"Where's Julian?" he asked pleasantly, as if he hadn't heard me.

"Julian is—" Actually, where *was* Julian? This fall, our twenty-year-old family friend and boarder had transferred from Cornell to the University of Colorado. Julian Teller's lifetime ambition, temporarily derailed owing to this change in colleges, was to become a vegetarian chef. Meanwhile, he was determined to pursue his B.A. no more than an hour away from us, his adopted family. "Julian is...let's see...it's Friday." Julian apprenticed in a Boulder restaurant on Tuesdays, Thursdays, and Saturdays, and his classes were..."Friday afternoons, he has film class. Then at night the class watches old movies. Afterward, he spends the weekend at a friend's apartment."

"Which means he won't be home."

"Look, Tom," I replied impatiently. "Please. I'll be fine. I'll probably still be up cooking when you get back tonight." I had lots of work to do at home, none of which required a commercial kitchen: preparing for an intake meeting with Arthur and baking cookies for a library party. The library wanted to throw a come-one, come-all holiday party for patrons.

I'd offered to bring the Christmas cookies. I was doing this volunteer food service so people would know I was still out there. So people would not think I had quit the food biz altogether. And what a price to pay for the Sunday reception: missing the Broncos play the Kansas City Chiefs! But I was determined to be a caterer full of the holiday spirit. And, with any luck, I'd have everyone fed and the place cleaned up in time to catch the second half.

Tom snapped open his cellular and called Marla. My best friend was not home. Tom checked his watch and announced to Marla's machine that she should cancel her plans for the rest of the day, drive to our house, and wait. "Goldy needs you," he concluded.

In spite of all that had happened that day, I smiled at the thought of hopelessly busy-with-life, immensely wealthy Marla Korman careening her Mercedes to our curb to await my arrival from Killdeer. Maybe she'd do it; Tom's message ensured she'd be eager for bad news. Meanwhile, I had Arch to speak to, a weekend crammed with nonpaying jobs, and looming questions about my former relationship with a parole board member, now mysteriously deceased.

Next Tom called Eileen Druckman's condo and asked for Arch. He handed me the phone.

"Mom?" My son's tentative, worried voice crackled across the connection. "Now can you tell me what happened?"

I told him a guy skiing Hot-Rodder was in an accident and I just had to talk to the patrol for a while. Was he sure he didn't want me to come get him?

"I'll be okay here, I guess." He sounded uncertain. An adolescent boy wants to be with you and yet despises mothering; he wants to make sure you're okay but doesn't want to appear to care. "What happened to the guy? Where was all that money coming from? Did somebody try to rob him?"

"Honey, I don't know. He died—"

"He's *dead*? Did he run into a rock or something?"

"Nobody has a clue. And yes, he was carrying a lot of cash; he was our buyer for Tom's World War Two skis. Listen, hon, I'll be coming back to Killdeer in the morning to meet with a client. We could ski together in the afternoon, if you want."

"Uh, no thanks." Ski with someone as uncool as your mother? No way. "Look, Mrs. Druckman wants to talk to you. I told her you witnessed an accident."

I groaned as Sergeant Bancock appeared at the door and summoned Tom to the outer office. Tom's lips brushed my cheek before he left.

"Goldy, what's going on?" Eileen's husky voice demanded. "Arch has been awfully worried about you, and so have I. There was an accident on the slopes? Someone died? Was it near the bistro, or further down?"

"No, it was closer to the base," I replied. "And I'm fine, thanks, there's no need to worry. I think a skier was going too fast on a closed run. He had a terrible fall."

"Arch said there was *money* all over the slope?"

"The man was carrying a lot of cash. It was disgusting. People were crazed, trying to grab it up."

Eileen muttered something about drunk skiers, then said she and Todd were looking forward to having Arch for another night. After the lunch rush, Jack was coming home to make them homemade spinach ravioli stuffed with pine nuts, napped with a Dijon mustard cream sauce.

With my stomach growling, I hung up. Parole for The Jerk. How was I going to research *that*? Not at the Killdeer Ski Resort, that much was clear. Tom still had not returned. A new hubbub emanated from the front office. *Now what?* I ventured out in search of more info.

Surrounded by ski patrol members and uniformed sheriff's deputies, my husband stood by a scarred oak desk. All the law enforcement folks seemed to be talking at once.

"Hello?" I called politely. "Would it be okay for me to take off?"

Tom murmured to a deputy and the deputy nodded. Then my husband turned and beckoned for me to come forward. When I joined them, Tom said, "Look, but don't touch. Please."

Perplexed, I stared down at the desktop. It was strewn with pamphlets, maps, memos, correspondence. Nothing on it looked especially unusual.

"Look at what?" I asked Tom.

With his fingertip, Tom carefully pushed back piles of paper, exposing an open greeting card. All the deputies and ski patrol folks craned down to make their own closer inspection. As a result, I couldn't read the thing.

"Wait." Tom's ocean-green eyes regarded me solemnly; he spoke deliberately. "Don't look at it yet, Miss G. I need to know *precisely* what Doug Portman said he had for me. Word for word."

"Well," I began. I shifted uncomfortably. "It wasn't that memorable. He said, 'I've got something for Tom in my car.' That's it. Why?"

Tom waved me forward. The crowd pulled back. As I leaned toward the opened card, Tom warned, "Don't even *breathe* close to it."

"What does the outside say?"

"It's a congratulations card. The outside message reads: 'Good Job!' "

Inside the card, an explosion of bright yellow stars was accompanied by the card's own greeting: *You're a Star!* Beside the yellow stars, where your thumbs grasp a card to open it, was something much more menacing.

Glued on both inside card edges were two perfectly round, filled pieces of plastic material. I frowned. From Med Wives 101, I recognized the plastic rounds as transdermal patches. Each was filled with a blue gelatinous substance. Patches of this type were usually used to administer pain or nausea medication through the skin, when the patient was unable to take a pill or give himself a shot. I looked more closely and saw a small, hand-printed message.

Thanks for nothing, Asshole! You're dead!!! There was no signature.

"What's that supposed to mean?" I demanded, mystified. "Was this card in an envelope? Was it addressed to someone?"

"It was in an envelope, an opened one, but there was no one's name on it," Tom said grimly. "This may be related to your coffee lady Cinda's story. Maybe this is the threat the guy was bragging about making. Threaten a cop? Threaten a parole board member? Anyway, I have to stay here and talk to these people. Then I'm going to take this card down to the crime lab." He shook his head. "If that blue jelly contains, say, anthrax, we could be dealing with something nasty. I've already called over to the coroner about getting the crime lab to run a couple of different drug screens on Doug Portman."

"So you think he..." I couldn't finish my thought.

"Might have been poisoned? Might have been close to dead before he hit that last mogul? Don't know."

My skin crawled. "Tom. Please tell me you didn't touch those patches."

"Nah. Sniffed 'em, though." Everyone laughed except me.

Irritably, I said, "Cinda told me that her waiter, Davey, talked to Barton Reed, the guy who was making the threats. Last night."

Tom riffled through the chaos on the ski patrol desk and unearthed a blank piece of paper. "Could you draw me a map to get to Cinda's place?"

It was while I was doing this that Hoskins and Bancock appeared at my side and announced I was free to go. They might be calling me later, they said again. As I handed Tom my crudely drawn map, Marla phoned. She eagerly informed Tom she'd be at our house at three o'clock, and did I need a bottle of cognac, prescription tranquilizers, or chocolate cookies and freshly ground espresso beans? *Whatever you think,* Tom told her, with a rich chuckle. That meant she'd show up with all of it.

Blisteringly cold sheets of snowflakes assaulted us on the way to my van. Words were blown out of our mouths into the swirling snow. When we finally found my vehicle, we moved Tom's skis out onto the snow-covered lot and searched in vain for my tire chains. I hadn't used them for three winters, and they weren't wedged into any of the van's crevices. We put Tom's precious skis and my battered ones back in and flung my equipment behind the front seat. Then Tom hugged me hard and murmured into my ear that he'd be home as soon as possible.

"Take it slow and you'll be fine," he assured me. "I'll call you. And Miss G.—until then, please try to stay out of trouble."

★   ★   ★

There's nothing like a Colorado winter to give you respect for nature's harsher side, I reflected as I piloted the van up the interstate's long climb to the Continental Divide. Vehicles of all varieties—with Nebraska, Illinois, Texas, and yes, Colorado license plates—littered the snowbanked shoulder of the ascent. Drivers struggling to dig out and chain up soon became caked with snow. They looked like miniature Abominable Snowmen.

In one place the guardrail was out. I shuddered to think of the thousand-foot plummet someone must have taken. Further along the shoulder, a man scooted beneath his station wagon. His prone body brought back an unwanted vision of Doug Portman's sprawled corpse. My van slid sideways. I grasped the wheel more firmly.

It was hard to concentrate on driving. First I focused on the aborted sale to Portman. Tom had said, *You know what that's going to mean, don't you?* Within the next day or two, I could surely expect a slew of unwanted, potentially embarrassing questions. *Why had you planned a private rendezvous with a parole board member? Why did you keep this meeting a secret from your husband? What connection did you have with the large sum of cash the dead man was carrying?*

How, I thought, do I get myself in these messes?

91

The taillights in front of me blinked scarlet in the blinding snow. I braked. My defroster whined as it labored—with little success—to keep my windshield clear.

The memory of the puzzlement in my husband's eyes made my heart ache. I couldn't shake the feeling that I had betrayed Tom, even if it was with that infamous cheapskate, Doug Portman, who'd died with cash pouring out of his bloody jacket.

I pressed carefully on the accelerator. Why had I ever gone out with Doug Portman? At one time, he'd saved Arch and me thousands of dollars. Would that come out, too? I groaned.

It had all started so simply. After I'd finally kicked The Jerk out, I'd hired Doug Portman. I was trying to take care of Arch, but making ends meet was a challenge. At the time I had no moneymaking job, only an apprenticeship in the Denver kitchen of a restaurant belonging to my late friend André Hibbard. When I'd needed money for groceries, for Arch's clothes or shoes, or to send Arch on a school field trip, John Richard had repeatedly pleaded poverty. This was a joke, but no matter how my lawyer tried to pry bucks out of the soon-to-be-ex, all we'd get were lies, delays, and more obfuscation. Finally, my lawyer had recommended I hire a forensic accountant to track down John Richard's true income and assets. When I called Doug Portman, he informed me he was an artist, and just did the accounting on the side. I'd told him he could illustrate his reports, as long as his work got me a good divorce settlement and decent child support.

He'd guffawed, that unforgettable, gasping hyena laugh that I'd quickly come to hate.

I shook off this thought and glanced outside. The snow had become a whiteout. I thought I must be near the Eisenhower Tunnel, but it was almost impossible to tell. I slowed the van to a crawl. When the whirlwind briefly thinned, a pickup truck in front of me slewed right, then left. I stopped and waited until the truck was underway again. When I touched the accelerator, my tires spun on the ice. Holding my breath, I backed up slightly, turned the wheel, and accelerated gently. To my immense relief, my van started forward again.

I sighed and thought back. Doug Portman had updated me weekly on the progress of his investigation. John Richard, who'd been having an affair with a woman in the St. Luke's choir, had enriched Miss Vocal Cords' bank account by a hundred thousand dollars. He'd also put his Keystone ski resort condo in his father's name. Doug had tossed a file on my kitchen table that proved John Richard had paid taxes on a sum several hundred thousand dollars *more* than what he'd told my lawyer he'd earned. *Forensics is the study of evidence,* Doug had announced pompously, *and I am a master of it.* He'd chortled. *Now you can prove how much this loser doesn't care what happens to you and your son. Want to go eat Chinese?*

Silly me. I'd said yes. At least somebody cares about me, I'd thought. When we went to dinner, Doug brought his portfolio: color photographs of his paintings. Over wontons and mu shu pork I commented politely on pictures of large, nonfigurative canvases which seemed to feature dull blotches of drab color. He declared his artwork was going to make him rich. It had been a reasonably painless evening that turned sour when the check came and Doug announced, *Your half comes to fifteen bucks.* Had I not cooed enough over his artwork? Surely he knew how broke I was? Did he treat all his female clients this way? Nobody, it seemed, wanted to treat me to anything.

The next time Doug presented me with a dismal report on John Richard's assets, he'd followed it with, *In the mood for some Italian?* After a *momento* of hesitation while I calculated my cupboard contents, I offered to prepare fettucine Alfredo. He wolfed it down, even asked for the recipe. Over coffee, I was politely enthusiastic as he showed me *another* fat portfolio, this of his representational paintings. All depicted historical weapons: the repeating rifle, the Colt .45, the bayonet. He said he was hoping to get a New York show for these works. Collectors would pay thousands for each painting! I murmured compliments.

The next week's discouraging report on The Jerk must have engendered some guilt on Doug's part. He pulled out tickets to a Denver showing of military memorabilia. Arch and Doug and I strolled past exhibits of samurai

94

swords, bloodstained maps of battlegrounds, state-of-the-art grenade launchers. I found it boring; six-year-old Arch had been in heaven. Doug sprang for vendor hot dogs outside Currigan Hall. He liberally squirted on ketchup and rattled on about his volunteer work at nearby Capitol Hill. It seemed Doug was campaigning for a friend who was running for the state senate. I dislike guns, I dislike hot dogs, and I find the state senate boring. Arch sagely assessed my mood while pasting mustard on his wiener; on the way home, he asked if the end of my relationship with Doug Portman was in sight.

Through the spinning flakes ahead, the tube of the Eisenhower Tunnel finally yawned. In the lane next to the van, another driver went too fast and careened off the median before straightening out.

When Doug had slapped his final report on my kitchen table, he'd assessed my rack of pots and pans and demanded, "What's cooking?" I'd smiled. I'd announced that nothing was on the menu but a trip to my lawyer. This had marked the end of my nonromance with Doug Portman, forensic accountant, artist, and bore. I'd received the house, a sixty-thousand-dollar divorce settlement, and a sizable adjustment in child support. Doug, with his ego, paintings, and plans, had been a man on the way up—and out of my life.

On my final approach to the tunnel, I tried to remember what Marla had told me about what had happened to Doug. He had married

Elva, just the kind of wealthy woman he needed. He'd given up accounting and moved to Killdeer, where he'd become involved in Elva's art gallery in addition to his own increasingly political commitments. His candidate had been elected; Doug himself had become involved in building high-end condos while writing about the arts for a regional newspaper. Someone *must* have told me he came to sheriff's department functions because he was connected to corrections. What I'd never guessed was that his political benefactor had made him *chief* of the state parole board.

If I was going to avoid even more suspicions about what was going on with my business and my life, I was going to need to find out more, I determined as I squashed down on the accelerator. And not only was I going to find out all about Doug Portman, I was going to find out the exact status of John Richard's stint behind bars.

Without warning, the van lurched forward. Wild honking burst from all quarters. A car had hit me from behind. I yelped as another hard thud shook the van and my teeth. More cars honked, but in the suddenly thicker snowfall I couldn't see the vehicles around me. My van slid across the left lane, where the bumper hit the divider with such force my neck snapped forward. I spun the steering wheel, but balding tires on ice have a life of their own. Another sickening thud sounded against my rear bumper.

It was a pileup, I realized helplessly. I was

the second domino, behind the pickup truck. But where was the truck? A grinding crash of metal on metal thrust me forward. I gasped as the van skated back across the lanes. Another *bang* resounded. The van skidded inexorably toward the guardrail. I saw a fleeting image in my rearview mirror, a horrified face. I braked again. It was hopeless. Another car whacked me broadside. My van crashed through the guardrail and I was airborne.

CHAPTER 7

Down, down, down the snow-covered hill the van flew. I was sure I would die. An internal brain screen flashed images of my younger self on the Jersey shore with my mother. Then I was holding Arch as a newborn. Pain shot across my back. Warm liquid ran up my arm. I saw Tom slipping the wedding ring on my finger. I thought, *But what will he have for dinner?*

The van slammed into something hard, jolting me forward. A wave of shadowy whiteness obscured the windshield. The van again bounced onto something hard—a boulder?—and shuddered. My vehicle flipped over, then flipped back. I was screaming. Then, with a terrifying *boom,* the van hit another rock. The windshield shattered. A shock wave of icy snow hit me in the face.

Suddenly, everything went still. I had the confused thought: *Arthur's intake meeting. I won't be able to cook this afternoon.* It seemed terribly easy to lie still and sleep.... *I'll bake the librarians' cookies tomorrow....*

I don't know how long I was unconscious. Suddenly, a distant voice called, "Hello?" My voice wouldn't obey my brain. I shook my head; snow slithered from my hair. I felt very, very cold.

Pawing and scraping sounds were audible overhead. "Hello?" the voice called again. I groaned and called back, "Yes," in a submerged voice. Actually, the rest of me *was* underwater, technically speaking. I wondered if I was frozen. I laughed weakly. Pain rippled through my chest and down my arm. Was there anyone else in the van with me, the voice asked.

"No," I tried to howl but it came out like a sob.

I should not attempt to move, the voice cautioned. I didn't want to move. I was breathing raggedly; my lungs hurt. Blood seeped down my arm. I squirmed: More snow fell away from my face. Suddenly, I was desperate to act. I reached up until my mittened hands were clear, waving in the blessed air. I called that I could get out on my own. Before I could do so, however, strong hands reached in and gently tugged me out of my prison.

The cold wind was a bitter shock. Something kept growling in my ear, like a huge mosquito. I was placed on a slanted stretcher. My head spun; my thoughts whirled. *Always use unsalted butter in baking.* Falling snowflakes burned my eyes. I was on a sled, not a stretcher, attached to a puttering, exhaust-spewing snowmobile. The sled was set at an angle because of the slope. I coughed—which hurt—and blinked. I couldn't see my van, but I could make out three men in uniforms. One of them was bent over my arm. I wrenched sideways on the sled to see what he was doing, but I was strapped in. The movement afforded me a look at my vehicle. The van looked like a squashed beer can—one that would never be recycled.

The men asked me my name and address. I almost giggled, thinking that this was the third time today uniformed people had come to my rescue. That had to be a record. I heard my rusty voice answering them, thanking them. I asked how my arm was, and heard: "Cut. Not too bad." They said I needed to go to a hospital in Denver. I mentioned my clinic in Aspen Meadow. It had an X-ray machine, a doctor on duty, and was an hour closer than Denver to our present location. "It's where I live," I added, although I had just told them that. "My home." *Home. My home. Oh, Lord, when will Tom finish our kitchen?* I started to sob, and the men clucked that I was lucky to be going anywhere.

Commotion on the roadway accompanied the arrival of two ambulances. Panicked, I asked if others had been in the accident. The officers looked at each other, then told me not to worry.

One fellow gently probed my neck. A lump of fear squeezed my throat shut as I peered down the hill. There was a smashed white pickup truck below my van. Its skewed, crushed cab was buried in snow. I couldn't see if anyone was in the front. The slope was strewn with debris and snow chunks churned up by the collision.

A horrific worry sprang into my consciousness: Had it been the pickup truck, and not a boulder, that had cushioned my van's landing? I said a silent prayer for the truck driver.

Two newly arrived paramedics checked my bones. In the swiftly falling snow, it was hard to get bearings, but from what the people around me were saying, it seemed the van and the pickup had landed on an outcropping that formed a cliff in the steep bank. Below us, the slope was precipitous, at least forty degrees, and formed a ravine with the high forested ridge running into the Divide. At the bottom of the deep gulch between the two hills, who knew how deep the snow was? Ten, fifteen, twenty feet? I shuddered.

Foul-smelling exhaust and the roar of the snowmobile engine announced we were about to go uphill. The snow was coming down so hard it seemed impossible to breathe. Glancing back at my wreck of a van, I thanked God that Arch had not been with me.

Crap, I thought crazily as the snowmobile

hauled me up the hill, *Tom's damn skis are still in the van. Leave them,* I thought just as quickly. *They've caused enough trouble already.*

Paramedics bustled me into the ambulance. One tended to me and monitored all my signs, while the other asked how I was doing.

"Not very well," I said. "Not very well at all."

Once we arrived at the clinic, my doctor checked for internal injuries and put a butterfly bandage on my arm. She told the ambulance driver to take me home. I should call her that night if I felt worse. I either thought or said, *Welcome to Aspen Meadow, an old-fashioned kind of town.*

This, then, was the scene that Marla told me she witnessed from the front seat of her Mercedes, parked in front of our house: an ambulance driving up—she knew I'd be in it, she said drily—followed by two handsome paramedics coaching me down onto our sidewalk. Me hollering that I was fine, to quit touching my arm. According to Marla, the hunky paramedics wisely declined to comment.

Beneath her fur coat, Marla's bulky body featured one of her pre-Christmas outfits, a forest-green silk shift highlighted with silver and gold threads, plus matching suede boots. She clucked, fussed, tossed her brown curls, and asked how I'd hurt myself *this* time. She shook her head when I said I'd been fine when I left Killdeer, but then there'd been this pileup....

She said I shouldn't have been driving. My van hacked and sputtered just getting across town, she pointed out. Forget making it home from a mountainous ski area. In a blizzard, no less. I agreed with her—what else was I supposed to do?—while she fixed me tea. As I drank a cup of strong, delicious English Breakfast, Marla brought a merlot out of our pantry. It had been a gift from Arthur Wakefield, who'd commanded me to sample it *only* with roast beef. Because of her heart medication, she couldn't have any. But she felt strongly that *I* should have some.

As I was finishing my first no-meat-accompaniment glass of wine, Tom called. I filled him in on my latest accident without too much detail, ignoring Marla's smirks. Tom said he was bringing Arch home from Todd's. My son was worried about me; he'd changed his mind about staying with Todd and wanted to be in his own place. Tom also said he'd called Julian. Julian was skipping his night of old films to join us for dinner—dinner that *he* would fix.

Marla told me to sit still while she set our oak kitchen table. She lamented that the library board was having a dinner meeting that evening, so she wouldn't be joining us. I watched her work. No question about it, the glass of merlot was killing the pain in my arm. I'd have to suggest tea with it to Arthur instead of beef.... Marla hugged me gently and left, promising to call.

Two hours later, Tom, Julian, Arch, and I dug into Julian's succulent, lemon-and-garlic-laced sautéed jumbo shrimp—his scrumptious version of scampi—served over spinach fettucine. I took a good look at Julian. His handsome, haggard face, dark-circled eyes, and earlength brown hair gave him the look of a typical sleep-deprived college student.

He sensed my mood. "Don't you like the shrimp?" he asked earnestly.

"It's out of this world," I replied, and meant it. But the events of the day had taken away my appetite. Arch and Tom, their mouths full, made *mm-mm* noises.

Julian put down his fork. "Goldy, now that your van's totaled, I want you to take my Rover. If I stay in Boulder, I don't need it." Julian's deluxe white Range Rover had been a gift from former employers. Before I could protest, he persisted: "My apprenticeship pays enough for me to share an apartment with some friends I've made. And I *will* be able to get around, oh mother of all mother hens."

"Julian," I murmured, "don't. Who are these *friends,* anyway?"

He laughed while Tom looked doubtful. Arch, stricken, exclaimed, "So you're moving out? You're *leaving* us?"

"Guys!" cried Julian. "If you're going to miss me so much, I'll come back every weekend!"

We agreed that I would take the Rover, and I thanked him. Julian beamed. I didn't know how difficult it would be to drive that vehicle for a personal chef assignment, especially with a bandaged arm. But the Rover *was* luxurious. More importantly, it had four-wheel drive. Julian then further mollified us with helpings of his pears poached in red wine and cinnamon sticks, surrounded with golden pools of crème anglaise. The first mouthful of juicy, spiced pear accompanied by the silky custard sauce was almost enough to make me forget my troubles. Still, I found that I couldn't take more than three bites.

When the dishes were cleared, I searched for and found a bottle of generic buffered aspirin. Tom announced that he was doing the dishes, no easy task, as our lack of kitchen drains still dictated use of the ground-floor tub. I was to relax, he insisted, and Arch and Julian should go do something fun.

Julian opened his backpack and pulled out a foil-wrapped package of his trademark fudge dotted with sun-dried tart cherries. I declined any, but Tom took two pieces before clearing the plates. With a mischievous smile, Julian offered a chunk to Arch. "Hey, buddy, how about a second dessert? Better yet, how 'bout I fix a batch of this Christmas fudge for Lettie? I can put in crushed peppermint drops instead of cherries."

Arch shot him a dark look. "No, thanks." Lettie was Arch's girlfriend, or at least he had been "going out with" this lovely, long-legged blond fourteen-year-old—the two never actually *went* anywhere—at the end of summer. To me, of course, Arch provided no updates on the status of the relationship. My only indications that he had any social life at all at Elk Park Prep were the carefully folded notes I found in his pants pockets when I was emptying them in the laundry room. Fearful that these papers were homework assignments that he would later accuse me of tossing—this had happened—I always unfolded them enough to read the first line. If Arch's small, vertical handwriting began, *This class sucks!* then I knew to toss the paper. He was communicating with *somebody*, anyway. Still, if we needed to plan for an additional Christmas present—Arch was notoriously last-minute on these things—I needed to know.

"So, is Lettie still in the picture?" I asked, noncommittally.

"Don't worry about it, Mom." Arch's eyes gleamed behind his glasses as he informed Julian, who now seemed repentant that he'd brought Lettie into the conversation, that he had something to show him. The boys disappeared. I swallowed three aspirin and wondered if there was any chance they could be contemplating Arch's ninth-grade reading assignment in Elizabethan poetry, or the homemade quantum mechanics experiment he was supposed to devise for his physics class. Probably not.

"Are you all right?" Tom said quietly, once he'd filled the bathtub with soapy water and the dishes were soaking. "You hardly ate a bite."

The aspirins weren't kicking in. "No, I'm not all right. But I will be soon. Thanks for asking." I wiggled my unfeeling fingers, rubbed my rapidly-blackening elbow, then tried and failed to move my neck from side to side. If I hadn't broken anything, how come everything hurt so much? Tom came over and gave me a healing kiss.

Just before eight o'clock, a state patrolman knocked on our door. Into our kitchen Tom ushered a tall, corpulent man with black hair so short and thin it looked like someone had ground pepper over his scalp. His name was Vance, and he wanted me to write down all I remembered about the accident. I scribbled what I remembered of the blur of events: cars skidding every which way, my inability to see what happened, being hit from behind, skidding, being smacked again and again and again. I'd hit another vehicle, crashed through the guardrail, and sailed down the hill. I begged for information about the truck's driver. The cop announced glumly that he'd died. My heart ached.

Officer Vance read what I'd written, put down the pad, and tapped the tabletop. "Tell me again what happened on the way *up to* the tunnel. *Before* the accident."

Patiently, I tried to visualize, then articulate, the happenings of those few minutes. The snow had been falling in sheets. Visibility had been wretched. What vehicles I could see were sliding haplessly on the ice. Then something had hit my van. All around me, cars were honking, thudding, spinning out of control. I'd careened down the hill, crashed into the truck, sunk into deep snow. I'd truly believed, I told the officer, that I was going to be buried alive in the white stuff.

As I related my story, neither Tom nor Officer Vance interrupted me. When I'd concluded, Officer Vance mused, "As far as you could see, then, there was a white pickup truck about ten yards in front of you. There was also a vehicle behind you."

"And one behind that, and one behind that." I waved my hand in a gesture of ad infinitum. The movement made my elbow howl with pain. "The noise of the crash was like books falling on your head. Thud, thud, thud, thud."

"But you couldn't see the cars behind you very well," the policeman asked, "because of the poor visibility, right? Are you sure you didn't hear that *thud, thud, thud,* and then your mind just supplied the image of books falling?"

I frowned and thought back. I knew this cop was trying to get at something. There *had* been a vehicle directly behind me. And yes, one behind that. That was all I could remember seeing. When I announced this, Tom pursed his lips. Officer Vance didn't blink.

"Right," Vance murmured. When Tom sat down at my side, Officer Vance slid the salt, pepper, and three unused serving spoons into a line. His thick, carrotlike fingers moved the salt cellar. "This is the white pickup." Then the peppermill: "This is you." The first spoon: "This is the guy behind you, another van." The second spoon: "Then there's another vehicle behind that van." He placed the last spoon in place. "Then here's somebody quite a bit farther back."

I concentrated on the objects, then moved the first two slightly to give the right scale of distances. But I had not seen a fourth vehicle, *somebody quite a bit farther back*. It had been snowing too hard.

Vance pointed to the last spoon. "The driver of this car farther back, a woman from Idaho Springs, was in a Subaru station wagon. Only she didn't skid into anybody. She was right behind another Subaru wagon, and the two of them were ten car-lengths behind you. Just before the accident, she swears that other wagon sped up wildly and *rammed* into the van behind you." Officer Vance moved the next-to-last serving spoon up toward the first spoon. "Then she heard the noise of cars colliding. She braked, and skidded. Ahead of her, the other Subaru sped up and rammed the van twice more. The snow made it hard for her to see exactly what had happened. In a fraction of a second, she saw the truck, and then your van, go over the cliff edge." He sighed. "By the time we got there, what with the snow and all the cars going by on the way to the tunnel, there weren't any skid marks left. Apart from what this woman said, we don't have a trace of the two vehicles behind you."

"I don't remember the cars behind me. Van, one or two Subarus, nothing."

Vance shrugged. "You were hit, you hit a truck."

"But...because of the snowfall, I didn't see the truck. At least, I didn't see it go over."

"The guardrail was busted in two places,"

he told me, "but aside from that, we don't have much physical evidence. The van behind you took off,"—he raised his shrewd, assessing eyes to mine—"and we can't find this Subaru the woman saw."

"So...are you telling me this accident was a planned hit-and-run?" I was incredulous. "That someone *deliberately* rammed the van behind me? Rammed it three times? Why would anyone do anything that insane?"

Officer Vance held up his hands. "That's what I was hoping you could help me with."

Tom reached over and gently clasped my fingers. "You witnessed a ski accident in the morning—"

"I didn't *witness* it," I protested. "I just...saw a guy lying on the slope. He died in the ambulance."

"In the road accident," Vance interjected, "we still don't know the identity of the guy in the pickup. We only know he's dead. Which makes the accident vehicular homicide." I moaned. "With the storm so bad, they won't be hoisting up either vehicle until the morning." He paused. "Did you see any vehicle, any person you recognized, anywhere on the road from Killdeer to the Eisenhower Tunnel?" Officer Vance demanded.

"No. Sorry."

"Did you witness any aggressive driving prior to your being hit?" Again, I shook my head. Officer Vance sighed. "This could have been a drunk. It could have been someone ticked off with the van driver, which would

109

explain why the van was long gone by the time we got there." When I stared at him in baffled disbelief, he picked up the pad, placed a card with his name and number on the table, and thanked me for my time. And if I remembered anything else... I nodded mutely and thanked him for coming. Tom showed him to the door.

"Do you think someone was trying to hit me?" I asked Tom, when he returned to the kitchen and poured milk and sugar into some cooked rice. "*What* are you doing?"

"Making a treat. I know you're bullheaded enough to try to cook tonight, and you can't do it on aspirin and an almost-empty stomach."

I sighed. "You didn't answer my question about the car accident."

He nodded and stirred the cooking mixture, which gave off a rich, homey scent. "I don't know. Hitting a van behind someone *else's* van isn't a very reliable way to kill someone on the road. Still, driving Julian's Rover is a good idea," he added thoughtfully. "As far as the roads go, the storm was breaking when Arch and I came through. No matter what, I feel more comfortable with you behind the wheel of a four-wheel drive. And speaking of the Rover, did you know General Farquhar had all the windows tinted very dark and bulletproofed?" I rolled my eyes at the mention of the super-paranoid military man, Julian's benefactor. Tom searched for a set of custard cups, then went back to stirring. "I want you to keep the cellular with you all the time. Watch who's around. Have somebody with you if you can. Just as a precaution, especially over in Killdeer, okay?"

"First of all, Tom, I can't even entertain the idea that that accident was a deliberate hit-and-run. The interstate was very icy. I could barely see the truck in front of me. And I think I'd have noticed somebody tailing me all the way from Killdeer. I mean, I'm grateful to be alive, but trying to execute the kind of move we're talking about, under those conditions, could be suicide."

"Miss G. Please. It's not difficult to take precautions."

"Sure, yeah, okay, I'll be careful." What did I have to lose? I already had a messed-up TV career, a ton of debt, no business, a wrecked van, and two mysteriously dead men: a parole-board member and a truck driver. Speaking of which. "Look, I need to call Arthur. The doctor said I could drive if my arm wasn't bothering me. So I'd still like to meet with Arthur tomorrow to arrange my personal-chef work for his party."

"I knew it," Tom said resignedly.

To demonstrate my resilience, I got up, zipped over to my kitchen computer, booted it, and searched for my notes on the assignment.

Tom shook his head. "Are you *sure* this is a good idea?"

But I was already dialing. Arthur answered on the first ring.

"Thank *God* you called, Goldy." His tone

was laced with mournful drama, as usual. "In the morning, I need you to be here by ten. I'll explain how I want things to go, and show you the layout of the kitchen before you start work. I've got dozens of callings to make about my wines—"

"Wait a sec," I interrupted as politely as I could. "Please, Arthur. I'm not sure I'll be able to be there by ten. There will be the ski traffic, and I have things to pack up, and I've got vehicle problems, because unfortunately I was in a car accident today—"

"But it's stopped snowing. You were in a car accident? For heaven's sake! There was an accident on the mountain today, guy was killed going down a closed black run. The Forest Service is closing Killdeer Mountain for a few hours in the morning to help the sheriff's department investigate it. That won't stop the ski traffic, unfortunately," he said mournfully. "A day for accidents. What a shame."

"Yes, indeed." I tried to make my tone noncommittal. "Maybe we can make our plans now, and you could just leave the key for me." I took a deep breath and waited for an explosion. I wasn't really expecting sympathy. I picked up the aspirin bottle and shook out a couple more. In Med Wives 101, we'd often told each other you could take up to six at a time. This was not advisable, medically speaking, but then again, being the wife of a medical student wasn't exactly advisable, either.

"I can't do that," Arthur replied, exasperated. "I live at 602 Elk Path in West Killdeer. Be here at ten. I want... I want the dishes you prepare to be *almost* done. Then I'll put on the finishing touches so my guests will think I slaved for hours."

"Ah, well, I've never—" I began, but he was gone.

I hung up the phone and frowned. Most of my clients start out anxious, I reassured myself. Once I serve them food, they're content. Only Arthur didn't want me to serve the food. He didn't even want me to finish cooking it. Ah, sufficient unto the day was the catering thereof. Or something like that.

With a flourish, Tom handed me a custard cup brimming with warm rice pudding. He'd sprinkled the pudding with cinnamon and garnished the top with a massive dollop of whipped cream. The cream melted slightly and slid sideways on the warm pudding. I took a bite: the dessert was dreamily thick, like a homey, melt-in-your-mouth porridge from heaven.

"Incredible," I said, and took another greedy bite. "I'm getting better already."

"That's why I made it," Tom said triumphantly. "Think the boys would want some?"

We listened. The faint thump of rock music reverberating through the ceiling was a sure sign the boys weren't listening to Tudor-style lute music.

"Better leave them alone," I replied. "After all, rice pudding is also great chilled."

Tom smiled appreciatively and dug into his own custard cup. "Julian seems good," he commented. "Tired, though."

"I'm worried about him."

"Miss G., you worry about everything. He loves being back in Colorado and he loves the film class, he told me so himself. Maybe he'll make how-to-cook-vegetarian videos after he graduates."

I smiled and scraped the bottom of the pudding cup. "Thanks for the treat. Can you possibly help me with the cooking I need to do for the rest of the weekend?"

"Cooking with you is only my *second* favorite thing we do together."

I laughed. From the walk-in, I drew out unsalted butter and eggs. Then I retrieved a bag of premium bittersweet chocolate chips and several bars of Godiva Dark from our pantry shelves. The library's Christmas Open House was in two days and I'd be away from my kitchen tomorrow. I asked Tom if he would chop the Godiva; he smiled and held out his hand.

I removed a pork tenderloin I'd started marinating the day before. Professional culinary literature urges the prospective personal chef to bring the first meal—a marvelous dinner using your best recipes—*gratis*. This is to show your client what a good and generous person you are. Arthur, if he'd been noticing, might already think I was a good and generous person. On the other hand, he probably thought I was a klutz. Still, that assessment could change once he ate his deliciously tender, herb-spiced, *free* pork dinner.

"Tell me about the parole board," I urged Tom, to distract myself from fretting about Arthur.

He sighed and continued to chop. "There you go again. Worrying."

I tapped buttons on my kitchen computer to bring up the chocolate cookie recipe I was working on. "Come on," I said, trying my best to sound reasonable. "I just want to know how the board operates. And I'm interested in your theory as to the reason Doug Portman had an anonymously written card containing a threat, and maybe some poison, too, and why he wanted to give it specifically to you."

Tom sliced the chocolate into dark, fragrant chunks. "First things first. There are six members on the state parole board, all appointed by the governor. Statutorily, two of them have to have a law-enforcement background. Portman didn't have a law-enforcement background, but I know he watched the newspapers. All the parole board members do. Every day, they're scared some felon they let out on parole might have committed a big crime. The board members really don't want that kind of thing coming back to haunt them. So." He pushed away the chopped chunks from the first chocolate bar and started on the second. "I think Portman got that card from someone *I* put behind bars, and *he* let out. But why would someone *he* let *out* come back and threaten *him*?"

I printed out the cookie recipe. "Maybe it's someone he denied parole to, who's finally out now. The name Barton Reed doesn't ring a bell? The guy at Cinda's?"

He shook his head. "I'd have to see a picture." He finished chopping the chocolate with a flourish, then rinsed his knife in the bathroom. When he came back, he gave me a long, gentle hug.

"You don't have to figure this out, Goldy," he murmured in my ear. "We should have the crime lab results back by Tuesday. Why not let go of this until then?"

"Whatever you say," I replied in a low voice. We both knew I never gave anything a rest, but dear Tom chose not to point this out at that moment. He merely mumbled something unintelligible, hugged me tight, and said he was going upstairs to check on the boys. I promised him I'd join him in a bit.

In truth, there was only one thing I could do to start cracking a case: Cook.

CHAPTER 8

I pressed the tenderloin through the plastic wrap. Before roasting, it had to reach room temperature, so the inside could cook along with the outside. I stabbed the pork with the sharp end of my digital readout thermometer, a help if you want to serve succulent, juicy meat but have a client who is trichinosis-phobic, then preheated the oven. I didn't want to take a guess as to the types of phobias Arthur held dear, but judging from our chats, fears about food were a distinct possibility.

Once the meat was in the oven, I set the beater to cream the butter for the cookies. Then I pulled out a bowl of wild rice that had soaked overnight. After one of our shows, Arthur had confessed he had wines to introduce to his best clients, and needed to do it at an in-home party, rather than in a bustling restaurant. He disliked cooking, even though he was pretty good at it. Could I help him?

Yes. And I would feed him in the bargain. I was taking a cereal concoction, the pork tenderloin, wild rice steamed in home-made beef stock, and a large salad of arugula and steamed asparagus. All free, to show my good-will.

Within ten minutes the kitchen was filled with the enticing fragrance of herb-flavored roast pork. I started the rice cooking in the homemade beef stock and turned my attention to the library-reception cookie recipe. As I carefully mixed dry ingredients into the creamy, bronze dough, my injured arm began to ache. My mind's eye raced backward to the van plummeting down the snowy slope. Really, it was a miracle I'd survived.

I mixed the chopped chocolate, dried cherries, chocolate chips, and nuts into the batter. A van behind me... Yes, I vaguely remembered now, it had been one of those shuttle vehicles

Snowboarder's Pork Tenderloin

2½ pounds pork tenderloin
  (2 tenderloins)
½ cup Dijon-style mustard
1 tablespoon pressed garlic (4 large
  or 6 small cloves)
¼ cup best-quality dry red wine
¼ cup extra-virgin olive oil
1 tablespoon dried thyme, crushed
½ bay leaf
¼ teaspoon freshly ground black
  pepper
½ teaspoon granulated sugar

Trim fat and "silver skin" from tenderloins. Rinse, pat dry, and set aside. Place all the other ingredients in a glass pan and whisk together well. Place the tenderloins in the pan, turn them to cover with the marinade, cover the pan with plastic wrap, and place in the refrigerator for 6 hours, or overnight.

Thirty minutes before you plan to roast the pork, remove the tenderloins from

the refrigerator to come to room temperature.

Preheat the oven to 400°F. Use a roasting pan with a rack; line the bottom of the pan with foil and place the tenderloins on the rack. Roast the tenderloins until an instant-read thermometer inserted in the center registers 140°F—about 20 to 25 minutes. Do not overcook the pork; the center should still be pink when served. Remove from the oven and slice.

Makes 10 servings

Chocolate Coma
Cookies

1 cup blanched slivered almonds
4 ounces bittersweet chocolate (2⅓
   1.5-ounce bars of Godiva Dark or
   1½ 3-ounce bars of Lindt bittersweet chocolate)
1 cup dried tart cherries
12 ounces semisweet chocolate chips
   (1 regular-size bag)
2 cups rolled oats
2 cups all-purpose flour
1 teaspoon baking powder
1 teaspoon baking soda
½ teaspoon salt
½ pound (2 sticks) unsalted butter,
   softened
1 cup packed dark brown sugar
1 cup granulated sugar
2 eggs
1½ teaspoons vanilla extract

Preheat the oven to 350°F. Butter two
cookie sheets.

In a nonstick pan, toast the almonds over
medium-low heat, stirring constantly,

for about 5 to 10 minutes, until they have *just* begun to turn brown and emit a nutty aroma. Turn out onto a plate to cool. Chop the chocolate bars into small chunks, no larger than large chocolate chips, and set aside.

In a large bowl, combine the cherries, chocolate chips, and oats, and set aside.

Sift together the flour, baking powder, baking soda, and salt, and set aside.

In a large mixing bowl, beat the butter until creamy. Add sugars and beat until light and fluffy, about 4 minutes. Add the eggs and vanilla. Beat the mixture until well combined, less than a minute. Add chocolate chips, chopped chocolate, cherries, and nuts. Using a sturdy wooden spoon, mix well by hand, until all the ingredients are thoroughly incorporated. Using a 1-tablespoon scoop, measure out cookies onto sheets, leaving two inches between cookies (about a dozen cookies per sheet).

Bake 12 to 14 minutes, or until the

cookies have set and are slightly flattened and light brown. Cool on sheets 2 minutes, then transfer to racks to cool completely.

Makes 6 dozen cookies

that ran between the ski resorts and Denver International Airport. But another vehicle close behind the van? I squeezed my eyes shut and tried to remember. Nothing came.

As I scooped the chocolate-cherry-nut-studded batter onto cookie sheets, I recalled reading many an article about high-country drivers fleeing scenes of weather-related accidents. Sticking around on a snowy, slick roadside in poor visibility could be more hazardous than taking off. At least, that's what hit-and-run drivers claimed after a snowstorm, if they were apprehended—a rare occurrence.

The thermometer beeped. I removed the sizzling pork, checked the timer on the luxuriantly scented wild rice, and slapped in the first cookie sheet. A wave of fatigue swept over me. It was past eleven. I had to finish the cookies and let the meat and rice cool. Then I could go to bed.

But something kept nagging at me—something besides the death of Doug Portman, besides the threatening poison patches, besides even the accident. What was it? I sifted through my emotions. What was I feeling? Numb.

I turned on the oven light. The cookie spheres were softening, the batter bubbling to a golden brown. I closed the recipe file on my computer and opened a new one, labeling it only "Unfortunate Friday." Then I sat and frowned at the empty screen until the timer beeped.

I removed the baking sheets. Tiny lakes of melted chocolate winked inside the crisp, golden cookies. While they were cooling I put in another sheet, then checked the rice: about fifteen more minutes.

Back at the computer, I typed:

1. What intersection of Tom and parole board member Doug Portman would lead to a death threat on Portman? Was the death threat even linked to DP's skiing accident? Does it have something to do with Barton Reed?
2. Why was Hot-Rodder closed? Who closed it? Did Portman ski down the run, knowing it was off-limits? Or was the run closed <u>after</u> he was on it? Who knew he had $8,000 cash on him? Was his death a bungled robbery? Why would it be bungled? How did Portman die, exactly?
3. What was Doug Portman's background in Killdeer? Who were his friends and neighbors? More importantly, who were his enemies?
4. Who hit my van?

Treat every puzzle with questions and chocolate, was my motto. And it worked, usually. Despite the fact that I'd already indulged in three desserts tonight, I had to taste one of my cookies, right? I *mm-mm*ed over the first bite, with its crunchy toasted nuts, tart sun-dried cherries, warm dark chocolate, and buttery, crisp cookie. I took another bite, and felt as if I must be going into a chocolate coma. So that was what I would call them: Chocolate Coma Cookies.

Hold on. *Treat every puzzle with...* I finished the cookie, licked my fingertips, emptied the steaming wild rice onto a wide platter, and removed the second sheet of cookies to a rack. What had I heard earlier in the day? I stared at the blinking cursor.

Don't feel sorry for me. An inscrutable face. An acidic tone. *I'm not sad...just puzzled.* I typed:

5. What is bothering Rorry Bullock? Is she still grieving her husband's mysterious death? Or is she embarrassed to show up pregnant and unmarried, three years after her husband's death?

I frowned at the computer. Maybe Rorry had remarried, and I just hadn't heard about it. Hold on: There *was* one person who *would* know the answer to that question. Marla.

I checked my watch: eleven-fifteen. Long years of church work had taught me that if you had even one compulsive talker on a committee of overly nice folks, the meetings can extend ad nauseum. If Marla had come home and gone to bed, she would have turned off her ringer and directed calls into her machine. So I wouldn't wake her up if I called, I thought happily as I punched in her numbers.

"Goldy? What in the world are you doing

up?" Marla had caller ID and loved to greet me with a breathless question.

"Cooking. How 'bout you?"

She groaned. "I can't drink because I'm on heart medication. But I keep thinking, if I had a drink and died, I'd never again have to listen to Karen Stephens talk for three hours without taking a breath." She groaned again. "It would be worth it."

"Listen, I saw Rorry Bullock today. Up at Killdeer."

"Oh, yeah?"

"Yes, as a matter of fact. I'd say she's about a week away from giving birth." I paused. "Did she remarry? Does she have a boyfriend? Why didn't you tell me she was pregnant?"

"Oh, that *doggone* prayer group and their insistence on secrecy," Marla groused. "Yes, she's pregnant, and we're praying for her because she doesn't have any more money now than she did when she and Nate were living in an apartment here in Aspen Meadow."

I asked tentatively, "And the father is...?"

"Hah! Ask Rorry! She definitely has not remarried, I can tell you that. Anyway, I'm convinced she hasn't come back to visit St. Luke's because somebody would tell her she should get married before she has the baby."

"Oh, please!"

"When do you want to get together? We could ski during the week."

"I'll call you. First, though, I'll let you get some sleep. Your fatigue is making you into a cynic."

126

I signed off and reread what I'd written in the computer. Satisfied that I had outlined the questions that had been troubling me, I wrapped the meat, packed up the cookies, and stored the cooled rice. It was nearly midnight. I could sleep for six hours, wake Arch to go see Todd, pack the Rover, and be on the road to Killdeer by seven. I crept upstairs and curled up next to Tom's warm, deliciously fleshy body. I heard a soft rustling sound and peered over his shoulder. A new torrent of flakes pattered against our windows. Lit by the street lamp, the blue spruce outside our window was swathed in snow. By morning, Aspen Meadow would be blanketed, and in one week we would have a white Christmas.

I snuggled closer to Tom. I had very little besides the revolver to put under the tree for him. I resolved to look for another gift in the Killdeer shops. A little shopping trip would cheer me up after I finished with Arthur. Of course, to get to Killdeer, I would first have to shovel out the Rover.

Make that, sleep for five hours.

When my alarm shrilled at five A.M., the darkness in the house seemed impenetrable. Out the window, the spruce had vanished. How much more snow had fallen? I shivered and checked my new clock. It was one of those digital jobs with a battery that kicks in when the power goes off. Through my early morning daze, I realized that that was precisely what had happened. I shivered, then concluded that with no power, there were no streetlights, no night-lights or—more crucially—no heat. Unless it was an extended outage, the contents of my refrigerator and freezer should be fine. Still, I wondered if we could afford to move to Arizona.

"Don't go," Tom murmured.

"Don't the Rockies train near Phoenix?" I asked. "When does spring training start?"

"What?"

"I'm talking about the baseball team, Tom."

He groaned, turned over, and pulled me in for a gentle hug that melted my body's residual stiffness from the accident. "End of February. You want to worry about sports, the Broncos are playing Kansas City tomorrow."

"I *want* to have an excuse to go to Arizona, and following our baseball team's spring training might be the excuse I'm looking for. At the moment, though, I have to pack up for my personal chef job."

"Not yet," he murmured into my ear. He moved his hands along my lower back. "You're freezing, for heaven's sake. Let me warm you up."

After carefully moving my sore arm, I yielded happily. What was there to worry about? The food was done, and if the Rover was four-wheel drive, why bother to dig it out? Besides, I thought as I kissed Tom's inviting mouth and rolled in closer to him, this was our favorite thing to do together, right?

Twenty minutes later, I felt much warmed and much revived. After a quick shower— there was still hot water in our tank, thank

God—I toweled my wiry-wet blond curls. Maybe the ghostly effect of the two candles I'd lit in the bathroom—our flashlights had vanished sometime during the kitchen remodeling—made me appreciate all we had. *Just think,* I reflected as I buttoned my catering uniform, *the medieval monks had it worse than this.* True, they washed and dressed by cold candlelight in the morning's wee hours, but without hot water or hotter sex, how good could *they* have felt when their day began?

To my surprise, Arch woke and slid from his bed without complaint. He wasn't cold, because he'd slept in his ski clothes. That was one way around a power outage.

I handed him a candle for the bathroom and then made my way downstairs. From their lair off the dining room, Jake the bloodhound and Scout the cat began to stir. In addition to the drains, one issue that had sent the county health inspector into the ozone layer had been our family's ownership of a dog and a cat. Per code, Tom had dutifully partitioned off a separate space in our dining room. Within this designated pet area, Tom had built a canine-feline exit to the out-of-doors. Our dining room looked like someone had stuck a large closet in it, but that was all right. *Think of a pet store next to a caterer's,* I'd said to the inspector, when I called to tell him of the change. He'd snorted and hung up on me.

Now Jake the bloodhound was eager to go out and bay at the darkness, but there was no way I was letting him loose this early. Scout the cat opened a sleepy eye, rose, sashayed to the bottom windowpane abutting our front door, and cast a disparaging look at the cold, dark snow. He moved off to his food bowl and meowed loudly. There was no telling Scout it was too early for anything.

While dripping copious amounts of hot candle wax on my right hand, I managed to spoon out cat food for His Majesty. Tom pounded down the stairs. He was carrying another candle along with boots, mittens, and a heavy jacket. He was going to start a fire and clear Julian's car of snow, he announced. While I held my candle up to the dark depths of the still-cool walk-in, Tom, whistling happily, wadded newspapers, snapped kindling, and piled up logs in the living room fireplace. By the time I had the food loaded in a Styrofoam box, my dear sweet husband had a blaze crackling. I came out to warm my numb hands and saw that he'd also filled his antique black kettle with water and hung it on the post he'd installed in the hearth while he was redoing our kitchen. Steam spiraled from the kettle.

"Listen," he told me, "I have a meeting this morning I can't skip. But if you can be back by four, I'll drive Arch back down to see his dad."

For heaven's sake. I had forgotten it was Saturday, Arch's regular jail-visit day. Taking Arch to see The Jerk always put me into a rotten mood, so whenever someone else offered to escort Arch on this dreaded mission, I jumped at the offer.

"Thanks, Tom. That'll really help."

He nodded and shuffled outside with Arch. Moments later, a sudden blaze of headlights lit the driveway and the Rover engine roared to life. Inside, a stiff wind howled down the flue. I could just make out Tom and Arch whisking what looked like ten inches of powder off the Rover. I strained to hear a faraway rumble that signaled the approach of a county snowplow.

"Ready to roll?" Tom, covered with snow, was halfway in the front door. "Got a box ready?"

"Yes, but I'll carry it out, thanks."

"Not with that arm, you won't." He stomped into the house, yanked off his boots and tossed them onto the mat, and sock-footed his way to the kitchen. Who was I to argue with a cop, especially one who was much bigger than I was?

Fifteen minutes later Arch and I sat in the Rover, travel mugs of creamy chocolate steaming between us. Tom's makeshift version, composed of kettle-dipped water, cocoa, sugar, powdered creamer, and milk, was actually quite luscious, like a hot chocolate *gelato*. Of course, as my mammoth fourth-grade teacher had told us, *Hunger makes the best sauce.* That teacher ought to know, my mother had commented drily.

Main Street had not lost power, and the thermometer on the downtown branch of the Bank of Aspen Meadow read four degrees. Snow had filled the street's gutters with two-foot drifts

131

that had been wind-sculpted into sharp-edged peaks. Streams of Christmas lights whirled in the snow and battered the windows of Darlene's Antiques & Collectibles and the Grizzly Bear Saloon. Seeing Aspen Meadow Arts and Crafts reminded me of the years when Arch and I had spent hours buying presents for his teachers. Arch had agonized over framed solitary gold-plated aspen leaves and pieces of bark painted with images of bull elk. When I'd asked him last week what cookies he thought I could make for his teachers this year, he'd curtly replied that *The other kids aren't bringing the teachers gifts.* Now I glanced at the decorated windows, and ached for those old times with my son, before *what the other kids are doing* dominated our lives.

"Arch," I said tentatively as he sipped his cocoa, "does Lettie have pierced ears?"

"Oh, no, Mom, don't start. Do *not* buy Lettie anything."

"I just asked—"

"Why do you want to know? Are you going to pierce them for her if she doesn't?"

"I just thought—"

"That you'd *buy* something for her for Christmas. The way you always do."

"Arch! I have never bought a female friend of yours a single thing for Christmas!"

"Remember those two Valentine's Days, when you went out and bought big baskets of candy and stuffed animals for girls you thought I was going out with?"

"But you *were*—"

He turned to face me. "I was *not* going out with them," he said fiercely. "I wanted to buy them bags of M&M's. But oh, no, good old *Mom* had to buy the most expensive baskets possible." His tone was scathing. "And then you were all upset when you found out I wasn't going out with the girl you just bought all that stuff for. Mom, you can't *buy* me a girlfriend."

I took a slug of cocoa and told myself to be patient. "I thought you told me Lettie *was* your girlfriend."

"Yeah, and I wish I hadn't told you *anything.*"

"Arch!"

"Don't buy her *any*thing!"

"Don't *worry!*" I shot back.

Arch turned toward his window with much aggravated shuffling of his down jacket. Suddenly I deeply regretted offering to take him snowboarding this morning, especially since I had just remembered Arthur Wakefield informing me that the mountain would be closed for a few hours for the Forest Service investigation into Doug's accident. I sighed and glanced at Arch. If he'd been so worried about me last night that he'd canceled his overnight with Todd, why wasn't he being nice this morning? Ah, adolescence. In any event, if Lettie wanted little silver pine trees dangling from her earlobes, the girl was out of luck.

We passed the lake, and I tried to put Lettie out of my head. Streetlights ringing the snow-covered sweep of ice revealed a lone fisherman with a lamp attached to his cap. I could not imagine how cold he was. No fish could taste *that* good.

I snuggled into my warm leather seat. The gorgeous Rover boasted every possible amenity, and gave a smooth ride, to boot. Julian had been wonderful to loan it to me. When it struck me that *Julian* could find out what Lettie wanted for Christmas, I instantly banished the thought. Perhaps I *was* trying to buy a Christmas present, a girlfriend, and happiness for my son.

No more.

CHAPTER 9

By the time I gingerly pulled the Rover onto the interstate, ski traffic was flowing steadily westward. Cars and trucks hummed through the Eisenhower Tunnel. Arch was asleep, or pretending to be. West of the Divide, the snow had finally stopped. A bank of thick white clouds clung to the far mountaintops. Above it, an azure-tinted sky promised sunshine. From the high drifts lining the roadway, wide swathes of snow blew across the lane dividers and obscured them. I was too timid to take my eyes off the road to see if there were any signs of my accident. The last thing I needed was to total *another* vehicle.

Tom had called the wrecker service that dealt with near-the-tunnel mishaps and asked them to tow my van to a secure storage lot in Dillon, near the tunnel. After I finished in Killdeer, I would pick up the historic skis on the way home. We wouldn't try to sell them again— of that I was absolutely certain.

When I made the turnoff for Killdeer, a red-tailed hawk swooped close to the Rover. I braked and Arch woke with a start. After a moment of getting his bearings, he pointed to a herd of elk along a rocky stretch of road only sparsely covered with snow. Since he'd turned fourteen, he'd ceased giving direct apologies. He simply resumed speaking as if nothing had happened. While I found this disconcerting, at least it was better than silence. Eileen Druckman complained that Todd gave her the silent treatment on a daily basis.

I turned onto Camp Robber Avenue, named after a wild bird frequently seen on the slopes. The killdeer was also a bird commonly seen in our state, and its distinctive "kill-dy, kill-dy, kill-dy" call could be identified by even the most inept birders, among whom I counted myself. But the loud, invasive camp robber ruled the slopes, boldly hopping onto picnic tables, pecking at leftover hamburgers, then carrying off its booty to nearby pinetops.

I passed a series of gray, white, and beige clapboard double-wide houses, actually massive duplexes marketed as condominiums. This was a misnomer, of course. Any half-house here possessed more floor space than our Aspen Meadow home.

I was surprised to see Eileen watching at a window when I pulled into her driveway. She wore a robe undoubtedly designed by the same guy who'd dressed Elizabeth II for her coronation. I glanced at my watch: eight-thirty. I'd made great time. Still, the anxiety in Eileen's face was worrisome. I told myself I could spend a maximum of thirty minutes here before taking off to find Arthur's place. But it was important to check on Eileen, and comfort her if she needed it. If Todd was in one of his silent phases and Jack was cooking at the bistro, my friend could be desperate for adult conversation. I'd been there myself.

But Jack answered the door. He was certainly a handsome dude, and I wondered again—although I'd never asked Eileen—exactly what had brought the two of them together. Disheveled half-braided dark hair surrounded his pale, unshaven, impish-looking face. His lustrous dark eyes were as big as Bambi's. His well-built, slim-hipped torso was shown off to good advantage by a turtleneck and printed chef's pants. A voice deep in my reptilian brain announced that this guy could melt women as easily as he did butter.

"Enter, O famed culinary one," he said with a mischievous grin. "I've made you a pecan-sour-cream coffee cake."

I grinned back. No matter what people tell you, caterers *do* get hungry. Ravenous, in fact. Arch tramped up the beige wool-carpeted stairs toward Todd's room without any kind of farewell.

"Want to have an early lunch at Cinda's?" I called after him.

"No!" floated down the stairs.

"Meet me at Big Map at two, then, buddy!" I called up. A door slammed. At that point, I didn't really care whether he'd heard me or not. Still, sour-cream coffee cake would do for my sudden need-to-kill-emotional-pain-with-calories.

Eileen, wearing what I now saw was a quilted pink satin robe, appeared from the living room.

"Goldy!" she exclaimed as she clasped me tight. "We're so worried." Her pressure on my banged-up arm made me howl with pain. Eileen pulled away. "Oh, my God, you're hurt!"

"Just a little surface cut." I had to get to Arthur's, so I decided not to go into a detailed description of the van being hit.

"Eileen, why don't you let Goldy relax?" Jack implored her with those eyes.

"I will, I will," Eileen protested. "But I do need to talk to you." She hesitated and stared at my arm. Sympathy and her own desires were clearly in conflict. "I need to ask you what we should do." What to *do*? *Hmm.* I followed Eileen and Jack from the high-ceilinged foyer to their spacious kitchen featuring mauve, lilac, and lime green tiles. The decor was what a designer had thought was Southwestern; it reminded me of a giant Easter egg.

Jack poured boiling water over coffee grounds in a sterling-and-glass French press, then set the timer. On the wall hung a small but intriguing framed collage made up of a complex design of photos of skis, orange-tinged snow-covered slopes, and open-chair lifts. I stared at it while Jack poured me a cup of coffee and placed it next to a piece of coffee cake. I thanked him and took a bite. The delectably buttery cake was laced with tiny bits of fragrant vanilla bean and the solid crunch of toasted pecans.

"Mm-mm," I murmured appreciatively, and took a sip of coffee. Marvelous.

"You've heard the mountain is closed because of the Sheriff's department and Forest Service looking into Doug Portman's death?" Eileen asked without preamble.

I nodded. "So are the boys just going to hang out here until Killdeer reopens?"

"No, I set them up with a snowboarding lesson in Vail," Eileen announced. "Semi-private, just the two of them. I'll take them and pick them up." I swallowed my coffee too quickly. Eileen read my thoughts and waved them away. "My treat. They'll be done by noon. We'll come back to Killdeer, give them some lunch, and Arch can still meet you at Big Map at two. They're only supposed to close our slopes for a couple of hours. The bistro will stay open, people just have to go up and down on the gondola."

I was suddenly worried for my old friend, tenderhearted, generous Eileen. Her problem must be serious if she wanted my advice, help, or whatever, in return for an expensive semiprivate snowboard lesson. I pushed away the half-eaten coffee cake and waited.

"We need to talk to you—" She stopped when Jack shook his head, clearly opposed to whatever she was about to share. "*I* need to talk to you, then," she corrected. "What do the cops know about that ski accident yesterday? The one where Doug Portman died?"

Surprised by her question, I squinted at another collage. This one hung on the kitchen wall. I was pretty sure it was by the same artist who'd done the one above the breakfast bar. Photos of large and small teacups had been set at all angles. It also resembled some of the detailed collages I'd seen behind the watercolors in the Killdeer Art Gallery the day before. Eileen cleared her throat.

What do the cops know about the ski accident? Why do you ask, Eileen?

"I really don't know," I said lamely. "They don't let me in on the status of—"

"Forget it," Jack interjected, as he looked sadly at the half-finished cake.

Eileen waved her hand. "Listen, Goldy... Jack's been out on parole for six months." She leaned forward, her eyes pained and earnest. "Portman was his caseworker, and—"

"*What?*" I couldn't compute what she was telling me, and looked from Eileen to Jack and back again. "You're out on parole? For what?"

"I was convicted of criminally negligent homicide. But I wasn't guilty of it," Jack announced matter-of-factly. He poured himself more of the fragrant coffee. No one said anything for several long moments. Jack sighed. "I used to be married. My wife, Fiona,

139

loved to ski as much as I did. Don't think I'm arrogant, Goldy, I'm just a really good skier. Fiona was more like low-intermediate. One day, we both had too much to drink at lunch. She wanted us to race to an out-of-bounds area beside a black run. It has a great view, and she'd been there once with her son." His voice had flattened, as if he were reciting his story under hypnosis.

"Jack, don't make yourself do this," Eileen implored.

Jack held up a hand. "Please, hon, you wanted advice from Goldy. She needs to hear what happened." He took a deep breath. "Fiona and I got to the overlook. A minute later, somebody crashed through the trees and attacked us. Fiona lunged for me and I tried to catch her, but she slipped away somehow. The attacker was wearing a ski mask. Whoever it was, was strong and fast. He or she hit me with a rock and I passed out." He stopped. "Then the attacker must have pushed Fiona over the cliff. Anyway, my wife...was killed."

"And you were convicted of homicide?" I asked incredulously.

"They had to have somebody to blame. The prosecutor said I shouldn't have let Fiona ski drunk, that I shouldn't have taken her down such a dangerous run. She had grabbed my hand when we were trying to defend ourselves against the attacker, and my mitten was by her body when the ski patrol came. They trampled the snow so much, they couldn't trace our attacker." He sighed again. "It was a day of unstable snow, too. But that didn't matter. The police didn't find enough evidence to charge anyone else, and I was sentenced to three years in prison. I served a year, was granted parole six months ago... I had a record of good behavior." He snorted cynically.

I felt an ominous tingling at the base of my spine. "If you were granted parole six months ago, what does this have to do with Doug Portman?"

Eileen narrowed her eyes at me. "So you haven't faced the parole scenario with The Jerk yet, have you?"

"No," I confessed. "Why?"

Jack grunted. Eileen said, "There were people who were opposed to Jack getting out when he did." When I looked at her blankly, Eileen added, "Jack's first wife had a lot of money. Her son is the one who filled her full of wine before she skied off Bighorn Overlook that day. Afterward, he went on and on about how Jack and Fiona weren't getting along. All crap: Arthur wanted my Jack to be liable for Fiona's death. Now the money's all tied up in court. But Jack isn't going to court, because he doesn't want Fiona's money and never did. Only crybaby Arthur doesn't *want* the million-dollar trust fund Mama set up for him. He wants the nineteen million she left to charity."

"Sheesh!" I said impulsively, then struggled to sort out what Eileen had just told me. *Arthur?* "You say Fiona's son filled her full of booze before she went out? Do the cops know this?"

There was a silence. Finally Jack said, "Fiona was drinking wines offered in a sampling by her son. He lives in Killdeer and is a wine expert. You're working with him in the show. Arthur Wakefield. You probably saw how he gave us the cold shoulder yesterday morning."

"Arthur *Wakefield*? You were his *stepdad*?" I was stunned. What if I had to work in close proximity with a relative of The Jerk's? Say that relative hated me? How would I cook, much less be a chef?

Jack shook his head. "Forget stepdad. We weren't even friends. Arthur showed up at my parole hearing, claimed he hadn't been able to sleep since his mother died, that he brooded about her death all the time, and so on, which wasn't true, if you judged by the fact that he never even came to our wedding, or called Fiona more than three times in the year before she died—"

"Oh, Goldy, I hate to bother you with our problems," Eileen interrupted in a rush. "It's just that we've been so upset... Look at this." She handed me a photocopied clipping from a Denver newspaper. "It's long. You can skip to the end if you want."

But I never skip to the end. I'd signed too many contracts to know the perils of that particular shortcut. I took a fortifying sip of coffee and began reading a letter to the editor that was headlined:

Kangaroo Court or Porkers' Parole?

When rough justice for rough crimes prevailed in the Australian outback, an out-of-doors court often had to be convened. Kangaroos sometimes hopped up to watch the trial. The big marsupials would sit on their haunches and silently observe the proceedings like solemn jurors. Hence the term "kangaroo court."

Although the criminal court system in Colorado may be slow and inefficient, families of crime victims CANNOT rest easily once the perpetrator of a crime has been placed behind bars. You think a three-year sentence may be light for the person who has killed your loved one. You think: At least it's a sentence. But it isn't.

The kangaroos have left. The pigs are on their way. If the killer of your loved one plays the parole board right, he could be out on the streets in a mere six months to a year. Surely the parole board is smarter than that, you think? Don't count on it.

Are you aware that in Colorado, a criminal has to meet with only one member of the parole board when his case is reviewed? Do you know that only that one member, who may be a newspaper critic who's donated heavily to the governor's campaign, makes a recommendation to the full board? And that the board, never having met with the criminal, or even read his file, follows the one member's recommendation ninety percent of the time?

Speak out, Colorado! Let's change the parole system. And while we're at it, let's make sure none of our current piglet parole board members are succumbing to the temptations that might be offered by rich criminals. Better yet, let's eliminate those parole board members altogether.

The letter was signed, *Arthur Digby Wakefield.*

This was a morning of surprises. I took another sip of coffee to steady myself. You didn't need a degree in psychology to see that Arthur Wakefield was dealing with a truckload of unresolved anger.

"May I keep this?" I asked. "To show to my husband?"

Jack nodded. His beautiful eyes bored into me. "Do you know what he means by 'succumbing to the temptations offered by rich criminals'?"

"No," I replied. "Do you?"

His pained face relaxed slightly. "Almost all the convicts had heard the stories about Portman. When Portman worked with me, he just heard what I had to say and decided to let me out. He even had a stenographer there. But what if a convict met with Doug Portman *without* the stenographer?"

I shook my head. Again I saw Doug Portman's bloodstained cash billowing out over Killdeer Mountain. I asked, "Do you know anyone who actually bribed Doug? Or tried to?"

Jack took a bite of cake and chewed it thoughtfully. "One guy, in for armed robbery, offered Portman a used Porsche that he'd kept hidden from the cops. That guy swore Portman just blew him off, pretended he didn't even know what he was talking about." Jack pressed his lips together, then went on: " 'Nother guy, said he knew Portman already had a Porsche, and that you had to offer him something bigger, or fancier, or funnier in that first meeting. Otherwise, he'd cross you off the list of people he'd allow to bribe him."

"Did you offer him anything?" I asked neutrally.

"I told him I didn't kill my wife, that the evidence was all circumstantial and conflicting, that I'd given up drinking. I had an excellent record of good behavior and no prior convictions." Jack paused. "I added that I'd give him free gourmet-cooked meals for life if he'd take my word for it." He smiled sourly. "Laugh? I mean, that guy split a gut. He said, 'What're you, a comedian?' Then he flipped through my record and said, 'G'won, get outta here. I never believe a crook, but I'm believing you. I read about you messing up? I'll visit the prison and kill ya myself.' "

Eileen expelled a nervous gust of air and shook her head. "Jack's doing great. He has a steady job at the bistro. Everybody loves him. Except Arthur, of course. Arthur wants the bistro to stock his wines, so he sucks up to *me*. Then he's spiteful behind Jack's back."

I frowned. "Is that why he was adamant that Jack not do the cooking show?"

Eileen sighed. "Arthur and Jack can't tol-

145

erate each other. Jack wanted to keep a low profile, and I knew you needed business...."

The way she said it, I sounded like a taxi driver whose cab everyone shunned. I turned to Jack. "What's it like working with Arthur in the bistro?"

"We hardly ever see each other, and when we do, we see who can ignore the other most effectively. You notice I'm usually not even there for the Friday show. When he comes in for lunch or dinner, I'm either in the kitchen or I'm off."

I nodded and thought for a minute. "What about those other convicts you just mentioned? The Porsche guy was refused parole by Doug Portman, but what about the one who said you had to offer Doug a big or unusual bribe?"

Jack shrugged. "Portman turned him down for parole. But then the con got cancer, so he just got out. Mad as hell at Portman, of course. The guy doesn't just have revenge in his mind, he's got it in his heart."

"Cancer?" I thought of the transdermal patches in the anonymous card found in Portman's car. *Thanks for nothing, Asshole! You're dead!!!* If these patches contained a high-potency painkiller such as those prescribed by oncologists, what were the chances that touching them would kill you? On the other hand, if you had such an advanced state of cancer that you had to have a transdermal patch filled with a powerful narcotic, would you be able to ski down a black run and murder a guy who'd denied you parole?

146

More questions for Tom.

I asked, "What's the name of the convict who had cancer?"

"Barton Reed. The guy used to be a church acolyte, but he went bad. He believes the cancer is God's punishment for his crimes."

Well, well. Remembering everything Tom had told me about investigations, I didn't let on that I recognized Reed's name. As I drank more coffee, Eileen slipped off her bright pink robe and threw it on a maple wheat-back chair. Underneath she wore a sheer, low-cut top swirled with gold and silver, along with matching billowing sheer pants. She scanned the kitchen, yanked open the refrigerator door, and retrieved a carton of orange juice and a bottle of champagne. The bottle's tilted cork indicated it had already been opened. She expertly poured both the juice and the champagne into a clean crystal flute to make a mimosa.

Then I noticed four orange-specked champagne flutes on the sideboard. If Jack had truly given up drinking, there was no way I was letting Eileen drive Arch anywhere.

Jack read my mind. "Uh," he interjected as he sought my eyes, "*I'll* be taking Eileen and the boys to Vail."

I watched him as he filled a china plate with golden orange muffins. The man was truly a fabulous cook. The time Eileen and Jack had invited Arch and me to spend the night, Jack had prepared a spectacular dinner in which he'd grilled chicken, flipped sautéing

147

asparagus, made hollandaise, and pulled out a spectacular baked Alaska faster than you could say *culinary school.*

I bit into a proffered muffin—it was tender, buttery, and moist with orange. "Very good," I said to Jack. "Do you share recipes?"

"Sure," he said proudly. He riffled through a card box and handed me a printed card: Marmalade Mogul Muffins, he called them.

"I'll make them for clients as soon as I'm reopened," I promised. "And I'll give you all the credit."

"Thanks," he said happily, and beamed at Eileen, who took a slug of the mimosa.

It worried me to see Eileen drinking again. I wondered how Jack felt about having first an older wife, then an older girlfriend, who overindulged in alcohol. Fiona I didn't know about, but Eileen never used to drink more than a glass of wine in an evening. Then, she'd caught her husband—the very successful president of a pharmaceutical supply company—mainlining heroin with his girlfriend in the Druckmans' home library. Eileen had started buying champagne by the case. At first she drank to console herself, then she drank to celebrate receiving ten and a half million dollars for the sale of her husband's company. He'd been jailed briefly on drug charges, been warned out of the medical supply business, and had moved to Florida.

And then Eileen had met Jack. She'd told me he made her so happy she didn't want booze. But with the death of Doug Portman, she seemed worried and morose. And drinking more than she should.

I asked Eileen, "What's the bottom line here?"

"Arthur Wakefield," Eileen replied promptly. She gestured at the newspaper article with her glass. "Arthur has not had an open conflict with Jack since Jack's been working for me. But now with Portman suddenly dead, I'm afraid Arthur'll try to use the local paper to stoke public opinion. Maybe he wants Jack out of town and my restaurant closed. Who knows?" Her voice turned bitter. "*I* believe Arthur killed Doug Portman yesterday, because he was so angry with him for granting Jack parole. Doug's death is bound to bring all kinds of negative attention to Jack's new life. I also believe," she added, almost spitefully, "that Arthur knocked Jack out and killed his mother, so he could try to inherit her millions before she made Jack a beneficiary of her will. But she'd already changed her will, and Arthur has never recovered."

I looked at Jack. He shrugged. He said, "That's all I could think about when I was incarcerated. Who hit me over the head? Who pushed Fiona over the cliff? And why?"

I'd heard a lot of theories this morning, too many to keep straight. On the other hand, I'd seen Tom barely nod at one hypothesis about a crime, laugh at two more, discard a fourth, and jot down his own ideas about a fifth.

"What I don't understand," Jack continued quietly, "is all these stories I've been hearing from folks in town. Portman had a ton of cash on him when he died. Why?"

I sighed and shrugged. I didn't want to tell them about my connection to Doug and the unconsummated sale of the skis. I finished my coffee and set the cup down on the saucer. "Thanks for the goodies. I'll report to Tom everything you told me."

I nodded to them and they smiled. From habit, I rose and put my dishes in the sink next to the dirty crystal glasses. When I turned back around, Eileen had clasped Jack's hand in hers.

I let myself out.

CHAPTER 10

Moments later, I was lost in a condo maze. Despite the curving roadways' fanciful names—Sweethearts' Summit, Lynx Lane, Mogul Avenue, and Snowcone Court—all the houses were painted monotonous tones of gray or beige, and featured yards piled high with identical mountains of snow. I was baffled *and* frustrated, as I hadn't yet mastered crucial details of driving the Rover, including how to signal. After fifteen minutes of winding around in search of Arthur's condo, I whipped the Rover onto a new, unmarked roadway and searched for clues to my whereabouts. Arthur had said he lived on Elk Path.

Bouncing along the snow-pocked street, I saw signs for the Elk Ridge Nature Trail and Picnic Area, and followed them to a parking lot. I wound between day-skiers unloading equipment from the backs of sport-utility vehicles. A couple of fellows directing traffic did not understand my question, and said I was *on* Elk Path. *Maybe the elk can find it just fine, but I'm having problems,* I longed to retort, but didn't.

It was nine o'clock. I wasn't due at Arthur's until ten. One sure way of finding any residence in Killdeer was to locate the street on the town map. It was a smaller version of Big Map, and it was conveniently located next to Cinda's Cinnamon Stop. Come to think of it, I could get a quadruple-shot espresso there, too! A mind-clearing detour could help, especially since I'd just discovered all kinds of things about Arthur Wakefield that had never emerged in our five weeks of work together.

I parked in one of the gondola lots, trod carefully across the snowpack to the Killdeer map, and found Elk Path. I had missed a turnoff that I had mistaken for a driveway; Arthur's house was less than five minutes away. I growled and headed for the back of a lengthy walk-up line at Cinda's. If no one was allowed to ski until the cops finished their investigation, I couldn't imagine what kind of boom was happening for the shop-keepers and restaurant folks at the base. From inside the shop, though, a waiter recognized me and waved. A moment later, he brought

151

out a quadruple-shot espresso. "PBS lady, right? No charge."

"Public television has *great* fans." I thanked my benefactor, a diminutive fellow with gray eyes set in a freckled face topped with curly red hair. I wondered if this was Davey, but he wore no nametag. I sipped the dark, hot, life-giving stuff. Fantastic. "What's your name? I want to tell Cinda how nice you were."

"Ryan," he said with a grin and a wink.

"Well, Ryan, is Cinda in?"

"Naw, she had a doctor's appointment for her knee."

"It's flaring up again?"

"Yeah. Old boarding injuries never really heal. She lives with a lot of pain. That's why she opened the shop," he added helpfully. "She can wash down a painkiller with espresso and feel sorta normal in twenty minutes."

I thanked Ryan again and moved off toward the Killdeer Art Gallery, where a floppy black-and-white ribbon bow tied on the door had caught my eye. Next to the bow was a calligraphy note.

We're open in honor of our dear departed critic, Doug Portman. Come in and see the artworks he honored as "Best of Killdeer" over the last five years.

When I peered into the gallery, I saw a fur-clad customer and what looked like a saleslady. I pushed through the door and tried to shed my nosy-caterer persona to take on the air of a short, female tycoon. A wealthy patron of the arts, just sipping her espresso...

The fur lady departed. In my backup quilted parka (my better one having been torn in my plummet down the hill) and black ski pants, it was pretty clear that I hadn't done anything in the presence of a tycoon except serve barbecued ribs. After ten minutes of being ignored by the saleslady, I wandered down "Prize Row," so indicated by another black-framed calligraphy note lauding the late Doug Portman.

I frowned at the twenty works displayed there. Maybe I was missing something, but I didn't like them. Then again, what did I know? I stared at the paintings. Some commonsense inner critic was announcing that the work Doug Portman had liked ranged from imitative to mediocre to terrible. I walked past a bad-rip-off-of-Peter-Max acrylic-painted canvas of a racing skier exploding through a snowbank, a Monet-ish drizzly watercolor featuring a rain-soaked elk, and a Dutch-style still-life of a gun cabinet full of rifles. Finally, there was a slashing-brushstroke oil of a bucolic cabin in a daisy-strewn mountain meadow. Bor-*ing*, as Arch would say. Yet from the right corner of each frame dangled a sometimes-dusty "Best of Killdeer" blue ribbon or bright red ribbon declaring, "Honorable Mention."

I finished my espresso and yearned for another. Failing that, I thought, eyeing the paintings, a shot of Arthur Wakefield's Pepto-Bismol.

I yawned and took a third trip down prize row. All but three First Prizes and two Honorable Mentions were still for sale for sums in excess of a thousand dollars. Signs announced that the others were on loan. This left me with a question: *If these prizewinners are so good, how come they haven't sold?*

But really, the problem was the pretensions of poor, dead Doug. His own paintings had been mediocre and derivative, and he'd believed they'd make him rich. How then could he judge what was good? I felt sorry for him, even in death.

When another five minutes elapsed and I still hadn't been asked if I needed help, I meandered to the rear of the store to find a trash can for my paper coffee cup. Beside a water cooler, above the garbage receptacle, three collages hung on the wall. They were all by the same person, the artist whose collages I'd seen at the bistro and in Eileen's home. For some reason, these works of art made me smile. "Spring Detritus" featured torn photographs of bright-white snow melting on churned-up soil, ski poles speared into patches of matted neon green grass, and dirty lilac mittens caught up in the teeth of a yellow snowcat. "Ski Patrol at Dusk" was crowded with images of ski runs in a blizzard, blurred in-motion images of athletic uniformed skiers, a snowmobile hauling a sled with an injured, faceless skier, and dark, forlorn-looking crossed skis, the signal for help.

Finally, there was "Celebrity on the Mountain." Pieces of photographs showed hordes of burly guards speaking into walkie-talkies, a stand of metal microphones gleaming in the sunshine, a photograph of half of the vice-president's face. The other half of the veep's face lay underneath an ad for a video-camera. I laughed aloud, and this finally brought a saleswoman to my side.

"Is there a problem?" she asked. Short and compactly slim, she wore heavy matte makeup on a face framed with chic-cut jet black hair. Her clothes, a black turtleneck and pants edged at the neck and cuffs with faux tiger fur, seemed to have been form-fitted.

"No," I replied with a very slight smile and a glance at my watch. I had been in the gallery almost twenty minutes. "No problem at all."

She considered the collages, then sniffed. "They make me want to puke."

"*Puke?* If you feel that way, why do you have them here at the gallery? I think they're wonderful."

She sneered at me. "They're saccharine. Do you prefer *decoration* to *art*?"

I looked back at the collages. "How're you defining 'decoration'?"

"Doug Portman, our critic, used to say Boots Faraday's art is *purely* decorative," the woman commented with an *if-only-you-understood* shrug. "We handle Boots because she accounts for half of our profits. Most of it goes to *decorators,* of course...."

"So is that how you define 'decorative'? Who buys it? Or what critic says it's 'decorative'?"

155

Her face turned smug. She looked me and my noncouture outfit up and down. "It's too complicated to explain."

"How much for 'Spring Detritus'?" I demanded impulsively.

Startled, the saleslady took a step away from me. "Uh, two-fifty. That's two hundred and fifty dollars. You're going to buy it? Today? Now?"

"Yes," I said. "Now," I added decisively. It would make a great Christmas present for Tom, debts be damned.

The woman took down the collage and swaggered to the front counter. I whipped out my credit card and ventured aloud, "To tell you the truth, I think the stuff Doug Portman picked as being good is pretty awful."

"You're talking about our town's premier art critic—"

"You knew him?"

"Of course. Unfortunately, he has just died. Yesterday. In a ski accident." She scanned my credit card. "There's no way you'd see Boots Faraday's work in Doug's Best of Killdeer picks."

"I'm sorry to hear Mr. Portman died," I murmured. "What happened?"

"I don't know exactly," she replied. She handed me my receipt. "Probably a snowboarder got going too fast and whacked him. That's why the authorities are up there investigating."

"Hmm." Arch railed against snowboarder prejudice. *If something goes wrong and they*

156

don't know why, he'd say, *they'll blame it on a boarder.*

"Will it hurt the gallery," I inquired pleasantly, "not to have the critic reviewing the art you display?"

"Of course it will. Doug loved to talk about art. He would come in and explain things. He was *brilliant.* And we had a major, major New York art critic in here, who just *raved* about Doug's picks."

"Really? Who was that, exactly?"

"I'm not at liberty to say," she replied, again smug.

"Ah, well." I tried to make my tone conciliatory. "Listen, do you have a card for this collage artist? I'd love to write her a little fan letter."

"If you're thinking of buying Boots Faraday's work direct, to cut us out, I'm just telling you, we're her *exclusive* agent in this town." The saleslady spat out her words. When I didn't respond, she rummaged reluctantly through a drawer and thrust a card at me.

While the woman wrapped the collage, I glanced casually at the card, then gaped at it. Not only were Boots Faraday's address, phone number, and e-mail printed on the card, so was a miniature picture of her. Boots was handsome and high-cheekboned. She flashed white teeth set in a powerful smile. And she had an enormous mane of ruffled blond hair.

I had seen her before. Where?

"*Now* what's wrong?" demanded the saleswoman when she returned and handed me the wrapped collage. "I can take the card back, if it's giving you as much trouble as our prize paintings."

I smiled, gripped Tom's collage, and walked away. I'd had enough art-appreciation-sniping for one morning. As I headed back to the Rover, a visual memory finally clicked.

I *had* seen collage artist Boots Faraday. Fleetingly, from afar. The previous morning, the day that Doug Portman had lost his life on these slopes, she'd been hanging artworks on the wall of Eileen's bistro. Then she'd sat down and watched our live filming of *Cooking at the Top* just like all the other guests.

I stowed the collage in the back of the Rover. Eileen Druckman owned several of Boots Faraday's works. Did Eileen know Boots Faraday? Had Eileen invited the artist to the PBS show? What about Arthur? Did he know Ms. Faraday?

Stop, I reprimanded myself. If the occasion arose where I needed to talk to Boots Faraday, I now had her address and phone number. And her picture. She shouldn't be that hard to find.

As I drove toward Elk Path, my mind came back to the image of the blond artist up the ladder. She was an artist deemed "decorative" and *not* the "Best of Killdeer" by a man who died very shortly thereafter.

Tom always told me to look for what was out of place. Boots Faraday was an artist, not a TV fan, and certainly not a foodie. So on the day Doug Portman died, what was she doing at the bistro? Anything besides hanging artworks?

CHAPTER 11

At five to ten, I pulled into Arthur Wakefield's driveway. Unlike the other houses along Elk Path, and undoubtedly pushing the limits of Killdeer's covenants, his residence was painted the darkest gray I'd seen all morning. Charcoal siding contrasted with pearly decks and a steep slate roof. The place had a Loire-Valley *château* feel to it, which was undoubtedly what *le wine-geek* had in mind. Or had his mother chosen the place—and paid for it—before she died?

Peering through my windshield, I wondered about doleful Arthur's agenda. If his mother had left him a good chunk of change, why would he need to work for PBS? Was the wine import business struggling? Or was Arthur living in a Killdeer condo for other, more personal reasons? His letter to the paper suggested a whole lot of rage. At least there was no Subaru wagon parked outside.

I hauled my box of goodies to the front door, balanced it on a silvery-gray railing, and rapped the gleaming knocker. I almost didn't recognize Arthur when he opened the door. Gone were the black *artiste* clothes, the Pepto-Bismol bottle, the menacing body angle. The man actually looked happy to see me. His black hair was freshly washed and fluffed. Unfortunately, his cheeks were still gaunt and translucent, and his eyes retained their haunted look. Arthur may have been a bit happier, but the man was neither well rested nor relaxed. Maybe he'd been penning another tirade to the paper.

"Uh, Arthur?" I rebalanced my box. "May I come in?"

"Yes," he rasped. "I'm glad you're here. I've been... I mean, I just couldn't wait for you to arrive."

"Are you all right?" When he shook his head, I crossed the threshold and edged around an expensive-looking, intricately patterned wool Oriental. *Another gift from Mom?* I wondered. The formal living room, all mahogany furniture and light walls hung with Old-Master-style oil paintings, was strangely impersonal. In the hallway, porcelain figurines adorned a mahogany end table. Nowhere did photos or memorabilia give a clue as to Arthur's background.

Something more astonishing adorned the walls: at least a dozen collages by Boots Faraday. I tilted my head at one, a montage of tall grasses, bushes, and evergreen shrubs, all sprinkled with snow. I peered close and read the title: "Winter Garden."

From behind me, Arthur gushed, "Boots is one of my best customers." I almost dropped my box in surprise. "It's coming into her busy season," Arthur continued airily, "Christmas and all. She'll be ordering cases and cases of wine for the showings in her house. She sells *tons* of her work that way."

"More than in the local gallery?" I asked innocently. I'd had a feeling that saleslady wasn't entirely forthright.

"Oh, please. Those Killdeer Gallery people think 'Western Art' is anything with a pony in it. Come on out to the kitchen, *please,*" he entreated. "And in answer to your earlier question, no, I'm not doing well today." I shot him a sympathetic glance. He looked piqued. "My first wine shipment was supposed to arrive and didn't. I'm going to have to postpone the party until Monday, which makes *me* look terrible. I tossed all night, trying to think how to re-invite people. Haven't had a thing to eat."

"Let's go, then!" I said heartily. Postponement was no problem for me: My calendar was depressingly open. No matter what the problems were, if Arthur was hungry, he was *mine.*

He pointed down the hall. I schlepped my box into a cheerful space with yellow walls, bright white tile counters, and a yellow-and-white floor of handmade tiles: hallmark of a noncook, because tiles spell major back pain. On the walls were bright tourist posters of France splashed with hues of lavender, yellow, and gray.

Arthur slumped into a ladder-back chair at his tiled breakfast bar, where eight or so bottles of wine sported jaunty ribboned bows and handwritten cards screaming *You're Invited, Again!* "I've got ten cases of wines sitting at Denver International Airport," he complained glumly. He stared at the wine bottles and a handwritten list next to them.

I raised my eyebrows. "Where at DIA?"

"Customs," he answered dolefully.

"Got a medium-sized pan?"

He gestured wearily to a bank of drawers. I located a saucepan and started cooking the oatmeal mixture I'd brought. I wanted to ask Arthur if he'd heard anything new about Doug Portman's suspicious death. More importantly, I wanted to see his reaction to my question. I also wondered fleetingly how we were supposed to do an intake interview if Arthur needed to 1) have something to eat and 2) spring valuable cases of wine from Customs. I stirred the creamy oatmeal mixture when it started to bubble. I couldn't ask him questions yet. I knew the dangers of trying to discuss business with, or elicit information from, a client with low blood sugar. I'd face crankiness, irrationality, and indecision. You don't get to be a successful food person without taking instant stock of such things.

Within five minutes the spicy orange-and-cinnamon oatmeal was hot and ready to be topped with a chunk of butter and spoonfuls of dark brown sugar. Arthur stirred in the melting pond of butter and sugar and hungrily scooped up enormous mouthfuls. It wouldn't help him deal with a bureaucracy, but it *would* get him through the next couple of hours. I sat down and pulled out my notebook.

"Gosh, this is fabulous," he commented. "You *have* to do this for our last show." Did

I detect color seeping into those cheeks, or was it wishful thinking on my part? He looked at me sheepishly, then scraped up the last of the cereal. "I realized in the middle of the night that I hadn't been very nice to you after you had your car accident. I'm sorry. This day has been crazy trying to figure out how I'm going to change the buffet. Are you okay?"

"I am, thanks. Actually, the car accident was the second terrible thing to happen to me yesterday. After our show, I...discovered the guy who'd been killed while skiing." Arthur raised his eyes questioningly. I said, "The guy was someone I used to know."

Arthur jumped up to rinse his bowl. With his back to me, he said warily, "How did you know Doug Portman?"

"Through my husband. Do you remember, he's in law enforcement?"

"Yes. Coffee?" he asked as he reached for a liter bottle of spring water.

"Sure, thanks. Did you know Portman?"

His face when he turned back to me was even more flushed. I was sure it wasn't owing to the oatmeal. "I guess you could say I knew him. You know, he lived here in town. But listen," he said with sudden energy, "you didn't tell me how *you're* doing." He stopped the coffee-making and beamed at me. "That's what I *really* want to know. Can't have my star in pain for our last show."

I sighed. "My arm's a bit banged up. The van's totally trashed. But I'm borrowing a vehicle, and I'm still alive, so I'm *very* thankful."

"Well, then. So am I." He returned to his coffee preparation. First he fastidiously poured the bottled water into an espresso-machine tank. When he opened an airtight crock, it went *pow!* and I jumped. Arthur giggled as he ladled out coffee beans. Next he pressed a button on his grinder, which growled like a motorcycle. He then dosed, tapped, and revved up the coffee machine. Half a minute later, he placed two tiny cups of hot, dark, foamy espresso onto the tiled bar. I took a sip, pronounced it marvelous, and refrained from any mention of how it was certainly the most noisily-produced cup of coffee I'd ever imbibed.

"Okay," I began, with a glance at the kitchen clock, then at my notebook. "When do you have to leave for the airport?"

"Five minutes." His eyes immediately turned anxious. "I'm not going to be able to discuss the food for the wine-tasting today. It's just..." He slurped his espresso, then squealed when he, too, glanced at the clock. "I also need to...*darn* it!"

"Need to what? Why don't you let me help out?" I offered. "There is that *personal* in 'personal chef.' "

"I need to deliver these wines with the new invites. I don't suppose you...never mind. Let me go get the buffet wine list. Then I really have to leave. We can finish planning on the phone."

As soon as he whisked out of his kitchen, I put the foodstuffs into his barren refrigerator. It looked as if Arthur never ate properly.

I washed our coffee cups and laid out instructions for reheating the pork dinner. I also glanced at the list of folks to receive the new bottles-with-invitations. It included the name *Boots Faraday. Hmm.* I'd just finished setting Arthur's dinner table—for one—when he returned. He'd slicked down his hair and wore a black turtleneck, black pants, and black sport coat. He handed me a piece of paper scribbled with foods and names of wines. Then his eyes shot to the beribboned bottles of wine. Indecision tightened his face. One of the best ways to get what you want out of people, I'd discovered, is to apply light pressure when they're in a hurry. I gave him a bright smile.

"Look, Arthur, can I do anything else for you? Since we're not going over the menu, I have until two. Why not let me help you?"

"I have to deliver these wines to people coming to the buffet."

"Let's see." I set aside the wines sheet and frowned at the list of guests. "Boots Faraday," I mused aloud.

"Boots is *very* well known in the Killdeer arts community."

"Sure, I know." That's why I wanted to weasel my way into her affections, I added mentally, because she was so well known with the local artsy-craftsy crowd. She might know more about Doug Portman than I'd ever learn from Arthur. I also wanted to find out what she was doing at the bistro the day of Doug's death. "Boots Faraday," I repeated pleas-

165

antly, as if the artist and I were big buds. "I bought one of her works for my husband for Christmas. I saw her up at the bistro before we started our show on Friday. I just didn't get a chance to say hello."

"Ah," he said, visibly relaxing. "So you know Boots, then."

"Not intimately—"

He waved this away. "All right, you know Mountain Man Wines in town?" I murmured that I would find it. "They'll do these deliveries. Have them send me a bill."

I nodded and asked, "How about the one for Boots? Can I take it to her?"

He shrugged. "She usually has lunch at the Gorge-at-the-Gondola Café, know it?"

"I can find it. Happy to be your wine courier, Arthur."

"Great. Here's the guest list and a general list of food for the buffet, then. Remember..." He blushed. "I...want the guests to think I did most of the cooking myself. So whatever you choose to prepare, make it something that *I* can very obviously be finishing when they get here." I shot him a serious look. "I just need them to think I'm a great cook, that's all. I'll say you helped me, don't worry."

"No problem, Arthur. I'll even write out the directions on a tiny piece of paper and you can eat that when your doorbell rings."

His smile was mirthless. "Good thing I've been working with you all this time. I'm used to your sense of humor." I repressed a sigh and thought, *Ditto, brother.* I tucked both lists

166

into my notebook. "With any luck," he added wearily, "I'll have the wines this afternoon. We can discuss the dishes themselves tomorrow. That won't be too late, will it?"

"Of course not." Never tell clients the problems they're causing you, even if you long to strangle them for their sudden changes of plans. As he packed up the wine-invitations, I said, "There's dinner in the refrigerator for you, Arthur. Gift from me. Instructions are on the counter."

"Okay, thanks." He spoke with more fatigue than gratitude. He glanced at the paper on the counter, then gave me a curious look. "That's what you did while I was changing? Wrote out all those instructions?"

"Well, yes—" *What did you think I was going to do, just sit here?*

"Hmm," was his only comment as his eyes flicked around his kitchen. I had the distinct feeling that he suspected I'd stolen something while he was out of the room. Without saying more, he picked up the box of bottles and led me toward the front door. In the hallway, he clumsily turned to check that a door beside the kitchen entry was locked. Then he glanced at one of the figurines on the hall table.

It was a Dresden shepherdess, I noted. *Gee Arthur*, I thought, *why not hoist a neon sign saying Valuables Here!* Why else would he lock a door inside his house? What did Arthur have that was so valuable?

Wines? *Duh, Mom.*

I carefully reversed the Rover down the snowy driveway, then waited as Arthur's garage door slid open and he backed out. No Subaru for him, but a huge, shiny, black Escalade, the Cadillac of four-wheel-drives. He'd decorated the grille with a bushy green Christmas wreath. His vanity plate read: *VinGeek.* Either he'd inherited a bundle or the wine business was great. But if either possibility were true, why would you work as a PBS floor director? Arthur was an enigma, I decided, as I drove into Killdeer to find the Gorge-at-the-Gondola Café.

I knew her as soon as I stepped into the restaurant: the golden mane of hair, the strong-featured, slender face. Boots Faraday even *looked* artistic. With her head tilted, she'd fixed her gaze out the window. She wasn't expecting me, so I watched her while coming up with my lines of introduction.

A sudden crash made her turn. Next to her table, a chubby, tow-headed toddler had tripped over his ski boots and toppled to the floor. He was crying with fear. Without missing a beat, Boots leaned over and scooped the boy up. In one fluid movement, she lifted him, boots and all, to his mother. When the mother declined to take him—he had to weigh over fifty pounds in those boots—Boots playfully threw the child up into the air and caught him. Both of them squealed with laughter.

So: artistic-looking, and strong as an ox. Her angular, British-film-star face was complemented by a long, lithe, muscular body.

Unfortunately, as soon as she had the delighted boy righted on his boots, she straightened and caught sight of me. If you could chill someone with a look, I'd say I'd just been flash-frozen.

I gripped her wine bottle and made my way resolutely across the crowded room. If what Tom had said the previous day was true, my own motives for meeting with Doug Portman could be called into question. I really needed to chat with Boots, to find out what she'd seen the previous morning, and, if I was lucky, what she knew. But did she know who *I* was? Why had I received that icy look? Boots Faraday did not exactly look thrilled at the prospect of chatting with me. My heart sank.

"You're the artist, right?" I blurted out when I arrived at her table. "Boots Faraday, the collage person? This wine and buffet invitation is for you. It's from Arthur Wakefield, but he had to go to Denver. A little problem with Customs."

Intense blue eyes assessed me: Was I friend or foe?

I introduced myself and said I was a caterer and personal chef, maybe she'd seen *Cooking at the Top!* She nodded slightly, and I plunged recklessly on: "I love your work. I've just bought one of your collages for my husband for Christmas. I'd *love* to hear a bit about how you create your collages. I'll pay for my own meal, of course. Or, do you not like to eat with fans?"

In the face of my obnoxiousness, she stared

169

down at her silverware and ran a long-fingered hand along the knife. Her face remained unreadable.

"It's okay if you don't want to lunch with a stranger," I gushed. "People are always wanting me to talk about recipes. Frankly, I'd rather *not talk* than hear tales about substituting cooking sherry for Dry Sack—"

She lifted her eyes at that, and smiled, Mona Lisa-ish. "You're the one with the eggshells in the cookies." Her voice was deep and pleasant. "I saw the show." She paused. "The annual fund-raiser in memory of Nate Bullock is very dear to my heart."

I placed the wine on the table. "Oh, really? How come?"

"Arthur probably told you Nate Bullock and I were good friends."

"That Arthur! No, he didn't mention it."

Boots glanced out the window again. Was she looking for someone? "I thought my old friendship with Nate Bullock was the reason Arthur asked me to do some collages for the set." She turned back and regarded me. Her formidable blue eyes were clouded, inscrutable. "You can sit down."

Her table afforded a panoramic view of the base of Killdeer Mountain. The investigators must have finished, for skiers and snowboarders now raced down the runs. When our waitress shuffled up, I ordered while Boots tucked the wine bottle into her large leather handbag. Boots said, "Ditto," to a Chicken Caesar Salad. Not sure where to

170

start with her, I launched us into an emotionally flat exchange of pleasantries about food, wine, and living in Killdeer.

Boots seemed enigmatic, almost on her guard. Maybe it was because she was famous and met adoring fans all the time. I gabbled on, pretending not to notice. By the time we were taking dainty bites of crisp romaine lettuce sprinkled with hot grilled chicken, freshly grated Parmesan, and butter-sautéed croutons, every innocuous subject had been exhausted.

I moved my plate aside. *Now or never.* How to broach the subject of Doug Portman without seeming nosy? On the other hand, I'd probably already hit the top of the Intrusivity Chart by crashing her lunch.

"The collage I bought was 'Spring Detritus,' " I began. "And I've seen your work all over. Being in a small town like Killdeer, was it hard to establish an art-making career?"

Her deep laugh was rich and seductive, and made me smile. Then she narrowed those startling blue eyes. "You must think I'm pretty dumb."

My smile melted. "Excuse me?"

The eyes once again turned chilly. "What's this about, really?"

I fiddled with the side of the plate. *Uh-oh.* "What is *what* about?"

"Just tell me what you really want to know. Aside from"—she raised her voice to mimic my question—"if it was hard to establish an art-making career?" Her eyes mocked me.

171

"Uh, I'm just a caterer who bought one of your—"

"Cut the crap."

"I—"

"Why are you here?"

"Well, I *am* doing a personal-chef gig for Arthur Wakefield, and he *did* ask me to bring you the wine. I bought one of your pieces and I *do* want to know about your career. And"—I took a fortifying breath—"since you're a local artist, then you must know, have known, Doug Portman. The local art critic."

She tilted back in her chair and narrowed her eyes. "You want to know if I knew Doug Portman? Why?"

"I...was supposed to meet him after the show yesterday," I confessed. "As you no doubt have heard, he was killed skiing down from the bistro before we could meet." Time to tell the truth. "The sheriff's department is classifying his accident as a suspicious death. That's why they had to close the mountain for so long this morning." Boots lifted her eyebrows. "As I'm the only one who seems to know why he was carrying a lot of cash when he died, the police are asking me a bunch of questions. Believe me, you don't want to be the one the cops are questioning, when it's a suspicious death."

"Really."

"Anyway," I continued, "once I figured out you were the artist who was hanging work yesterday morning, I was wondering if you saw anything…you know, strange. With Doug, I mean."

"No, I didn't," she replied immediately, then looked away, out the window.

"No, you didn't? Did you see Doug at all? Was he talking to anybody during the show? Did he seem upset? Sick? Can't you tell me anything?"

She swiveled to face me. "I read that article on you, you know. The one in the *Killdeer Courier* that Arthur placed to publicize your cooking show."

"An article? Actually, publicity for the show is Arthur's department—"

"You should have read the article," she interrupted me sharply. "It said you were a caterer, and that you were starting in the personal chef business." I shook my head and opened my eyes wide, as in *So?* "And that's not all. Let's see—'Goldy Schulz is also known for occasionally, and unofficially, helping her husband—a homicide investigator—solve crimes. So if she cozies up to you for a chat, you might want to call your lawyer.' "

"Is that why you think I did Arthur's wine delivery for him? To cozy up to you?"

"Isn't it? Everyone knows I was no friend of Doug Portman. Doug Portman was a rotten judge of art who thought he was very smart. His ignorance hurt people. Including me. So what's the *real* point of you asking me about Doug Portman at the bistro?"

"Whoa. Listen. I do love your work. I do want to know how you got started. And it would be helpful if you could tell me if you saw anything suspicious on Friday. That's it. You don't want to talk, just say so."

She snorted impatiently. "I'll let you know if I mind talking. Regarding your first question. I tried to make a living as a painter of large abstract oils. *Critics,* including Doug Portman, loved them. I didn't sell a single one."

"That's too bad—"

She lowered her voice and held up an imaginary magazine. " 'Ms. Faraday's groundbreaking canvases depict violence with passion, color, and ontology.' "

"Doug said that?"

"Are you kidding? Doug Portman wouldn't have known the difference between 'ontology' and 'on-line trading.' Those lines were from some Denver critic. Anyway, I needed to pay the rent, so I tried my hand at making collages. Some critics dismissed them as 'craftwork.' Most ignored them. Unfortunately, our one local critic, Doug Portman, hated them because they were small and intimate, not grand or *grandiose.*"

"I'm sorry."

Her smile was a thin slash. "Don't be. I sold every one of those first collages. I even enjoyed ignoring Doug when he referred to my work as"—here she lowered her voice again—" 'saccharine and domestic.' I formed the Killdeer Artists' Association, so the artists in town could network to make money instead of being jealous and competitive. Eventually, a few magazine writers did pieces on my work, and I received a stream of orders. Now I have a tidy little business, and I don't give a hoot about passion and ontology." She speared a piece of chicken. "Ready for the answer to Question Two? No, I didn't see anything Friday morning."

Watch it, I warned myself. I stalled by taking a sip of water. Actually, I *had* thought of a couple more questions, on the subject of Nate Bullock and his pregnant widow. If Boots Faraday felt so close to Nate that she came to the annual fund-raiser held in his name, maybe she knew what was going on with my old friend Rorry.

"I admire your spunk," I commented with a smile, then pretended to ponder a bit. "The Bullocks used to live in Aspen Meadow, where I'm from. You mentioned an artists' association. Is that how you got to know Nate?"

"Yes, I met Nate through KAA." Her answer was curt, as if she were suddenly under legal cross-examination. "He was a good cameraman, but public television doesn't pay that much. He joined the artists' association when he was trying to make some extra money. Then he died."

"Nate wanted to make extra money? Doing what?"

Her face turned rigid. "I really can't say."

"But...he's been dead for three years. Look, Boots, Rorry was my friend. A long time ago, we taught Sunday school together. She seemed so terribly unhappy yesterday—"

Boots snarled: "Don't get me started on

Rorry," then seemed to regret it. After a moment, she continued in a steadier voice: "I'll tell you why Nate wanted extra money. When you taught Sunday school with Rorry, was she complaining about wanting to have children, but not being able to afford it?"

I thought back. Had she? I only remembered her wistful admiration for Arch, then a toddler. "No...but that was years ago. I'd love to get in touch with her again—"

"She works for Killdeer Corp. I think she's still in the same trailer where she and Nate lived. Shouldn't be hard to find."

"Was Nate trying to make that extra money when he died?"

Boots glanced out at the gondola whizzing along, high above the beautiful, treacherous mountain. "I told you: I can't say exactly. He had some film ideas, he had his PBS work. That's what I know."

I got the distinct feeling that that was *not* all she knew. But I said only, "Rorry is pregnant now. Do you know if she's seeing someone?"

"Man, you don't quit, do you? I don't know anything about Rorry Bullock's social life. She doesn't confide in me." She took a bite of salad and regarded me warily over her fork. "The gallery called and told me you were in this morning. You turned your nose up at their show and went straight to my stuff. Now all of a sudden you're my biggest fan, pumping me with questions about my career, Doug Portman, and Nate and Rorry Bullock. Why?"

The waitress reappeared. I ordered a double espresso and a brownie with vanilla ice cream. Boots declined anything.

"I just wanted to find out more about Doug Portman. That's all. Asking about Rorry popped into my head when you mentioned Nate. Honest."

"And why do you want to know about Portman?"

I sighed. "I told you that already. If you don't want to believe me, don't."

Again she tilted her chin back in appraisal. "How do *you* take to criticism? I find myself wondering what you thought of the first two sentences under your photo in the Killdeer paper? 'Some call her the corpulent Queen of Cream. But this caterer is one tough cookie'?"

I shook my head. The Killdeer paper was not part of my regular reading material, I was happy to say. Which was probably a good thing, since discussing it filled Boots's voice with vitriol. How she must have hated Doug Portman, with his uncomplimentary critiques. I replied tentatively, "I'd say I'm a *tad* shy of corpulent—"

"I know why you wanted to have lunch with me," Boots interrupted. "You don't care about my work. Or the artists' association. And you certainly don't give a damn about Nate Bullock. You think I killed that son-of-a-bitch know-nothing wannabe critic, Doug Portman."

"Did you?"

"No. But I wish I had. Am I a suspect?"

177

"No, you're paranoid. *I'm* higher up on the list of suspects than you are."

"Were you there when he died, Goldy?"

"No."

"Then why is the sheriff's department asking *you* about his so-called suspicious death?" She grinned maliciously. "I mean, if you don't mind *me* asking a question or two."

"My ex-husband is in jail. Doug was a member of the state parole board. I was skiing with him. It looks peculiar."

My dessert arrived and we fell silent. When the waitress left, Boots demanded, "Why do the cops even think it's a suspicious death in the first place?"

I sipped my espresso. I couldn't tell her about the medical patches and the threat, couldn't tell her about the mysterious closure of the run, or the blood all over the snow. "I don't know exactly."

Boots pursed her lovely lips. Then she said, "Baloney."

I shrugged. The anger in her was making me nervous.

She stood, snatched up her jacket, and flipped her blond hair over her shoulders. "Go to hell, tough cookie."

CHAPTER 12

Well! Let's do lunch any ol' time. I finished the brownie, sipped my espresso, and reflected on Boots's news that my crime-solving exploits had been written up in the local paper. How had I missed that? The waitress returned and told me the blond lady had thrown a fifty-dollar bill at her. I told her to keep the change.

I got directions to Mountain Man Wines, where the manager said he would happily deliver the rest of Arthur's bottled invites. By the time I got to Big Map, a light snow had begun to fall. Pink-cheeked skiers, their boot buckles clanking, headed past me, bound for lunch after a brisk morning on the slopes. And speaking of food, not only had my meeting with Boots Faraday been less than perfect, I had to assess my first day as a personal chef as a failure. Arthur had not given me a check, had not signed a contract, had only given me a vague list of foods I could put together for his wine-tasting buffet. He was going to call, though, and wanted me to do the buffet Monday. Wonderful.

I passed a line of skiers waiting for the gondola. I clambered up to the bottom of Base View Run, where skiers and snowboarders had to stop to take off their equipment before heading back to the gondola or across the foot-bridge. At the far left of the run's end stood Big Map, a fifteen-by-eight-foot plastic-covered diagram of the ski area. Arch was not there.

I wiggled my toes to keep warm. As the bottom of a run is a precarious place to spend any time just standing around, I worked my way through the snow to get closer to the map. To my right, hooting, calling skiers and snowboarders produced waves of snow as they made sudden hockey stops and stepped out of their bindings. Children, fat as dough-boys in their brightly colored down jackets, wheeled this way and that, searching for parents from whom they'd become separated on the hill. Occasionally an out-of-control skier or snowboarder would biff—slang for *crash*—into one of the kids and send him sprawling. Two ski patrol members standing near the map called warnings, helped the children up, and yanked the tickets of particularly reckless skiers and boarders.

Arch knew where to find me, so I didn't waste time trying to spot him among the hordes descending the last leg of the run. I turned to the map and ran my fingers along Widowmaker and Jitterbug Run. My eyes inexorably turned to Hot-Rodder, where Doug Portman had died. With all the stamping around done by the patrol as they tried to rescue Doug, there couldn't have been much of a crime scene left for the police and Forest Service to investigate.

My eyes wandered over the diagram to Elk Valley, where Nate Bullock had died three years ago. *Nate wanted to make extra money. Doing what? I really can't say....* Striped red lines indicated both the valley and the ridge above it as out-of-bounds for skiing. Just to the west of Elk Valley lay a green-dotted area labeled *Area III Expansion.* On the map, I retraced my route this morning along the main road and then to the parking lot by the Elk Ridge Nature Trail. If I had come out the other side of the parking lot the first time, I could have found Arthur's condo without a hitch. Speaking of directions...

Near me a ski patroller was carefully buckling yellow straps around a transport sled. I called a greeting down and received an answering smile from the patroller, a young woman with a thin, tanned face.

"I don't want to interrupt you," I began.

"You're not. Have you lost somebody? Do you need help?"

I told her I was just waiting for my son. "But I do have a couple of questions about the map, if you don't mind." I introduced myself and said that yesterday I'd done a fund-raiser for Nate Bullock up at the bistro.

"Yeah," the patroller said mournfully, "I knew Nate. Everybody did." Her genuine sadness seemed a contrast to Rorry's bitter words from yesterday: *I'm not sad. Just puzzled.* And then there had been Boots's angry comment: *Don't get me started on Rorry.*

I turned back to the map. "What I can't figure out is why a high-country-wise person like Nate would go into a dangerous area like that."

She shrugged. "There hadn't been a slide

there in thirty years. Nate probably thought he'd be okay."

I glanced at the slope. "Rorry Bullock, Nate's widow? She's an old friend of mine."

The patrolwoman put her hands on her knees, sprang up agilely, and brushed snow from her legs. She was about my height, with dark blond hair poking from beneath her red hat. She moved with a graceful, unconscious athleticism, and as usual at the ski resort, I felt horridly uncoordinated and chubby. But not corpulent. At least, I hoped not.

"Yeah," she said, "Rorry's getting close, now. With that baby about to pop, I'm surprised she came up to the bistro yesterday."

"But she did," I said. "Unfortunately, I was so busy yesterday that I didn't get a chance to talk with her very much. I know she's an employee of Killdeer Corp and lives in a trailer, but I don't know where she works or have her exact address or phone number any more. Any ideas?"

The patrolwoman harnessed the sled to her shoulders. "Last I heard, Rorry was working the night shift at the container ware-house. I'm pretty sure her number is listed. Oh, and she has the only green-and-white mobile home in Killdeer." She expertly stamped snow off her boots, signaling that she was ready to go.

"Ah," I said hesitantly. "Do you think it's okay to talk to Rorry about the avalanche? I kind of got weird vibes from her yesterday."

The patrolwoman shrugged inside her harness, then pointed to two patrol members working the bottom of the slope. "Ask Gail. The tall one. She knows Rorry pretty well. She was also on the search team that found Nate."

I thanked her and galumphed between skiers and boarders to Gail, whose windburned, leathery face was framed with long, shiny black hair pulled off her forehead with a thick red band. I scanned the slope—still no Arch. As I introduced myself to Gail, I recognized her: she was the woman who'd pulled me up from the snow yesterday morning, when I'd fallen after disembarking from the gondola. She recognized me, too, and said I'd done a great job on the Bullock fund-raiser. *How about that,* I thought. *A compliment, for a change!*

I told her I was looking for my son and his friend, both snowboarders, both late. Gail asked for their description and said she hadn't seen them, but she'd keep an eye out.

"The patrolwoman over there by the map?" I asked. "The one with the sled? I told her I was a friend of the Bullocks. She mentioned you were on one of the search teams that went out for Nate."

Gail nodded sadly. "Yeah, I was."

"Uh, Rorry and I were real close before she moved to Killdeer. I'd like to hook up with her again, bring her some casseroles for when the baby arrives. But she seemed to be in an awfully bad mood when I saw her yesterday..."

"That figures. The memorial is hard on her, I think. And of course, losing Nate, and then their baby, that was horrible, too."

I'm not sad, Goldy. Just puzzled.

"Uh," I ventured, "the patrolwoman over there said an avalanche hadn't come down Elk Ridge for thirty years."

Gail shrugged. "You get the right snow conditions, a slope steeper than thirty degrees, a trigger, it could happen anywhere. That's why we set explosives on some peaks. We want to anticipate slides."

"But there wasn't an explosive trigger for the avalanche that killed Nate. Or was there?" Before she could answer, I heard a familiar yell: *Mom!* followed by *Goldy Schulz!* just in case there was any doubt what *Mom* was being summoned.

From the other end of the run, Arch waved at me with both hands. "Hey, *Mom!*" He and Todd, their snowboards leashed to their ankles, scooted toward me. Snow clung to Todd's hat, jacket, pants, and mittens. His lowered chin indicated discouragement, pain, and embarrassment. He must have taken an awfully bad fall. At least he hadn't had to be carried off the slope. Speaking of which.

"The other patroller said you were on the team that actually brought out Nate's body," I said to Gail.

Gail flipped her glossy hair back and scowled at the mountain. "There was a report, all public record, if you want to look it up. I read about you in the paper, wanting to do your own investigations."

I shook my head. "I want to know what's bothering Rorry. I just don't want to say

184

something to her that would hurt her feelings—"

Gail's voice softened. "We believe there was a *human* trigger for the avalanche. So you might not even want to mention the slide to Rorry."

"*What?*"

She looked away. "It's all public record," she repeated. "There were three sets of tracks at the Elk Ridge trailhead that day. It's a well-marked hiking area in the summertime, but this was winter, with seven inches of new snow. We saw two sets of boot prints going up, one Nate's, one somebody else's. Snow-depth was almost identical, so there's reason to believe Nate went up with somebody. Still, it's not impossible that the other person came up later. It's just unlikely—"

I stopped her. "Why is it unlikely?"

"If you follow someone else, you usually step *in* their tracks. It makes it easier to walk. Nate's and this other person's tracks were side by side."

"Somebody else was hit by the avalanche that day, but didn't get killed? Or was killed and never found?"

"No," Gail corrected patiently, holding me with her dark eyes. Arch and Todd were twenty feet away. "Somebody went partway up the path with Nate. Then his companion or whoever split off and went *up* the ridge. Nate descended to the valley. We don't know why he went there. His footprints led into the slide. We didn't find him for five hours. By then, he'd suffocated."

"And the third set of tracks?"

Again I got the dark eyes. "Nate's companion came back down. Running, from the look of the tracks. We never found out who he was. Or she. I don't know if anyone ever told Rorry about the second person on the slope that day. Probably she knows anyway. So as I say, you might not want to talk to her about it." She strode away to admonish a skier who'd slammed into an entire family.

Openmouthed, I struggled to process what I'd just been told. Two sets of tracks up? One down? Did Rorry indeed know about Nate's companion? And who could it have been? Why hadn't that person ever shown up?

"Mom!" Arch was panting. His flushed cheeks were wet with melted snow. "Todd got hit by a lady skier. She bounced off him and crashed into me. Major yard sale and I'm not kidding. Then *she* yelled at *us* for getting in *her* way. I told her, 'Y'ever heard of *Yield to the downhill skier?*' and she shouted, 'You're *not* a skier!' "

I consoled him while he brushed clumps of snow from his shoulders and complained of prejudice against snowboarders. Poor Todd shuffled up and I asked if he was all right. His ambiguous *I guess* was followed by a request to take him back to his condo, which I did.

Arch fell asleep in the Range Rover within five minutes of our leaving Killdeer. By the time I pulled into High Country Towing in Dillon, he was snoring. A man in oil-splashed coveralls unlocked the gates to a lot crammed with vehicles, all of which had seen better days. When I caught sight of my ruined van, an unexpected lump rose in my throat. My trustworthy vehicle, its *Goldilocks' Catering, Where Everything Is Just Right!* now crumpled and illegible, had been my companion through years of catering. The van's sorry state seemed an omen of the loss of my business. I patted the bumper and bid it a silent farewell. Then, before the overall-guy could call the local mental health center, I scooped up Tom's skis—miraculously unharmed—as well as my own ski gear and my backpack, and roared toward home.

Arch woke up as we pulled into our driveway. I needed to talk to Tom about all I'd learned, about Barton Reed, the cancer-suffering convict; Jack Gilkey, the paroled chef; Arthur Wakefield, the wine-loving antiparole activist; and Boots Faraday, the savagely unfriendly artist who'd hated the town's art critic. But visiting time at the jail was almost over, and Tom had promised Arch he'd take him down to see his father. Before they left, Tom added that he wanted to help me make dinner, so I should wait until he returned to start.

I thanked him and hauled the precious skis upstairs, where I screamed bloody murder when I tripped over what turned out to be Arch's physics experiment. Once I'd stored the still miraculously unbroken skis, I stomped back to the hallway, seething. A god-awful mess awaited me. According to the skewed label, Arch had meticulously dropped bleach on black fabric to demonstrate the random spatter patterns of quantum mechanics. I, unfortunately, had kicked the bucket of bleach down the carpeted hallway and taken out not only our gold shag rug but a pile of blue jeans waiting to go into the laundry. With rags, I blotted what bleach I could from the ruined rug. Then I threw the jeans into the wash—they'd be okay for painting and gardening—and hung the grossly spotted and experiment-ruined black fabric in the bathroom.

I tried desperately to be a good mother in the teach-your-kids-and-support-their-interests department, but every now and then my failure quotient became awfully high. Regardless of American sentimentality toward motherhood, I longed to create a Mother's Day card that told the truth: *You can't win.*

In the kitchen, I typed Arthur's wine list and suggested foods into my computer. Then I contemplated my next few culinary events. I checked the number of cookies I had made for the following day's library reception. I decided that in addition to the wrapped platters of almond Christmas cookies and Chocolate Coma cookies, I should make Jack's delicious marmalade muffins and more of the gingersnaps I'd muffed on television. When you fall off a horse, you should get right back on, right?

I took out unsalted butter to soften and made sure I had whole nutmeg, then hunted for my molasses and cider vinegar. By the time Tom came in, loaded with bags containing chilled cans of pasteurized crab and a dozen different sauce ingredients, I was loading scoops of buttery, spicy cookie dough onto baking sheets.

"Aha!" he said expansively as he pulled me in for a hug. "The Queen of Cream tackles gingersnaps again!"

"*You* read the article in the Killdeer paper?"

"Yeah, somebody faxed it to me," he replied absentmindedly. "How're you doing? You're *not* corpulent, by the way."

"Thanks." I sighed. "How was The Jerk?"

"His usual self. I felt sorry for Arch, so I bought some lean ground beef and—don't kill me—Velveeta and picante to make him some Chile Con Queso. We can have it with chips and vegetables. He always orders it in restaurants, so I figured I'd give it a go for him."

I laughed. "Great. So much for corpulence. I'll thaw some halibut steaks for us, too. The queso will be good. I need some comfort food myself, since I had to say good-bye to my van today. It was awful."

"We will *buy* you another van."

"You don't understand. It was so sad."

His green eyes searched mine. "Hey, Miss G., y'know how many prowlers I've wrecked?" The slight scent of his aftershave made me shiver.... Whose idea was it to have dinner *before* you went to bed?

I said, "Is this a statistic that's going to upset me?"

"Six wrecked. Four totaled."

"Ah."

"What are you making there, Queen of Cream?"

"Marmalade Mogul Muffins," I said happily. That was the thing about Tom: You never could stay in a sad mood for very long when he was determined to cheer you up. I removed halibut steaks from our freezer while Tom sautéed the ground beef for his Mexican appetizer. Then I pulled my zester over plump oranges, whirred the fragrant strands of zest in a small electric grinder, and measured out thick, best-quality marmalade.

"Mind if we invite Marla over?" I asked. "All this back and forth to the ski area, I haven't seen or talked to her. She loves halibut."

"Okay," he said as he stirred picante sauce into the lake of melted cheese and browned beef. "Only tell her not to come until six, I need to talk to you first."

"Sounds sexy. I need to talk to you, too. Suppose we could do it somewhere else?"

He grinned. "Later. Call Marla—"

At that moment Arch screamed from upstairs that he wanted to know *who had ruined his experiment*! I called back that I had, because he'd left it where someone could trip over it in the hallway. I was rewarded with a slammed door. I sighed. Well, we could all make up at dinner. Hopefully, Tom's queso dip would smooth over my son's mood.

"Call Marla," Tom said calmly, "then I'll tell you about this artist who filed a complaint against you today."

Chile Con Queso Dip

1 pound lean ground beef
12 ounces English-Cheddar flavor
  Velveeta, or regular Velveeta
½ cup medium picante sauce (or ½
  recipe of the tomato, onion, and
  chili sauce from Sonora Chicken
  Strudel, well drained)
Corn chips and crudités

In a wide frying pan, sauté the ground beef over medium-high heat, until brown but not overcooked. While the meat is cooking, cut the Velveeta into 1-inch cubes. When the beef has browned, add the Velveeta cubes, turn the heat to medium-low, and stir until the Velveeta has melted. Turn the heat to low and add the picante sauce or the Mexican strudel sauce. Heat just until bubbly and serve with chips and/or crudités.

Marmalade Mogul Muffins

½ pound (2 sticks) unsalted butter
1¾ cups sugar, divided
4 large eggs
2 cups buttermilk
4¾ cups all-purpose flour (High altitude: add ¼ cup)
2 teaspoons baking soda
2 teaspoons baking powder
½ teaspoon salt
2 tablespoons orange zest, minced
1 cup best-quality bitter orange marmalade (recommended brand: Harry and David Wild & Rare Bitter Orange Marmalade)

Preheat the oven to 350°F (High altitude: 375°).

In a large mixer bowl, beat the butter with 1½ cups of the sugar until well combined. Add the eggs one at a time and beat well. Add buttermilk and mix thoroughly.

In another bowl, mix together the flour,

baking soda, baking powder, and salt. Add the dry ingredients to the butter mixture. The batter will be stiff. Stir in the zest and marmalade. Using a ⅓-cup measure, divide the batter among 28 muffin cups that have been fitted with paper liners. Using the last ¼ cup of sugar, sprinkle a teaspoon or so over each muffin.

Bake 15 to 20 minutes, or until a toothpick inserted in the center of a muffin comes out clean.

Makes 28 muffins

"*Who* did *what*?"

But Tom was ripping open a bag of chips. I phoned Marla, who declared she was famished, thank you very much, and what kind of wine should she bring to go with the halibut? Not that she could drink any, but maybe Tom and I would, she said. I racked my noggin for a stored tidbit of oenophilic advice from Arthur Wakefield, and told her a full-bodied, spicy white. Marla promised she'd be over in twenty minutes, armed with the vino.

Tom asked: "Miss G., did you pretend to be an undercover cop, and have lunch with a woman named Boots Faraday so you could grill her on the Portman case?"

"Oh, sure, Tom." The oven timer beeped. I gently levered the crispy cookies onto waiting racks, then put in the muffin cups. "I invited Boots Faraday to lunch and said, 'I'm an undercover policewoman. Don't tell anybody. I do have a bunch of questions for you, though. Don't tell anybody *that*, either.' "

Tom asked, "Want to make a pasta dish to go with the halibut?"

I nodded, angrily chopped garlic and onion, and tossed them into a pan shimmering with heated olive oil. "I did not pretend to be *anything* with that woman." I didn't want to tell Tom about the collage I'd bought him, because now I was wondering if the gallery had a return-for-cash policy.

"Watch yourself, because *that woman* has served time for assault."

"You're kidding." I set water on to boil

for orzo pasta. Then I chopped a few ounces of smoked ham and a couple of tomatoes, and stirred them along with some whole-grain mustard, Madeira, white wine, marjoram, and oregano into the headily fragrant, sizzling garlic mixture. A spicy pasta dish would go wonderfully with the halibut. When the sauce was simmering, I asked, "Boots Faraday assaulted somebody?"

"Seems she did a series of artworks for a client. Man owned a snowboard store, he used a snowboard as a down payment on half a dozen collages *featuring* snowboarders. When Ms. Faraday finished them, the guy said he'd changed his mind. He didn't want the collages anymore, but he told her to go ahead and keep the board. She could even hang the collages in Killdeer restaurants, he added happily."

"For heaven's sake."

"Now, most reasonable people would take their complaint to small-claims court. Not our Ms. Faraday. She drove her Chevy Suburban smack into the guy's truck. Broke both his legs, which put a stop to his snowboarding that winter. At first, she claimed she didn't know who the fellow was she'd hit. But since his truck was custom-painted with the words *Killdeer Boards,* nobody believed *that.* She spent ten days in the clink. The rest was a suspended sentence."

"Hmm." I showered orzo into the boiling water and set the timer. "Did she have any parole-type run-ins with Doug Portman?"

Tom shook his head. "But he was the art critic, and at least half a dozen people have told us she hated his guts because he didn't review her work favorably. She even tried to get him fired from the Killdeer paper, but they ignored her, probably because they weren't paying him very much to write his columns."

"I didn't interrogate her. For the record."

"No, I know," Tom said with a broad smile. "You were probably just being your usual nosy self. Figured that as soon as I got word of the complaint." He stirred the bubbling cheese concoction; my stomach growled.

"Boots Faraday wasn't the only one I was nosy with today." I told him about Jack Gilkey being out on parole for his role in Arthur's mother's death and Arthur's taking very public exception to Jack's release.

"Let me guess who granted Gilkey parole," mused Tom.

"Yep. And guess who Portman did *not* grant parole to."

"Barton Reed," replied Tom promptly. He was heating water for a chafing dish. "I know, I looked him up today. I arrested him for fraud a while back. And by the way, John Richard has written to the board asking for an early parole date. But it'll be at least a month before they even consider letting him out."

I sighed. "So do you think Barton Reed might have killed Portman?"

"We're a long way from knowing that, Miss G."

I set the table, lightly dressed a salad of

romaine and Bibb lettuces, and set out slices of a five-grain homemade bread Julian had left for us.

"I do have a question for you, though," Tom said after further thought. "Seems Ms. Faraday, too, read that article in her paper about your more-or-less successful career as an amateur sleuth."

"Don't get me started on *that*. Publicity, as I told Ms. Faraday, is strictly Arthur's department."

Tom stirred my orzo. "Uh-huh. But a lot of people did read the article. Maybe one person who read it decided to rear-end your van. Maybe they were worried you'd go nosing into Doug Portman's death." I sighed. "Just a theory," Tom added. "Speaking of Portman, we got a preliminary drug screen back on him. He had touched the patches, but they'd already been used, so there was just a trace of opioid in his system. Not enough to kill him. No, *that* particular job was left to whoever smashed him in the head with a big rock found tossed off the run. He was hit repeatedly, apparently. Rock had stuff on it that you don't want to hear about while we're fixing dinner. One thing it didn't have on it were fingerprints, sorry to say."

"So it was murder, then?"

"It was murder, definitely," Tom said grimly. "They think somebody knew he took that run and was waiting for him. Saw him go by and quickly put up the poles and ropes closing the run. Then skied down and did him in."

I hadn't liked Doug Portman, but I suddenly felt heavy with sadness. Tom gave me a long hug.

He poured the steaming queso dip into the chafing dish and lit the Sterno underneath. I'd given him the chafing dish for Father's Day. Tom had done more positive things for Arch in two short years than The Jerk had done in the preceding twelve. So he'd deserved a Father's Day gift.

"Snow, snow, snow!" cried Marla as she came in and threw off another full-length coat, one she'd assured me was fake fur, although I had my doubts. Underneath, she wore a Christmasy crimson dress streaming with sewn-on ruby-colored beads. "Where's that son of yours? I brought him some Christmas candy, that ribbon stuff. Tell him I want to know what kind of candy his girlfriend likes, too. I'm putting in another big order next week. Yum! I *swear* it always smells *great* in this house!"

I decided against telling her that the subject of a gift for Arch's girlfriend was a sore one, and called him. He clomped down the stairs and accepted Marla's gift of candy with guarded enthusiasm. When she bustled over to open the Gewürztraminer, he squinted skeptically at the thick, brightly colored candy ribbons, unsure whether the confection was too babyish to consume in public. I ignored him and broiled the halibut steaks. Before long we were digging chips into Tom's hot dip and agreeing that halibut was perfect with a

198

spicy orzo dish. Funny how—when you're not being filmed—cooking is much easier.

"How many more shows?" Marla asked, as if reading my mind.

"One, right before Christmas."

"I heard about yesterday. Portman's suspicious accident was on the news," she commented matter-of-factly. "I'm sure Elva the ex-wife didn't do it, though. She's found a new boyfriend and they're in New Zealand. He's real cute, she sent me a picture." She looked at me ruefully. "Is there anything *good* about your work in Killdeer?"

"Free skiing," Arch and I said in unison, and we all laughed.

"I know it's heresy, and I *do* ski, but I'm not sure it's all the fun it's cracked up to be." Marla shook her head as she accepted a second heaping plate of pasta from Tom. "I mean, it's expensive, you get cold, you fall. I say, why not go straight to the après-ski food, wine, and hot tub, and skip the stuff on the slopes?" Arch rolled his eyes. Marla went on: "About the fundraiser. You did a great job, Goldy. It wasn't your fault the mixer blew up on you. I mean, I called in a pledge, and it wasn't even because I felt sorry about Nate Bullock. I couldn't bear that show, *High Country Hallmarks*. The only hallmark the high country has gotten in the last decade is Neiman-Marcus."

I smiled.

Marla munched salad and considered. "I do feel sorry for Rorry Bullock, I suppose. You know, when you work in Killdeer, you can't afford to have decent housing. It's like Aspen that way. The rich folks have driven the cost of housing out of sight—I hear some workers have to live in tipis in the woods all winter. Can you imagine that? Rorry lives in a trailer park, but it's not much more secure than a tipi. St. Luke's is raising money to help her buy a new car. Can you believe somebody borrowed her car without even asking? Banged it into something and then just left it parked by her trailer! What a drag!"

"That's terrible!" I exclaimed, and thought of my own accident. "When did it happen?"

Marla shrugged. "Not sure when. Recently, though. I'm glad the church is going to help her buy another one."

Tom said, "How'd you hear all this?"

"She's on the prayer list, but the money request isn't confidential," Marla replied as she licked the last of her salad dressing from her fork. "Thank goodness! I'm so tired of keeping secrets!"

I couldn't help laughing; neither could Tom. Arch grinned, too, perhaps remembering how Rorry had showered him with hugs when he was little. He announced to us all that he was going to do another physics experiment. He shyly added that he was sorry he'd left his stuff in the hall. Then, to my astonishment, he opened his bag of ribbon candy to share with everyone.

CHAPTER 13

The next morning, I stood in my beautiful-but-drainless kitchen and admired the heaping platters of library reception cookies and muffins. Even when things aren't going very well, I consoled myself, it's best to bake. I fixed myself an espresso and filled small vases with cheery sprigs of holly and ivy for the library tables. Tom came in, kissed me, then whipped together a golden German pancake that puffed so hugely even Arch smiled. By seven-thirty, I had everything packed into the Rover and we were ready to roll.

As the Rover chugged behind Tom's Chrysler, snowflakes swirled down from an ominous charcoal sky. Despite the fact that we were heading for the much-complained-about early Sunday service at St. Luke's, Arch seemed less sullen than usual. That might mean Lettie was coming to the service. Then again, maybe it was the pancake.

Marla waved to us from a pew near the front. As we slid in next to her, I shot her a look of surprise. She usually did not get up to attend this service. Maybe her prayer-chain duties demanded she haul herself out of bed at dawn so as not to miss any rumors. Marla hated to think people were having crises without her knowledge.

I focused on the liturgy. At least, I tried to. An unidentified worry gnawed at me. I'd always told the Sunday schoolers to hand their problems over to the Almighty. Now I tried to take my own advice.

When we reached the beginning of the intercessory prayers, one of the ushers handed the priest a note. This practice of passing forward written prayers had been presented as *a way to bring us together.* It smacked a bit of TV-evangelist-land, but never mind. The priest solemnly intoned that we needed to pray for a former parishioner who was struggling with a pregnancy. This far-flung member of our parish family, he added, had also had her car stolen and vandalized.

"You see," Marla leaned over to whisper. "I told you."

Rorry. Questions about her behavior were what bothered me. And now this. *When,* I wondered, *when was her car stolen and smashed?* I would call her as soon as I finished at the library, and make that formal offer to bring casseroles to freeze until her baby arrived. Maybe she'd open up and tell me why she was in such a snarly mood at the fund-raiser in honor of her dead husband. Maybe she'd also share what had happened to *her* vehicle, so close to the time when mine had been struck.

The service ended. I hugged Arch. Tom kissed my cheek. Arch had spent Saturday snowboarding and visiting his father at the Furman County Jail, only to come home to a wrecked science project. So this afternoon, he was starting over on the project and memorizing the lines from Spenser he was supposed to recite in English class this week. Tom would take him home, before going down to the department for a few hours. He wanted to check up on the information I'd given him. Marla asked what type of goodies I would be serving at the library. I told her they were delicious, guaranteed to please, and plentiful. What more could a caterer give? She said she'd be first in line. I took off.

Our small-town library, with its brick walls, steeply pitched copper roof, and two peaked reading towers, was an enchanting spot. I was alone in this opinion, though: Hundreds of letters to the local paper had protested the year-old structure as unmountainish. Unless public edifices looked like lodges, Rocky Mountain folks found them repulsive. Ever-resourceful Marla wrote in that we should call the place the "Château de Volumes." No one took her up on it.

I squinted through the snowflakes and was surprised to see a very large banner hung across the library entrance. HOLIDAY RECEPTION—REFRESHMENTS! it screamed. Might as well have said FREE CHOW! On the other hand, the thickening snow might deter the hordes. Tom liked to tease that I was unhappy if there were too *many* folks, and miserable if there were too *few*. In other words, like the original Goldilocks, I was too picky.

As it turned out, the event was wonderful, or rather, *just right*. Over a two-hour period, about sixty well-bundled patrons tramped into the reading tower, shed coats, boots, mittens, and scarves, cozied up to the gas fireplace, and indulged in cookies, muffins, and each other's company. Marla gushed to every single guest that these were the *best* treats in the universe. People enthusiastically replied, Yes, the best indeed. My heart warmed, especially when a dozen patrons begged me to do their Christmas parties. Rather than shamefully admit to my official closure—with my business shut, I could only give munchies away, I couldn't sell them—I replied that my personal chef work and the TV show in Killdeer had me fully booked up to the new year. To which Marla, ever the optimist, added that I was compiling a waiting list for February. She urged patrons, *Call Goldy and order your special Valentine's Dinner, delivered right to your door!*

When I shot her a blank look, she winked and gave me a thumbs up. At least ten people swore they'd give me a ring. What would I do without Marla?

The afternoon's only wrinkle came as I was packing up. One of the librarians told me in a low voice that I should not forget to pick up the books I had ordered. When I said I hadn't ordered any books, she said that I had a whole packet of material at the front desk. It had been there since late yesterday, she added. Must be late-arriving reference material for Arch's physics project, I thought. I packed up the Rover, then made my way to the counter.

"There must be some mistake," I told the checkout librarian as soon as I leafed through the contents of a manila file folder and glanced at two rubber-banded books, both labeled for me. "I didn't request these."

"Library card, please." Without looking at me, she held out her hand for my card. I riffled through my wallet, confessed I couldn't find the card, and waited while she tapped keys on her computer, frowning. After a moment, she asked me if I was Goldy Schulz and recited my street address. When I said yes, she frowned some more, tapped more keys, then said I must have forgotten I'd ordered the books and articles, because I'd certainly used my card to request them.

Doggone it. I looked down at the books in my hand: *Avalanche Awareness* and *The Stool Pigeon Murders.* The first was a safety manual. The second appeared to be a true-crime slasher story, complete with grisly photographs of corpses left in Boston parking lots. The stool pigeons, apparently, had witnessed crimes, turned in the criminals, and been slaughtered for their civic-mindedness. I set these aside and opened the file with its typed label: GOLDY SCHULZ. The bumper stickers it contained said: *Want to Die?* and *Friends don't let friends kill themselves.*

What in the *world*?

I flipped carefully through a sheaf of photocopied pages. There was no note, not a single indication of who had sent them. The half-dozen articles in the file were from the *Killdeer Courier,* the weekly *Furman County Register,* and the *Denver Post* and *Rocky Mountain News.* Some paragraphs had been highlighted in neon green. I flipped back to the beginning, then cursed softly: Now fingerprinting the pages would be impossible. Then again, a whole slew of librarians had probably already touched the pages. And maybe I was getting a trifle paranoid. Was leaving stuff for somebody else at the library in some way threatening? An invasion of privacy? Could you be booked for impersonating another library patron? I gnawed my cheek while contemplating the true-crime slasher book. Whatever it was, it didn't make me feel good.

To the librarian I said, "Do you have any idea who left these for me?" When she shook her head, I asked if she would be willing to ask the staff if they'd received the manila folder from someone they remembered. The librarian took the file and disappeared. She came back to say one of the volunteers had reported to a staff person that the file had been in the drop box that morning. That meant that someone had left it sometime after closing on Saturday and before opening on Sunday. I tucked the folder under my arm, pressed some leftover cookies on her by way of thanks, and took off for home.

Tom had left an apologetic message on the tape. His captain wanted to see him; he'd be tied up longer than he expected. He'd be listening to the football game on the radio. Maybe he'd be home by the fourth quarter. Would I cheer for both of us?

There was another message, a long one, from Arthur Wakefield. I retrieved his wine list with suggested foods as I listened. He'd been able to rescue all but one of his wines from Customs. Still, he was planning on show-casing all five vintages, and a truck should deliver the sauvignon blanc Sunday after-noon.

He needed food for a dozen people, he went on. He'd invite four more people. He knew he'd only put fish, chicken, and red meat on the list—not very helpful—so this phone call was to spark my thinking. But remember, *he himself* needed to finish the cooking.

He loved the pork I left for him. He'd bought some pork tenderloins, and I should certainly make that dish again to go with the Châteauneuf-du-Pape. I should bring the ingredients for the marinade, though, then mix them with the red wine at his place. I scrib-bled madly.

A lot of folks had asked him, Arthur went on airily, about the yummy-looking crab cakes I'd made on TV. He wanted something Mex-ican to go with the zinfandel, but not the egg rolls, since he didn't want to be running back and forth for appetizers. So please fix a Mex-ican main dish, he said vaguely, with chicken. Also a fish dish. He'd picked up some fresh sole and spinach while he was in Denver, could I do sole Florentine to go with the chablis? I nodded to his taped voice and con-tinued to make notes.

Last, Arthur said, could I please make the gingersnaps from the program? He'd gotten a great deal on that wonderful, lush Sauternes, and wanted to give the snaps another try. Had a lot of folks asked him about the cookies from TV, too, I wondered? He didn't say. He *did* say that he'd pay for the foodstuffs, plus give me forty dollars an hour for labor, and another hundred for the time and travel I'd put in so far. Not bad. I rewound the machine and made sure I had the food requests right. I had a lot of cooking to do at his place tomorrow, no question about that.

I set aside Arthur's directives and gripped the anonymously sent file from the library. I was trying to decide where to sit down and study it when Arch marched into the kitchen. He asked if he could do his splatter pattern with water mixed with confectioner's sugar, dropped onto a cookie sheet. Great idea, I replied. Much better than bleach, anyway.

To give Arch privacy, I fixed myself an espresso and took it along with three cookies and the articles from the library into the living room. I muted the football half-time show and stared at the unopened file. Had The Jerk ordered this weird collection of material for me? My ex-husband had found ways to sabotage me from jail before.

I sipped the thick, dark coffee, especially welcome on a snowy day after working an event, and started reading the first article, dated three years before and headlined: UNSTABLE SNOW MAY HAVE CAUSED TWO DEATHS IN KILLDEER. In it, I read of avalanche victim Nate Bullock, host of PBS's *High Country Hallmarks,* who had died the previous day in an avalanche in an out-of-bounds area. One source, who asked not to be identified, claimed Nate had gone to the valley to track lynx. But Nate had not left a marked map, the way a pilot might file a flight plan, so no one, not even his wife, had been quite sure what he was doing or where he was going the day he died.

On nearby Bighorn Overlook, the article went on to say, Fiona Wakefield—heir to the Wakefield corn oil fortune, and an intermediate skier—had died in a fall off a snow-covered cliff that was less than fifty yards out-of-bounds. Estimation of time of death for both Wakefield and Bullock was two in the afternoon.

I frowned. The two of them died on the same day, at the same time? Nobody had mentioned this to me, although Jack Gilkey had mentioned the unstable snow that day.

The next article stated: QUESTIONS LINGER IN TWO KILLDEER DEATHS. Mysteriously, this writer claimed, both Bullock and Wakefield had not been alone. When the ski patrol had found Jack Gilkey, his skull had been bloodied and he'd been dazed. The patrol had discovered his wife one hundred feet below him, over the cliff. Dead. Gilkey had claimed he and his wife had been attacked by a strong-built, ski-masked person. The three of them had struggled; Jack had been knocked unconscious; Fiona had gone over the cliff edge. In trying to rescue Fiona and Jack, the ski patrol had obliterated any sign of other prints in the snow.

In the case of Nate Bullock, the patrol, Forest Service, and sheriff's department had found a set of boot prints beside Nate's, going into the out-of-bounds area. This I already knew from patrolwoman Gail. But only Nate's body had been found in the search. No one else had been reported missing.

The third article screamed: SNOWBOARD TRACKS ON ELK RIDGE VANISHED INTO AVALANCHE ZONE. It was possible, the writer hypothesized, that Nate Bullock had hiked partway up the mountain with a snowboarder. The two had then parted ways, Nate tracking in the valley, the snowboarder ascending the ridge. Had the snowboarder triggered the avalanche that killed Nate?

WAKEFIELD WIDOWER QUESTIONED focused on Jack Gilkey's account of the circumstances surrounding his wife Fiona's tragic death. More details of Fiona's last day had emerged: Fiona had had too much to drink at lunch, she'd boasted she could beat her husband to the Bighorn Overlook, a roped-off area just off one of Killdeer's advanced slopes. The over-look faces the out-of-bounds area that includes Elk Ridge, the writer added parenthetically, and skiers occasionally ducked the boundary line to take in the view. Those pristine moun-tain forests of Elk Ridge, the article reported, were now earmarked for ski-area expansion. According to Jack Gilkey, Fiona had skied ahead of him and ducked the rope. Fiona and Jack arrived at the overlook, then were attacked by someone bursting from the trees.

Jack tried to help his wife and was knocked out himself.

QUESTIONS PERSIST IN DEATH OF HEIRESS cited the postmortem drug screen, which showed a blood-alcohol level in Fiona's body that made her legally drunk. GILKEY CONVICTED OF CRIMINALLY NEGLIGENT HOMICIDE added that a mitten belonging to Jack had been found clutched in Fiona's hand. He had let her drink too much; he had let her go down a run she wasn't qualified to ski. The nail in Jack's coffin had been the fact that the ski patrol had apprehended him at the overlook the day *before* Fiona died. They'd yanked his ticket and warned him away from that spot. But the next day, he and Fiona had raced to the same out-of-bounds overlook....

Since by law a person who in any way causes another person's death cannot benefit from it, the article concluded, Jack Gilkey was not inheriting Fiona's millions. Neither was her son Arthur, however. If Jack for any reason did not inherit, Fiona had specified that her money should go to charity: the Public Broadcasting System.

Finally, WAKEFIELD HEIR FILES COMPLAINT recapitulated Arthur's furious claim that Jack Gilkey had exerted "undue influence" on Fiona Wakefield in the making of her will. Before Fiona's remarriage, Arthur had been the sole beneficiary of a twenty-million-dollar estate. Suddenly, Arthur had become, instead of the heir to an immense fortune, the recipient of a paltry million-dollar trust fund. But nineteen million was not going to PBS if Arthur Wakefield had anything to say about it. The article added that ski patrol had verified that it had been Arthur Wakefield who had sent the patrol to the overlook, to try to find his missing mother. They'd found her all right, but she was already dead. Her neck had broken in her fall.

I stared at the silent television. Mile-High Stadium was a mute chaos of orange and blue. The Broncos scored a field goal; the crowd went wild; the station cut to commercial.

Who had left these articles for me? Why? What connection did Fiona have to Doug Portman? Could it have anything to do with my discovery of Doug's body? But what? Portman had granted parole to Jack Gilkey; Portman had also been despised and vilified by Arthur Wakefield. What did that have to do with the avalanche that snuffed out Nate Bullock's life?

I shuffled through the material again. *The Stool Pigeon Murders* had nothing to do with anyone or anything I knew about. Had someone been a stool pigeon? Who?

And then there was the avalanche book. I flipped through it: *Always test the snow in a slide area before traversing it. If you are caught near an avalanche, grab a tree, rock, or anything solid. Carry an avalanche beacon in all wilderness areas.* Great.

Three years ago, Nate Bullock and Fiona Wakefield had died on the same day, at the same ski area, albeit not on the same slope. Two days ago, Doug Portman, parole board member, had been murdered on a Killdeer ski run. An ex-con had been mouthing threats against the police. My van had been hit, perhaps deliberately. Could there be any connection between the deaths of Fiona Wakefield, Nate Bullock, and Doug Portman? Is that what someone was trying to tell me? If there was a connection, what was it, and how could I uncover it? Waiting for another anonymous library delivery was a slow way to solve a case.

Impulsively, I punched in the numbers for Arthur Wakefield's Killdeer condo. I'd pretend to have questions about his wine-tasting menu, then I'd ask him point-blank if he'd taken my library card. Then I'd ream him out.

Unfortunately, his machine picked up. Arthur's throaty-voiced recording featured Chopin piano music and a lofty greeting: He was off searching for the perfect pinot; when he found it, whoever was calling could come over for a glass. I left a brief message asking him if he wanted a salad with all these main dishes; please give me a buzz.

Through an entire series of downs in which Kansas City drove to the ten-yard line and then fumbled, I scanned the two books and reread the newspaper articles. My bafflement only grew. Arthur had connections to Nate through PBS, and to Doug Portman, whose work on the parole board he reviled. Jack Gilkey, of course, had been married to Fiona and been paroled by Doug Portman. Did Jack's new lady love, my dear old friend Eileen Druckman,

213

know all of this information? Was it my duty to make sure she did?

I frowned at my watch: Sunday afternoon, where would Eileen be? Probably on her way back to Aspen Meadow, so Todd could make it to Elk Park Prep in the morning. Would Jack be with her? With any luck, no.

I put in a call to the Druckmans' country club residence and reached Eileen on the first ring. After we chatted about the ninth-grade Elizabethan poetry assignment and the quantum mechanics mess—Todd had dropped pebbles onto, and broken, a glass coffee table—I took a deep breath and asked if she'd tell me: How exactly did she meet swashbuckling Jack Gilkey?

Eileen chuckled. "Through John Richard."

"My ex-husband?" I was stunned. "You met Jack through The *Jerk?*"

"Oh, come on, Goldy." She was instantly defensive. "Am I a welfare lady who visits convicts because that's the only way she can get a date?" I said nothing. "Don't you remember," she went on, "last summer? When Tom was trying to fix up your kitchen? You asked me to take Arch down to visit John Richard a couple of times, since you hate to do that."

"Eileen. Sorry. Of course I remember. I just didn't think you'd be getting involved with him. I mean, John Richard."

Her tone softened. "Goldy, I *know* John Richard was terrible to you." Terrible doesn't begin to cover it, I thought. The man is *in jail*

214

for assault. Eileen went on: "But I think he's changed. Anyway, John Richard was awfully nice to me. When I said I was thinking of buying a new business in the ski area, maybe a restaurant, John Richard said I was in luck, there was a chef right there in jail with him. This chef had been messed up royally by his lawyers, John Richard said, and I should meet him. I did, and now Jack and I are together, and I can't remember the last time I was this happy."

"Did you check the facts of his case?"

There was a pause. "Gee, thanks, friend." But Eileen's voice had hardened again. "I've already told you: Jack didn't kill Fiona. Somebody else did. I think that son of hers murdered her, hoping to get her money. Or maybe he hired someone to kill her. He just didn't know she'd already rewritten her will so that either the money went to Jack, or it went to PBS. Now he's asking the probate court to set aside the will. And Arthur wants to look like such a good little boy to the probate court. He *loves* PBS, that's why he works for them for practically nothing. He *wouldn't* mind if the money went to public broadcasting, but really, it's *his.* Please, spare me!"

"Eileen—"

"For heaven's sake, Goldy! Do you really believe I'd be living with a *killer*? Would I make my own son vulnerable?"

"If you'd just—"

"I believe Jack. He did not kill his first wife. He's a good man trying hard to rebuild his life. I even offered him money for lawyers to appeal his conviction. He said no. He said, 'That's not the way to be healed.' "

I shook my head and turned my attention to the television, where I watched the Broncos execute a successful down-and-in pattern. I asked, "Are you planning on marrying him?" I wanted to add, *Since he seems to prefer older, wealthy women,* but thought better of it.

Eileen snorted. "Goldy! For heaven's sake!" She raised her voice a notch. "Listen to me. Here's how nice Jack is." On the screen, the Broncos punted, and the illuminated billboard at Mile-High exploded with the words *Defense! Defense!* "Jack doesn't have any money. He *wants* Fiona's money to go to charity. Even Doug Portman was convinced of Jack's goodness, that's why he let him out of prison. Jack is a good man. That's what petty, greedy, deceptive Arthur Wakefield *really* can't stand."

"Okay, I just wanted to hear what you were thinking about this.... You know, we always talk about everything—"

"I'm sorry, Goldy. I don't want to fight with you. I just...was so unhappy until Jack came along. At least you didn't say that Jack's with me because of my money, and that if I didn't have any, he'd find somebody half my age."

"You are smart, funny, and beautiful. What more could a man want?"

"Yeah, yeah. Look, if Jack *were* after my money, don't you think he would have asked me to marry him by now? And if he really intended to harm Fiona for *her* money, don't you think he would have taken out a fat insurance policy on her or something?" She sighed. "Not to worry, my dear friend. How's the planning going for your last show?"

I laughed and admitted the planning so far was zilch. We decided on times this week when our sons could work together to finish up their science projects before Christmas break. Hopefully, neither would burn the house down in the process. We hung up smiling. Thank God. Old friendships are too important to lose...especially over vague rumors and unsubstantiated suspicions. Speaking of old friendships—

I called Information, got Rorry Bullock's number, and punched buttons. Rorry sounded very surprised to hear from me.

I said, "We prayed for you in church today. You're having trouble with your pregnancy?"

"Still in Med Wives one-oh-one, eh, Goldy?" she shot back. "It's just a little separation of the placenta. I'll be fine."

"And they said something had happened to your car?"

"Borrowed and trashed. This trailer park is the worst place for security in all of Killdeer, and we don't have anything like what's in the rich folks' houses!"

I murmured my sympathy, and offered to bring her some casseroles the next day. Once again, food worked its magic. Rorry softened instantly and said she'd love them. After I left the dinners, she added, would I mind driving her to work at the Killdeer warehouse? I'd passed the warehouse, one of the dark-painted service barns owned by the Killdeer Corporation, when I'd been looking for Arthur's condo. No problem, I'd be glad to take her to work. When I got off the phone, I realized I'd forgotten to ask her what precisely had happened to her car. I did not call her back because at that moment, Tom walked through the door.

It was the end of the third quarter; the Broncos were leading ten to zip. To my surprise, Tom shuffled heavily into the room and glanced at the score without much interest.

"Tom?"

He sat on the couch and set three sheets of paper on the coffee table. Then he turned and took my hands.

"Tom? What is it?" His expression frightened me.

"Someone broke into Portman's condo the day he died. He'd lived alone since Elva divorced him, so it was definitely *his* stuff somebody was after." Tom sighed. "If anything's missing, we have no way of knowing. We seized all the files that were there, and we've ordered his bank records. We're trying to fit up a series of deposits with his parole recommendations, but so far we haven't figured out if he was up to anything."

"Do you think he *might have been* taking bribes, then?"

Tom nodded. "Portman was under investigation. A number of prisoners in Cañon City and at the Furman County Jail have told investigators how he asked them for money. He always did it when the stenographer wasn't there. He always wanted the money to be brought to him personally by a relative or friend. And judging by the stuff in that condo, the guy was loaded. Even with his side business of dealing in military collectibles, and the bit he got from being a critic, there's little chance you could live the way he did on sixty thou a year from the parole board."

"So he didn't get a big divorce settlement from Elva?"

"Not according to our court records. They didn't have a prenuptial agreement. She sold her gallery and kept the proceeds. She's on record as saying she hoped he'd have to go digging ditches. Plus, he gave up the forensic accounting when he got the parole board job."

"What about Jack Gilkey?" I asked. "Did you find any connection between Doug and Jack?"

"Nothing yet. If Gilkey gave Portman money in exchange for an early release, we can't find any record of it. We talked to Jack, and to Eileen, very informally, and both say Portman really liked Jack, and that there was no money involved. We checked out Jack's alibi for the times of both Portman's death and the break-in. There's one person who remembers being with him for most of the lunch *prep*. Four people were with him while they were cooking the meal itself. By the time Jack got off work, Portman's place had been burgled. The receptionist at Portman's condo complex said a man in a uniform came in around noon, showed ID, claimed he was there to check the security system. She didn't see him come out, so she figures he was the one who broke into Portman's place. Eileen says she was skiing most of the day. But she was alone, no witnesses."

"So her alibi isn't airtight," I said reluctantly. "What about Arthur Wakefield?"

Tom shook his head. "Swears he was skiing alone. No alibi for the time of Portman's death, no alibi for the time of the burglary."

I thought for a minute. "Could Doug have kept another office, apartment, or house, where he might have hidden records of bribes? A lot of folks have condos in Killdeer as second homes."

"Not that we've been able to determine. He only listed the Killdeer condo with the parole board for an address. Now here's something puzzling: Portman hadn't quit the parole board, but it looks as if he was leaving or moving, because most of his belongings were in boxes. His military memorabilia were carefully packed in about forty or so boxes marked *Store.* Whether that meant *put these in storage* or *sell these at a store,* we have no idea. We're still looking into it." I nodded, mystified. Tom glanced at his first sheet, then paused. Finally he asked, "Goldy, how many antiques dealers did you contact about selling the Tenth Mountain Division skis?"

"I called a guy in Lodo, a couple on South Broadway, and a woman in Vail. Not one of them was willing to give us more than five thousand dollars, and then they wanted to take a commission on top of that. Wholesale, they called it. But everyone *said* the skis were worth at least ten thousand. So I figured we— *I*—ought to be able to sell them on my own."

"So you offered them to Portman. Because you knew from your dating days that he had an interest in that kind of thing."

I nodded, but, watching the expression on Tom's face, felt increasingly uneasy.

He went on: "But you didn't want to tell *me* that Portman was our buyer, because you'd dated him before we met, right? And you felt funny about that, contacting an old boyfriend, even though he wasn't a boyfriend."

"I didn't feel funny, I felt foolish." When Tom said nothing, I mumbled, "Yes, something along those lines."

"So you struck a deal with Portman for the skis."

"He was willing to pay eight thousand—"

"Which was close to the amount of cash they found on him, and scattered on the slopes."

"Tom! Why is *that* a problem?"

Tom pressed his lips together and stared at the swirling, silent action on the television. "You were selling valuable skis to a parole board member with no intermediary. Meanwhile, your ex-husband is in jail, facing parole in the not-too-distant future. Think about that. You were selling skis to a man who might be in a *position* to do you a *favor* down the road, by *denying* your ex-husband parole."

"At the time, I didn't even *know* Doug was on the parole board!" I protested.

"Someone might say you were trying to influence him."

"I was *trying* to pay for new drains—"

He held up his hand. "Miss G. Your plan to sell the skis to the parole board member included your agreeing to charge him *less than the full market value* of ten thousand dollars for them. You were doing him the *favor* of selling him a valuable item for two thousand dollars under market price." His green eyes, full of pain, studied me solemnly. "How do you think that makes you look?"

"I don't care, because what you're saying is ridiculous!" I cried hotly. "You can't honestly think that I would do such a thing!"

Tom did not reply. Unable to bear the look on his face, I glanced at the television. Kansas City jumped offsides but the penalty wasn't called.

"Miss G.," he said. "You didn't warn *me,* but now *I'm* warning *you.* You better *pray* that the sheriff's department figures out who killed Doug Portman. And why." He sighed. "Your home kitchen's closed for repairs. Now you're involved in what could be interpreted as shady dealings. The press gets hold of this, it might get so slanted against you, your client base could dry up. Permanently. And if you're *prosecuted* for this—" He broke off abruptly.

"The district attorney is not going to pros-

222

ecute me for trying to influence Doug Portman, is he?" I demanded. "That's absurd!"

The phone rang. Tom rose to answer it. "You never actually completed the sale to Doug, so it's doubtful you'll have to face prosecution," he answered slowly. Then he hesitated; the phone bleated. "But, Goldy—it does look very bad."

CHAPTER 14

Tom was sitting at the table, scribbling in his trusty spiral notebook, phone tucked under his ear, when I entered the kitchen. The game was in overtime, the score tied. I didn't care. I was angry my kitchen was closed, furious my van had been destroyed, and remorseful that I hadn't been brave enough to tell Tom who was buying his skis. And why was all this happening? Because, years ago, I'd dated Doug Portman. And then, unabashed, I'd offered to do business with him. I'd figured, *he's the perfect buyer for the skis.* I'd thought, *This money will solve all our problems, and quick.* Sure.

I looked around the kitchen. *Action is better than inaction.* Or something like that. I carefully moved Arch's still-wet, splatter-frosted cookie sheet onto another counter, then stared at my old recipe card box. Tom continued to talk on the telephone.

I flipped through the box of stained recipe cards, my old standby before the kitchen computer. What dishes would comfort and nourish Rorry Bullock when she came home from the hospital with her newborn? Two reliable casseroles beckoned from a time before I entered the catering business: lasagne and Swedish meatballs. On one of the walk-in's side shelves, I miraculously located fresh oregano, basil, and thyme. Serving meatballs and lasagne could jeopardize my upscale reputation, I reflected while removing ground beef, ricotta, Fontina, whipping cream, eggs, and mozzarella from the walk-in. Rorry wouldn't tell on me, would she?

"Okay, got it. Yeah, sure, send it now. Thanks." Tom hung up. "We know what opioid was on the patches. A drug called Duragesic."

"Oh, brother." Duragesic was a very powerful painkiller, administered through transdermal patches. The potency of the drug diminished over a period of time, at which point a cancer patient or other chronically ill-and-in-pain patient put on another patch.

"You use or even *touch* more than one Duragesic patch at a time, you're probably going to die," Tom added grimly. "But there wasn't enough on those *particular* patches to kill anybody."

"So why would you threaten a law enforcement person, in this case the head of the parole board, with something that wouldn't work?"

"I don't know," he said. "Maybe you thought it would work. Maybe you just wanted to scare the guy to death." He slid his finger down the list of names he'd written in his notebook. "Eleven people I've arrested over the last four years have treated their cancer pain with Duragesic. Five of them were denied parole by Doug Portman. One's in remission in Lamar, one's a roofer in Pueblo, one's in a Colorado Springs hospital on life support. One guy died. The last one, man of thirty, was paroled last June by someone else. He'd been denied twice by Portman. But Barton Reed violated his parole three weeks later by assaulting a big guy wearing a Red Wings jersey. He swore the Detroit fan taunted him. But Reed still went back to jail for another six months anyway." Tom shook his head. "He's been out for a couple of weeks."

I set a pot of water on to boil for the pasta. "How's his health?"

"He's in remission now. Last May, while he was still in jail, he was in so much pain he was on…*Duragesic.* " Tom's fax rang. A moment later the machine spat out a high-quality photocopied photograph. Barton Reed, wide-faced and menacing, a dozen crosses and oval-shaped earrings strung along the edge of each ear, leered off the faxed page. The photocopy undeniably captured the likeness of the man I remembered seeing last summer at Aspen Meadow Health Foods, the man I'd dubbed the Earring King. Last June, he'd been putting together an herbal remedy for his illness. When Cinda had talked to me about him on Friday, he'd been putting together something altogether different: a threatening card with death as its message. What had Jack Gilkey said? *Reed has revenge in his heart.*

I poured green-gold olive oil into a sauté pan. When the heat made the oil glisten, I tossed in chopped onions and crushed garlic cloves. They sizzled, turning the air mouthwateringly pungent. "So...what was Reed's original offense?"

Tom cocked one of his bushy eyebrows. "Did you know our friend Barton was a hot snowboarder for a lot of years? Don't get me wrong, that wasn't what got him into trouble. He toured the freestyle circuit here and abroad. That takes money—for travel, lodging, entry fees, you name it. In winter, he based himself in Killdeer. In summer, he would search Aspen Meadow and the other wealthy areas of Furman County for elderly women in the last stages of cancer."

I added the ground beef to the pan and soon the scrumptious aroma of beef sautéing in garlic and onion filled the kitchen. I was beginning to feel a little better, perhaps because I was cooking. Or maybe it was because we were talking about somebody else's problems. I said, "Rich, elderly women with cancer? Why target them?"

Tom perused my Swedish meatballs recipe card, washed his hands, and whisked together eggs and cream. "To steal from them. He'd tell these women's families that he knew a doctor down in Mexico, an American genius with a pedigree as long as a prosthetic leg. Reed's very convincing line was that Doctor Genius had given up on the FDA ever approving his cancer-healing miracle drug. Why wouldn't they approve? these people would ask. Because the AMA didn't want their oncologists to go out of business, Reed claimed."

"For heaven's sake."

"At Doctor Genius's luxurious healing spa in Oaxaca, Barton assured his clients, their terminal relatives could be healed. They'd be back home in six months. He showed pictures, offered testimonials, the whole bit. He had a background as a lay preacher, and was *very* convincing. Each family handed over sixty thousand dollars—ten thousand a month for the first six months. They'd send Granny off with Reed, and that was that. They got glowing reports from Doctor Genius, from Reed, even from a purported resident chaplain. But never heard a word from their beloved grandmothers."

"Which should have been their first clue."

Tom nodded. "Finally, one relative went down to find out what was going on. The women were being kept in dreadful conditions in a sub-par nursing facility. No phone, no medical treatment, no chaplain. And needless to say, no genius doctor. Barton Reed had to hang up his snowboard so he could be incarcerated for three long years." He paused. "Where's the allspice?" I handed it to him. "Here's the irony," he continued thoughtfully. "After

Sonora Chicken Strudel

2 tablespoons vegetable oil
3 cups seeded and chopped tomatoes
2 garlic cloves, pressed
8 ounces (2 small cans) chopped
   green chiles
1½ cups chopped onions
⅛ teaspoon cumin
2 cups cooked, shredded chicken
1¼ cups grated Cheddar cheese
1 cup lowfat or regular sour cream
1 teaspoon salt
½ pound phyllo dough (approximately), thawed
¼ pound (1 stick) unsalted butter,
   melted

In a wide frying pan, heat the oil over medium-low heat until it shimmers. Reduce heat to low and add tomatoes, garlic, chiles, onions, and cumin. Cook, uncovered, stirring occasionally, until the mixture is thick, about 30 minutes. Set aside to cool slightly.

Preheat oven to 400°F. Butter a 9x13-inch glass pan. In a large bowl, combine the chicken, Cheddar, sour cream, and salt. Stir in the tomato mixture. Pour this mixture into the pan.

Working quickly with the phyllo, lay one sheet at a time over the chicken-tomato mixture and brush thinly but thoroughly with the melted butter. Continue until you are almost out of butter, then lay on a last piece of phyllo and brush it with the last of the melted butter. With a sharp knife, cut down through the layers of phyllo in 12 places to make 9 evenly spaced rectangular servings.

Bake 20 to 30 minutes, or until filling is hot and phyllo is puffed and golden brown. Serve immediately.

Makes 9 large servings

less than six months behind bars, Barton Reed was diagnosed with testicular cancer. Parole board member Doug Portman had no sympathy."

"Or Barton Reed had no cash to fan the flames of Doug Portman's sympathy," I commented sourly.

Tom whirled cornflakes in the blender; he added them, along with dried minced onions, to the egg mixture. "Our guys are picking up Reed now for questioning. Miss G.—I want you to stay away from Reed. The man is fueled by rage." Tom seasoned the crumb mixture and stirred it into his bowl of fresh ground beef. His large, capable hands formed scrumptious-looking meatballs. He placed them in rows on a jelly-roll pan and popped the pan into the oven. I stirred tomatoes, red wine, and herbs into the sauté pan for the double batch of lasagne sauce. While it was coming to a simmer, I browned two packages of chicken thighs in olive oil and set them to stew with onions, carrots, and bay leaf. These would form the base for the Sonora Chicken Strudel to be served at Arthur's buffet the next day. Soon the old-fashioned scents of stewing chicken and spicy tomato sauce were wafting through our kitchen. Heavenly.

I layered the cooked pasta, grated cheeses, and rich tomato sauce into two pans—one for us, one for Rorry Bullock—then set the table. When the lasagne was bubbling, I called Arch. He made one of his silent appearances in the

230

kitchen and nodded approvingly at the pasta dish. When Tom cut into the lasagne, a lake of melted Fontina and mozzarella spurted out over the delicate layers of ricotta and tomato-beef sauce. Sauce and melted cheese oozed between the tender pasta. I savored each bite. Best of all was watching Tom and Arch help themselves to thirds.

When we were finished eating, Arch stood up from the table and hugged me. "Great dinner, Mom."

This sudden display of affectionate enthusiasm made me wary. "Thanks..."

"All right," Arch began, in a preamble-to-an-announcement tone. "Lettie's dad is driving the two of us to school early tomorrow, since we're writing up our theories on the physics project together. Her father is picking me up at seven A.M." He pushed his glasses up his nose and gave me a *very* serious look. "When Lettie arrives, Mom, please do *not* ask her what she wants for Christmas. Okay?"

"No problem," I replied. "If you want, I won't even let her in. Does she have a thick winter jacket? So she can wait for you outside?"

My son considered this question. "I don't know. But you can invite her into the kitchen."

Tom smiled at me and winked. I said, "So, if Lettie is coming inside, what would she like for breakfast?"

"Will you *stop*?" Arch implored.

Now what did I do?

Monday morning dawned cold and dark. At six, I scooted across our chilly wood floor and checked the thermometer outside our bedroom window. It seemed stuck at seven degrees. With any luck, we'd make it into the low twenties by afternoon.

I moved through a slow yoga routine, showered, dressed, and went down to the dark kitchen. I fed and watered Jake and Scout, then convinced them to go outside and quickly return from the snow to their own space. Sitting at the oak table, I sipped a much-welcome cup of coffee and made a list of dishes to be prepared and packed up.

First I would make a salad, just in case Arthur wanted one. Then I'd be on my way to his place, to prepare the Sonora Chicken Strudel, plus the dish I was now dubbing Snowboarders' Pork Tenderloin, Chesapeake Crab Cakes, and Julia Child's Sole Florentine. Then I'd deliver the meatballs and lasagne to Rorry, pray for reconciliation, and hope for a nugget or two of information as well. I frowned at my list and wondered if I had any baby blankets, bibs, or other paraphernalia of Arch's still around. Rorry Bullock wasn't on the parole board; I could do her a favor without getting into trouble, couldn't I?

I was still trying to remember where I'd stowed Arch's baby things while I creamed soft—not rock-hard—butter with brown sugar

232

and mixed in apple cider vinegar, eggs—broken without mishap—and molasses, to make the snaps. Oh, yes: The blankets and clothes were in a box in the attic. I mixed flour and spices into the cookie dough, scooped balls of spicy dough onto a cookie sheet, and ran upstairs to find the box marked *Baby Stuff*. I raced down with it, placed it in the Range Rover, then rushed back to retrieve the first cookie sheet. The snaps had flattened and crinkled on top. The gingery aroma in the kitchen absolutely demanded another cup of coffee and a taste-test of the soft, dark cookies. *Mm-mm*. They were really more of a molasses cookie than a gingersnap, but older clients always had to worry about denture problems, Arthur had informed me, and *nothing* should be too crunchy. I ate another cookie to confirm the texture was perfect. Whether I called them molasses cookies or gingersnaps, I definitely should have them for breakfast more often.

Soon I had packed the stewed chicken along with the other ingredients for the strudel. Next to them, I placed the marinade components and miscellaneous items for the fish and crab dishes. Amazing how much you can accomplish when you're enjoying what you're doing.

Promptly at seven, Lettie's father pulled up in his black Jeep. Lettie, a leggy fourteen-year-old with blond French braids, a sweet, lovely face, and perfect teeth, strode up our sidewalk. She wore a white blouse, red plaid kilt, black leather car coat, and ankle-high black boots. The picture of a teenage model—which she was.

"Hey, Mrs. Schulz!" she said brightly when I opened the front door. I had yet to discover how the old Southern version of *hello* had migrated westward, but never mind.

"Hey," I replied congenially. "Come in."

Lettie stepped across the threshold, closed her eyes, and inhaled. "It always smells *so* great in here!"

"Can I offer you a cookie? Some juice? It's all ready—"

"That sounds—"

"Hey," came Arch's growled greeting from the top of the stairs.

Lettie sparkled. "Good morning, Arch."

"How about a snack?" I ventured.

"We need to go, Mom," Arch answered sternly. Today he wore baggy khaki pants, an oversized green sport shirt, and a sleek black vest. He'd combed his dark brown hair back with mousse; it stood in short spikes. If I hugged him a bit carelessly, my cheek would be speared. Not that I would be so thoughtless as to hug him this morning. Rule #32 when dealing with a teenage son: *Never* touch the coiffure.

I hustled back to the kitchen, tucked two tiny boxes of apple juice and four bagged cookies into Arch's backpack, then handed him the pack in the foyer. I mumbled, "Treats inside." Arch glared and shook his head: *Stop talking, Mom.* Lettie waved gracefully as she bounced down the sidewalk. Arch did not look back.

I rechecked the foodstuffs going to Arthur's place, kissed Tom twice, and set out. After I crossed the Divide, the sky lightened. Approaching Killdeer, smoke from wood-fires hovered in the valley and turned the air pleasantly acrid. By nine I was pulling into the Elk Ridge Nature Trail parking lot. It was chock-full of brightly clad day-skiers. They were pulling out their skis and poles, calling to each other as steam issued from their mouths, and jouncing along merrily in their ski boots toward the bus stop.

As I wended the Rover through the lot to get to the turnoff to Arthur's, I passed the glistening humps of snow that marked the base of the Elk Ridge trail. I felt a twinge of jealousy for the skiers. The mid-December day seemed made for skiing: the sun glittered off pristine slopes, the sky extended endlessly in a cloudless periwinkle dome, a light breeze carried fresh, sweet air off the peaks, and five inches of new powder topped an eighty-five-inch base. What more could you want?

Let's see, I answered myself playfully as I pulled into Arthur's driveway. How about a friendlier relationship with my son? But I doubted that was really possible with a four-teen-year-old boy. Well, what else would I like? How about a new van, and my business restored? And oh, yes, to find out what had happened to Doug Portman, and why someone had left me a pile of articles about two other Killdeer deaths from three years ago.

The doorbell bing-bonged into the depths

235

of Arthur's condo. I realized I was going alone into the house of a man I worked with, but didn't know very much about. Remembering Tom's admonition I put down the box I was carrying—causing my injured arm to yelp with pain—and pulled the cellular phone out of my pocket. I dialed my husband's sheriff's department answering machine and announced to the tape that I was at the doorstep of Arthur Wakefield's place. It wasn't exactly protection, but it was something. Arthur pulled the door open. As usual, he was clutching a pink bottle of antacid.

"Come in, come in," he said.

"Good morning, Arthur! I was just letting my husband the *cop* know where I was."

He shot me a curious look, noticed the box at my feet, struggled to get the Pepto into his pocket, then took the carton. "I'm in a phone battle with a supplier. Might have to go over to Vail to look for some cases of the sauvignon blanc."

"I'm sorry," I murmured. Being a wine importer did not sound like a whole lot of fun.

"You can set up in the kitchen. Need me to carry in any more boxes?"

"That's okay, Arthur, I can handle it." Thankfully, the phone rang. Arthur dumped the box into my hands and rushed to take his call.

In the barely-used-but-beautiful yellow-and-white kitchen, it was slow going finding the utensil drawers, cupboard for baking sheets, and bowl and cutting board cabinets.

At least Arthur had made a neat design of the buffet schedule, with meticulous notes beside each entrée concerning its placement. Now I just had to teach him how to finish the dishes themselves.

"I heard you had some trouble with Boots Faraday," Arthur said grimly as he rushed into the kitchen and slammed the portable phone onto the tile counter.

What had Boots Faraday done after we'd met? Spent the rest of the afternoon calling people to complain about me? "I delivered your wine and stayed for lunch. Unfortunately, she didn't seem to like me very much. And by the way, you didn't tell me you ran an article that described me as a crime-solver, for goodness' sake."

"Sorry, sorry, that's show biz. Hype. Look, I'll talk to Boots. The Bullock thing is *extremely* sensitive to her. Rorry is convinced to this *day* that Boots was having an affair with Nate. I'm sure they weren't. Boots was just trying to help Nate with some business venture. But Rorry was so jealous that Nate got paranoid. Boots started calling him from pay phones and using coded messages, and that just made matters worse. She'll come to her senses, don't worry. I'll get her to apologize—"

"Please forget it, Arthur." I hesitated. "What business venture was Boots helping Nate with?"

Arthur shrugged. "Come on, Goldy. It's all I can do to keep the wine business straight."

And speaking of *business,* I was desperate to

237

ask Arthur about his love/hate connection with PBS. But I figured that his TV work, along with his vintages and his complaints to the probate court, was what kept him on antacids. "All right, then," I said pleasantly, "We've got a lot of cooking to do here. Should we start? Please? How about with the salad? I made one of mixed field greens. Didn't dress it, though."

"Thank you. Sorry I didn't call you back about that. Field greens would be marvelous. No vinegar in the dressing, remember." He gestured at the row of bottles. "Unfortunately, I have only the single bottle of Sancerre for you to make an oil-and-wine vinaigrette." He sighed and flipped through his Day-Timer. "I'm up to fourteen people, by the way. Two of my customers just returned from Mexico and they want to come. That's no problem, is it?"

Rule of catering: *Never panic in front of the client. Especially on the day of the event.* "Um, fourteen people," I said, stalling. I'd planned on four main dishes—crab, sole, pork, and chicken. Unless we had massive food allergies, that was no problem. "That's fine," I replied cheerfully. "And the clients are...?"

"In the trade. I've got two wholesalers coming," Arthur ticked off on his manicured fingernails, "plus nine of the best customers west of the Divide. And of course, three retailers, who will fill the orders for the customers. Two of the retailers own wine shops, and the third is a restaurateur, *not*, I might add, your friend Eileen or her dreadful chef."

"Jack Gilkey," I supplied gently, and Arthur grimaced. "I was wondering if you'd be in the mood to talk about him—"

He turned away and opened the refrigerator. "Sorry, but I thought you said we needed to talk about the food. Ah, here we go. Two pork tenderloins." Pulling out a shrink-wrapped packet and a box of phyllo dough, he placed both on the counter, then frowned at the wine bottles as if they were chess pieces. Finally he pulled one forward. "Here's the Châteauneuf du Pape—"

"Wait. If you're finishing the dishes later—"

"I already told you that," he said crossly.

"Phyllo goes back in to chill."

He sighed hugely, stuffed the slender box on a refrigerator shelf, then energetically twisted the cork out of the red wine. He bonged the bottle onto the counter. "For the pork marinade. It's a big red from the southern Rhône, just the ticket for a rich meat dish."

"Okeydoke. Please, Arthur, Jack Gilkey is living with one of my closest friends. I really need to talk to you about him."

Arthur whirled away from the refrigerator. "So, was Boots right? All you want to do is *interrogate* people?" he snarled.

"Arthur, calm down. You and I are friends. Somebody sent me books and articles anonymously. To the Aspen Meadow Library. Was it you? The articles were all about your mother's death."

Arthur snorted and turned back dismissively to his refrigerator. "You think I have time to do that kind of thing? If I want you to read something, I'll *give* it to you, Goldy." He pulled out a butcher-paper-wrapped package and slapped it on the counter next to the pork. "This is your sole."

"Arthur, we work together. Please talk to me."

He whirled, his face furious. "Jack Gilkey is a gold digger. He married my mother for her money. He was twenty years younger than she was, handsome, attentive, quite the flirt. He systematically got her to cut me out of her will, set up a *minuscule* trust for me, and made himself the beneficiary. My mother must have felt slightly guilty about all this, so if Jack predeceased her, the money would go to public television, since I'd learned to read watching *The Electric Company.*" He rolled his eyes. "I didn't find out any of this until after her death, I'm sorry to say. Only none of Jack Gilkey's planning and organization worked, because he was a *bit* too obvious. I'm just glad a jury could see through his story. End of subject."

"Do you think he bribed Doug Portman to get out of prison early?"

Arthur laughed. "I'm sure he did."

"Where'd he get the money?"

Arthur put his hands on his hips. "Well, crime-solver, whose dear old friend has scads of money, where do you *think*?" The phone rang and he grabbed for it. I could tell from the expression the news was not good: the cases of Sancerre still had not arrived.

Eileen had given Jack money to bribe

Portman? I didn't believe it. I washed my hands and pulled out the covered container with the stewed chicken. I separated succulent chunks and strands of chicken and studied the French posters on the walls.

When Arthur hung up, I said, "Look, Arthur, let's forget about Jack Gilkey for the moment. Doug Portman's death puts *me* in a compromising position. I was about to sell him some valuable skis, at less than their market value. He was a parole-board member, and now it looks as if *I* was trying to buy a favor."

"What kind of favor?"

"A favor as in *please keep my ex-husband behind bars.* All I was trying to do was get a quick sale for the skis. But it still looks very bad."

Arthur's dark eyes twinkled. "And you without a wholesale license."

"Don't joke."

"I didn't send you any articles, Goldy. But Doug Portman *was* on the take. Guess what Portman said to me?" His tone turned vicious; his black eyes narrowed. "That he'd keep Gilkey behind bars, but it would cost me twenty thousand dollars a year. Problem was, my mother's millions were going to *Sesame Street,* and I couldn't spare an extra twenty thou a year."

"The trust-fund background was in the articles left for me," I told him. "The article also said that you were challenging the will, claiming Jack had unduly influenced your mother."

"He did. He turned my mother against me,

discouraged her from seeing me, changed their phone number every week, fired the family lawyer, you name it. He thought he could kill her and inherit, so no one would be the wiser. He just didn't figure he'd get caught. Mother allowed him to swindle her because she wanted that handsome snake-oil salesman to love her."

I folded sour cream, grated cheddar, and spicy picante sauce into the chicken. "Kill and inherit? *Kill* is a strong word."

Arthur seemed intent upon assembling wineglasses on the tiled counter next to the array of bottles. "I don't use the word lightly. I wish to God the prosecutor could have proved premeditation on Jack's part, but she couldn't. I'll guarantee you this, though: Gilkey will marry Eileen Druckman for her money. You'd better watch out for your friend."

"I know. And I'm sorry to bring up painful memories."

Arthur sighed. "I sure do wish I'd taped Portman's call to me about paying him to keep Gilkey behind bars. Now he's dead. So it's up to me to prove Portman was taking bribes. Then my claim to have the will set aside is infinitely strengthened. Gilkey will be proven once and for all to be a bounder, and I'll be able to—" He abruptly stopped talking. His eyes rested on the poster on his wall.

"Be able to what?" I kept my tone lighthearted as I began to measure out the marinade ingredients. "Travel to France? Go live in Tuscany?

My fantasy is to eat my way through Italy on a six-month walking tour. The exercise works off the meals."

After a moment, Arthur said softly, "My dream is right there." He gestured toward the travel poster, the lavender-surrounded village with its high church steeple.

"To go to France? To live there?"

"Not just France, Goldy, but a particular place." He stared lovingly at the poster. "I'm going to buy a vineyard in the town of Bandol, in Provence. Here, let me have you taste something." He reached for a corkscrew, then disappeared to another part of the house. When he returned five minutes later, he carried a bottle of red wine. "I just want you to try this."

"Arthur, please. It's not even nine o'clock in the morning."

"Just a sip." He uncorked the bottle and poured a half-inch in each of two wineglasses. I sighed. Two rules of catering were in conflict: *Do not drink alcohol on a job, especially in the morning* and *The more you need the client, the crazier the client will act.* Arthur dramatically proffered me a glass; we toasted each other silently; I took a sip. It was delicious. Even *I* knew enough about wine to call this red hearty, spicy, and just the ticket for getting your morning off to a great start.

"That's my future you're drinking," he told me, very seriously. "My *wasted* future," he added glumly.

"Why 'wasted'?"

Arthur cocked his head. "What do you taste in the wine? What spices?"

"I'm not that good at—"

"I will tell you what you're tasting." He clattered his glass onto the counter. "You smell lavender. You taste rosemary. Basil. Bay leaf. You taste *Bandol.*" He gestured at the poster. "A corner of it, anyway." His voice cracked. "Bandol is a lovely Provençal village, where I could have bought an operating vineyard for two million dollars. I keep that picture here to remind me what Jack Gilkey stole from me. I could be growing my grapes and relaxing each evening with my view of the sea. But Jack Gilkey ruined that. And your buddy Doug Portman let that killer out of prison."

"Doug Portman was not my buddy." *And the sheriff's department also thinks he was taking bribes,* I added mentally. But I did not know how much of what Arthur was telling me was true, so I kept my mouth shut.

"Yes, yes. It doesn't matter now, does it?" He felt in his pocket for his Pepto and pulled it out. He did not drink any of it, thank goodness. After staring at it for a moment, he stuffed it back into his other pocket.

I had one more question for Arthur. "If you're trying to deprive public broadcasting of your mother's fortune, why do you work for them?"

He sipped his wine. "Because a love for public television was something my mother and I shared. Yes, I want the money. But I can't

244

turn my back on something that was dear to my mother and me. You know? Her favorite show was Nate's *High Country Hallmarks.* And they died the same day."

I set the wine down, murmured sympathetically, and wondered if I could ask Arthur to fix me one of his perfect espressos. My brain was starting to spin, after only three sips of wine. Unfortunately, the phone rang again. Arthur refilled his glass as more disastrous news was delivered: the cases of Sancerre, including the one intended for tonight's party, had been left on the loading dock of a warehouse in Glenwood Springs. The only way they could be in Killdeer that night was if Arthur drove over and picked them up. He banged down the phone.

"I have to go," he said frantically.

"I'll be done in a couple of hours. I can lock up for you," I assured him. Arthur groaned and patted the Pepto-pocket. "I do it all the time for absentee clients, Arthur. And I'm bonded."

He frowned at the food on the counter. "Well...all right. I know how to heat up the pork, but what about the rest of it?"

"I'll write it all out for you."

His face relaxed. "Thanks, Goldy." His face tightened again. "Just do the food. I'll get out the other wines when I come home."

"Okay, but you'll never be back before five, and you should chill the whites for—"

"No, thanks," he said abruptly as he opened drawers and scanned the kitchen counters. "Don't get me wrong. I *am* grateful for what

245

you're doing. Looks like my checkbook's in the car. Can I pay you Wednesday? In fact, can I take you to lunch at the bistro? Wednesday is Gilkey's day off. We can talk about the last show. Save Thursday, please. I want you to make that oatmeal you gave me, maybe a bread...."

"Sounds great."

"Afterward, we could ski together, if you want."

I laughed. "Sure. But I'm strictly a slow-going blue-run skier. And I rarely have wine with lunch."

His puzzled look said *Are you joking?* But he merely mumbled, "See you at the bistro Wednesday at noon," grabbed his keys, checked the locked door in the hallway, glanced at the Dresden shepherdess figurine on his front table, and took off.

I studied the three "sample" bottles on the counter. Why did he have a fit when I offered to get out the *rest* of the wines? As his Escalade roared down the driveway, I began mixing the crab cake ingredients, thinking hard. Arthur probably didn't want me fetching the wines because wine geeks are notoriously secretive about their cellars. I rolled the crab cakes in crumbs and slid them into the refrigerator next to the strudel, then peeked out the front window. The Escalade was nowhere in sight.

The door in the hallway was indeed locked. I hesitated. If I snooped around, but didn't steal anything, could I lose my bonding? If I snooped around, and Arthur came back and caught me, would he break a wine bottle over my head? Would it be full or empty?

I won't steal a *thing,* I promised myself. If he comes back, I'll just say I was looking for the wines. To try to help him out, I'll tell him. What I wouldn't tell him was that his locked door and furtive ways had me convinced he was trying to hide something besides chardonnay. And that always provokes me to find out if I'm right.

First I checked his leather jacket for the key. His "lost" checkbook was sticking out of one of the pockets. I remembered his visual check of the Dresden shepherdess on the table. I lifted the delicate china piece and found a small brass key beneath it. When I unlocked the door, it opened onto a carpeted staircase.

I tiptoed down, holding my breath, and found myself in a long hallway lined with color photographs. This lower level held two guest rooms, a bathroom, and another closed door. The wine cellar?

Someone desperate for information, valuables, or *something* had broken into Doug Portman's apartment the day he died. The sheriff's department had discovered no evidence linking Portman to alleged under-the-table payments, although they had yet to search through his sealed boxes of military memorabilia. If an uncategorized piece of art or an antique weapon had been within reach of the burglar, it could have been stolen. If there had been files or papers in the condo, they could have been removed. Most significantly, if

there had been any immediately recogniz-
able clue as to what Doug Portman was up to,
it had vanished. Who needed something
belonging to Doug Portman? Needed it badly
enough to burglarize a dead man's home? If
you had nineteen million dollars riding on
finding evidence of Portman's wrongdoing,
wouldn't you rush to go through the place? And
if you'd killed him, wouldn't you know you had
only a few hours' jump on the cops?

I gulped. How well did I really know Arthur?
He had been friendly when he wasn't nerve-
wracked, which was most of the time. Did I
really think he was capable of killing someone?
Hard to tell.

I turned the knob on the closed door at
the end of the basement hallway. Locked.
Did Arthur have the wine-cellar key on him,
or was it hidden down here? Where had he kept
the key to the basement? In the hallway,
under a figurine.

I walked up and down the hall, much the
same way I'd strolled past the "Best of Killdeer"
show at the art gallery. Here, finally, were the
family photographs that one would have
expected to see on the upper floor. All had dates
underneath. Several of them featured Arthur
a decade ago, standing beside a tall, good-
looking woman whom I recognized from the
articles left for me: Fiona Wakefield. She
smiled with her son from the Bridge of Sighs
in Venice, from the steps of the Parthenon.
There was a picture from the Sixties, taken in
front of the Waldorf-Astoria. In this one,

Fiona had her arm around a handsome man I assumed to be Arthur's father.

But one photograph in particular caught my attention. In sunglasses, clad in bright snowgear, Fiona smiled on a snowy mountaintop. There had been someone standing next to her, but that person's image had been neatly sliced away; all that remained were the tips of another pair of skis. A penned-in date indicated a time four years ago.

The person cut out of the picture had to be Jack Gilkey.

The photograph was mounted in an acrylic frame. *Gilkey stole my future,* Arthur had told me. I carefully lifted the framed photo off the wall. Something clinked to the floor. I looked down: At my feet was a gleaming key ring. Dangling from the ring were a door-size brass key and a small steel padlock key.

CHAPTER 15

Now that I had the key, the locked door opened easily. Behind it, a padlocked gate barred entry to the cold, gloomy cellar itself. I undid the padlock and removed it, then creaked the gate open.

I groped for a switch; overhead lights blazed through the gloomy space. The walls were made of Colorado river rock. Stacks of crisscross-style bins held hundreds of wine bottles, each lying on its side. My shoes crunched against the stone-paved floor as I moved cautiously forward. The cellar was not a square, it was not even symmetrical: It had angled walls and dark corners. I shivered. How much had it cost Arthur to put in this storage bunker? Worse, through these thick walls, how would I even hear him if he came back?

I quickly scanned the bins for anything besides wine. Ignoring the cold, I crossed to a near wall where a bin contained two file folders. I flipped through the first file: it apparently contained a log of what was stored in the cellar. The second file was stuffed with papers detailing outflow from Arthur's supply—to whom the wine went, when, and how much. I moved on to a set of shelves built into the rock wall. This held two rows of empty bottles; names and dates were scribbled on each label. The labels were difficult to read, but seemed to be records of when the bottles had been consumed. The man obviously carried wine-obsession to new heights. On the floor were more empty labeled bottles, as if Arthur had run out of room for his souvenirs.

A foot away from the empty-bottle rack, he'd mounted a color poster of limestone cliffs next to a dark blue sea. The poster-photograph looked familiar. I suddenly realized I was looking at the Mediterranean: This was another view of the French village of Bandol.

I keep the picture here to remind me.

The four corners of the poster were affixed to the wall with gummy adhesive. I peeled up

the bottom right corner, then the left, and discovered what I'd suspected: behind the poster
was a double set of shelves just like the one
with the empty bottles. For some reason,
Arthur had emptied out these shelves and
put the bottles on the floor, to make an
impromptu—and hidden—storage area. Why?

Disappointingly, only one shelf contained
something: four letters and a UPS package.
I was not surprised to see that every single item
had been addressed to Doug Portman. Nor was
I shocked to note that every one had been slit
open and, presumably, read.

I worked my way through the letters first.
Their postmarks indicated they'd been mailed
in the first two weeks of December. One was
from a potential buyer in Minnesota who
wrote to say he was interested in unjacketed
bullets from the Civil War. Another was from
someone wanting to sell Doug a rifle complete
with bayonet. The earliest postmarked letter
was from Mexico. It was from one Juanita Mar-
tinez, and explained in formal English that
Señor Portman's guest villa awaited him.
Señor would be able to do business in the town,
Puerto Escondido. Spanish for *Hidden Port;*
I knew that much. I also knew Puerto Escondido was not a high-profile American tourist
destination.

Finally, there was the UPS package, stamped
with the return address of Copper Mountain
Worldwide Travel. Inside was a ticket and a
note. The ticket was a round-trip to Puerto
Escondido with a departure date of the twen-

tieth of December and an open return. The scrawled note from the travel agent said: *Mr. Portman, This time of year, it's much cheaper to buy a round-trip ticket. Thank you for your check.*

Heart pounding, I stuffed the ticket and note back in the UPS packet, then folded the letters and tucked them back in their envelopes. I placed the pile on the stone shelves exactly as I'd found them and reattached the poster to the rock wall. Then I fled the dreary cellar, turning off the lights and relocking as I went.

Safely back in the kitchen, I poached the sole, braised the spinach, and made the easy sauce for the sole Florentine. I whisked together a wine-only vinaigrette. Then I wrote out all the directions for Arthur. He had to be very careful to brush each delicate sheet of phyllo dough with melted butter, I admonished, and stack the buttered sheets on top of the chicken to make a puffed, crispy strudel topping. I wrote out directions for reheating the crab cakes and sole and tossing the salad. Last, I locked the heavy front door, swung it closed behind me, and walked quickly to the Rover. My brain whirled with questions.

Doug Portman had been leaving Colorado, going one-way to a small town on the Pacific coast of Mexico. He'd used the travel agency of a nearby resort town. He had found himself a villa and business opportunities. He'd been packed. All this Arthur Wakefield had discovered when he'd broken into Doug's condo the day he was murdered.

Arthur Wakefield was in the process of battling to have his mother's will reversed. He desperately needed to prove Jack Gilkey had had undue influence over his mother before she died. Clearly, he believed that if he could prove Jack Gilkey had had undue influence over *anybody,* that would strengthen his case. If nineteen million clams were at stake, wouldn't *you* want a strong case? So Arthur had broken into Portman's condo to see what he could find.

Why would Doug Portman be leaving, anyway? Had he gotten wind of the investigation into his parole board activities and decided to take a powder? Was it possible that Arthur had discovered Doug's travel arrangements— through the travel agent or some other source— and killed him? After the fact, why rob the condo? Could someone *else* have discovered Doug's departure plans, and tried to stop him, permanently?

I shifted gears and headed toward the trailer park that perched on the outskirts of Killdeer. Maybe Rorry Bullock would enlighten me on some of these people. I would certainly welcome some illumination. The more *I* tried to figure out what was going on in this mountain town, the more muddled I became.

Actually, I decided when I once again lost my way on the too-quaint, too-curvy streets of Killdeer, what I really needed was caffeine. Cooking, wine-tasting, and snooping were too much to handle before eleven o'clock in the morning, even if you were the toughest cookie in the Rockies.

The sunshine and fresh snow had lured so many day-skiers that their cars filled the lots near the gondola. I backtracked to the Elk Ridge lot and walked to Cinda's. It wasn't a bad trek if you weren't wearing ski boots. Twenty minutes later I was bellying up to the coffee bar and wondering if I didn't deserve four shots instead of two. And how about a luscious cheese-filled croissant to go with it? After all, I hadn't had any lunch.

Cinda, her cottony-pink hair held back with twisted rubber bands, opened her pale eyes wide when she spotted me. She beckoned with a ring-studded hand and then whispered ominously in my ear: "He's *here*. The snowboarder. Barton Reed."

"Here, now?" Then I added, "May I have a four-shot espresso and ricotta-stuffed croissant to clear my vision?"

Cinda said, "It's the guy who made the threat, remember? My other waiter, Ryan, and I have just been talking about it. Barton Reed used to be big in the snowboard circuit, and he drove us all nuts with his temper. Then he went to jail on a fraud charge. Now he's back, and the law enforcement guys found some threatening card he supposedly wrote. So *I* don't want to have to deal with him." She hustled off. Since it was late-morning coffee-and-hot-chocolate time, her shop was mobbed. She returned quickly, however, balancing a tray of goodies for me: a cup brimming with steaming, *crema*-topped espresso, a plate with a hot, flaky, ricotta-oozing croissant, and a jar of plum preserves. *Zowie!* I took a sip of the coffee and looked around the shop. I instantly recognized the chunky-faced profile and spill of earrings: Barton Reed.

"Did he *say* anything to you when he came in?" I whispered to Cinda.

"Yeah. The cops picked him up yesterday," she replied *sotto voce,* "but then let him go. His fingerprints weren't on the threatening card, and it wasn't his handwriting. But it *looked* like his handwriting. Then he came in here and demanded to know if *we'd* told the cops he'd threatened some cop. We played dumb. A couple of other shopkeepers told me Barton's been making threats all over town. So he can't be sure who spilled the beans to the cops."

"Why is he here now?"

"Says he's looking for somebody. He's clutching a cross. Maybe he's waiting for a vampire."

I started in on the flaky, hot croissant. It was superb. "You said he was waiting for somebody? Could he be waiting for Doug Portman? Does he know Portman is dead?"

"He didn't say. But he must, everybody in town knows. I'm telling you, that guy's lift doesn't go to the peak." She tapped her forehead meaningfully. As she did so, Reed shuffled to his feet and stomped toward the exit. At the door, he stopped and turned. He held Cinda and me briefly in a withering glare.

"Who could he be looking for?" I wondered in a low voice.

"I sure don't know." Cinda shook her pink-filament hair. "But it's not likely he'll be opening up his soul to any of our waiters again soon."

I didn't like the feeling this gave me. I thanked Cinda for the coffee, told her I'd see her later, and backed away from the bar. Before heading for the Rover, I made a visual check of the lift ticket windows, repair shop walk-up, and crowds going into and out of the Karaoke and Gorge-at-the-Gondola cafés. No Barton Reed. No, wait.

He was across the creek, standing in line for the gondola. With the crowd around him, I couldn't see if he was carrying a snowboard. Had he spotted the person he'd been waiting for, or had he given up?

If the sheriff's department had released Barton Reed, there was nothing I could or should do. I asked for directions to Rorry's trailer park at one of the lift ticket windows, then trekked back to the Rover.

The West Furman County Mobile Home Court—so named to distinguish it from any connection to the much-sought-after appellation *Killdeer*—was surrounded with a snow-laced five-foot-high chain-link fence. The fence was hung with fierce no-parking warnings, and the entry was flanked with signs informing the unwary that the motor court was for residents and their guests only; other vehicles would be towed and their owners fined. All the ski resorts had parking problems. No doubt some skiers thought nothing of

256

leaving their vehicles here, in the low-rent district.

Where the rest of Killdeer featured picturesquely winding roads, the snow-covered-but-unplowed roads of the employees' trailer park were laid out in ramrod-straight gridlines. I pulled in behind a red Subaru wagon. *Hmm.* Like its neighbors, the Bullock trailer stood perpendicular to the curb. Green and white siding peeled away from a sagging bay window; the trailer's bottom rim was patched with rust. There were no signs of life.

I hopped out of the Rover and walked up to Rorry's red car. The front bumper was crumpled, the right headlight gone. I fingered the cold metal of the impacted area. Rorry claimed somebody had stolen her Subaru, then smashed it up. I believed her. It hardly made sense that a pregnant woman would risk her unborn child to wreck a caterer's van. I edged back over the thick ice to the Rover, loaded up the casseroles I'd made, then carefully made my way to a rickety wooden staircase that led to an unpainted aluminum door.

There was no doorbell, but the door opened the moment I started to shift the dishes around to find a way to knock.

"Bummer about the car, huh?" Rorry said wistfully. "It's my fault, I guess. I shouldn't have left the keys in it." She wore a navy blue knitted maternity dress with thick cables and an uneven hem. Her skin was the color of mashed potatoes; her light brown eyes looked cloudy; her hair, blond and thin, curled softly around her face. She looked like an unhappy ingenue. If my arms had not been full of covered casseroles, I would have given her a hug. She pulled the door open as wide as it would go.

"Yeah, bummer," I agreed, with a backward glance at the red Subaru. I decided not to mention what had happened to my van. *When possible,* I'd learned, *do not upset a very pregnant woman.*

"It's the second time I've been a crime victim in this park," Rorry said bitterly.

"The *second* time?" I prompted as I followed her to the tiny kitchenette.

Rorry opened the freezer section of a small refrigerator. "The first time was after Nate died. When I had to go down to see the coroner, some kid broke in and stole our TV and Nate's videocamera. The cops caught him with the television, but he denied stealing the camera. The little creep."

"For heaven's sake," I muttered as I tucked the casseroles into the only freezer space free of icy stalactites and stalagmites. Respect for personal property was a very low priority in Killdeer, it seemed. I shook my head, turned, and gave Rorry a long, tight hug. I told her I'd be right back.

"Do you still love coffee?" she asked when I returned with the box of baby blankets.

"More than ever."

She pressed a button on an ancient drip machine to start a pot brewing. Rorry had always invited me in for a cup of coffee, even when she and Nate had lived in a tiny Aspen

Meadow apartment. Back then, he'd had a little business making videos of recitals, high-school graduations, and weddings. Apparently he and Rorry had also badly wanted children, and now... On the counter, a torn herb-tea package and half-full glass mug of green liquid indicated the mother-to-be wasn't indulging in caffeine these days. Next to them stood one of those porcelain coffee-bean containers and a grinder from an expensive mail-order coffee bean house. Low-income folks, I'd found, always bought a few food luxuries in case someone dropped in.

Rorry waved at her minuscule living area. "Please, sit down. And thanks for the casseroles and baby blankets."

"No problem. It was fun putting it all together. And it's nice to know someone can make use of Arch's things." I walked into the wood-paneled living area, where the linoleum of the kitchenette gave way to green shag carpet. This space featured a miniature sagging green-and-gold brocade couch, two stained gold chairs, and a fruitwood-veneer coffee table with a small pile of cardboard coasters featuring beer logos. The furnishings were all from that Seventies-era style known as "Mediterranean." It must have been in that decade, I reflected as I sat on the couch, that this trailer had been built and sold as a furnished home. If Killdeer could spend millions expanding onto adjacent slopes, why couldn't they subsidize low-income housing for their workers?

"Here you go." Rorry set a large mug of steaming coffee on one of the cardboard coasters. She winced. "Don't look at the rug. My boss back at Aspen Meadow Carpets would have had a fit."

"I won't tell," I vowed, "if you promise not to squeal to my food-snob clients that I brought you meatballs." She laughed and sipped her tea. I drank some of the coffee and pronounced it delicious.

Rorry smoothed the blue dress over her huge belly, then said, "Thank you for being so nice, Goldy. I don't deserve it, after how bitchy I was to you." Her light brown eyes held mine. Flecked with gold, puffy from lack of sleep, they were weary and apologetic. And sad.

"Don't worry about it, I can handle bitchy. Remember when the president of the Episcopal Church Women objected to our class doing Ezekiel-in-the-Valley-of-Dry-Bones in the narthex? Now *that* was *bitchy*."

She smiled thinly and shifted with obvious discomfort in her chair. "We had fun with that class, didn't we?" When I nodded, she pulled a miniature bottle of lotion from a pocket, squirted some onto her right palm, and rubbed her hands with a nervous wringing motion. "We did Ezekiel after we did Joshua and the walls of Jericho," she mused. "We were a pretty rambunctious group." She took a deep breath. "I still stay in touch with St. Luke's through the prayer chain. That was a great community. In Killdeer, there's nothing like it. You've got the very rich and then you've got their servants, who live in trailers at the edge of town. Guess what category I fall into?" She laughed humorlessly.

"If you don't like it," I blurted out, "why do you stay?"

"We used to love to ski." Rorry's voice was unexpectedly defiant. What had she said at the fund-raiser? She was *just puzzled*. Her mood swings were bewildering. Or maybe not. After all, she was nine months pregnant and, as far as I could tell, alone. "I suppose you've heard the rumors," she went on bleakly. "That's one way that Killdeer doesn't differ from Aspen Meadow. The gossip mill runs around the clock."

"Nope, haven't heard any rumors. And I'm a servant, too, you know."

"But you're dying of curiosity, and so is everyone at Front Range PBS. They sent you."

"*Nobody* sent me, Rorry," I told her. "I saw you Friday...and suddenly missed our friendship. So I called."

She stared at the low, stained ceiling and went on as if I had not spoken. "The TV people won't tell me anything. Oh, sure, they have their annual *do* in memory of Nate. They're not raising funds for *me*, because the FCC says they can only raise money for themselves. For *equipment!* What a joke!"

"Rorry, I don't know what—"

She banged her mug down on the battered coffee table and glared at me. "Nate's the father of this baby I'm carrying."

"Ah." Either she'd been artificially insem-inated, or she was losing her mind.

She read my expression accurately. "The first time we conceived, we had to freeze his sperm and go through artificial insemination. I was seven months pregnant when I had the mis-carriage. Then last year I read an article, about women laying claim to the frozen sperm of their deceased lovers. So I decided to use what I had left of Nate." When she scowled, her eyes crinkled in anger. "Use it before his *girlfriend* did, that is—"

I gagged on my coffee and remembered what Arthur had told me about Rorry's sus-picious nature, about her claims Nate was having an affair with Boots Faraday. "You think another woman would actually—"

Rorry held up a hand. "Nate said he and Boots Faraday—the collage artist, do you know her?" When I nodded, she raised a thin blond eyebrow. "Nate said Boots was giving him business advice. Then he went out-of-bounds to film something, and *she* said he was tracking lynx. Unfortunately, the wildcat population doesn't buy a lot of videotapes, so I *doubt* a film of tracks was his so-called mon-eymaking idea." She *tsk*ed and asked, "Do you know anything about tracking wild animals?"

"Not a thing, I'm happy to say."

"You hear of a sighting," Rorry continued in the same aggressive tone, as if determined to prove something to me. "You go where the trail might be and you look for scat. You find it, you start filming."

"Rorry, I'm not following you—"

She heaved herself up, crossed to the kitchenette, and pulled something out of a drawer. Wordlessly, she thrust an envelope at me. I pulled out a much-crumpled note. *Meet me at the Ridge trail at 2:00. Make sure nobody sees you. And remember your equipment, pal.* The handwriting was slanted and feminine.

Rorry, bitterly triumphant, announced: "Lynx *don't* buy videos, and they *don't* write notes, no matter *how* endangered they are. Arthur Wakefield and the TV people claim Nate was not doing a tracking project for them. But they didn't know what he was doing, so the spin, the story, the *myth* came out of the Killdeer Artists' Association and Boots Faraday." She raised her voice to a mocking falsetto. " 'Brave Outdoorsman Loses Life Tracking Vanishing Colorado Wildlife.' What crap! The only prints on that trail were from a man and a woman. Nate and his girlfriend, Boots. *Bring your equipment,* puh-leeze. They sneaked into the out-of-bounds area to make love. Where no one would see."

"There's no hay to roll in in Killdeer Valley, Rorry." She shook her head dismissively. I persisted. "But the footprints diverged. One set went up, one went down."

"So you *have* heard some rumors." Her eyes blazed.

"Not rumors, but information. From the ski patrol. After the fund-raiser, I was worried about you. So I asked a patrolwoman to tell me

263

about the avalanche. I thought it might help me understand what was going on with you. That's it." I took a deep breath. "But if their paths parted, maybe he was just keeping her company—"

"Maybe he was planning on getting undressed at the bottom of the hill and waiting for her," she said hotly.

I bit the inside of my cheek. My old friend had clearly spent three years of sleepless nights worrying over details, trying to piece disparate data bits into a coherent theory of her husband's death. She hadn't grieved properly because she didn't know what had happened. Worse, too many unknowns had left her with a sense of betrayal deeper and more devastating than grief.

"Rorry, the Killdeer Artists' Association said that Nate was trying to diversify, to provide a better living—"

"Oh, don't give me any of Boots Faraday's bullcrap. I've heard her line about Nate wanting to raise money for us, blah, blah, blah. Boots is a great skier and snowboarder and a successful artist. She called here and called here and called here before Nate died. Each time, she tried to hide her identity. Why? She's sexy as can be, as I saw when I went to one of the association's meetings with Nate. She was flirting all around, trying to get everyone to sign a petition, to get rid of Doug Portman. You saw her at the fund-raiser on Friday, didn't you? You see, she just can't get Nate out of her mind. She's obsessed. I think she's the one who wrecked my car, then returned it just to torment me."

"Rorry, you're an old friend." I asked gently, "Why did you decide to have Nate's baby, *now*? After all these years?"

She pressed her lips together, struggling to keep the emotion in. Then she answered, "I lost one baby when he died. And...I miss Nate terribly, even with all the...unanswered questions. The baby is for me—for *us*. I decided to have the baby now for what Nate and I could have been." Before I could reply, she pulled back her sleeve to check her watch. "I need to go. Can you still take me to work at the warehouse? I'm doing a double shift today. A coworker can bring me home later." Before I could ask whether doing a double shift was a good idea, she excused herself to freshen up.

I sighed quietly, picked up our mugs, and fit them into the trailer's small, packed dishwasher. When Rorry returned wearing snow boots, a jacket, and a hat, we took off for the Killdeer warehouse.

The enormous supply area was only a quarter-mile beyond the turnoff for the path to Elk Ridge and Elk Valley. I didn't want Rorry to see the signs to the place where her husband died. To distract her, I asked her to tell me about her work.

"It's not very exciting," she said with a laugh. "I just track the inventory for the supplies going up the mountain." We pulled into the parking area of several mammoth, brown-painted warehouses. Two heavily clad workmen were unloading boxes from a truck bearing the logo of a Denver wholesale food supplier. Numerous signs warned not to park, not to enter, not to do anything but go away. "That's the central storage area for produce, meats, canned goods," Rorry said as she pointed beyond a row of snowcats. "The tracks for the canisters start up there and go straight to the bistro. It's pretty efficient, really. Well, gotta go." She hesitated before opening the car door. "Goldy...I'm sorry to burden you with all my troubles."

"Rorry," I tried one final time, "it's possible that even if Nate did go up the ridge with a snowboarder, it was completely innocent. He could have been filming something else, and then things went wrong—"

"Then where's his camera? Sony VX-One Thousand, digital-video, industry-standard for filming out-of-doors? You gotta have a camera if you're going to film tracks or skiers or just do clips of trees. Suppose the kid *didn't* steal it when he took our television. If Nate was carrying that camera, the avalanche team or groomers or *somebody* should have found it, shouldn't they? They found Nate's hat, fifty feet from his body. They even found the note still inside his jacket." She raised her eyebrows and held out her hands. "Don't know? Me, either. And if his little hike was so innocent, why wouldn't his girlfriend come forward afterward? 'We weren't making love, we were just hiking and chatting about public television! Then he went down the hill, and I went up!' "

"Rorry—"

She unsnapped her seatbelt. "Look, thanks for your concern. The casseroles will be great. I'll call you when the baby comes." She struggled to find her next words. "Please, Goldy. If I could turn Nate's death into a Sunday school lesson in redemption, believe me, I would. But I can't."

"If you could just find this person—"

Her golden eyes blazed and her cheeks flushed with anger. "I don't *want* to know who it is anymore. Or to see her. I'm pregnant again. I have to stay calm. My husband was unfaithful to me, I barely have enough money to live on, and my car's been wrecked. But I am *not* going to lose this baby. I'm not stupid, Goldy. Nate's girlfriend never came forward because she didn't want to admit she was *screwing* a man with a *pregnant wife.*"

With that, Rorry climbed out of the car and slammed the door. She walked away clumsily, her shoulders slumped, her head bent. Somehow I knew there were tears in her eyes. *You have* not *thought of every angle,* I wanted to call after her.

The girlfriend—or whoever the snowboarder was with Nate that day—had triggered an out-of-bounds avalanche. But Rorry was wrong. The snowboarder hadn't stayed silent because of an affair with a man with a pregnant wife. The snowboarder hadn't come forward because she—or he—had started an avalanche that had *killed* a man with a pregnant wife.

267

CHAPTER 16

I drove out of Killdeer feeling as low as I had since the health inspector closed my kitchen. Poor Rorry. I was personally acquainted with the bitterness that welled up after betrayal. Yes, indeedy, I reflected as I moved into an unplowed lane on the interstate, a husband's cheating could poison your whole outlook. Not only that, but I also had firsthand experience in the no-income, no-vehicle department. But I was lucky: Now I had a husband with an income, and a friend who'd loaned me a car. Rorry was vastly, vastly unlucky. Had someone stolen her car and deliberately wrecked it? Why would someone do that? Had it been her Subaru that had hit the van behind mine? Or would that be too much of a coincidence? In any event, I kept a kestrel-eye on the Rover's rearview mirror. One catapult off a cliff per week was all I could handle.

When the Rover crunched over the snowpack in our driveway, Arch and Todd were outside throwing snowballs at each other with the intensity of a full-scale military battle. I powered down the window and asked for a truce, just until I could get into the house. Arch galumphed to the car to ask if I remembered Todd was spending the night. Of course, I replied. They had to finish their stanza memorization of "The Faerie Queene," Arch explained. Todd and Arch disliked memory

268

work, so they were coaching each other. And, Arch added, Tom wanted to talk to me.

I jumped from the Rover. "He's home?"

"Yeah. The kitchen drains were delivered and he's putting them in." My son turned and took huge footsteps through the deep snow to get back to packing snow-missiles.

"How'd the work with Lettie go?" I called after him.

"Fine!" he yelled before throwing a new white grenade. So much for sociable chitchat.

Tom was sprawled on his back on our kitchen floor. Strewn by his legs were two dozen plumbing tools and pieces of dismantled cherry cabinet. The top half of his torso disappeared beneath the sink.

I leaned down. "How's it going, O multi-talented mate?"

With a grunt, he slid out and heaved himself upright. His face and work clothes were filthy. Undaunted, he smiled hugely, white teeth in a portrait of grime.

"Your pipes and drains arrived." He got to his feet. "I'm not assigned to any cases now, so I convinced the lieutenant to let me take two vacation days and put 'em in."

I hugged him, hard. "Thank you!" In my enthusiasm I backed over a wrench and almost crashed onto Arch's second spatter-pattern experiment, the dried frosting on a cookie sheet. "But, why can't we hire a plumber? There's no reason you should have to—"

Tom winked, set me upright, then lowered himself again to the floor. "Don't trust me, eh?" He slid back under the sink. His muffled voice said: "I'm doing it because I want to know *exactly* what kind of plumbing we have. I'll be done in a few hours."

"Tell me what your heart desires for dinner. Anything."

"Ah, Miss G., I am very much in the mood for a curry. I bought some fat raw shrimp, peeled and deveined, in the hope that you would make *just* such an offer. But you're going to have to do the sink work in the bathroom. Want me to come out and help?"

"Of course not. Shrimp curry it is. But listen, I've got something to tell you—"

"I want to hear it, but there's something I forgot," his hollow voice boomed. "You need to call your buddy the wine guy before six."

Uh-oh. Had Arthur discovered the raid on his cellar? And what would my husband the cop think of my subterranean foray?

"Actually, Tom, Arthur Wakefield is who I need to talk to you about—"

"Call him first, okay? I promised you would."

It was five-thirty. A long chat with Arthur would make preparing a curry dinner impossible. I washed my hands in the ground floor bathroom, then rinsed the shrimp and half a pound of fresh, plump mushrooms. After drying, trimming, and chopping the mushrooms, I minced shallots, onions, and garlic, swirled oil in a wide sauté pan, and tossed in all the vegetables. They sizzled and filled the room with a yummy scent. Once they were tender, I measured in curry powder and flour, stirred the pungent mixture for a couple of minutes, then removed it from the heat, crushed dried thyme over it, and poured in homemade chicken stock, cream, and dry white French vermouth. I suppressed a smile. Only a true wine geek would insist on pouring fifty-dollar-a-bottle Grand Cru chablis into curried shellfish. Still, by the time I added the shrimp, this thick, flavorful dish would be a suitable reward for Tom's hard work.

He again reminded me to call Arthur; I promised him I would as soon as I started the raisin rice. In another skillet, I sprinkled rice into sputtering melted butter, stirred until the kernels were toasted golden brown, and dropped in a handful of moist raisins. Then I poured in more homemade chicken stock, lowered the heat, and gently placed a lid on top.

"Sure smells fantastic up there," was Tom's sub-sink comment.

"Thanks." I punched in Arthur's number, tucked the phone under my ear, and gathered my dishes to rinse in the bathroom. He answered on the first ring.

"My guests are due in ten minutes," he said hurriedly. "I have my wines ready. Your wonderful food is heating. Thank you for everything," he gushed.

"No problem, Arthur." Compared to his attitude that afternoon, he sounded suspiciously mellow.

"I feel awful for not paying you. We're still on for lunch Wednesday?"

I felt a frisson of unease. "You bet—"

"Wednesday will be three years since Mother's funeral," he interrupted dolefully. "I...I want to show you the spot," he said quickly, then hung up.

Show me what spot on the anniversary of his mother's funeral? The spot where she was buried? The place where she died? Now *there* was a cheerful incentive to join the man for lunch.

"Tom," I called downward, "may I talk to you about this Killdeer mess?"

"Yes," came his echoing-inside-the-pipe voice.

I started filling bowls with sour cream, chopped peanuts, chutney, coconut, pineapple chunks, chopped hard-cooked egg, and more raisins. "Doug Portman was about to leave for Puerto Escondido before he died. It's a small town on the Pacific coast of Mexico. I, uh, I found his plane ticket hidden in Arthur Wakefield's wine cellar. So I'm a *tad* concerned about having lunch with Arthur on Wednesday."

"*What?*" Banging on metal was followed by a groan as Tom worked to extract himself again. By the time I'd finished setting the table, he was leaning on the marble counter and giving me a skeptical look. "What *did* you do, exactly?"

I checked the refrigerator for beer—our preferred drink with curry—and soft drinks for the boys. "Look, I know I wasn't supposed to snoop around Arthur's place, but the man is obsessed with the Portman case."

"I know, I know, everybody in the Department of Corrections is sick of Arthur Wakefield and his letters about Portman. But *you're*
the one who decided to go through his stuff."

"I didn't steal anything." Tom grunted
and I went on: "Look, he's got nineteen million dollars at stake. My best guess is, when
you're trying to get a will set aside because you
think someone exerted undue influence over
your rich mother, you try to make that influ-
ential someone look *bad*. Very bad. In this case,
that person is Jack Gilkey, who was granted
parole by Doug Portman. So you also want to
find out everything negative you can about
Doug Portman. If Arthur can *prove* Portman
took a bribe to grant Gilkey parole, he'd be
in better shape to have his mother's second will
overturned. Of *course* he'd steal Portman's mail,
if he thought it might help him find out exactly
what Doug was up to. If you want to get a war-
rant," I added hastily, "the ticket-issuers
were Copper Mountain Worldwide Travel."

"Oh, Miss G., why do you do this to me?
Tickets don't prove anything by themselves.
You want to lose your bonding? Did you
think about that?" But he was reaching for the
phone.

"I didn't take the ticket," I repeated stubbornly.

Tom did not reply. He was using his
answering-machine voice to ask Marla if she
could meet me at eleven o'clock on Wednesday
at Killdeer, to ski for a couple of hours and
have lunch. He'd phone again later to confirm.

273

"What are you doing?" I demanded of him. "Marla hates skiing."

Tom hung up and regarded me intensely. "Yeah, but she's a good skier, I've seen her. I want her there."

"*Why?*"

"Because I *don't* want Arthur Wakefield to make any unexpected moves on a caterer who's broken into his wine cellar and riffled his papers. You better *pray* he didn't discover what you did," Tom commented as he moved off to clean himself up.

"Arthur will never know if you don't tell him," I shot back.

Discouraged, I scraped the moist, tender raisin rice onto a heated platter and covered it. Then I stirred the shrimp into the curry and called Todd, Arch, and Tom, who emerged showered, dressed, and smelling as sweet as ever. He seemed to have forgiven me for my morning's escapade at Arthur's. Or if he hadn't, he was letting it go for now.

Everyone busied themselves with the condiments. I sprinkled peanuts onto my chutney-topped bowl of curry and took a bite. The crunch of nuts combined with the succulent shrimp robed in its spicy-hot, luscious sauce was out of this world. Tom winked at me in thanks. Somewhat dramatically, Arch announced that he and Todd would like to recite their Spenser to us tonight. They were, he informed us, splitting a stanza. I looked at Tom and he grinned. They would begin right after dinner, Arch concluded.

They'd have their backs to us, though, as they couldn't yet handle an audience's faces.

When we'd finished, Tom scraped the dishes and insisted on washing them in the bathroom. Pretending to be flipping through a cookbook, I took surreptitious delight in watching Todd and Arch huddle over Spenser's *Complete Works*.

Todd had stuck by Arch during the worst of my trials with The Jerk; in return, Arch had invited Todd to sleep over numerous nights after Eileen kicked her husband out. Todd, shorter than Arch but heavier, still had endearingly cherubic cheeks that were now deeply flushed at the prospect of performing. His unevenly shorn black hair had nothing to do with style and everything to do with his unconscious habit—developed after his father's troubles were exposed—of tugging out his shiny curls. But he'd stopped pulling his hair out, Arch had assured me. I stared down at the cookbook, then peeked back up. Even though the two boys had gone from bikes to fantasy-role-playing games to snowboarding, they were still best friends, and I was glad of it. Friendship was a great blessing; we all needed to remember that. With a pang, I thought of Rorry.

Tom returned. The dishes were soaking in the tub. Arch announced that they were ready to begin.

"Book Five, Canto Two, Stanza Thirty-nine," Todd began stiffly as he faced the convection oven. He cleared his throat twice, then woodenly recited:

> *"Of things unseen how canst*
> *thou deem aright,*
> *Then answered the righteous Artegall,*
> *Since thou misdeem'st so much*
> *of things in sight?*
> *What though the sea with waves continual*
> *Do eat the earth, it is no more at all...."*

He turned and nodded uncomfortably at Arch. I held my breath and glanced at Tom. Should we be encouraging and clap at this point? Tom gave a tiny warning shake of the head. Arch stood facing the stove and began:

> *"Nor is the earth the less, or loseth ought,*
> *For whatsoever from one place doth fall,*
> *Is with the tide unto another brought:*
> *For there is nothing lost, that may be*
> *found, if sought."*

"Excellent, Arch! Todd, wow! *Fantastic!*" Tom and I gushed, clapping wildly.

Todd reached up to scratch his fuzzy scalp, then remembered not to. Instead, he nabbed the Rockies baseball cap he usually wore, but had politely removed for dinner. "Thanks, Mrs. Schulz. My mom liked it, too. She said I didn't need to work with Arch tonight, but I told her I did." I suddenly remembered Arch's remark—made when Jack had fixed us dinner at Eileen's condo—that Todd spent tons of time at our house because he didn't like Jack Gilkey. How would Todd fare if Eileen married Jack? If they did tie the knot, I only hoped poor little Todd would do better than Arthur Wakefield had.

The boys clattered off, promising to practice in front of each other. Tom disappeared, then reappeared carrying clean dishes, which he dried and clanked back onto shelves. Then he pulled out invoices to check that he'd received all the plumbing supplies he'd ordered. I stared at our shiny silver-and-white marble counters, darkly glowing cherry cabinets, and butter-golden oak floors. I had no more professional cooking to do until this week's final PBS show.

I sighed. When I had a big event to prepare for, I always complained. Without work, I ached for it.

I quickly fixed myself a cup of cocoa. Unfortunately, the hot, creamy chocolate drink did not stave off the sudden pangs of emptiness. *No work* felt like *no life*. Whenever I was up to my elbows in *coulibiac* and flourless chocolate cake, I fantasized about the crocheting I would one day do, the beaches Tom and I would one day stroll. But here I was, as free as I had ever wanted to be, and my big worry was whether eight-thirty was too early to go to bed.

Outside, snow had begun to fall. I gathered my ski equipment, packed it into the Rover, and said good-night to Tom. The boys—who had traded Elizabethan poetry for rock music—thanked me for dinner, swore they had their verses *nailed,* and promised to go to bed soon. I took a long, hot shower and fell into bed.

But slumber eluded me. Hours crept by as I stared at the snowflakes swirling around our street lamp. The pounding music stopped. Tom slid into bed. I did fall asleep at some point, because when the telephone jangled through my consciousness, it sounded very far away.

I blinked at the clock: The business line was ringing? At six-fifteen on a Tuesday morning? Somebody must want a catered holiday dinner *wicked* bad.

Tom groaned. "Want me to get it? It's probably the department—"

"They never call on this line." I fumbled for the receiver and mumbled my business greeting.

"Goldy Schulz of Goldilocks' Catering? This is Reggie Dawson of the *Furman County Register.* " The voice was high and brittle, almost a falsetto. Reggie *Dawson*? I was not a regular reader of the *Register,* so the name rang no bells. The paper paid poorly, and staff turnover was high, I knew. Every now and then, I did an extremely low-budget going-away party for one of the reporters who'd been let go.

"You have regular business hours, Mr. Dawson?" I hissed. "Could you call me back? I'm not catering any business coffees or lunches at the moment—"

"The way I heard it, Mrs. Schulz, you might be out of the catering business entirely."

Now he had my attention. I wished desperately we had caller ID on our phones. "What are you *saying?*"

"Four days ago, Douglas Portman died while skiing at Killdeer. You discovered his body, and you had prior ties to Portman."

"So?"

"We've received information that you were renewing a romantic relationship with Portman. Can you confirm or deny this?"

Well! I'd watched a press conference or two in my day. "Deny," I said fiercely.

"Were you rendezvousing with Portman because you wanted him to do something for you?"

"Like what?" My mind was reeling, and I was shivering in the early morning cold. Could there be an easy way to end this conversation? Was it better to talk to an obnoxious journalist, or cut him off? *The wife of homicide investigator Thomas Schulz, local caterer Goldy Schulz,* I imagined reading, *whose abusive ex-husband, Dr. John Richard Korman, is serving time for assault, refused to answer questions regarding her secret relationship with parole-board chief Douglas Portman. ...*

Reggie Dawson persisted: "Did you bribe Portman to ensure that your ex-husband would stay incarcerated?"

"No. Of course not. Look, could you call me back—"

"Was that the favor he was going to do for you?"

"There was no *favor*—"

"Does your current husband, top cop Tom

Schulz, know about your extramarital involvement?"

"There *is no,* there *was no,* extramarital—"

"Was your involvement with Portman another attempt on your part to crack crimes in Furman County?"

I didn't answer right away, because I was not going to be interrupted again. To my surprise, this time the reporter waited for me to reply. Finally, into the lengthening silence, I said firmly, "I was skiing with Doug Portman. Period."

"So now you're trying to cover up your relationship with Doug Portman?"

My mind flitted to the undervaluation of the skis. "There is absolutely nothing to cover up."

"Were you doing some kind of deal with Portman so you could bail out your failing business?"

"Now, listen here, Mr. Dawson, there *is* no failing business. I have a TV job in Killdeer—"

"Mrs. Schulz! Given what you've experienced in Killdeer, don't you think it's dangerous to be snooping around while your son snowboards alone?"

Icy fear washed through me. My mouth opened; no sound came out. Wording of state laws covering *implied threats* and *explicit threats* swam up from my unconsciousness.

I said, "Listen, you, you—"

But the line was dead.

*   *   *

Now sleep was officially impossible. Fingers shaking, I flipped through the phone book: no Reggie or R. Dawson or Dausson or anything close to it in the entire Denver metropolitan area, including all of Furman County. Tom brought me a pen and clean pad of paper. He urged me to write down every word of the conversation. While I did this, he called the department to see if they could expedite ID on the call. They promised to try.

Tom fixed me coffee, then started frying bacon for the boys. A lump had formed in my throat. I couldn't even swallow coffee. Once the boys were digging into bacon and toast, Tom clasped my hands in his.

"Miss G. Do you want the boys to stay home while I finish the plumbing?"

The boys squealed in protest. There was nothing to *do* at home, and today they were supposed to get their classroom ready for the Christmas party! I said if Tom felt they would be safe, they should go to school. Tom called the department again and was assured a deputy could be sent to the school to protect some kids who'd been threatened. In response to the proliferation of high school shootings, Elk Park Prep parents had insisted on the erection of a new security gate attached to the electrified fence, and the round-the-clock presence of an armed guard in the school. Tom would also alert the guard to the possibility

281

of danger, and instruct him to call the sheriff's department at the first sign of suspicious activity. Okay?

"Yes. Thanks." Even to my ears, my voice sounded full of doubt. Just before eight, Tom and the boys took off through a drapery of snowflakes. As soon as they pulled out, I called the food editor of the *Furman County Register*. There was no Reggie Dawson working there. Dawson could be doing something freelance, my friend added. But she doubted it.

So did I, I thought as I put on several compact discs of Christmas carols and gathered all the presents I still needed to wrap. Still, it was hard to stop thinking about the events in Killdeer. Who was my early morning caller? Why was he asking questions about my relationship with Doug Portman? Had he truly been threatening Arch? Or had I just misunderstood?

I unfurled foil paper and shiny ribbon, and began snipping, folding, and tying. Did Arthur Wakefield know that his attempt to publicize my presence at *Cooking at the Top!* in the Killdeer paper had backfired so miserably? On the other hand, could it have been Arthur on the phone? If what Rorry had said about the rumor mill in Killdeer was true, then anyone could know by now that my business was in jeopardy; that Arch snowboarded in Killdeer; that my ex-husband was in jail.

I labeled the gifts for Tom, Arch, Marla, and Julian, and slid them under beds and into other hiding places. Returning to the kitchen,

I took out unsalted butter, sugar, flour, and double-strength vanilla, to start on the cookies for the neighbors. Still the questions from "Reggie Dawson's" call replayed in my head.

Was your involvement with Portman another attempt on your part to crack crimes in Furman County? Ridiculous, I thought, as I beat the butter and sugar into a fluffy mass. Of course not. Doug Portman had been killed before I could chat with him, sell him skis, or retrieve something from his car to show to Tom.

Once I'd mixed in the other ingredients and rolled out the dough, I stared at it. *Wait a minute.* Did someone think *I* knew what Doug Portman had been up to? Did someone think I hadn't been there to sell Doug skis— but to do something entirely different? Like what? Act as a go-between with the police department? Expose Portman's bribery scheme?

I put these thoughts out of my head as I cut molded stars, bells, Santas, and Christmas trees out of the smooth, buttery dough. Soon the kitchen was enveloped in the homey scent of baking sugar cookies. Once I'd cooled, frosted, and decorated the treats, I placed a dozen on each of ten paper Christmas plates, wrapped them in cellophane, and delivered them to the neighbors. My spirits soared as each neighbor offered thanks, hot cider, and hugs.

When I returned home, the phone was ringing. I picked up only to hear heavy breathing followed by a click. I pressed buttons to trace the call, then hung up and sighed.

Tom had been right to warn me to be cautious: I was finally convinced that the accident with my van had not been an accident, but a deliberate attempt to get rid of me.

CHAPTER 17

The next morning, I boarded the gondola just after ten. The previous day had ended without mishaps or additional anonymous calls. Still, all the way to Killdeer, I'd worried about Arch and whether he'd be safe at school. I'd worried whether "Reggie Dawson" would threaten, appear, bully, or harm me. Tom insisted that that kind of call was usually intended to keep someone *away* from an investigation. Since the caller had asked specifically about my relationship with Doug Portman, was that investigation what he wanted to keep me away from?

As the suspended car zoomed up Killdeer Mountain, I smiled politely at my fellow passengers—five chicly-clad skiers from Virginia—and reflected on what I'd learned thus far about the deaths at Killdeer. "Reggie Dawson" may have been trying to warn me away from the Portman case. But any *one* of his prying questions could engender negative stories about me. Publicity like that would make the reopening of Goldilocks' Catering impossible, building code, drains, or no.

Three years ago, Fiona Wakefield and Nate

Bullock had died at this resort—within hours of one another. Both deaths had occurred under mysterious circumstances. Jack Gilkey had been convicted of contributing to his wife Fiona's death. A snowboarder accompanying Nate Bullock had vanished from the face of the earth.

Far below, out the window, I could just make out where Hot-Rodder intersected the catwalk. Hot-Rodder Run. Four days ago, Doug Portman, a not-unanimously-popular local art critic and chief of the state parole board, had died there. Portman's death had also been shrouded in bizarre circumstances, not least of which was that someone had left him a death threat on a greeting card.

Portman must have felt law enforcement closing in on his profitable scam. Doug Portman had planned a Mexican escape—when someone closed a ski run and killed him.

Other strange occurrences might or might not be related to these three deaths, I reflected as we rolled up the last segment of snowy slope. Right after Portman was killed, someone had stolen and then returned Rorry Bullock's Subaru. Her car might have been the one used in an attempt to dump me over a cliff. Why use Rorry's car? What was the connection?

One ex-convict, cancer patient Barton Reed, had been denied parole by Portman, and had been mouthing public threats against him. Another ex-con, Jack Gilkey, had been terrified of what Portman's death could imply for his future. Arthur Wakefield, son of one of the earlier victims, was enraged with Portman for letting Jack Gilkey out on parole, and was working with all his might to get his mother's will set aside. Arthur had also been tracking Portman's movements, and had broken into Portman's condo to snag his mail, which included the ticket to Mexico.

The gondola car slammed open. I waited until the happy visitors had exited before I hopped out, retrieved my skis, and crunched onto the apron of snowpack surrounding the gondola structure. I stabbed my poles into the hard white surface and slotted my boots into my bindings. *Let it go for now,* I ordered myself. All around, enthusiastic skiers called to each other and sped off down the runs. I might not have a clue about what was going on in the Portman murder investigation, what had happened to Nate Bullock in Elk Valley, or how Fiona Wakefield had died. But I was here for the day. Inside a hooded charcoal-gray ski suit from the Aspen Meadow Secondhand Store, nobody would recognize me. It was just a few days before Christmas, and I was going to give myself the gift of having fun skiing, by golly! Sheesh.

Monday's storm had blown eastward. Blinding sunshine flashed from between swift-scudding wisps of cloud. Whenever the sun shone, the snow turned to glitter. A gust of mountain air made my skin tingle. I took off on a blue run and felt the heady rush of sudden descent. Down right, down left, down, down, down…the skis obeyed, effortlessly whispering back, *swish bend swish bend.* Soon I was flying. In the best skiing, the body, mind, and skis are one. If your mind wanders, so do the skis, and your body pays.

"Hey, girlfriend! Not so fast!"

The call came from behind me. I hockey-stopped, throwing a four-foot-high wave of snow onto the yellow boundary cord, by the sign for Jitterbug Run.

"Goldy, for crying out loud!" squealed the voice. "I don't want to hit you!"

Marla skied up beside me. I laughed and gave her a clumsy hug.

"So you're going to be my bodyguard for the day. Is skiing a good pastime for heart-attack patients?"

"My cardiologist *swears* exercise is good for me."

"And downhill skiing is okay?"

"It's better than skateboarding, which I told him was my first choice." Marla's chosen attire for the slopes this morning was an ultra-glamorous one-piece purple ski suit twinkling with shiny yellow squares. With this she wore a bright purple-and-yellow ski hat, streamlined yellow goggles, custom-made boots, and what looked like a new pair of skis.

I asked, "How'd you know where to find me?"

"I remembered the runs we took last year. Plus, Tom said you'd be dressed like a piece of granite." She grinned. "So when is this dangerous lunch? I'm starving. Oh, and I called Eileen. After lunch, she's going to tag along with us on her *snowboard*. We're supposed to meet her at two at the bistro."

Oh, brother. "Is Jack coming with her?"

Marla wrinkled her nose as she readjusted her goggles. "Not sure. I hope not. I don't want some hotshot skier making me feel old."

"Let's go then, ancient one."

We flowed into a rhythm of long slaloms. Marla really was a marvelous skier. She held herself confidently, maneuvering with adept turns and aggressive grace over the bumps. Her chief objections to the sport were the cold and the crowds. As neither was a problem this day, we could swoosh past each other, laugh, and feel the exhilaration of blue skies, smooth slopes, and speed. Finally we pulled up by a black square denoting an advanced run.

"Race ya," she squealed.

"No way."

"One, two, three, *go*!"

And we were off. Two minutes later we collapsed at the bottom. Marla had beaten me handily. We giggled all the way down the catwalk to the gondola.

On the way back up, we had a car to ourselves, and I quickly filled her in on what I'd learned about the Bullocks: the artificial insemination, Rorry's suspicions about Nate's infidelity. Marla looked dubious. As far as she knew, Nate Bullock had not been having an affair. Then again, they had not moved in the same circles.

"So pregnant Rorry is the one I'm supposed to be protecting you from today?" she demanded. "That's why Tom called and asked me to keep you secure?"

I laughed. Since we were lunching with Arthur, I couldn't tell her about my surreptitious foray into his wine cellar, and risk she'd make a verbal slip. "Tom just worries about me since the van accident. Plus, Arthur makes both of us a little nervous."

"I will protect you!" Marla vowed as she took off down the slope.

We skied three more fast runs before heading for the Summit Bistro. I'd forewarned Marla that Arthur wasn't expecting her, in case he was less than charming. But when we stomped through the wooden doors, Arthur, leaning against a stucco wall by the ski boot check, grinned broadly.

"Do you enjoy wine?" he asked Marla solicitously after I'd introduced them.

"I used to, but it doesn't go with my heart medication," she replied with a twinkly smile. "But if you recommend a particular vintage, I'll order a case for my cardiologist."

"Let's go, then," Arthur said as he whisked us toward the table he'd chosen. To Marla, he murmured, "Remind me if there's a retail wine merchant in Aspen Meadow...."

When our waitress appeared, Marla ordered shrimp brochettes with no oil and no butter. Arthur said he'd have the same, but with the fats. He cheerfully pulled a large silver flask from his pack while I ordered vegetarian chili in a bread bowl. For someone commemorating the anniversary of a tragic death, I thought he seemed awfully chipper.

"Arthur," I began, "I know this day is significant for you, I mean with your mother—"

"Wait a minute, I *know* you!" Marla cried. Folks at neighboring tables glanced our way. Marla, unfazed, continued: "Your mother was Fiona Wakefield. Fiona and I used the same hair colorist in Denver."

Arthur unscrewed the flask. "How long ago was this?" he asked evenly.

"Four years." Marla reflected momentarily, then plunged on. "So *you're* the one who works with Goldy on the PBS show?"

Arthur nodded and poured equal amounts of red wine into the bowls of two wineglasses on the table. "A robust Côtes du Rhône," he intoned reverently, placing a glass in front of me. Well, I guess this was going to be one of those rare times when I had wine with lunch. Anything for the client, as they say.

Marla exclaimed, *"Now* I'm putting it all together! Fiona used to tell me about your work. These days, Goldy keeps me up to date. I just didn't connect the two."

Arthur lifted his glass. "To the memory of my mother Fiona," he intoned.

Marla snagged her water glass. The three of us clinked glasses solemnly. The wine was very good. Arthur used words like *fruity, perfect for a picnic*. After a few swigs, even Arthur's ability to irritate me faded. I had a sudden warm vision of the three of us enjoying a wine-tasting tour of France. Another sip or two, and I was thinking maybe I *could* beat Marla if we took that advanced run again!

"How well did you know Mother?" Arthur asked Marla.

"Not that well," Marla replied. "I remember how proud of *you* she was. Fiona used to say there were only a handful of people in the world who were able to make the kind of wine-tasting distinctions her son could."

Arthur blushed. Why had I never thought of laying a little flirtatious flattery on my wine-importing floor director? No question about it, Marla was in her element. Flirting with Arthur was her way of playing body-guard.

I smiled a little too broadly and a headache loomed from nowhere. Unfortunately, no basket of bread and plate of butter pats graced our table. I'd skied four runs and chugged a glass and a half of red wine on an empty stomach. Tipsiness, apparently, was one of the consequences of stupidity.

Which brought me to the question of exactly how much wine Fiona had drunk just before she died three years ago. I wondered what the chances were that Arthur would share *that* information with me.

"Ah, Arthur," I asked, forcing myself to focus on the business at hand, "didn't you want to talk to me about this week's show? We wouldn't want to repeat what happened last time, when there was so much disorganization, and then Doug Portman—"

"We can't tape on Friday, which is Christmas Eve." He stopped to pour himself more wine. I covered my glass with my hand.

"Not tape Christmas Eve," I repeated. "Good idea. So—?"

"Tomorrow afternoon," replied Arthur. He tore his eyes away from Marla. "Taping will be at four. Arrive by three-thirty. Can you manage it? Also, I've been meaning to tell you how well my wine-tasting went." He dipped into his backpack again and handed me an envelope. "This is your check."

I thanked him and zipped the check into my ski jacket pocket. "So, tomorrow," I prompted him, "what will we be doing?"

"We don't want to guilt-trip folks to buy turkeys at the last minute. Could you do a very simple holiday breakfast? No eggs to coddle, no casserole to bake. An easy bread recipe, if that would work. And your wonderful oatmeal. Then you can wiggle your hips over a big bowl of sliced fruit and some hot, sizzling Canadian bacon. Voilà! Merry Christmas."

"No problem," I replied, despite the fact that no *easy bread recipe* leapt to mind. But I had learned not to voice worries to Arthur. I looked around again for our waitress, so I could beg for a bread basket. She was nowhere in sight. My eyes caught a glimpse of someone else, though, and my skin pricked with gooseflesh.

Barton Reed sat hunched at a table next to a window. He was staring out at the gondola, the ski racks, and the folks making their way to the bistro. Just the way he had at Cinda's Cinnamon Stop, he was clutching something in his hand and seemed to be looking for someone—someone in particular. When he turned to scan the restaurant, I ducked.

The waitress placed sputtering kabobs of grilled shrimp, cherry tomatoes, and onion quarters in front of Marla and Arthur, and a bread bowl heaped with steaming chili in front of me. While she was placing a basket of rolls onto the table, I glanced uneasily at Barton, whose earrings sparkled in the chandeliers' light. He had poured a bottle of Mexican beer into a tall glass and was sipping it while keeping his eyes glued to the out-of-doors. One of Reggie Dawson's questions played through my mind: *Were you meeting Portman because you wanted him to do something for you?*

What exactly did Barton Reed want?

"Actually," Arthur was saying to Marla, "I was going to take Goldy to that very spot after lunch. Would you like to come?"

I tried to ignore Marla cooing at Arthur that *it would mean so much to her to be included!* I spooned up some chili. It was a hearty mixture of corn, pinto beans, black beans, and tomato, all wrapped in a spicy south-of-the-border sauce. I wondered if I could duplicate it.

And it was pretty good with the Côtes du Rhône, I had to admit, although I knew better than to drink any more of the fruity wine. I sipped water while polishing off the chili as Marla told Arthur about her pre-heart-attack holiday in Provence. Arthur listened devotedly, asking if she'd tried this, that, or the other wine. We ordered coffee as Arthur delved into a narrative of a tasters' boat ride he'd done in Germany, along the Rhine.

"Don't fall for this guy," I murmured to Marla as we retrieved our ski boots. "I'm not sure he's aboveboard."

She tugged her purple-and-yellow hat over her curls. "Jeez, not to worry! I'm trying to *protect* you!"

Arthur joined us before I could reply. "Now, where'd I leave my skis?" he asked as we came out the bistro door.

Just then, a gaggle of boisterous six-year-olds pushed toward the three of us. Marla teetered away as two of them elbowed past. Arthur reached out to help Marla get her balance. Unfortunately, he miscalculated his momentum, overcompensated to avoid collapsing on the kids, and careened into me instead. With a clattering of ski boots and a flurry of hats, goggles, and mittens, Arthur, Marla, and I spilled ass-over-teakettle down the metal steps.

"Wipeout!" the kids chorused gleefully.

Arthur muttered evil words in the direction of the ski school instructor, who swiftly shepherded his young class away before more damage could be done.

"Maybe you should have some more coffee," I said to Arthur. "After all that wine—"

"Maybe that instructor should control his group!"

"Arthur—"

"Let's go!" As if to prove he was fine, he took wide, purposeful steps in the direction of the racks.

Once we were buckled into our skis, Arthur announced that we needed to head down Bighorn, a black run, to get to the overlook. He added that we'd be able to switch over to a green—easy—run, aptly named Easy-as-Pie, once we left the overlook. To my surprise, he schussed expertly to the top of Bighorn and waved for us to follow.

"As long as it gets us to Big Map by two," Marla replied loudly.

Bighorn turned out to be a precipitous mogul field. The bumpy slope was so steep you couldn't see past the first two hundred feet, where it curved to the right. Taut cords marking the out-of-bounds wooded areas bordered the slopes. When surveying the moguls, I tried to rid myself of the unhappy thought that each one represented a skier's grave mound.

Arthur maneuvered nimbly through the bumps. He jumped and turned, jumped and turned, as if he were having great fun. I knew the strength it took to keep one's skis rigidly parallel, as he did, to plant one's pole with great exactness in the middle of each mogul. He was an expert, there was no doubt about it.

At the far right and left of runs like this, there was usually a narrow, smooth path without moguls. With misgivings, I pushed off behind Marla, and the two of us executed short, tight slaloms down the run's right side. Fiona and Jack, I reflected as cold wind slapped my face, must have been very good skiers.

Finally, we came around the curve on the empty run. Arthur loomed in front of us. He looked creepily triumphant. I was suddenly glad Tom had asked Marla to accompany me. The enigmatic Arthur Wakefield, an unexpectedly strong skier, could definitely mow someone down. His hand pulled up the boundary rope. He was not even remotely out of breath.

"This way, ladies," he announced as he pointed to a slender trail winding through thickening pines. Beyond the trees lay a glimpse of blue sky. "This only goes about twenty yards, then you're on the overlook." He pointed to a wider, more gently sloping path. There were logs piled across it. "The ski patrol blocked off the old path."

"This is illegal," I commented to Arthur as we ducked the rope. "Ever heard of the Skier Safety Act, boss? We could be ticketed and thrown off the slope for the day. Or worse."

"I know," Arthur replied grimly. "Don't I know."

I summoned a firm voice. "Would you go first, please?" He shot me another skeptical look, then skied ahead on the two-foot-wide trail through the trees.

Marla poled her way up next to me. She was breathing hard. She peered in disbelief at the path Arthur had just taken. "What is this, a frigging obstacle course?"

The ground on the trail path alternated

between deep clumps of snow and slick ice. I carefully made my way over the bumps. With my goggles on, the scarce sunshine in the woods brought sudden twilight. I had agreed to come here because I wanted to know more about Arthur and the deaths three years ago. But I was wary, and intended to remain extremely cautious.

Soon the trees opened onto a granite ledge. I slid to a stop on the ice-covered outcropping. Realizing I was just fifteen feet from the edge of the precipice sent my heart into my throat. I breathed deeply to steady myself; my eyes watered from the frigid wind. Despite the danger nearby, the panoramic sweep of snow-capped peaks, forested valleys, and ice-sculpted ravines was undeniably stunning. To our left, skiers in a back bowl resembled gnats floating down a hill.

"Wow," said Marla. "I never knew this view was here."

"The ski patrol doesn't want you to know," Arthur told her. "That's why they closed the old path." He pointed to smoke rising from a small building on a hill to our right. The plain beige edifice, which looked as if it had once stood in the middle of a forest, was now surrounded by hundreds of tree stumps. "That's the expansion area. The resort is under tight construction-loan deadlines, so they're working night and day to clear it. Killdeer needs to start lift construction in the spring. Over there," he added, pointing to a small cabin at the edge of the construction area, "Killdeer Corp has stationed a full-time security guard, just in case any environmentalists take violent exception to the expansion plans."

He raised his eyebrows at us and pointed higher up the peak to the right of the construction area. That mountain featured a bare shelf of trees clustered around a sheer dropoff. "That's Elk Ridge," said Arthur. "The steep area below the ring of woods is a leeward-facing, thirty-two-degree slope." He swept his mittened hand down to a wide, partially wooded, gently sloping valley below the ridge. It looked like a postcard of a pristine, snowy meadow. "That's where the avalanche came down three years ago, the one that killed Nate Bullock." Moving parallel to the dropoff near us, Arthur worked his way to the edge. I stayed put and motioned for Marla, standing next to me, to do the same.

"Not to worry," she muttered, her eyes on the perilous drop-off. Arthur kept moving forward.

"Careful, Arthur." The words were out of my mouth before I noticed. Motherly habits die hard.

Arthur knelt on his skis and gestured to the area below the dropoff. "There," he said, "is where Jack Gilkey pushed my mother to her death. In court, Jack insisted *I'd* given her too much to drink, that someone—*me,* he meant to imply—came out of the trees and hit him so hard with a rock that he fell unconscious into the snow. Then whoever this Mr. Atlas

298

was, he pushed my mother over the edge." He looked at us. "Do you actually think one person could incapacitate a strong man and push an athletic woman to her death?"

"It's possible," I said grimly, thinking back to the terrible stories of spouse abuse and murder that I'd heard since my years of ridding myself of The Jerk. Arthur gave me a black look.

"No, Arthur, Goldy doesn't think one person could do all that," Marla said hastily. "Let's go back."

I asked sympathetically, "How much wine had Jack given your mother at lunch?"

He shrugged. "Three glasses of a spätlese Riesling that I'd recommended. And no, I wouldn't have given them a bottle if I'd known he was going to taunt her to race here. Race *here*? Why would you do something so foolish?"

Why indeed? I murmured that I did not know, and recalled Jack's claim that *Fiona* had initiated the race idea. And I'd believed his explanation: that his wife had had too much to drink, that she had challenged him—her young, virile husband—to race to a dangerous spot, to prove—or so it seemed—that she, too, was young, virile, and sexy, since she was willing to take risks.

That weirdly victorious expression again swept over Arthur's face. "Don't you want to see what those articles were talking about, Goldy? The articles you thought I left for you?"

"She doesn't." Marla said it firmly. "And

299

if she gets any closer to that edge, I'll have another heart attack."

Arthur took a last long look over the side of the outcropping, his face unreadable, then got to his feet and skied quickly past us, toward the run. When we found our way out—Arthur checked for lurking ski patrol members before we sneaked back onto Bighorn—he showed us how to get onto Easy-as-Pie. "Matter of minutes." He turned back to the rope. "I'm going back in for a bit."

Marla and I shook our heads in sympathy...and bafflement. Arthur nodded to us, as if he'd made the point he intended to make. He asked me to call him that night about the exact menu they'd put on the graphic for the next show, then scooted under the rope. Soon he disappeared through the trees.

"That guy is weird," Marla commented as she adjusted her goggles. "Plus, he drinks too much."

Eileen was waiting for us at Big Map; she waved enthusiastically as we skied up. Wearing a skintight royal blue ski suit and a red-and-royal-blue tasseled dunce cap, she looked the epitome of *cute as a button*. No matter what Arthur Wakefield thought of Jack Gilkey, he had clearly wrought a transformation in Marla's and my old friend.

"Come on, come on, we don't have much time," Eileen chided gaily. "Jack's going to meet us at the bistro at twenty to three. Feel okay on Mission Hill? It's a very smoothly groomed intermediate run."

Marla and I said Mission Hill sounded fine. With our skis stored in the gondola rack, and Eileen's snowboard lying across half her metal seat, we rumbled back up the mountain. Once we'd unloaded and found the run, it was just a matter of minutes before the three of us were laughing and shouting, spraying snow on each other, and yelling "Wahoo!" every time we sped past each other down the slope.

Jack Gilkey caught up with us the second time we ascended in the gondola. Under her breath, Marla muttered, "I'd forgotten how yummy-looking that guy is." Jack, dressed in a fashionable beige-and-black ski suit and a dunce cap to match Eileen's, seemed cordial, even a tad shy, toward Marla and me. His solicitude and affection for Eileen was obvious. I watched as he cautioned her to slow down, sternly, like the mother hen Arch often accused me of being.

Eileen knew how to ride a snowboard, I'd give her that. She must have been practicing every day for years to be able to make the jumping, leaping, twisting moves she did that afternoon. Marla and I laughed at her antics, while Jack skied cautiously behind her. Maybe this trying-to-prove-you're-virile thing was a universal phenomenon in May-September relationships. Who knew? They were having a great time. We all were.

One thing about intermediate ski slopes: There's a lot of yelling. Kids call to their parents to wait for them, and vice versa. Usually it's all good fun. Sometimes it isn't. Hus-

301

bands and wives scream at each other to speed up or slow down. Ski school instructors try to keep their charges in an orderly line behind them, calling out directions like a caterpillar head noisily instructing its lengthy tail.

An occasional skier wears a Walkman, even though it's illegal. These skiers want to block out the noise, or time their ski maneuvers to the bars of Strauss waltzes or Three Dog Night. I don't listen to a Walkman, but I do ignore the yelling. It's distracting and can make you fall.

So I didn't hear a bawled caution. At least, not the first one.

Yelled warnings of "Look out! Move! Get out of the way!" finally got my attention, however. I brushed snow from my goggles but couldn't see what the problem was. I skied to the far side of the run. More screaming erupted as I looked up the hill and tried to determine the source of the commotion.

In her sparkly suit, Marla was easy to spot on the opposite side of the run. A ski school class had stopped in its tracks. A gaggle of snowboarders in backward baseball caps flew down beside me. Further up the slope, a lone snowboarder was hurtling down the hill. He was headed toward a skiing couple not far from me....

The startled couple moved one way, then another to get out of the speeding snowboarder's way. Each time they sped up and turned to avoid him, he changed direction. It was like watching a torpedo homing in on a target.

The couple, I suddenly realized with horror, was Eileen and Jack.

"Eileen!" I screamed. "Jack! Get out of the way! *Move!*" What could I do? "Hey, snowboarder!" I shrieked. *"Stop!"*

Eileen and Jack turned back, then started to scoot toward the trees. Down the boarder came, faster and faster. Was he drunk? Was he crazy?

The snowboarder hit Eileen and Jack with all the force of a speeding bowling ball. Two bodies went flying. The big boarder struggled to right himself, then kept going down the hill. As he came nearer, I feared for a moment he was going to hit me, too. Then I realized he was slowing down.

He stopped inches away from the tips of my skis. Then, almost in slow motion, he toppled sideways and then backward into the snow. Cautiously, I made my way to his side.

When I removed his dark goggles, Barton Reed's eyes were closed. The sound of wailing drifted down the hill. Jack Gilkey was crying, calling desperately for help. He was leaning over a blue-clad body sprawled in the snow.

Eileen.

CHAPTER 18

The ski patrol took Eileen and Barton down the mountain in sleds. The two patrol members would tell us only that Eileen was unconscious. Barton was nearly so, and had a broken leg. How fast was the boarder going, the patrol wanted to know? *As fast as any downhill racer I've ever seen on television,* I told them. *It wasn't the kind of collision where folks get covered with snow. It was the kind of crash that leaves limp bodies. Lifeless bodies.*

The patrol wouldn't let us near Jack, whom two other patrolmen were treating for shock. Marla and I got permission to leave and skied down. As we lugged our equipment to our cars, I filled her in on what I knew about Barton Reed. That he was a convict. That he was in remission from cancer. That he had had a possibly deadly resentment for Doug Portman, and apparently also had it in for Eileen or Jack or both.

We headed eastward in convoy, Marla in her four-wheel-drive Mercedes behind the Rover. Overhead, two Flight-for-Life helicopters thundered eastward. The ski patrol members had told us where Eileen and Barton were being taken: Lutheran Medical Center in Wheat Ridge, northwest of Denver. I tried to keep my eyes on the road while punching in our home number on the cellular.

"Eileen's been hit," I began without preamble when Tom answered. "On the slopes. I saw it coming. I didn't—" My voice cracked. "I couldn't do anything."

"Slow down, Miss G. Someone hit Eileen? What was it, a skiing accident? Is she all right?"

"She's unconscious. Oh, Tom. Barton Reed hit her. He was watching for her and then he hit her. With his snowboard. It was deliberate. I saw it." Emotion closed my throat. I struggled for control and said: "The helo's taking her to Lutheran now. Reed, too. Oh, Tom, why would he *do* a thing like that?"

"I don't know. Look, Wheat Ridge is in Jefferson. I'll call someone from the Jefferson County Sheriff's Department to be there at the hospital when they arrive. You...think I should pick up Todd from school and bring him down? What about Arch?"

Of course Todd should go to his mother. I told Tom so. "But I have to warn you, she looked terrible. All limp. Would you..." I couldn't say it. Tears welled in my eyes. "Would you see if...if the priest from St. Luke's can come down, too?" Best to prepare for the worst.

Ninety minutes later, Marla and I careened side by side into a hospital parking lot. Belatedly, I realized I'd tossed my ski boots in the Rover's hatch and driven to Wheat Ridge in my socks. By the time I'd tied up my sneakers, Marla was opening the Range Rover door and peering inside.

"Goldy? Can we *walk* in there instead of running? I can feel my blood pressure rising."

305

"You shouldn't go in. Just stay out here and relax."

"Are you *kidding*? The best place to *be* when you're having a heart attack is *inside* the hospital."

"Marla—"

"I *am* kidding." We walked across the snow-packed road to the hospital. Low, dark clouds obscured the view of the Front Range. Marla asked, "Did you see what happened?" I nodded, and she went on: "I've been thinking about it all the way over here. Like TV. Instant replay." She shuddered. "It wasn't what it seemed."

The automatic doors opened. A rush of warm antiseptic air washed over us as we entered the high-ceilinged hush of the hospital's lobby. As we headed for the information desk, I asked, "Wasn't what it seemed in what way?"

Marla faced me. "That snowboarder, the one you said you knew? Barton Reed. He was headed for *Jack*. Not Eileen."

"How'd he miss?"

"Who knows? I saw it right from the start. Reed was perched at the top of the run. Eileen had boarded to the side. Jack was traversing the run. Reed took off *toward* Eileen. But he was on a snowboard. To gain momentum, he would have to go fast one way, then turn, still cruising fast, and fly over to hit Jack. Jack was *too far away* for Reed to go straight down the fall line to whack him." I suppose I looked puzzled, because she continued:

"Goldy, listen. A snowboard is different from skis that way. To build up momentum, if he was aiming for Eileen, he would have gone *left,* not *right,* and then doubled back to hit her."

I struggled to recall what I'd seen. I didn't know enough about snowboarding to analyze the way Barton Reed had come down the slope. Had Jack seen the danger? I *thought* he'd reversed direction to protect Eileen, or at least to get her out of harm's way. Had he been trying to protect himself instead?

The woman at the information desk informed us that Eileen Druckman was in critical but stable condition in Intensive Care. Internal injuries, head injuries, what? I pressed. The woman replied that she did not know. Starting soon, Eileen could have family-member visits, two people at a time, for ten minutes per hour. As Marla and I rolled up the elevator to Intensive Care, I again tried to dredge up the memory of precisely what I'd seen on Killdeer Mountain. If you didn't know much about snowboarding—and I didn't—interpretation was not possible. To be perfectly honest, I didn't know how much *Marla* knew about snowboarding, either.

Plus, what did I really know about any relationship between Barton Reed and Jack Gilkey? When I'd dropped Arch off on Saturday morning, Jack had known about Reed's sentence. He'd also known that Portman denied Reed parole.

I had never thought to ask how he'd come by his information.

Tom and Arch were standing in the ICU waiting room when we arrived. Todd, though, was nowhere in sight. I was so happy to see Arch I hugged him before he could protest.

"Mom. Please. Stop."

"I've been worried about you."

"Why? *I* wasn't skiing. *I* was in school." I must have looked defeated because he made his tone brighter, more comforting. "It's okay. A nurse just came out and told us Eileen's awake, but real weak. She's got a concussion. Todd's in there with her. Oh, and Tom says that Todd can stay with us. You know, indefinitely. Until his mom's better."

"Of course he can."

Arch's smile was joyful. He adored company. Then he *hrumph*ed and raised an eyebrow at me. "Jack's in there with her, too. Crying, crying, like a big baby. And he's not even a family member."

"Well, hon..." I couldn't think of what to say.

Tom came to my rescue. "I'd *love* a hug." He wrapped me in his arms. The relief of his company was exquisite. "The priest was in a counseling session and couldn't come. But I promised I'd call the church phone with updates." I murmured that that was fine. With Eileen conscious and being cared for, I wasn't quite so panicked.

"Hey, Arch, old buddy," Marla interjected. I'd almost forgotten she was beside me. "I've spent so much time here in Lutheran Hospital I know the location of every place where

308

candy, cookies, and soda pops are sold. What's more," she added as she drew her leather change purse from a pocket and jangled it, "I have the means of entry. I do need company, however."

With little success, Arch again tried to hide a smile. "All right." To Tom and me he announced, "I'll bring Todd something, too."

As soon as they left the waiting room, I ran Marla's theory about the accident by Tom.

He pursed his lips thoughtfully. "Did *you* think Barton was aiming for Jack?" I mumbled that I did not know enough about the dynamics of snowboarding. Tom drew his cellular out of his pocket and punched buttons. *Jail,* he mouthed to me. While he was on hold, a large Hispanic family entered the waiting room. All looked desperately nervous and worried. I counted the number of kids and adults and matched it to the available seats—an old caterer's habit—and realized not all of them would be able to sit down while awaiting the fate of their loved one, because Todd and Arch had left their books, schoolbags, coats, and other paraphernalia all over the place.

Since Tom was still on the phone, I moved the boys' stuff. Whether the two of them would do any schoolwork while we were here was extremely doubtful. When I tried to lug the huge load over to our couch, the cursed quantum mechanics spattered-cookie-sheet experiment crashed from a bag, spewing thousands of bits of dried frosting all over the waiting-room carpet. A stray chunk pelted the eye of a twentyish male member of the Spanish-speaking family, and he cried out. I snagged some tissues and hurried over to his side, mumbling one of the few Spanish phrases I knew: *"Lo siento, lo siento."* *I'm sorry.* He grinned and wiped his eye. My Spanish was very rusty, but it seemed the rest of his family was reprimanding him for overreacting, clucking to each other that Diego was *such* a crybaby. I told him again that I was sorry, and Diego announced in perfect English: "No problem. I was just surprised."

Oh-kay. I returned to where the cookie sheet was perched beneath a mountain of school equipment. When I tried to extract it, Arch's Spenser book toppled from his bag, pulverizing several hundred of the hardened icing pieces. I stomped to Tom's side and savagely threw the remaining books and bags onto the couch. Except for Diego, the Hispanic family watched openmouthed, certain, I was sure, that I had a relative in emergency psychiatric care.

Amused and still on hold on the telephone, Tom gave a silent clap to my temperamental performance until he finally reached the person he was seeking. He asked about the location and duration of incarceration for Jack Gilkey and Barton Reed. He drew out his spiral notebook and jotted down something, thanked the person providing the information, then disconnected.

"Four years ago," Tom told me in a low voice,

"Cañon City was already running well over capacity. That's when Reed began serving his fraud conviction. Because there was no room for him at the state prison, he was incarcerated at the Furman County Jail. And you already know that when Gilkey was found guilty of criminally negligent homicide two years ago, he was also sent to the county jail. They were in the same section, on the same floor, as John Richard Korman." He flipped his notebook closed. "So you have to figure Gilkey hadn't just heard a story about Reed being denied parole. He knew the story because they knew each other. When Jack was granted parole, I bet it didn't go over too well with the former champion snowboarder."

"Darn it," I grumped, as frustrated by this information as I was with the schoolbook mess. "If only the Furman County cops could get evidence to see if Portman was dirty. The guy *must* have kept records. Well, maybe not. But if Barton Reed had some information about Jack Gilkey, or Doug Portman, that we could get out of him, it sure would answer a lot of questions." *And deal with the early-morning innuendoes from Reggie Dawson,* I added silently.

Tom raised his bushy eyebrows. "Our guys are going through forty-six boxes of military memorabilia, Miss G. Lotta stuff in there, lotta places to hide things like files or computer disks."

"I know, I know. But the more I try to figure out what happened with Doug Portman, the more questions come up. What's the *truth* about the death of Fiona Wakefield?" I looked out the waiting-room window. Dark, silver-edged clouds did not spell anything but more snow. "Who triggered the avalanche that killed Nate? Or was it even triggered by a person? If it was, where is that person? Why did Barton Reed try to kill somebody today? And exactly *whom* did he try to kill? Dog-gone it!"

Tom shook his head. "I forgot to tell you, that collage lady called you today. Boots Faraday. Wants to see you the next time you come to Killdeer. You're supposed to give her a call."

"Oh, peachy. I can't wait." I thought for a minute. "Have your guys talked to Barton Reed?"

"Not sure."

"May I visit him? Am I allowed to?"

Tom pursed his lips and considered. Finally he said, "You can visit him. But he's got a badly broken leg, he's lost some blood, and he's in pretty bad shape. He's immobilized and can't hurt you. I don't want *you* hurting *him*, though." I gave him a sour look. "If Reed gets better, he may face criminal charges for assault," he told me, then paused. "There's a Jeffco deputy at his door. Room ten-nine-teen. The deputy knows me, just tell him you're my wife. The only person I've told him *not* to let in is Jack Gilkey."

I didn't need prodding. Tom promised he'd take care of Arch and Marla, and especially Todd, when they returned.

At the door of 1019, I identified myself to

a young Jefferson County deputy and asked to see Barton Reed. The deputy inquired about ID, meticulously scrutinized my driver's license, then told me to go on in. I knocked gently. From within came a groan.

If Reed didn't want company, I would leave immediately. Even aggressively snowboarding convicts deserved hospital privacy. I pushed open the surprisingly heavy metal door.

A single small light illuminated the form in the bed. Barton Reed's right leg was thickly bandaged and suspended. His head and left arm were also swathed in gauze. Flecks of dried blood clung to his forehead and cheek. All of his jewelry had been removed; tiny dark holes freckled his ears. The earrings lay in a dish on a metal bureau. On top was a silver cross on a tarnished chain.

"Barton?" I whispered.

He was breathing heavily. *"Henh?"*

"Do you want me to leave? I'm just here to visit."

He mumbled something that sounded like, *"Who you?"*

"Goldy Schulz," I replied. I moved closer to the bed so he could see me. One of his eyelids was blackened, swollen shut. The other eye—clouded and blue—opened and regarded me blearily. I went on: "I first saw you last summer. At Aspen Meadow Health Foods. You were getting an herbal cancer treatment." He shook his head, and I wondered how much painkiller they'd given him. "And I was at Killdeer today. I saw the accident."

His groan was deep and guttural. "You from...the church?"

The question took me back. "The church?"

His face was sheened with sweat. "I'm gonna die."

"Of course you're not," I said, panicked. "Let me call a doc—"

"Nah." The sole blue eye assessed me. "Why're you here?"

"I just wanted to see you—"

He sighed. "Is she dead?"

I swallowed, then said, "Who?"

"Lady I hit." His bulging eye questioned me.

The lady I hit? So he didn't know Eileen Druckman? Had he not been aiming directly for her? "No. She's hurt, but hanging in there."

"Is he...dead?"

I hesitated again, torn between wanting to get information and trying to be pastoral to a man who believed he was dying. "Who?"

"Kee-rist! You an owl or somethin'?" This question sent him into a fit of spasmodic coughing.

"Gilkey?" I said when his paroxyms abated. "Were you aiming for Jack Gilkey?"

Reed started coughing again. "Is he dead?" he repeated hoarsely.

"Do you mean Jack Gilkey? No, he's not dead. Do you mean Doug Portman? Yes. Did you hit him, too, the way you hit that lady?"

"I'm dying," Barton Reed repeated dully. "There's no hope."

"There's always hope."

He turned his head away.

Since he didn't seem to want to talk about Jack Gilkey or Doug Portman, I said brightly, "You're quite a snowboarder. Maybe when you get better—"

"She wouldn't do the half-pipe with me anymore. Said she was hurt but that was…crap. Just chickened out."

I knew better than to say *Who?* a third time. I decided to try the Rogerian technique, one of the few remembered remnants from a mostly-useless psych degree. The famous shrink Carl Rogers had maintained that you should always repeat what the patient says. See where it leads. I repeated dutifully, "She said she was hurt."

"She was the best. Got hurt. Wanted to be famous. Never happened."

"It never happened."

"Is there an echo in here?" Barton turned from the window and batted his good eye at me. A puzzled look came over his face. "Is he dead? I gotta know."

I folded my hands and tried to think of what to say. Barton Reed was confused. He was convinced he was at death's door. He craved information or absolution or *something,* and I just didn't know how to provide it.

He groaned. "You from the church?" he repeated.

"Yes, I am."

"Then pray for me."

I took his bandaged hand in both of mine

and clasped it. *No matter what, give what you've got,* Rorry and I always told our class. God can take a couple of sardines and five hard rolls and turn it into a feast, and God can help you pray with an incoherent criminal in physical and spiritual pain.

"Our Father," I began; he mouthed most of the prayer with me. When we finished, he was asleep, and I hadn't learned who "he" was in his insistent question: *Is he dead?* I figured I could come back and visit him the next day, and hope he'd be more coherent.

But it did not happen. The next morning, Tom and I received a call: Barton Reed had died of a heart attack at midnight.

CHAPTER 19

That morning, Thursday, after we got the call, I prayed for Barton Reed. Then I cleared my mind and did my yoga before pulling myself into the shower. I couldn't focus. Again and again I saw Barton Reed, crouched, hell-bent, racing down the slope, sending Eileen sprawling. The previous night, I had not been allowed to see Eileen. The doctor told Todd his mother was doing so well she could probably be out of Intensive Care today. Todd, subdued and shaken, had come home with us. He'd spent the night in Arch's room, in Julian's old bed.

Jack Gilkey, his eyes red and swollen, had informed us that *he* was spending the night at the hospital. He asked Tom to call the bistro so someone else could do the lunch shift the next day. Before we left Lutheran, the Hispanic family took notice of poor Jack. They told us the grandfather of their clan had been in a car accident, and they, too, would be spending the night in the waiting room. Diego offered Jack hot homemade tamales. The last I saw of Jack, he was holding a tamale in one hand and a Dos Equis in the other.

Now, as I toweled off, I wondered how he was doing. Sleeping on a couch always seems convenient until you've done it for six or eight hours. I slipped into warm clothes and descended to the kitchen. Tom, who was poring over a plumbing manual, set it down to fix me a double espresso topped with a soft dollop of whipped cream. I sipped it and stared out the bay window in my no-longer-commercial kitchen. Too much had happened. Too many people had been hurt. No break, no light, appeared on the horizon. Outside, as if echoing my gloom, a steady snowfall that had begun during the night showed no sign of letting up.

"I'm taking the boys to school," Tom announced. "They want breakfast at McDonald's first. Can I bring you something?"

"No, thanks. Are they *sure* they want to eat out? I have to put together breakfast dishes for today's show, and I can offer them something good in about half an hour...."

Tom touched my shoulder. "Todd says he doesn't want to sit around. He's asked the doctor to call him at school if there is an emergency." He smiled mischievously. "And both boys are *desperate* to get their Spenser presentation over with so they can have their Christmas party. Nothing like the lure of Christmas cookies."

"Oh, Lord!" I exclaimed. "I forgot to make anything—"

Tom picked up a foil-covered platter from the marble counter and crinkled up a corner. Underneath the silvery wrapping lay dozens of crisp brown Chocolate Coma Cookies, each one studded with dried tart cherries, toasted almonds, and dark chocolate chips.

"What in the—?"

"Miss G., you wanted your recipe tested, didn't you? After I finished putting in the drains—"

"Tom! You're *done*?"

" 'O, ye of little faith,' " he began as the boys catapulted into the kitchen howling that they'd fed the animals, could they *please* go get some breakfast burritos? Todd and Arch both seemed better, each buoyed by the other's presence, each enthusiastic about the prospect of their upcoming holiday party. They did not want to discuss Eileen's condition, but only asked me to send them good vibes for their presentation. I promised I would.

Tom set two cookies on a small china plate and left it by my espresso. The crunch of almonds, tang of cherries, and rich, luscious chocolate woke me right up. I decided to call the upcoming day's TV menu "Feel-Your-Oats Holiday Breakfast." Rashers of crisp Canadian bacon, a bowl of icy vanilla yogurt, and a mountain of fresh fruit would go perfectly with the two starchy dishes I'd decided to prepare—spicy Swiss oatmeal and homemade bread. By seven-thirty, I had called early-rising Julian. He was flattered to fax me his new five-grain bread recipe. I thanked him, then proofed yeast while measuring out the cereal. A fresh, dimple-skinned orange, a new jar of Indonesian cinnamon, and more tart cherries beckoned to go into the oats.

By nine-fifteen, I was actually humming to myself, a sure sign the culinary work had once again helped me get life back into per-spective. I realized the time set for Arch and Todd's presentation was only half an hour away. I checked that the bread dough had risen properly and sent the boys a silent prayer of encouragement.

The phone rang. Concerned that it might be the hospital calling about Eileen, I picked up rather than letting the machine answer. It was not the hospital. It was Boots Faraday.

"Look, Goldy," she said without preamble, "Arthur Wakefield insists I owe you an apology."

"What?"

"Arthur's an old friend, and he didn't mean any harm by running that article about you." She paused, struggling, I supposed, to adopt an unfamiliar apologetic tone. "I...I heard about your friend Eileen Druckman, and that awful Barton Reed, and that you were there when it happened. I realized that you really *are* in the middle of a mess."

"Yes, it's bad," I admitted. But why call me? Unless, of course, she wanted to confess that Doug Portman's mean critique of her work had driven her to kill him six days ago.

"There's something I didn't tell you," Boots went on. "I...I...don't know whether it's relevant. But...I've decided to tell you anyway—It doesn't matter anymore." She took a shaky breath. "I do know what Nate was doing the day he died. It wasn't tracking lynx. That was just the standard story he told me to put out if he ever got caught."

"Got caught doing what?"

"Filming in Killdeer's out-of-bounds area. He...didn't think he'd get killed, of course." She sighed. "He was trying to make money, before his baby arrived. He...was making a sports-genre video."

"A *what*?"

"An outdoor sports film, haven't you ever seen them? You can catch them on the sports channels. The most popular around here are the extreme snowboarding videos. They show boarders leaping and spinning and jumping off ledges and generally risking death for a ride."

"Okay, yes," I said, remembering the big screen at Cinda's. "But...what kind of money could you hope to make from one of those?"

She laughed at my naïveté. "*Big* money. The good ones sell for fifty to a hundred

320

thousand. For the great ones, you can make two hundred fifty thousand to half a million."

"You're kidding!"

"No. Nate had talked to a distributor who was a friend of mine, a collage client. The distributor wanted to see a rough cut of whatever extreme snowboarding film he could do. But Nate didn't want to get Rorry's hopes up, so he begged me not to tell anybody."

"Was Barton Reed the snowboarder who was with him?"

"I...don't know."

"Were you the boarder?"

She groaned. "Of course not. I don't engage in risky behavior. By the way, that includes sleeping with married men, in case Rorry has been filling you in on her paranoid baloney."

"Why are you telling me all this?"

"Listen," she said brusquely, "I've been trying to protect Nate's good-granola-guy reputation for three years. Don't you think *died tracking lynx* sounds better than *died making money*? But I wanted you to know the truth. I don't know if it will relate to any of your problems."

Or your problems, I thought, such as my wondering if *you* triggered the avalanche, and that's why you've been lying for three years. After a moment, I asked, "Did Nate or Rorry know Doug Portman?"

"Nate knew about Portman through the artists' association. I'm not sure whether Rorry knew Portman or not. I just wanted you to know the truth about Nate. Because Arthur asked me to talk to you," she added stiffly. "And he's a good friend."

"Thanks, Boots." I didn't say, *Is it the truth?* Or, *Is Arthur more than a friend to you, by any chance?* I said only, "You...don't know anything more about Doug Portman, do you?"

"Only that he wouldn't have known a decent piece of artwork if he'd run into it." She banged the phone down before I could comment.

I slid the bread into the oven, set the timer, and simmered some of the cinnamon-orange oatmeal mixture to test it. I took a bite of the creamy concoction with its moist tart cherries. Heavenly. I was about to spoon up some more when the phone rang again. Boots, I figured, remembering more truth.

"I hear you're still trying to figure things out up in Killdeer," came the raspy voice of Reggie Dawson.

I exploded. Enough was enough. "Who *are* you? You're not a journalist. I checked. What do you want?"

"If you don't want your son hurt, you better start skiing at Vail, caterer. Quit being such a busybody."

"You leave my family alone!" I hollered, but whoever it was had hung up. I pressed buttons to trap the caller's number, and prayed that the telephone company's central computer had indeed registered the call. Then I called Tom's voice-mail and told him there had been another threatening call, and could the department please try to trace it, again?

Thoroughly unnerved, I called Elk Park Prep. Yes, I was assured, Arch Korman and Todd Druckman were fine. No intruder could get into that school, the receptionist told me, what with all the metal detectors and video cameras that had been installed over the summer. But hearing the anxiety in my voice, she put me on hold and went to check on Arch's exact location. When she returned, she said Arch and Todd were just going into English class. Oh, yes, I replied, as relief washed over me. The Spenser report was due in fifteen minutes. I thanked the receptionist and hung up.

The comforting, homey scent of baking bread wafted through the kitchen. Outside, snow fell. I told myself I'd done everything I could to figure out who "Reggie Dawson" was. Arch was safe, and Tom would find the threatening caller. And nail him.

I fixed myself a cup of espresso laced with cream and ordered myself to think positively. At nine-forty-five, I sent good vibes to the boys as they faced the class to perform. I tried to send a telepathic message to Arch to look only at kids he knew would *not* laugh when he began. I visualized him standing confidently and speaking clearly.... *Whatsoever from one place doth fall, is with the tide unto another brought: For there is nothing lost, that may be found...* Wait a minute. "Found *if sought*," I said aloud, and stared out at the falling snow.

Numerous times, I'd heard an avalanche described as a "killer tide." A tidal wave of snow that comes down the mountain.

I thought of Arch's physics experiment. Most of the frosting had spattered on the cookie sheet. But a very few drops, in places only one, had spattered far away. This was what had happened in the hospital waiting room, when Diego had been hit in the eye by a very errant chunk of dried frosting. That's quantum mechanics. Or quantum physics, if you prefer.

He was filming a sports-genre video, Boots had said.

His camera was stolen along with the TV, Rorry had insisted. But the TV had been the only item recovered.

Whatsoever from one place doth fall, is with the tide unto another brought. ... In the killer tide of an avalanche, maybe some things—one item in particular—had followed the patterns observed by quantum physicists and spattered far away.

I chugged the last of the espresso and dialed the main number for Killdeer. After an eternity of punching numbers for menu options, I was finally connected with a woman in Killdeer Security.

"I'm calling about a missing item," I began.

"Let me get into my program for the Lost and Found," she said pleasantly. Computer buttons clicked. "How long ago was the item lost?"

"Three years."

She gurgled with laughter. "We only keep items sixty days, ma'am. Then they get sold at a police auction or sent to a shelter in Minturn. Sorry."

"Wait a sec," I replied. "Let me think. Look, I have another question. What happens to all the stuff that gets rolled up into an avalanche? You know, besides sticks, rocks, and trees? Say a person goes down and you find his body without his skis. Do you ever find the skis? In the spring, maybe?"

"Hmm." The poor security woman tried to sound as if she were pondering my question, but her dubious tone said she thought I was some kind of nut. "Well..."

"Look," I said patiently. "The snow slides down. Say it knocks down a house. Do the chimney bricks and furniture end up at the bottom of the hill? How and when do you clean up the debris left by an avalanche?"

"Actually, in an avalanche everything gets thrown all over the place."

"So how does the debris get picked up?" I persisted. "I mean, not just from an avalanche, but from the whole ski area?"

She sighed. "When our maintenance guys groom the slopes in the spring, they scoop up everything they find. Wallets, jewelry, hats, mittens, you name it. Those items get logged into our Lost and Found for sixty days. You mentioned an avalanche. Where did it come down?"

"Elk Valley. Three years ago."

Her voice stiffened. "I see." After a pause, she went on: "Even though it's an out-of-bounds area in the winter, Elk Valley is used in the summer as a nature trail. Each year before the trail is opened, our maintenance team

325

cleans up the valley. The items they might have picked up would have come to Lost and Found. For sixty days. *All* items would have been logged in, and logged out to go to charity." She added tentatively, "Unless the item happened to be very valuable. We keep jewelry in the safe for longer. Up to a year."

"And your log goes back how long?"

"Five years."

"Can you do a computer search," I said, feeling my heart start to race, "for a certain log entry? I'm looking for a—" What was it Rorry had said? "A Sony, um, VX-One Thousand. A videocamera." Quantum mechanics, I reminded myself. The camera might have been thrown anywhere. Might have been found anytime. "It might have been turned in at any point in the last three years. If it went to a shelter or police auction, I can try to track it down. I just need to know if you *ever* had it."

She tapped buttons. "Okay...nothing from three years ago." More clicking. "Nothing from last year." She paused and tapped some more. "Hmm," she said at length. "How about that."

"What?"

"Our construction workers in the expansion area were cutting down trees this September. They found a camera inside its case under a pine tree and turned it in."

"Is it a Sony—"

She wouldn't let me finish. "So, it's yours? Were you caught in that avalanche?"

"I, I—It's not important after all this time, is it?"

326

"Yeah, it is. There are initials on the case. Can you identify them?"

My heart was pounding in my throat. *"N.B."*

She said, "Yes. Is that you?"

"No. It was Nate Bullock's camera. He was killed in the avalanche."

"Okay," she said blithely. "Bring ID to prove you're a family member, and you can get it between nine and four any day of the week." She hung up.

My skin was cold. *Bring ID to prove you're a family member.* I tried to call Tom on his cellular but the mountains were obscuring the signal. Even if I could talk my way into claiming Nate's camera, would it actually work after all this time? Wait: Julian's film class. I reached for the phone.

"Hey!" Julian cried. "Twice in one morning. How'd the bread come out?"

I turned on the oven light and peered in at the risen, golden-brown loaves. "Almost done. And the *scent* is heavenly."

"Great," he said, pleased.

"Listen," I said, "I have a video question for you."

"Shoot," he replied. Then he laughed. "Sorry. Film joke."

"If cassettes have been in a camera, or in a case, *outside,* for three years, would they be usable?"

"Gosh, Goldy. First bread, now old cameras. The stuff you come up with." He reflected for a few seconds. "Was the case protected?"

"Under a tree."

"Wait, let me ask my roommate." He left the line for a few minutes, then came back. "Okay. The film should be all right unless the camera's rusted shut and moisture has gotten into the apparatus itself. Just the cold alone shouldn't hurt it. In Colorado, some folks even keep their film cassettes out in their garages, to keep them fresher. But...why do you need to know this? Are you going to film your cooking show in the snow?"

"I'll tell you Christmas Eve."

He laughed again. "Whatever."

I hung up and contemplated the problem in front of me. I desperately needed to prove I was a family member. I punched in the numbers to Rorry Bullock's trailer. She picked up and dropped the phone. Then she declared in a gritty, sleep-saturated snarl: "Whoever you are, you better have a *great* reason for waking me up. Otherwise, I'm going to kill myself for forgetting to shut off my ringer."

I identified myself and apologized. Working a double shift that included nighttime, of course she'd be upset to be roused.

"It's okay," she said grumpily. "Goldy. I'm glad you called. I broke off a chunk of the frozen lasagne and heated it in the microwave. Fantastic! The baby loved it so much he twirled around in utero. I thought I was going into labor."

I laughed, then asked seriously, "Rorry, could I come over this afternoon? I might have some answers to your questions about Nate. But...I need you to claim his camera from Killdeer's Lost and Found."

"Someone found his *camera*? It's in the Lost and Found after three *years*?"

"This fall, workers in the expansion area discovered it under a tree. They turned it in. Because it was valuable, it's been in a safe there ever since."

"I, I can't...."

"Please, Rorry." I made my voice calm, comforting. "Please listen. You don't have to do anything with the camera. But *I* need it, to see if there's anything left of the tape Nate was making." When she said nothing, I went on: "Four people have died after suffering accidents at that ski area. Nate, Fiona Wakefield, Doug Portman, and now a guy named Barton Reed—"

"The snowboarder? That guy who went to jail?"

"He died of a heart attack last night at Lutheran. After being in a terrible snowboarding accident."

"But how can a tape that's three years old...tell you anything?"

"I don't know if it will," I admitted. "But every time I try to figure out what's going on, questions come up over what happened that day Nate died—"

"Have you found out who his girlfriend was?" she interrupted.

"No. Or if he even had one. But I did find out that he really was trying to make a sports video."

"A sports video? What are you talking about?"

"I don't know exactly—"

"I'm not sure I want to see the film," she interrupted me. "I mean, not if it can be viewed. Not with the baby so close. It's like a snuff film. Of my dead husband. I can't do it."

"Rorry. Please. This is important. Because I knew that guy Doug Portman, because I was on my way to meet with him the day of Nate's memorial, all kinds of nasty questions are coming up now about *me*. I may *never* get my business back if I can't figure out what's happened—what's *still going on* up at Killdeer. Losing my business is not as bad as what you've gone through in losing Nate, but it hurts. And I, too, have a child to think of." She groaned. I continued desperately, "Just claim the camera with me, will you? Please? I'll do the rest. You don't have to watch a thing."

She was silent. My heart sank. She was going to refuse. "Okay," she said, to my surprise. "When will you be here?"

I told her I should arrive around one, that we could go up together to the Killdeer Lost and Found at Ski Patrol Headquarters. I remembered the state of her car, and promised I'd take her to work, too.

"You're doing the PBS show at four?" she asked.

"Yeah, it's been rescheduled because of Christmas Eve. I don't have to be there until three-thirty."

"Why don't you just spend the night here afterward? Then you won't be driving back to

Aspen Meadow so late. You could look at the tape, then take me to work for the four-to-twelve shift. I've got someone who'll bring me home. You could do your show, and come over afterward. You'll have the place to yourself until I get off at midnight." She paused. "Unless you don't want to stay in my ratty trailer, of course."

I swallowed, thinking of "Reggie Dawson." I didn't care about staying in a trailer, but I *was* worried about Arch. And then of course, there was all the preparation I had to do at home tomorrow, Christmas Eve. But I was worried that Rorry needed company, especially right before the holiday. If Tom would agree to be with Arch around the clock, then I would stay with Rorry. I could leave before dawn tomorrow morning and arrive home early enough to thaw the turkey and find the stockings we always hang by the fireplace. "Sure, I'd love to stay with you. Thanks. See you at one, then."

I left a message on Arthur's answering machine detailing the exact menu graphic and food preparation I needed for our last show. *Very easy*, I assured him, in conclusion. *See you at three-thirty.*

It was going to be a full day. No time for lunch, anyway, so I made two peanut-butter-and-cherry-preserves sandwiches for Rorry and me. If the baby loved lasagne, he was going to *flip* for PB&J. While I was wrapping them in wax paper, I put in a call to Tom. Would he have arrived at the sheriff's department by now? Did he have a meeting? Miraculously, he picked up.

"Hey, Miss G., I was just about to call you. Don't panic. First of all, I left the boys off and they're fine. I called Lutheran, too. Eileen's doing better. They've moved her into her own room. She's resting comfortably, as they say. The nurse told me Jack finally left the hospital and went back to Killdeer," he added, "so he's not sleeping on the waiting room sofa anymore. And those anonymous phone calls: Made from a pay phone in Killdeer, our guys tell me."

Doggone it. I told him of my plan to do the show and spend the night at Rorry's. Considering the weather, Tom replied, that was probably a great idea. And yes, he would pick up Arch and stick to him like epoxy until I came home.

I also told Tom of my find—make that *potential* find—at the Killdeer Lost and Found. He tapped the receiver, a *click click click* sound that did not betoken approval.

"What's the matter with that?" I demanded. "I'll bring the camera, the case, and whatever's in it straight back to you."

"I'm trying to figure out if this film could be considered evidence. If it is, you should be leaving it alone."

"If it's evidence of *malfeasance,* if it's *anything,* you'll have it first thing tomorrow. But I'm the one who has articles left anonymously, I'm the one getting threatening calls. I've got a bigger stake in finding out what's going on up there than you all."

"I have a stake in protecting my wife. Doesn't that count?"

"Look, Tom, all I'm doing is looking at something, if there is something. Then I do the show and come home first thing tomorrow morning."

Worry threaded his voice. "Are you going to have somebody you trust with you today, all the time?"

"I'll be with Rorry, then I'll be onstage for PBS, then I drive back to Rorry's. Then I drive home."

"After the show, have somebody walk you to the Rover. *Not* that wine guy; he might have discovered you found the ticket he stole from Portman's place. Call me the moment you get to Rorry's. And lock all the doors."

"Tom, it's a trailer. There's only one door. And it's a ski town, not the inner city."

"In the past week, Killdeer Ski Resort has had more unexplained accidents and deaths per capita than the worst ten-block stretch in Denver."

I said, "Now there's a happy statistic."

CHAPTER 20

Gusts of wind whipped waves of snow on the windshield as I drove out of Aspen Meadow. Because of the poor visibility, I drove slowly up the interstate's right lane. With its high center of gravity, the Rover rocked with each blast. On the ascent to the Eisenhower Tunnel, a whining eighteen-wheel rig loomed abruptly and my foot slammed the brake. The Rover skidded onto the shoulder—and stalled.

I restarted the car and contemplated what the wind and snow would mean for riding the Killdeer gondola. But as I emerged from the west side of the tunnel, the breeze softened. By the time I reached Killdeer, snowflakes were swirling thickly but gently to the whitened earth.

Rorry was watching for me from her trailer's bay window. She clambered down her steps and waddled through the snowfall to the Rover. She wore a fluffy-white-fur-lined pink maternity ski suit. She looked like the Easter bunny.

"I can't wait to get this over with," she said bitterly as she slammed the passenger door and settled into her seat.

"The pregnancy or getting the film?"

"Both."

"Buck up. I brought you a sandwich."

We munched our sandwiches and drank bottles of water as I drove cautiously toward the mountain base. Because snow was still falling fast, I splurged and parked at the close-in pay lot. It was the least I could do for Rorry, who made her unwieldy way through the street of shops, and stopped at Cinda's to go to the bathroom.

A sudden storm will drive all but the most die-hard skiers home, or at the very least, into mountain-base cafés for tequila, steaming hot chocolate, or both. True to form, Cinda's was mobbed with skiers slamming down drinks while watching one of Warren Miller's extreme skiing videos. Knowing what I now knew about Nate's last tape, I averted my eyes. Cinda, whose hair held some of the hues of Rorry's ski suit, offered us free Viennese coffee with a shot of rum.

"Or rum flavoring," she told Rorry. "Might be better for the baby." Rorry declined. I promised Cinda that I would have a celebratory Bacardi-coffee, heavy on the Bacardi, when I finished my last show that afternoon. She told me to break a leg.

Rorry and I had our season tickets scanned and clambered onto the gondola. As we ascended, the wind picked up dramatically, thrashing the snowfall sideways like thick confetti. Our gondola car quivered and swayed. When the wind abated slightly, a few skiers and boarders were visible battling their way down the runs. Between the runs, clusters of whitened pines nodded and bent in the wind.

Rorry's face was pinched, the circles under her eyes dark and deep. She squirmed on the cold metal seat. I remembered that last month of pregnancy all too well. You didn't suffer just an occasional pain, but almost constant physical unease, whether you were walking, sitting, or sleeping. I couldn't even *imagine* the discomfort of a jarring ride on a cable car.

When the gondola shuddered to a halt at the turnaround, Rorry groaned as she heaved herself up and out the clanging doors. I felt guilty about asking her to walk to the lodge to claim Nate's camera, and was tempted to take her ID into the Lost and Found myself. Maybe I could bluff my way through. But before I could put the thought into words, she was barreling ahead of me and I had to plow through ten inches of fresh powder to catch up.

A mob of skiers was clamoring to gain entry to the lodge. Rorry looked back at me in confusion. I pointed to the bistro. It would be inconvenient to go through the restaurant to the Lost and Found, but easier than trying to push through the people-jam at the main doors.

The aromas inside the restaurant were tantalizing: Roasting beef melded with tarragon, rosemary, and the scent of baking bread. Several of the diners were dipping into steaming bowls of what looked like cream of asparagus soup topped with spicy grilled prawns. My peanut-butter-smeared psyche howled with pain.

The first person I saw was Jack Gilkey. With his tall chef's hat set at a slightly rakish angle, his handsome face filmy with sweat, he was placing bowls of the delicious-looking soup on the hot line. A half-dozen servers jockeyed to be first to shout more orders at Jack and whisk away with their soup orders. Jack caught sight of me, then smiled broadly and gave a thumbs-up sign—referring to either Eileen's improved state or the state of his prepping for this afternoon's show—and went back to ladling out food.

"You're friends with the chef?" Rorry demanded under her breath.

"He's living with an old friend of mine, Eileen Druckman. She owns the bistro."

Rorry exhaled in disgust. "He's a *jerk.*"

We pushed through the side door and walked down the hall to the Lost and Found. "What makes you say that?"

"Jack Gilkey," Rorry responded hotly, "is like the teacher who's nice to the parents but treats the kids like dirt. When he thinks you have something he wants, or you're his superior, he's as sweet as chocolate pie. You work for him, you're *dung.* A couple of our guys who load the canisters won't come up here anymore, 'cuz Gilkey blamed them when he forgot to order all the ground beef for a day. He even tried to get them fired. Gilkey knows he needs to fax the right forms down to us at the warehouse, but when he screws up, he's always looking for somebody to blame." Her voice was tight with anger.

In the Lost and Found, we were greeted by none other than Joe Magill, the brusque Killdeer Security fellow who'd asked me so many questions after the death of Doug Portman. Rorry dug into the Easter-bunny ski suit for her wallet while Magill asked what we needed. I gestured to the Lost and Found sign and said I had called about a camera and case, initials *N.B.* on the case. Magill tapped suspiciously on his computer, scowled at the screen, and tapped some more. He was about to say something when Jack Gilkey poked his head in the door. He was holding a plate laden with a grilled filet mignon, Duchess potatoes drizzled with melted butter, bright green edible-pod peas, and a small *salade composée* of marinated cherry tomatoes and baby corn. Agh!

"Here's your lunch, Joe," he said to Magill.

"You're the man," Magill replied, taking the plate, "you're too much!" He frowned at us. *If you two would just leave,* his expression clearly said, *I could eat.*

Jack turned to me. "You've heard the good news about Eileen?" When I nodded, he said, "I'm going down to see her tonight. Want to come?"

"Can't, sorry. I have to do the show, and then—"

"Okay, that's something else I need to talk to you about," he interrupted. "I've got your five-grain-bread dough rising, plus a loaf baking now. The cereal's in a green plastic bowl in the refrig." He made a face. "Arthur Wakefield brought the menu up. He's having lunch here with one of his wine customers."

I thanked him and he retreated quickly. Sure enough, he had not said a word to Rorry, or even taken any notice of her. She raised a telltale eyebrow at me: *You see? Dung.*

"Ladies," Joe Magill said with a tinge of impatience, "I'm not seeing your camera case in our inventory."

"That's impossible! I called Killdeer

338

Security just this morning. They said it was here!"

"Said it was *here*," Magill replied with exaggerated politeness, "or said it was in the Lost and Found *safe* at the *base*?"

"Oh, phooey," muttered Rorry, as she turned away. I was so angry that the Killdeer Security woman had not told me this on the phone that I said nothing. *If you bite off a bureaucrat's head, what do you get? Three more bureaucrats.*

The main entrance was still crammed with skiers. The impossibility of fighting through them meant that Rorry and I had to retrace our steps. Unfortunately, it was my bad luck to run into Arthur Wakefield as I pushed open the door to the bistro. And I do mean *run into.*

Arthur sprawled backward, but managed to tuck his silver wine flask under his arm. My first paranoid thought was that he must have been watching me through the door's glass square. He just hadn't retreated quickly enough when I'd pushed through the entrance. He righted himself with dignity, then begged us to come over to his table for a minute. More bad luck: Arthur was having lunch with Boots Faraday. Boots smiled at me and nodded awkwardly at Rorry, who'd stiffened instantly at the sight of her.

"So, what are you two doing up here? Scoping out the last show? Having lunch?" Arthur, seemingly oblivious to the female hostility, asked his questions as he wiggled up next to us, unscrewed the flask, and poured white wine into two glasses. I looked longingly at their plates of baby-vegetable strudel napped with a creamy sauce, probably béarnaise. Arthur leaned in close to my shoulder, sniffed, and cried triumphantly. "I smell peanut butter!" He looked at both of us expectantly. "How about some ten-year-old Grand Cru chablis, then?"

Rorry moaned in disgust. "I go out, nine months pregnant, and all everybody offers me is *booze.*"

Boots's expression said: *Didn't I tell you this woman was difficult?* She said abruptly, "Did you get my *message,* Goldy?"

"I didn't get your message, I just talked to you a few hours ago—" But I stopped when Boots shot me a stern look. Aha: She was trying to ask me if I'd told *Rorry* her story about Nate making an extreme sports film the day he died.

"That's okay." Two spots of color flamed on Rorry's cheeks; she was glaring at Boots. "You don't have to try to send Goldy some kind of secret *message,* the way you used to do with Nate and your early morning calls. I know your code. One ring means, *Call me back.* Two rings mean, *Meet me for lunch.* He finally told me, you know." Rorry's tone was angrily triumphant. Boots looked flabbergasted. "He swore it was all innocent. That you were just afraid of my jealousy. If it was all innocent, how come I had the phone company trace your calls to a *pay phone* outside the

Killdeer Art Gallery? Why didn't you call from your house? Too afraid I had caller ID?" She whirled on Arthur. Startled, he cradled the wine to his shoulder. "Are you *married,* Arthur? That's the kind of guy Boots goes for."

Arthur's voice squeaked, "Rorry, please! Boots Faraday is a customer!" Boots clamped her mouth into a forbidding line. Arthur gulped, set the wine flask down, and frowned. He repeated his question: "What exactly are you and Rorry doing up here, Goldy?"

Luckily, Rorry remembered my warning about not divulging the purpose of our trip. I told him I just wanted to make sure Jack and his staff were prepping the last show. Arthur nodded, and Rorry announced that we had to go. During the gondola trip down, I endured Rorry's litany of complaints about Boots Faraday, who, Rorry insisted, had tried desperately to break up her marriage.

"Boots does have a really nice body, for an older woman," Rorry conceded as the car door opened at the base. "I even thought Nate might have been doing a porno film of her, and she'd use photo clips from it in one of her stupid collages."

"Well, we'll find out, won't we," I commented as we headed for the building marked *Base Security—Patrol Office* and pushed through to the Lost and Found. Rorry, again distinctly uncomfortable, insisted she had to sit down.

"Are you all right?" I asked desperately.

"Yes, it's just that damn woman," Rorry

replied as she lowered herself into a padded chair. "She gives me indigestion."

"Item?" inquired the patrolman behind the desk. It was Hoskins! These people must run on a six-day rotation, I thought. My helper from the day of Doug Portman's accident asked if I was doing all right, and if my son was okay. I told him we were both fine, but that my friend and I desperately needed help finding something. Hoskins said seriously, "And the item is..."

"A camera case." Rorry reached up to slap her ID onto the counter. "Initials *N. B.* It's in the safe, we called."

Hoskins tapped keys on his computer, disappeared, then returned with a dirty, crumpled case made of heavy-duty gray fabric, frayed in places. When Rorry saw it, she cried out in surprise and alarm, and began to weep. Damn, had I done the wrong thing? She held out her hands and I gave the case to her. She hugged it to her huge belly, rocking back and forth and sobbing as if her heart were broken.

"Rorry," I said softly as I knelt down beside her chair. "I'm sorry. What can I—"

"You want me to get a paramedic in here?" Hoskins asked me. "She doesn't seem well."

"She's not going into labor. Could you please just get her a glass of water?"

"Take the camera," Rorry moaned when Hoskins had left. "See if the cassette's in there, watch it somewhere, and then let's get out of here. I can't take any more in one day. Please, Goldy."

When Patrolman Hoskins returned with water for Rorry, I asked if there was a VCR in another office where I could watch something quickly. He shook his head, then asked dubiously, "Are you sure your friend is going to be all right?"

"Yes, I think so. This camera belonged to her dead husband, and... It's a long story."

"You need a VCR?"

"Yeah."

Hoskins lifted his chin at the wide front window. "Cinda's got a couple of VCRs at her place. Why don't you try her?"

Of course. I thanked him and went back to Rorry. I unzipped the case and checked the camera, which was spotted with rust. The word *Sony* was still visible. I rezipped the bag, patted Rorry's shoulder, and murmured that I would be right back.

The snow seemed to be letting up a bit as I made my way to the Cinnamon Stop. The café was still hopping with business, though, and a video showing a freestyle snowboarding competition was drawing *ooh*s and *aah*s from the enthralled crowd. I shouted my request to Cinda, who was steaming milk for a latté. Did she have an extra machine in the back where I could watch a film?

She gave me a puzzled look, then cried "Sure!" and muttered something to the waiter I recognized as Ryan. He pointed to a door and I waded through the boisterous crowd to join him.

"You need help with a video?" Ryan asked.

"Yeah, my friend's pregnant and about to pop. My Lamaze teacher gave me a childbirth video," I improvised blithely, "and I need to see if it's in good enough shape to show."

Ryan shrugged, as if my lie were the most ridiculous thing he'd ever heard, which it probably was. He turned on the VCR while I struggled to open the camera, first with my fingernails, then with a pair of scissors from Cinda's desk. When the latch finally gave, the shears snapped. Ryan took the cassette and showed me how to operate Cinda's VCR.

Fast-forwarded, Nate Bullock's tape was spotty with visual static. When the film opened with the first shot, the snow-capped rustic sign for Elk Valley and Elk Ridge, I grabbed the remote control from Ryan and hit "Stop."

Ryan turned to me. "Lamaze at a ski resort? What is this, 'Cliffhanger Childbirth'?"

I opened the office door to usher him out. "It's women's stuff. Not a place you want to go, Ryan."

He muttered something like *You can say that again* and zipped out. Worried about Rorry in the present, and what this video was going to show me about the past, I took a nervous breath. Then I hit the Play button.

Nate Bullock's garbled-but-familiar PBS voice gave me a jolt. I couldn't make out a word of what he was saying. From the tone of it, it sounded like an introduction. After the shot of the sign, his next shot was of the path beyond it. Next the camera panned to his companion, whom I couldn't quite make out.

344

Rorry was right about one thing: She was a female. The woman had a snowboard slung under her arm. Nate went from a long shot to a close-up.

I cried out: A conservative form-fitting navy-blue ski suit, no psychedelic outfits. A short cap of brown hair, no spill of pink curls. No jewelry. But her athleticism, her pretty face with its freckle-sprayed pixie nose, her bright, lopsided smile: All these were unmistakable.

Cinda Caldwell.

Barton Reed's words in the hospital echoed in my brain: *Said she was hurt, but that was crap. Just chickened out.* Of course, Cinda was the most famous female snowboarder in Killdeer. Young, pretty, and as adept at snowboarding as anyone. *She was the best. Got hurt. Wanted to be famous. Never happened.*

No, it never happened, I thought as I watched. Nate expertly clicked off the camera and then resumed taping from the valley. Cinda was far above, on the right edge of Elk Ridge. Nate zoomed in on her doing a smooth right to left, then left to right maneuver on the steep white slope. Cinda's flowing movements were as effortless and breathtaking as big-wave surfing.

Nate's garbled voice came on again; the tape clicked off. The next time Cinda appeared she was up higher, near the top edge of the steep, forest-lined bowl that Arthur had pointed out to Marla and me the day before. Nate zoomed in. Poised unafraid at the edge of the bowl, Cinda's face was happy but determined. Then her concentration broke. She stared, puzzled, into the distance. A look of horror spread over her face, and she gestured to the camera.

"Over there," I could lip-read her saying. She pointed and mouthed the words again. Nate lowered the camera. You could hear him yelling. Then the camera rose and panned vertiginously. I blinked and realized I was looking through treetops at Bighorn Overlook. In the distance, Cinda screamed. Her voice sounded as if she were underwater.

A small noise made me jump. The office door had opened. Cinda, her flaming pink hair backlit by the café's bright lamps, stood rigidly in the oblong of light. She stared at the initials on the camera case in my hands, then lifted her eyes to meet mine.

She said, "What are you going to do with that? Get *me* killed, too?"

CHAPTER 21

"No," I said immediately. "At least, I'm trying not to. Is this film why you quit snowboarding? You were afraid?"

"Yes. Still am. Not to mention feeling guilty about Nate."

I took a deep breath. "And do you feel afraid because you saw who pushed Fiona Wakefield over the cliff?"

She sighed. "Yes. But all I saw was people struggling on Bighorn Overlook. Does the tape show what happened?"

"I haven't gotten that far."

Cinda closed the door, muffling the noise of the café behind her. "What are you planning on doing?"

I shrugged and glanced at my watch. Desperate as I was to see the rest of the tape, my fear of interruption and my desire to protect evidence, not to mention my need to do the last PBS program, dictated that I not view any more of the tape just then. I needed to find out what Cinda knew, and then I needed to split. Fast. "I haven't got immediate plans," I answered noncommitally.

"Goldy, please. Don't turn in that tape. It'll be the end of me. I was hoping you could figure out what happened, and leave me out of it—" She bit her lip.

"What are you talking about?" I stared at her. "Leave you out of it? You were so eager to get me to figure things out, you left the articles and ordered *The Stool Pigeon Murders* and the avalanche book, didn't you?" She nodded bleakly. "For crying out loud, Cinda, you took my frigging *library* card?"

"It dropped out of your wallet here a few weeks ago. I'd been *meaning* to give it back to you. But then you got involved looking into Portman's death. And I thought, well, Goldy's the one who's supposed to be so good at solving crimes, why not let her solve this one?"

347

"Did you call me pretending to be a journalist named Reggie Dawson?"

She grimaced. "Of course not." She sighed. "Look, I know you're angry, but please, think about what I've gone through since the avalanche. That day changed my life, for the worse. Who killed Fiona Wakefield? And did whoever do it see *me* up on the ridge? Did Nate tell anyone that *I* was the one he was filming? Does anyone know *I'm* the one who started the avalanche that killed Nate Bullock?"

"What do you think?" I asked her. Again, I was aware of the tape in her VCR. I was also aware that I suddenly did not trust Cinda Caldwell.

"I followed Jack Gilkey's criminal trial," she was saying. "I don't think Gilkey knew *I* was the one snowboarding in the out-of-bounds area on Elk Ridge. But Gilkey, or whoever pushed his wife off the overlook, knew *some* snowboarder was on Elk Ridge. It was in the papers when Nate died. In jail, Gilkey befriended my old buddy Barton Reed. Maybe it was just to be friendly, but Gilkey asked Barton a million questions about scofflaw snowboarders in Killdeer. Barton wrote me about his new friend; told me the two of them would be out soon; we could all go snowboarding. I wrote back that I hadn't done any boarding since my knees gave out the year before."

"Why didn't you tell me all this last week, when you were so upset that Barton had made a threat against someone in law enforcement?"

The freckled skin around Cinda's pale eyes crinkled in sudden fury. "Oh, *sure*. And then have the cops ask me, 'How do *you* happen to know so much about Fiona Wakefield's death, Ms. Caldwell?' And I say, 'Well, Officer, I think I saw something just before I caused an avalanche in an out-of-bounds area, an avalanche that killed a PBS star!' Do you think that kind of confession would keep me out of prison?"

How long had I been away from Rorry? How was I going to manage to be up at the bistro in less than an hour? "Look, Cinda, I have to go—"

"I *had* to tell you what Barton said!" she continued, impassioned. "Do you think I don't have any conscience left? Barton had cancer, he was half crazed, he wanted to kill some guy in law enforcement. I couldn't be responsible for *two* deaths! Why don't you play the tape? Then we can see what's what."

"No," I said firmly, as I ejected it from the VCR, slotted it back into Nate's camera, and zipped up the case. "I need to leave. Meanwhile, Cinda, you *have* to come forward and talk to the authorities. This tape can help, and you must help, too. We *have* to find out who really killed Fiona—"

"If it was Jack, he can't be tried for the same crime twice," she countered stubbornly.

"I know, but listen. Eileen Druckman is one of my best friends. If it *is* true that Jack cold-bloodedly killed his wife, then Eileen has to know. She has to dump him, before it's

349

too late. If it was Arthur, he needs to be arrested and punished. If it was Barton Reed, then we can close the case. If it was Boots Faraday, then she can get ready to teach art classes in prison."

"I *can't*," said Cinda, her jaw clenched. "I'll go to jail for the rest of my life." She held out her hand. "Give me the tape, Goldy."

"No."

At that moment the office door opened. Cinda and I froze. Rorry Bullock's huge belly came through first. She looked blankly from Cinda to me. Behind Rorry, Ryan's head appeared. He peered over Rorry's shoulder.

"Hey boss," he said desperately. "I've got four people out here screaming for vanilla lattés, and I can't find a new bottle of extract."

I announced: "Time to go." Hoisting the camera case, I made an internal bet, the kind that always drives Tom crazy when I tell him about it later: Cinda would not risk exposing herself in front of Ryan. Nor would she wrench the case from my hands while Rorry was there. She knew she'd have a struggle on her hands, one she was bound to lose.

Rorry, the very pregnant widow of the man whose death Cinda had inadvertently caused, said, "Goldy, I need to go to work. And you need to do your show," she reminded me.

"Oh, yes, your show," said Cinda.

Doggone it. "See you later," I gushed as I pushed past Cinda to lead Rorry out. "Thanks for letting us use your tape player."

"Well?" Ryan stage-whispered as we made

our way to the exit. "Did you see what you need?"

I was acutely aware of Cinda's rigid form behind us, her ears tuned to our every word. "Not yet," I replied loudly. "Maybe the tape's too screwed up."

Anything to stall for time.

The sun was struggling through parting clouds as Rorry and I crunched through the new snow to the car. Her questions spilled out. *You see who the snowboarder was?* No. *Was Nate really filming a sports video?* Yes. *How did the avalanche start?* Not sure, I replied tersely. Probably from the construction noise that day. She paused, then asked in a low, husky voice, *Did you see him die?* No, I replied honestly. I really need to look at it again, I added grimly, and have the police analyze it.

When I dropped her at the warehouse, I asked her once more if she was doing okay. It had been a successful trip, but arduous. Yes, yes, she assured me quickly, just fine. She handed me a spare key to her trailer and said a co-worker would be bringing her home about midnight. Then she disappeared behind the large warehouse doors. It was hard to tell if she was satisfied with my answers about the tape. Probably not, I reckoned, since half of them were lies.

As I drove away, I tried to figure out the best way to get to the bistro, where the show would be filmed. The new, unplowed snow was too deep to try to get up the back road in the Rover. I wasn't going to ski down. So I had to take the gondola both ways. But how would I avoid Cinda's, with its panoramic view of the path to the gondola?

I decided to park in the Elk Ridge lot. Then I could walk back through the trees to the creek, find the first way across, and head straight to Big Map. I had on thick waterproof leggings and good boots, and could probably move pretty fast. But Cinda was younger and much stronger than I was. Bad knees or no, I didn't want to tangle with her.

I glanced at the camera case on the passenger seat beside me. What should I do with the cassette? Would it be safer with me or safer in the car? In the past week, it seemed as if everyone I'd come to know in Killdeer had had their place or their automobile broken into. I couldn't risk leaving the tape in the Rover: I stuffed it into a small opaque plastic bag inside my cooking-equipment bag.

The parking lot was three-quarters full of cars and emptying quickly. Folks had had enough of skiing. They wanted to beat Denver's Christmastime rush-hour traffic. I remembered Tom's warning not to be alone. To get up to the bistro for the final episode of *Cooking at the Top,* I would have to take the least public route possible.

The trailhead, filmed as Nate's establishing shot, offered food for thought. In the film, these signs appeared without posted warnings. Now, the arrows to Elk Ridge and Elk Valley were covered with a sign stating *Closed for Winter——No Entry.* Beyond the trailhead, a formidable wooden barrier stretched from one sheer rock outcropping to another. But there was something else that offered possibilities....

A bright orange sign posted beside the trailhead screamed *Construction Workers Only!!!* and marked the beginning of what must be, under the plowed snow, a dirt road. Did the construction road wind around to the gondola? Was I willing to chance it?

From the Rover, I could see the plowed road was not without security: tall poles abutted huge snowdrifts on both sides. Bands of padlocked horizontal chains attached to each pole were undoubtedly designed to ensure no scofflaw skier or boarder squeezed through to get to the ridge. But whatever project manager had overseen the installation of the poles into dirt bases—rather than wide, deep, cement bases—must have been from a warmer climate. Our state's heavy snowfall guaranteed that any mailbox, road sign, or metal pole pushed into shallow dirt was going to heave out sooner or later, as the ground froze, thawed, and refroze. In this case, the heaving had happened sooner, and one of the poles now leaned precariously into the road. This left a gap that I bet was big enough for a short, only-slightly-pudgy caterer to squeeze through.

I shouldered my bag resolutely, hopped out of the Rover, locked it, glanced all around, and made for the construction road. After squeezing between the pole and drift, I trotted along the pocked, snowpacked road. Thank God I wouldn't be skiing down tonight, and was therefore free of skis, heavy ski boots, and poles. Then I made a surprising and unhappy discovery. The road meandered up twenty yards and then forked. Did the left side go over to the gondola? Was I willing to find out? I didn't have time.

The right side of the fork swung up and joined, or rather, *became* the path that led to Elk Ridge and Elk Valley. The path, formerly a narrow hiking trail, had been widened to accommodate two vehicles. I couldn't imagine how the nature-loving summer hikers were going to react to this transformation, but it wasn't going to be pretty. By the time the Sierra Club could drag Killdeer into court early in the summer, the lifts and runs would be built. No wonder Killdeer had undertaken the challenging winter construction schedule.

So I had a problem: It was ten to three, and I needed to get to the bistro by three-thirty. Since the dirt construction road did not lead to the gondola, I needed to go through town. *Damn.*

I scuttled back to the parking lot and the main road. The Victorian-style boutiques in Killdeer were mobbed with last-minute Christmas shoppers. I melted into the frantic crowd. Shielded by the mob, I stayed as far away from the Cinnamon Stop's windows as possible. Eventually I was chugging up the mountain in a gondola car next to a skier complaining about the snowstorm and how long it had taken to blow through. Across from us, three teenagers, more philosophical about the weather, were singing carols in harmony. While the wind still gusted fitfully, the snow had thinned to flurries. The sky rolled with new dark clouds that parted and thinned in the west. By morning, with any luck, it would be clear, and they would have plowed the interstate back to Aspen Meadow.

Once off the gondola, I surveyed the bistro. Smoke curled out of the two chimneys. Late-day skiers straggled out to catch one last run. *Stay with someone,* Tom had warned. It would not be smart to take the hidden cassette directly into the restaurant. I could be mugged or pickpocketed by "Reggie Dawson" or any other unsavory character, and lose the evidence forever. Reflecting, I gnawed the inside of my cheek and then set off for the lower entrance, the one that led to the bistro's storage areas. At this time of the day, workers should be down there sorting and packing the day's trash into canisters. They wouldn't mind a servant coming through the servants' entrance, would they?

The two lower-level barn-type doors were partially open. My entry with my toolbag raised the eyebrows of the pair of grizzled, hulking workers. Both were so swaddled in scarves, hats, heavy gloves, layers of sweatshirts, and what looked like padded dungarees, that they were unrecognizable.

"I'm one of the cooks," I explained to one

as I squeezed past the first stinking canister. He nodded apathetically and turned back to his work, while I scuttled along the tunnellike, neon-lit hallway. It was dank and cold. I was surprised at how depressingly subterranean the concrete basement was, at how tired and raggedly clad the workers had been. The bistro's storage area was as unglamorous a workplace as the bare trailer park was a living area. As I bustled into a freezer-lined room and tucked the cassette between boxes of frozen chocolate cakes, I wondered if the rich folks who played on the manicured slopes outside had any idea of the economic underside of their vacations. The workers labor all day and night, dress and eat poorly, and are crammed into freezing trailers at the edge of town. Not something for the resort owners to be proud of.

I rushed up the steps and, panting, came through the uncrowded kitchen, where the six-person evening staff was bemoaning the fact that one of the two walk-in refrigerators was out of order. It would take twice as long to prep for the evening meal, they complained, as they set about cutting leeks, carrots, onions, and celery into julienne. I set my bag down and asked one of the cooks if Jack Gilkey was here. No, Jack had gone to Denver to see Mrs. Druckman in the hospital. The food for the show lay prepped on a sideboard, the cook added. He pointed to a counter. The other cooks began to snigger, and I thought I caught one of them saying, "At least he isn't here to take the credit for our work, the way he usually does."

I slipped into my jacket and uniform for the show, then inspected Jack's—or his subordinates'—impressively organized foodstuffs, all labeled: a loaf of Julian's crusty golden-brown five-grain bread sat next to the yeast, molasses, and other ingredients. The cereal and its ingredients were similarly laid out. Beside these was a platter lined with grilled Canadian bacon and plump sausage links. At the end of the counter, a crystal plate was adorned with concentric circles of fresh sliced ruby red strawberries, golden pineapple, and emerald green kiwi, all dotted with fat blueberries and raspberries. My stomach reflected on the long-ago peanut butter and jelly, and sent up a distress signal. *Later,* I promised myself.

Jack had left me a note: *Goldy—I'll give Eileen your love. Break a leg! J.* I guessed I was one of the people Jack looked up to. Or was hoping to get something from, as Rorry claimed? I wouldn't mind working with him one bit, if I could be sure he was a good guy.

Hopefully, Nate's video would tell all.

I scurried out to the hot line with the first batch of ingredients. Would the bistro audience be disappointed to be receiving only oatmeal, bread, Canadian bacon, and fruit for their nine bucks? I didn't know. Boots Faraday, now apparently a regular at the show, was seated serenely by the fireplace. So, unfortunately, was Cinda Caldwell. My heart lurched.

357

Arthur strode toward me, clipboard in hand. He appraised me menacingly. I felt myself blushing. Finally he said, "I suppose you know the chef's gone to see the owner in the hospital." He made it sound as if I had put Eileen there.

"Not to worry, Arthur. Jack left everything done."

Arthur narrowed his eyes skeptically, then handed me the visual they would post for the menu. There was the usual Front Range PBS logo, followed by:

Feel-Your-Oats Holiday Breakfast
Celebration
Platter of Strawberries, Kiwi, Pineapple,
Raspberries, and Blueberries
Skiers' Swiss Cereal
Grilled Canadian Bacon
Toasted Thick-Sliced Five-Grain Bread
Butter, Jams
Champagne, Coffee

"You have to put that it's Julian Teller's five-grain bread."

"This is public TV," Arthur replied stiffly. "No advertising." Before I could protest, he added: "Are you going to tell me what Rorry Bullock was *really* doing up here today?"

Startled, I answered, "She was seeing how the other half lives, Arthur." When he *hrumph*ed, I tapped the menu. "Make it 'Julian's Five-Grain Bread,' and it won't be an advertisement because you're not using his last name. If you don't, I'm

Skier's Swiss Cereal

1 cup rolled oats
1 teaspoon very finely chopped
    orange zest
½ teaspoon cinnamon
2 tablespoons dried tart cherries
2 cups skim milk
Brown or granulated sugar
Cream, butter, or milk

The night before you plan to serve the dish, in a glass bowl, combine the oats, zest, cinnamon, and cherries. Stir well, then stir in the milk. Cover with plastic wrap and refrigerate.

The next morning, place the mixture in a medium-sized saucepan and bring it to a simmer. Lower the heat and cook, stirring frequently, for 4 to 6 minutes, or until the oats are tender and the mixture is thick. Serve immediately, either as is or with brown or granulated sugar, and cream, butter, or milk.

Makes 4 one-half cup servings

Julian's Five-Grain Bread

2 cups five-grain cereal (available
   either in the cereal or the health-
   food section of the grocery store)
   or rolled oats
2⅓ cups water
2 tablespoons unsalted butter
¾ cup dark molasses
¾ cup milk
1 teaspoon dark brown sugar
5 teaspoons (2 packages) active dry
   yeast
2 tablespoons bread-dough enhancer
   (optional) (recommended brand:
   Lora Brody's, available at
   Williams-Sonoma)
4 cups bread flour (or all-purpose
   flour), plus up to 1 cup more flour
   for kneading (if required)
2 cups whole wheat flour

Butter two 9x5-inch loaf pans.

Place the cereal in a large bowl. Bring
the water, butter, and molasses to a

boil. Pour this mixture over the cereal and set aside to cool to 100°F.

Heat milk and dark brown sugar to 100°F. Pour into a large bowl and stir in the yeast. Allow to proof, about 10 to 15 minutes.

Mix the cooled grain mixture into the yeast mixture. Combine the optional bread dough enhancer with the first cup of bread flour and stir into the yeast mixture. Beat the other 3 cups of bread flour and the whole wheat flour into the mixture, beating well to combine. Place the dough in an oiled bowl, turn dough to oil the top, cover with a clean kitchen towel, and let rise in a draft-free spot, at room temperature, until doubled in bulk, about 1 hour.

Add as much of the additional bread flour to the dough as needed to make a dough that is not too sticky to knead. Knead on a floured surface until the dough is smooth and satiny, about 10 minutes.

Divide the dough into 2 pieces and place them into the pans. Cover with a towel and allow to rise until almost doubled.

Preheat the oven to 375°F. Bake for 50 to 60 minutes, or until the loaves are deep brown and sound hollow when knocked. Remove the loaves from the pans and allow them to cool completely on racks.

Makes 2 loaves

not going to talk about the champagne. It's too dry to serve with this sweet food, anyway."

Arthur's groan of protest attracted stares. Then he grunted assent and whisked morosely away. Fifteen minutes until showtime: I concentrated on transporting ingredients. The crowd grew more boisterous with each minute. A tech handed me the mike wire and I threaded it through my jacket. *I'm almost done,* I thought with an unexpected pang of regret. As challenging as Arthur and the whole TV gig had been, the thought of jumping into the abyss of *no work* after the New Year brought a lump to my throat.

And so I did the show. Without a single calamity or disaster. I realized I hadn't thought of a single sexy thing to say about the food except that molasses was reputed as an aphrodisiac, and oats were widely used in the diet of the British Isles, and didn't the Brits, after all, know lusty, ribsticking food? Finally, after nibbling on the bread, swishing my hips about, and taking an eye-rolling bite of the oatmeal, I beamed at the camera and crooned, "That's comfort food for you. And doesn't everyone want to be comforted and loved at this time of year?"

To my astonishment, and to Arthur's consternation, the audience broke into spontaneous applause. Tears welled in my eyes as I smiled at the camera and Arthur made his wild *Cut* motion. The taping was over. The audience divided into those leaving and those staying for treats. I hustled out to the kitchen, eager to be on my way back to Rorry's for a hot shower and a glass of some wine that Arthur would no doubt disdain.

The kitchen staff was clustered around a problem with the oven. I barely noticed them as I made my way to the clothing closet by the broken refrigerator. Feeling triumphant, I took off my apron and hung it up, then bent to unbutton my jacket. Then I sensed a movement behind me and my blood ran cold. *Always have somebody with you.*

Something hard and heavy hit my skull with such force that black lightning formed in front of my eyes. Startled, I opened my mouth to cry out. The heavy object crashed down on my head again. My knees buckled and I hit the floor. Something sticky was slapped over my mouth. Duct tape? By the time powerful arms dragged me into the refrigerator, I could see nothing. Understand nothing. The hard, cold floor of the walk-in rose up to slap my cheek. I remember unholy anger, intense, sudden grief for Arch and Tom, then nothing.

CHAPTER 22

An echoing storm of pain was my first indication I had regained consciousness. A scarlet fog covered my eyes. When a cough convulsed my chest, I gagged. My mouth was taped hard and tight. I was painfully cold, chilled to the core, lying on my side on an icy floor. Another cough snagged in my throat. I felt myself choking and beat down panic.

"Where is it?" demanded a husky voice close to my ear.

The tight duct tape mangled any response I could make. Suddenly, without warning, the cold, dense darkness lifted; a door beside me opened. Far above, a tiny fluorescent light made my eyes ache. I moaned. Strong hands hitched under my armpits and roughly hauled me out of the dark space. I struggled to get to my knees; my hands were taped together. I was in the bistro kitchen. Out the window, the sky was black. It was late at night. The lodge would be deserted.

Out of nowhere, a hand slapped me hard across the face. I reeled. It was the kind of hit I used to take from John Richard. One hand pulled my hair hard to tilt my head back, while another hand yanked the duct tape off so roughly I knew my cheeks were bleeding.

I blew a mouthful of vomit all over Jack Gilkey. He cried out and swung at me again. I dodged—one thing I'd learned in my years with The Jerk.

His glossy dark brown hair was loose and wild, his handsome face menacing, gray with shadow. He grabbed me in a choke-hold around the neck. His mouth brushed my ear. "Where's the tape, bitch?"

My brain thumped and throbbed. The building seemed to echo the vibrations in my head. "The videotape," Jack snarled.

"If I tell you," I managed to say, "will you let me go?"

In answer, he tightened his grip around my throat and shook me hard. Black spots danced in front of my eyes. I made a squeaking, submissive sound.

"Is it here with you? In this building?"

"Yes," I said, when he shook me again. *Think.* "Yes, yes, let me take you to it."

"No."

"It'll take you hours to find it. Maybe more."

He didn't reply. Panic gripped my gut. Then he said, "Get up," harshly, with just a shade of doubt. In this I took comfort. Apparently, Chef Well-Organized didn't have a plan to cover this exigency. *Think.* How could I get away from him? The agony in my brain made mental work impossible.

"Please undo my hands," I whispered. I could feel blood trickling down my cheek. "I'll fall if I can't get balanced."

"No way," he snapped. Then he lifted his flannel shirt, revealing a flat stomach—and a small pistol. He pulled the gun out of his waistband. "Don't move unless I tell you to, don't fall, don't run, don't yell. If you do, I'll kill your son at your house in Aspen Meadow, once I lure your husband out of the house. You understand?"

"Yes," I said angrily, still trying to think. On my feet, I shuffled through the long, shadowy kitchen. Why had the TV people left without checking on me? They must have figured I'd gone down on the gondola. I should have kept somebody with me. Why hadn't I paid more attention to Tom's warnings? Hindsight. "What are you going to do with me?"

"Easy. You're going to die hitting a tree. You hiked out of the bistro, got confused, and *bam*. We'll get more snow by morning, nobody will ever know it wasn't an accident. *Move.*"

I shambled groggily toward the hall that led to the storage-area stairway. *Think.* What do cops advise in a situation like this? *Talk to the criminal. Use his name.*

"Jack," I begged, "Eileen's my friend. I was just trying to help her—"

"Yeah, sure," he said, prodding the gun painfully into my back to push me forward. "I knew you were looking for something, and guessed it had to do with Nate because today you brought Rorry here. I quizzed Magill, found out about the camera, and figured out what you were doing." His voice deepened. "You're not on Eileen's side. You're on the cops' side, that's why you came here in the first place. To set me up, figure out Portman's scheme. You're not going to steal Eileen from me, trying to prove to her I killed Fiona."

Reggie Dawson's call echoed in my brain: *Was your involvement with Portman another attempt on your part to crack crimes in Furman County?*

"But you did, didn't you? You killed Fiona. That's what's on the tape. How'd you kill Doug Portman? I thought you were prepping for lunch on Friday—"

367

He laughed and shoved me. "You give your staff a ton of prep, they don't notice whether you're there or not."

"Jack, were you the one who hit my van on the interstate—"

He opened the door to the storage area. He didn't need to answer; of course he'd tried to get rid of me. He just hadn't been successful the first time. "Get down those stairs," he commanded.

"Jack," I said softly, "did Eileen know you bribed Portman so you could be paroled early?"

"She knew and she didn't know." He announced it triumphantly. "I needed ten thousand a month for six months, but she never asked what for." He gave me a shove. *"Alimony?"* Another shove. *"Child support?"* Shove. *"Surely not bribery, Jack?"* He laughed sourly. "Don't ask, don't tell."

We'd reached the first landing. The foul smell of trash rose up to greet us. "Please, Jack," I begged. "Please stop, I have to rest." I leaned against the wall and closed my eyes. "So, you framed Barton Reed? Your old prison chum? You knew he had cancer, knew he'd had the Duragesic, knew he hated Portman?"

Jack shrugged. He was so marvelously good-looking, it was hard to believe he was so evil. "Portman said he sniffed an investigation coming. He was skipping out. What if they got him, with all that money I'd paid? He'd go to prison. If he did, so would I. I had to get rid of him. Making it look as if Reed had done it seemed like a good idea, since he didn't have long to live anyway. Reed figured out what I'd done. Too bad. So he tried to get back at me, mow me down on the slopes. And he nearly killed Eileen instead. I could have killed him for that—I wasn't married to her yet."

"And you needed the money from Eileen that you didn't inherit from Fiona."

Jack shrugged, then poked me with his ugly little gun. "Time to get moving."

The pistol in his hand was a .22, accurate only at close range. Six shots, unless he had more ammunition. We were coming down to the rail that led to the canisters. I had to run away from him, hide, run out onto the slope, hope I could get away from him—something, or else I'd die, like everyone else who'd stood in Jack Gilkey's way. I had to *act*.

I tensed my leg muscles and kicked Jack's washboard stomach with all my might. He gasped in pain and surprise and banged into the wall. Then I jab-kicked him hard in the back; he fell to his knees. I ran, clumsily, stupidly, as fast as I could. I ran for my life. Down the steps. Down the hallway. Down the rail toward the canisters. I could hear Jack stumbling down the stairs after me, cursing.

Five canisters were lined up. Oh, when did the night crew arrive? No telling. I squeezed along the wall and tried to figure out which one to duck into. The one farthest from Jack, of course. It was poised right at the large double doors, and it was half full of food scraps and garbage. Beyond the front canister was darkness made silvery by moonlight. I clumsily climbed up the sides, jumped into the canister, and slithered down into the trash. It was all I could do to keep from gagging.

I heard a shot. Jack was firing into the canisters. One shot, two, three. This was going to be it, I thought, and prayed for Arch and Tom. With taped hands, I used my body to burrow as deep as I could into the trash. I thought I was going to vomit again.

Then, without warning, there was a loud *kee-chunk*, and the canister quivered violently. I could hear male voices in the distance. The night workers? Were they coming? I was surrounded by rotting lettuce and meat fat. Would the workers hear me if I squirmed to the top of the garbage? Could I risk calling to them, with Jack—armed—so close to the canisters? No. *Clink. Ke-chunk, clink.* It was the clank of metal doors being closed on trash canisters, followed by the whir of the descending gondola.

Behind me, a loud pop was followed by a zing. Another shot. Jack was shooting at my canister. *Pop-zing.*

I could hear Jack howl. Then my stinking, packed canister swung out into the darkness.

The night air was stingingly cold. But I'd escaped Jack. I knew the gondola operators at the top could stop the cars, but they could not *reverse* their motion. That could only be done by the operator at the bottom. So even if Jack knew I was in this canister—and he didn't—

he wouldn't be able to bring me back. With a startling suddenness the canister dropped and I was swaying, out of range of Jack's lethal little .22. Would he hurt the canister workers? I doubted it. He had only one target tonight: me.

I wriggled between two bags of mind-numbingly smelly garbage. My head hurt, my cheeks hurt, everything hurt. The stink was inconceivable. I'd never get the smell out of my hair, I thought, and giggled insanely. The canister had holes in its walls and top. Through the holes overhead, a distant light was shining. The canister shook; an almost full moon came into view.

Down, down the canister rolled. In my mind's eye, I saw the gleaming container, suspended twenty feet above the ground, streaming noisily through the night.

I had to get the tape off my hands. My only choice was to feel with my tongue around the duct tape till I came to an edge. Then I began, slowly, laboriously, with my teeth, to tug off the tape. The blood running down my face didn't make the task any easier. But at least biting and wrenching the tape off, centimeter by centimeter, took my mind off the cold, the smell, the canister swaying and creaking in the frigid wind, high above the mountain.

When I finally had the tape off, the canister clanked onto the track, then began to move laboriously toward the warehouse. I was on the ground, but where? How long had I been on the gondola? Ten minutes? Twenty? What had Jack been doing? I knew he kept ski equipment at the bistro. Would he try to ski down in the moonlight? How long would it take for him to get his equipment on—five, six minutes? How long to schuss down from the top? The fastest I'd ever made it was six minutes, and I was nowhere near the expert skier Jack was.

Suddenly the canister shuddered and stopped. I clambered up through the trash to the metal door. My heart sank. Through the holes of my cage, the moonlight on the slope showed the canister was only halfway down the track to the Killdeer base. I wasn't even in *sight* of the warehouse. Jack must have stopped the lift engine from the peak. Dammit.

I peered down through the holes in the metal. The moonlight illuminated much of the mountain, including nearby woods and what looked like a catwalk or cleared path of snow. With blood pounding in my ears, I pushed on the container door. It swung open.

I leaped out and looked all around. Had Rorry missed me and called Tom? Would he call someone to go looking for me?

I tried to get my bearings. The cleared path was not a catwalk, I realized. It had a plastic orange fence going up one side... The construction road! If I followed it, I would get down to the Rover where I had a spare key in the wheel-well.

I hobbled over to the road and started to run. Within seconds, my chest burned with the exertion and the cold. Did I hear something? I stopped, panting, looked up the moonlit slope, and saw the shadow of a lone skier. I turned and again ran. Could I possibly make it to the Rover before Jack caught up with me? My brain cursed my agonized legs. How far to the parking lot? Maybe fifteen minutes, if I could keep up this brutal pace. I ran and ran, and after an eternity, reached the fork that led back to the parking lot and trailhead to Elk Ridge. Wheezing, I stopped and tried to catch my breath.

Scritch, scratch. Scritch-scratch. Very regularly, the sound came from behind me. *Scritch-scratch.* I glanced back. Jack, on skis, was poling swiftly along the snow-covered road, cross-country-style. He was perhaps fifty feet behind me. *Damn.* I moved my legs as fast as they were able to go. But I knew in my heart I'd never make it to the Rover before he closed the gap.

And he had at least two more shots left.

With sudden decision, I ran up the snow-packed road of the left fork, toward the construction site. On skis, Jack could go swiftly downhill; as fit and muscular as he was, he could traverse flat terrain quickly as well. But he could not go uphill on skis, unless he was Superman. I had to get to the guard's cabin first.

Low clouds, silvered by the moonlight, rolled across the sky. How far was the cabin, if the dirt road ran right across the valley? A half-mile? A mile? Jack would have to stop; he would have to remove his skis *and boots.* No one could run in that clunky footwear. *You can beat him,* I told myself. *All you have to do is run.*

I looked over my shoulder. *Scritch-scratch, scritch-scratch.* Jack was gaining on me. I even thought I saw him smiling at me.

"Goldy!" he called placatingly. "Stop! Let's talk!"

Yeah, sure. I ran up the track. A sudden pool of darkness swallowed me and I slowed. Tall pines loomed on the right side of the construction fence, casting black, swaying shadows on the road. *Run,* I ordered myself. *But whatever you do, don't fall. If you do, you'll die.*

Behind me, the sounds of Jack removing his ski equipment were barely audible. *Damn it.* I couldn't believe he would still follow me. He couldn't be tried again for Fiona's murder. Why not run away, rather than risk exposure? Because he'd told me he had killed Doug Portman. Because he desperately wanted Eileen's money. The tape would show Eileen and the world that Jack had murdered his first wife to get her fortune. Eileen would dump him; he would go to prison for murdering Portman and the truck driver he'd killed on Interstate 70, when he'd been trying to nail me.

I came to the spot in the road where it veered upward and became the old hiking trail. I did not know how far the trail went before it diverged—a high side leading to Elk Ridge, the low, level side heading through the valley. As I ran, I peered into the darkness. Was the faint light I saw the guard's cabin far, far up the hill? Or were my eyes playing tricks?

The wind whispered in the pines. In the moonlight, I could make out lodgepole pine branches littering the slick, snow-hard road. The branches had been blown down by the wind. I would have to be careful; stepping on them would alert Jack to my location. Had he found the road yet? How fast could he go in stocking feet? He was almost ten years younger than I was, and an athlete. Grimly, I quickened my pace.

Minutes later, winded and puffing, I was wondering if, in the dark, I had missed the turnoff to Elk Valley. Then, as I fought down panic, it suddenly appeared on the left, and stopped me in my tracks. The left-hand split to the old hiking path was completely blocked with a gigantic pile of dead trees. The sign posted on the trees saying *Warning——Avalanche Area——Do Not Enter!* filled me with alarm. I couldn't climb over the pile of trees...it was eight or nine feet high. But going through the valley was the fastest way to the expansion area—and the security guard's cabin.

To my consternation, I suddenly realized the construction road ran *over* Elk Ridge. For a moment, the wind ceased shuffling through the trees. Behind me, the faint huffing noise drew nearer. Jack was coming.

I whispered a prayer. Then I headed up the hill.

How far to the cabin now? Twenty minutes? I tried not to think. *Just head upward.* Up, up, up, no time for rest, despite the fact that my sides were screaming with pain.

Ten minutes later, the wide, shimmering expanse where Cinda had started her fatal run in Nate's film opened up on my left. It was startlingly beautiful, like a giant's sugar bowl, steeply tipped, frozen hard, glittering in the moonlight. And—people will never learn—running straight across the steep, concave space were the unmistakable paths of half a dozen ski tracks. At the other end of the ski tracks, set perhaps twenty feet into the pines, the lights of the security guard's cabin glowed yellow in the shadows. I could just make out the path of the construction road. It ran across the treed top of the ridge, then curved right down to a parking lot surrounding the cabin.

I looked behind me. Jack was about a hundred feet back, running methodically, despite socks, despite ice and snow.

Think. The fastest way to the cabin was straight across the steep bowl, the way the ski tracks ran. But I could never go that way. It was too dangerous, especially after all the new snow we'd had. Still, I didn't have time to go over the forested ridge and make it to the cabin. Even if I could run straight on the road the whole way over, Jack would come straight across and cut me off.

Stay in the trees, I decided. *Above the bowl, but below the road. It's the only safe way. Hug the shadows, stay off the moonlit side of the road. When you get near the cabin, call for help.* I ran.

At the top of the ridge, I dared another glance down. Jack had left the road and was running through the bowl, in the skiers' tracks, about a hundred feet back. He knew where I was headed, and he intended to get there first. Worse, he was wearing shoes. He must have brought them in his ski jacket pockets, along with his pistol. The man was not going to be deterred.

Well, neither was I. "Help!" I screeched as I pelted down the center of the road. A third of a mile left. "Help! Security! Come out of the cabin! Help! On the road, above you! Help!" Despite the fact that wood smoke whipped out of the metal-pipe chimney, no face came to the window, no door opened. My heart pounded madly. Dammit! Was the guy deaf?

Jack was two-thirds of the way across the tracks. He ran as nimbly as Mercury, as Pan, as every Greek god who'd ever been known for speed. Badly winded, I continued my bumbling pace. A quarter-mile to the cabin. The wind had picked up again. There was no use yelling for someone to rescue me, because it wasn't going to happen. I was going to die on this mountain. Just like Nate and Fiona and Doug.

Pow. Jack, only forty feet away, both hands gripping the pistol straight in front of him, had fired at me. I tried to zigzag as I ran, but each step brought me closer to him. We were both racing down the sides of a triangle; the cabin was where we would intersect.

Thirty feet from the cabin, totally out of breath, I hugged a tree and stopped, bent over and wheezing.

"You're not going to make it, Goldy," he called fiercely as he kept advancing toward me, aiming the gun. Fifteen feet away. He was almost to the edge of the bowl. I clung helplessly to my tree. "Good-bye!" he screamed as he fired again.

The frigid air boomed and reverberated with the explosion. I squeezed my eyes shut as terror closed my throat.

An image of church school with Rorry floated into my mind. Our teaching: the fall of Jericho. *Joshua.* I looked up: The moon skidded drunkenly between the branches. Had I been hit? Jack's shot echoed and re-echoed in my head. *After the Hebrews blew their horns.* The earth was moving, the moon was wobbling in the sky. *The walls came tumbling down.* I gripped the tree and turned my head to the groaning, trembling slope. A mammoth slab of ice and snow had dislodged from the mountain. *Joshua's troops made the noise.* The monumental size of the slide, like a skyscraper imploding, was beyond belief. The avalanche's deafening rumble pained my ears. A mist of snow burned my eyes. *The walls came tumbling down.* My knees gave out beneath me as I held onto the tree. A fifty-foot vertical wave of snow was roaring downward, toward us.

A vast cloud of mist exploded upward. Darkness flashed inside it. Jack Gilkey screamed and fell. Then he was sucked into the killer white tide of the avalanche that rushed past me and swept him away.

CHAPTER 23

A helo carried me out. At the roar of the avalanche, the guard in the cabin, who'd been listening to a football game on the radio and was therefore deaf to my cries and the sound of gunfire, came bursting outside. He phoned for help.

On the way to Denver, I told two sheriff's deputies all I knew about Jack Gilkey and his deadly, double-dealing relationships with Fiona Wakefield, Doug Portman, and Barton Reed. The paramedics insisted I go to the hospital to be checked for frostbite, injuries, and shock. I kept assuring them that I was fine. But they did not believe a wildly shivering woman whose face and clothes were covered with blood and garbage.

"Lady," one of them said, "at this point you couldn't *buy* a ticket straight home. That ankle looks badly bruised. Did you fall on it when you were holding on to the tree?"

I nodded numbly and looked down at the snow-covered Continental Divide far below, the sparkling rows of tiny cars going east and west, ruby lights one way, diamonds the other. *You can't buy a ticket home.* That was really the problem, wasn't it? Trying to buy your way into anything. Jack had tried to buy his way out of a prison term by bribing Doug Portman; like Fiona Wakefield, Eileen Druckman had thought her money could bring her a handsome young husband who would really love and cherish her. Nate Bullock had tried to provide a better lifestyle for his beloved pregnant wife by making a video that had killed him. Even I was not immune, with my misbegotten attempts to use earrings and treats to purchase a girlfriend for my dear Arch. And hadn't the lure of money made me ignore my scruples and try to sell Tom's skis to Doug Portman?

All that night and the next day, Friday, I was cossetted, bandaged, medicated, questioned, and scolded. With Arch and Todd Druckman in tow, Tom raced to the emergency room to meet me. Todd hurried off to see his mother; Arch brought me soft drinks from the soda machine and (bless him!) some of Julian's life-restoring fudge. Tom gave me updates and called Rorry to tell her I was all right. I learned that Jack Gilkey's body had been dug out by Killdeer Ski Patrol's Avalanche Rescue Team. Arthur Wakefield was being charged with breaking and entering and mail theft. The latter was a federal offense. Arthur, Tom said, had hired a lawyer who was a teetotaler.

During a break between X-rays, I visited my old friend Eileen. I had told the authorities that I wanted to be the one to give her the bad news about Jack. Gently, I did so.

Todd comforted her. She patted his head and kept sobbing that she was *sorry, just so sorry.* Todd said he was fine! And besides, the nurses had announced he could spend Christmas with her, on a guest sofa in her hospital suite.

And then Eileen cried some more, but this time with happiness.

Christmas Eve, bandaged, weak, and awkward on my crutches, I slid into a pew next to a surprised Julian and Marla. Tom and Arch joined us. In the pew behind us, three of my former Sunday school pupils were giggling in their home-fashioned shepherd costumes. They tapped my shoulder and twirled for my approval. I gave them the thumbs-up. Tom kissed my cheek, Marla handed the kids sticky chunks of ribbon candy, Julian winked at everyone. Even Arch smiled. *You can't buy what you want,* I reflected. *It all comes as a gift.*

"I've got three news items," Tom whispered as the organist warmed up for the prelude of carols. "Ready?" I inhaled the sharp, invigorating smell of Christmas greens and nodded. "First," he said, "we found a computer disk with all of Portman's records. It was tucked inside a cigar box belonging to a Civil War general. Second, we found Nate's tape where you left it in the bistro freezer. Cinda Caldwell confessed to being out-of-bounds with him when he died." He tilted his head at me and I nodded. "She was all weepy, said she'd plead guilty to whatever they wanted to charge her with. The district attorney told her thanks, but the statute of limitations had expired on out-of-bounds excursions. And to her surprise, causing an avalanche that killed somebody who was also out-of-bounds is not a crime. She said she was going to give lectures on winter sports safety, donate some of her shop's profits to avalanche victims worldwide. I mean, the woman has gotten *religion.*" He took a deep breath and pulled a folded piece of paper from his pocket. "And this, Miss G., is your certificate of reinspection. You passed. The inspector is smitten with your drains. Almost as much as I am smitten with you."

I hugged him so hard he chuckled like Santa. The service started and the packed church surged into song. We prayed and heard Bible lessons. At the Intercessions, an usher handed the priest a note. He opened it and beamed at the congregation.

"A former parishioner," he told us, "has given birth to a seven-pound, thirteen-ounce boy. Joshua Nathan Bullock was born to Rorry Bullock at three-thirty this afternoon."

Everyone smiled and clapped. The tiny white lights on the church's ceiling-high Christmas tree twinkled and glimmered. I reached out to embrace Arch, and to my surprise, he reciprocated with an enthusiastic, tight hug.

"That's the best bit of news yet," I whispered to him.

"Merry Christmas, Mom," Arch whispered back, and I hugged him harder.

What a gift, I thought, *to have a son.*

INDEX TO THE
RECIPES

ABOUT THE AUTHOR

DIANE MOTT DAVIDSON lives in Evergreen, Colorado, with her husband and three sons. She is the author of nine bestselling culinary mysteries, including *Dying for Chocolate, The Main Corpse,* and *The Grilling Season.*